Junius

# The letters of Junius

Complete in One Volume

Junius

**The letters of Junius**
*Complete in One Volume*

ISBN/EAN: 9783744716420

Printed in Europe, USA, Canada, Australia, Japan

Cover: Foto ©Andreas Hilbeck / pixelio.de

More available books at **www.hansebooks.com**

# THE

# LETTERS

## OF

# JUNIUS.

Complete in ONE VOLUME.

---

A NEW EDITION.

---

WITH A COPIOUS INDEX.

STAT NOMINIS UMBRA.

---

LONDON:
PRINTED IN THE YEAR 1786.

# CONTENTS.





LET.

4     C O N T E N T S.



LET. XLV.

# DEDICATION

## TO THE

# ENGLISH NATION.

---

I DEDICATE to You a collection of Letters, written by one of Yourselves for the common benefit of us all. They would never have grown to this size without your continued encouragement and applause. To me they originally owe nothing but a healthy, sanguine, constitution. Under *Your* care they have thriven. To *You* they are indebted for whatever strength or beauty they possess. When Kings and Ministers are forgotten, when the force and direction of personal satire is no longer understood, and when measures are only felt in their remotest consequences, this book will, I believe, be found to contain principles worthy to be transmitted to posterity. When you leave the unimpaired, hereditary freehold to Your children, You do but half Your duty. Both liberty and property are precarious, unless the possessors have sense and spirit enough to defend them.—This is not the language of vanity. If I am a vain

man,

man, my gratification lies within a narrow circle. I am the fole depofitary of my own fecret, and it fhall perifh with me.

If an honeft, and, I may truly affirm, a laborious zeal for the public fervice, has given me any weight in Your efteem, let me exhort and conjure You never to fuffer an invafion of Your political conftitution, however minute the inftance may appear, to pafs by, without a determined, perfevering refiftance. One precedent creates another.—They foon accumulate, and conftitute law. What yefterday was fact, to-day is doctrine. Examples are fuppofed to juftify the moft dangerous meafures; and where they do not fuit exactly, the defect is fupplied by analogy.—Be affured that the laws, which protect us in our civil rights, grow out of the conftitution, and that they muft fall or flourifh with it. This is not the caufe of faction or of party, or of any individual, but the common intereft of every man in Britain. Although the King fhould continue to fupport his prefent fyftem of government, the period is not very diftant at which you will have the means of redrefs in your own power. It may be nearer perhaps than any of us expect, and I would warn You to be prepared for it. The King may poffibly be advifed to diffolve the prefent parliament a year or two before it expires of courfe, and precipitate a new election, in hopes of taking the nation by furprife. If fuch a meafure be in agitation, this very caution may defeat or prevent it.

I cannot doubt that You will unanimoufly affert the freedom of election, and vindicate your exclufive right to choofe your reprefen-tatives.  But other queftions have been ftart-ed, on which your determination fhould be equally clear and unanimous.  Let it be im-prefled upon your minds, let it be inftilled into your children, that the liberty of the prefs is the *Palladium* of all the civil, politi-cal, and religious rights of an Englifhman ; and that the right of juries to return a general verdict, in all cafes whatfoever, is an effential part of our conftitution, not to be controuled or limited by the judges, nor in any fhape queftionable by the legiflature.  The power of King, Lords, and Commons, is not an ar-bitrary power *.  They are the truftees, not the owners, of the eftate.  The fee-fimple is

in

* This pofitive denial, of an arbitrary power being vefted in the legiflature, is not in fact a new doctrine. When the Earl of Lindfay, in the year 1675, brought a bill into the Houfe of Lords, *To prevent the dangers which might arife from perfons difaffected to government,* by which an oath and penalty was to be impofed upon the members of both houfes, it was affirmed, in a proteft figned by twenty-three lay peers, (my lords the bifhops were not accuftomed to proteft), " That the privilege " of fitting and voting in parliament was an honour " they had by birth, and a right fo inherent in them, " and infeparable from them, *that nothing could take it* " *away,* but what, by the law of the land, muft withal " take away their lives, and corrupt their blood."— Thefe noble peers (whofe names are a reproach to their posterity) have, in this inftance, folemnly denied the power of parliament to alter the conftitution.  Under a particular propofition, they have afferted a general truth, in which every man in England is concerned.

in US. They cannot alienate, they cannot waſte. When we ſay that the legiſlature is *ſupreme*, we mean, that it is the higheſt power known to the conſtitution;—that it is the higheſt in compariſon with the other ſubordinate powers eſtabliſhed by the laws. In this ſenſe, the word *ſupreme* is relative, not abſolute. The power of the legiſlature is limited, not only by the general rules of natural juſtice, and the welfare of the community, but by the forms and principles of our particular conſtitution. If this doctrine be not true, we muſt admit, that King, Lords, and Commons, have no rule to direct their reſolutions, but merely their own will and pleaſure. They might unite the legiſlative and executive power in the ſame hands, and diſſolve the conſtitution by an act of parliament. But I am perſuaded You will not leave it to the choice of ſeven hundred perſons, notoriouſly corrupted by the Crown, whether ſeven millions of their equals ſhall be freemen or ſlaves. The certainty of forfeiting their own rights, when they ſacrifice thoſe of the nation, is no check to a brutal, degenerate mind. Without inſiſting upon the extravagant conceſſion made to Harry the Eighth, there are inſtances, in the hiſtory of other countries, of a formal, deliberate ſurrender of the public liberty into the hands of the Sovereign. If England does not ſhare the ſame fate, it is becauſe we have better reſources than in the virtue of either houſe of parliament.

I ſaid that the liberty of the preſs is the

*palladium* of all your rights, and that the right of the juries to return a general verdict is part of your constitution. To preserve the whole system, You must correct your legislature. With regard to any influence of the constituent over the conduct of the representative, there is little difference between a seat in parliament for seven years and a seat for life. The prospect of your resentment is too remote; and although the last session of a septennial parliament be usually employed in courting the favour of the people, consider, that at this rate your representatives have six years for offence, and but one for atonement. A death-bed repentance seldom reaches to restitution. If you reflect, that in the changes of administration which have marked and disgraced the present reign, although your warmest patriots have in their turn been invested with the lawful and unlawful authority of the crown, and though other reliefs or improvements have been held forth to the people, yet that no one man in office has ever promoted or encouraged a bill for shortening the duration of parliaments, but that (whoever was minister) the opposition to this measure, ever since the septennial act passed, has been constant and uniform on the part of government.——You cannot but conclude, without the possibility of a doubt, that long parliaments are the foundation of the undue influence of the crown. This influence answers every purpose of arbitrary power to the crown, with an expence and oppression to the people, which would be un-

necessary

neceſſary in an arbitrary government. The beſt of our miniſters find it the eaſieſt and moſt compendious mode of conducting the King's affairs; and all miniſters have a general intereſt in adhering to a ſyſtem, which of itſelf is ſufficient to ſupport them in office, without any aſſiſtance from perſonal virtue, popularity, labour, abilities, or experience. It promiſes every gratification to avarice and ambition, and ſecures impunity.——Theſe are truths unqueſtionable.—If they make no impreſſion, it is becauſe they are too vulgar and notorious. But the inattention or indifference of the nation has continued too long. You are rouſed at laſt to a ſenſe of your danger.—The remedy will ſoon be in your power. If *Junius* lives, You ſhall often be reminded of it. If, when the opportunity preſents itſelf, You neglect to do your duty to yourſelves and to poſterity,——to God and to your country, I ſhall have one conſolation left, in common with the meaneſt and baſeſt of mankind:——Civil liberty may ſtill laſt the life of

JUNIUS.

3

PRE-

# PREFACE.

THE encouragement given to a multitude of spurious, mangled publications of the letters of *Junius*, persuades me, that a complete edition, corrected and improved by the author, will be favourably received. The printer will readily acquit me of any view to my own profit. I undertake this troublesome task, merely to serve a man who has deserved well of me, and of the public; and who, on my account, has been exposed to an expensive, tyrannical prosecution. For these reasons, I give to *Mr Henry Sampson Woodfall*, and to him alone, my right, interest, and property in these letters, as fully and completely, to all intents and purposes, as an author can possibly convey his property in his own works to another.

THIS edition contains all the letters of *Junius*, *Philo Junius*, and of *Sir William Draper* and *Mr Horne* to *Junius*, with their respective dates, and according to the order in which they appeared in the Public Advertiser. The auxiliary part of *Philo Junius* was indispensably necessary to defend or explain particular passages in *Junius*, in answer to plausible objections; but the subordinate character is never guilty of the indecorum of praising his principal. The fraud was innocent, and I always intended to explain it. The notes will be found not only useful, but neces-



sary.

fary. References to facts not generally known, or allufions to the current report or opinion of the day, are in a little time unintellligible. Yet the reader will not find himfelf overloaded with explanations. I was not born to be a commentator, even upon my own works.

It remains to fay a few words upon the liberty of the prefs. The daring fpirit, by which thefe letters are fuppofed to be diftinguifhed, feems to require that fomething ferious fhould be faid in their defence. I am no lawyer by profeffion, nor do I pretend to be more deeply read than every Englifh gentleman fhould be in the laws of his country. If, therefore, the principles I maintain are truly conftitutional, I fhall not think myfelf anfwered, though I fhould be convicted of a miftake in terms, or of mifapplying the language of the law. I fpeak to the plain underftanding of the people, and appeal to their honeft, liberal conftruction of me.

Good men, to whom alone I addrefs myfelf, -appear to me to confult their piety as little as their judgment and experience, when they admit the great and effential advantages accruing to fociety from the freedom of the prefs, yet indulge themfelves in peevifh or paffionate exclamations againft the abufes of it. Betraying an unreafonable expectation of benefits pure and entire from any human inftitution, they in effect arraign the goodnefs of Providence, and confefs that they are diffatisfied with the common lot of humanity. In the prefent inftance, they really create to their own minds, or greatly exaggerate, the evil they complain of. The laws of England provide as effectually as any human laws can do, for the protection of the fubject, in his reputa-

tion,

tion, as well as in his perfon and property. If the characters of private men are infulted or injured, a double remedy is open to them, by *action* and *indictment*. If, through indolence, falfe fhame, or indifference, they will not appeal to the laws of their country, they fail in their duty to fociety, and are unjuft to themfelves. If, from an unwarrantable diftruft of the integrity of juries, they would wifh to obtain juftice by any mode of proceeding more fummary than a trial by their peers, I do not fcruple to affirm, that they are in effect greater enemies to themfelves than to the libeller they profecute.

WITH regard to ftrictures upon the characters of men in office, and the meafures of government, the cafe is a little different. A confiderable latitude muft be allowed in the difcuffion of public affairs, or the liberty of the prefs will be of no benefit to fociety. As the indulgence of private malice and perfonal flander fhould be checked and refifted by every legal means, fo a conftant examination into the characters and conduct of minifters and magiftrates fhould be equally promoted and encouraged. They who conceive that our newfpapers are no reftraint upon bad men, or impediment to the execution of bad meafures, know nothing of this country. In that ftate of abandoned fervility and proftitution, to which the undue influence of the crown has reduced the other branches of the legiflature, our minifters and magiftrates have in reality little punifhment to fear, and few difficulties to contend with, beyond the cenfure of the prefs, and the fpirit of refiftance which it excites among the people. While this cenforial power is maintained, to fpeak in the words of a moft ingenious foreigner, both minifter and ma-

B 2

giftrate

giftrate is compelled, in almoft every inftance, *to choofe between his duty and his reputation.* A dilemma of this kind perpetually before him, will not indeed work a miracle in his heart, but it will affuredly operate, in fome degree, upon his conduct. At all events, thefe are not times to admit of any relaxation in the little dicipline we have left.

BUT it is alleged, that the licentioufnefs of the prefs is carried beyond all bounds of decency and truth:—that our excellent minifters are continually expofed to the public hatred or derifion:—that, in profecutions for libels on government, juries are partial to the popular fide;—and that, in the moft flagrant cafes, a verdict cannot be obtained for the King.—If the premifes were admitted, I fhould deny the conclufion. It is not true, that the temper of the times has in general an undue influence over the conduct of juries. On the contrary, many fignal inftances may be produced of verdicts returned for the King, when the inclinations of the people led ftrongly to an undiftinguifhing oppofition to government. Witnefs the cafes of *Mr Wilkes* and *Mr Almon.*—In the late profecutions of the printers of my addrefs to a great perfonage, the juries were never fairly dealt with.—*Lord Chief Juftice Manffield,* confcious that the paper in queftion contained no treafonable or libellous matter, and that the fevereft parts of it, however painful to tbe King or offenfive to his fervants, were ftrictly true, would fain have reftricted the jury to the finding of fpecial facts, which, as to *guilty* or *not guilty,* were merely indifferent. This particular motive, combined with his general purpofe to contract the power of juries, will account for the charge he delivered in *Woodfall's* trial.

He

He told the jury, in so many words, that they had nothing to determine except the fact of *printing and publishing,* and whether or no the *blanks* or *inuendos* were properly filled up in the information;—but that, whether the defendant had committed a *crime,* or not, was no matter of consideration to twelve men, who yet, upon their oaths, were to pronounce their peer *guilty,* or *not guilty.* When we hear such nonsense delivered from the bench, and find it supported by a laboured train of sophistry, which a plain understanding is unable to follow, and which an unlearned jury, however it may shock their reason, cannot be supposed qualified to refute, can it be wondered that they should return a verdict, perplexed, absurd, or imperfect ?— *Lord Mansfield* has not yet explained to the world, why he accepted of a verdict which the court afterwards set aside as illegal; and which, as it took no notice of the *inuendos,* did not even correspond with his own charge. If he had known his duty, he should have sent the jury back. —I speak advisedly, and am well assured that no lawyer of character in Westminster-hall will contradict me. To show the falsehood of *Lord Mansfield's* doctrine, it is not necessary to enter into the merits of the paper which produced the trial. If every line of it were treason, his charge to the jury would still be false, absurd, illegal, and unconstitutional. If I stated the merits of my letter to *the King, I should imitate* LORD MANSFIELD, *and* * TRAVEL OUT OF THE

B 3

RECORD.

---

* The following quotation from a speech delivered by *Lord Chatham* on the eleventh of December 1770, is taken with exactness. The reader will find it curious in itself, and very fit to be inserted here. " My Lords, The verdict given in Woodfall's trial, was " *guilty of printing and publishing* ONLY: upon which two mo- " tions were made in court;—one, in arrest of judgment, by

" the

RECORD. *When law and reason speak plainly,* we do not want authority to direct our understandings. Yet, for the honour of the profession, I am content to oppose one lawyer to another, especially when it happens that the King's ✓ orney General has virtually disclaimed the doctrine by which the Chief Justice meant to insure success to the prosecution. The opinion of the plaintiff's counsel (however it may be otherwise insignificant), is weighty in the scale of the defendant—*My Lord Chief Justice De Grey,* who filed the information *ex officio,* is directly with me. If he had concurred in *Lord Mansfield's* doctrine, the trial must have been a very short one. The facts were either admitted by *Woodfall's* counsel, or easily proved to the satisfaction of the jury. But *Mr De Grey,* far from thinking he should acquit himself of his duty by barely

" the defendant's counsel, grounded upon the ambiguity of the
" verdict;—the other, by the counsel for the crown, for a rule
" upon the defendant to show cause, why the verdict should not
" be entered up according to the *legal* import of the words. On
" both motions, a rule was granted, and soon after the matter
" was argued before the court of King's Bench. The noble
" judge, when he delivered the opinion of the court upon the
" verdict, went regularly through the whole of the proceedings
" at *Nisi Prius,* as well the evidence that had been given, as his
" own charge to the jury. This proceeding would have been
" very proper, had a motion been made of either side for a new
" trial; because either a verdict given contrary to evidence, or
" an improper charge by the judge at *Nisi Prius,* is held to be a
" sufficient ground for granting a new trial. But when a motion
" is made in arrest of judgment, or for establishing the verdict
" by entering it up according to the legal import of the words,
" it must be on the ground of something appearing *on the face of*
" *the record:* and the court, in considering whether the verdict
" shall be established or not, are so confined to the *record,* that
" they cannot take notice of any thing that does not appear on
" the face it; in the legal phrase, *they cannot travel out of the*
" *record.* The noble judge did travel out of the record; and I
" affirm that his discourse was *irregular, extrajudicial,* and *unpre*
" *cedented.* His apparent motive for doing what he knew to be
" wrong, was, that he might have an opportunity of telling the
" public *extrajudicially,* that the other three judges concurred in
" the doctrine laid down in his charge."

barely proving the facts, entered largely, and I confefs not without ability, into the demerits of the paper, which he called *a feditious libel.* He dwelt but lightly upon thofe points, which (according to Lord Mansfield) were the only matter of confideration to the jury. The criminal intent, the libellous matter, the pernicious tendency of the paper itfelf, were the topics on which he principally infifted, and of which for more than an hour he tortured his faculties to convince the jury. If he agreed in opinion with *Lord Mansfield,* his difcourfe was impertinent, ridiculous, and unreafonable. But, underftanding the law as I do, what he faid was at leaft confiftent and to the purpofe.

If any honeft man fhould ftill be inclined to leave the conftruction of libels to the court, I would intreat him to confider what a dreadful complication of hardfhips he impofes upon his fellow fubjects.—In the firft place, the profecution commences by *information* of an officer of the crown, not by the regular conftitutional mode of *indictment* before a grand jury.—As the fact is ufually admitted, or in general can eafily be proved, the office of the petty jury is nugatory.—The *court* then judges of the nature and extent of the offence, and determines *ad arbitrium* the *quantum* of the punifhment, from a fmall fine to a heavy one, to repeated whipping, to pillory, and unlimited imprifonment. Cutting off ears and nofes *might* ftill be inflicted by a refolute judge ; but I will be candid enough to fuppofe that penalties, fo apparently fhocking to humanity, would not be hazarded in thefe times.—In all other criminal profecutions, the jury decides upon the fact and the crime in one word ; and the court pronounces a *certain* fentence, which is the fentence
of

of the law, not of the judge.  If *Lord Mansfield's* doctrine be received, the jury muft either find a verdict of acquittal, contrary to evidence (which, I can conceive, might be done by very confcientious men, rather than truft a fellow-creature to *Lord Mansfield's* mercy); or they muft leave to the court two offices, never but in this inftance united, of finding guilty, and awarding punifhment.

But, fays this honeft *Lord Chief Juftice*, " If " the paper be not criminal, the defendant (tho' " found guilty by his peers) is in no danger, for " he may move the court in arreft of judgment." —True, my good Lord, but who is to determine upon the motion?—Is not the court ftill to decide, whether judgment fhall be entered up or not? and is not the defendant this way as effectually deprived of judgment by his peers, as if he were tried in a court of civil law, or in the chambers of the inquifition? It is you, my Lord, who then try the crime, not the jury. As to the probable effect of the motion in arreft of judgment, I fhall only obferve, that no reafonable man would be fo eager to poffefs himfelf of the invidious power of inflicting punifhment, if he were not predetermined to make ufe of it.

Again :—We are told, that judge and jury have a diftinct office;—that the jury is to find the fact, and the judge to deliver the law. *De jure refpondent judices, de facto jurati.* The *dictum* is true, though not in the fenfe given to it by *Lord Mansfield.* The jury are undoubtedly to determine the fact, that is, whether the defendant did or did not commit the crime charged againft him. The judge pronounces the fentence annexed by law to that fact so found; and if, in the course of the trial, any question of law arises, both the counsel and the jury must, of necessity, appeal to the judge, and leave it to his decision. An *exception*, or *plea in bar*, may be allowed by the court; but, when issue is joined, and the jury have received their charge, it is not possible, in the nature of things, for them to separate the law from the fact, unless they think proper to return a *special* verdict.

IT has also been alleged, that, although a common jury are sufficient to determine a plain matter of fact, they are not qualified to comprehend the meaning, or to judge of the tendency, of a seditious libel. In answer to this objection, (which, if well founded, would prove nothing as to the *strict right* of returning a general verdict), I might safely deny the truth of the assertion. *Englishmen* of that rank, from which juries are usually taken, are not so illiterate as (to serve a particular purpose) they are now represented. Or, admitting the fact, let a special jury be summoned in all cases of difficulty and importance, and the objection is removed. But the truth is, that if a paper, supposed to be a libel upon government, be so obscurely worded, that twelve common men cannot possibly see the seditious meaning and tendency of it, it is in effect no libel. It cannot inflame the minds of the people, nor alienate their affections from government; for they no more understand what it means, than if it were published in a language unknown to them.

UPON the whole matter it appears, to *my* understanding, clear beyond a doubt, that if, in any future prosecution for a seditious libel, the jury should bring in a verdict of acquittal not warranted
ranted

ranted by the evidence, it will be owing to the falfe and abfurd doctrines laid down by *Lord Mansfield.* Difgufted by the odious artifices made ufe of by the Judge to miflead and-perplex them, guarded againft his fophiftry, and convinced of the falfehood of his affertions, they may perhaps determine to thwart his deteftable purpofe, and defeat him at any rate. To *him* at leaft they will do *fubftantial juftice.*——Whereas, if the whole charge, laid in the information, be fairly and honeftly fubmitted to the jury, there is no reafon whatfoever to prefume that twelve men, upon their oaths, will not decide impartially between the King and the defendant. The numerous inftances, in our ftate-trials, of verdicts recovered for the King, fufficiently refute the falfe and fcandalous imputations thrown by the abettors of *Lord Mansfield* upon the integrity of juries.—But even admitting the fuppofition, that in times of univerfal difcontent, arifing from the notorious maladminiftration of public affairs, a feditious writer fhould efcape punifhment, it makes nothing againft my general argument. If juries are fallible, to what other tribunal fhall we appeal? —If juries cannot fafely be trufted, fhall we unite the offices of judge and jury, fo wifely divided by the conftitution, and truft implicitly to *Lord Mansfield?*—Are the judges of the court of King's Bench more likely to be unbiaffed and impartial, than twelve yeomen, burgeffes, or gentlemen, taken indifferently from the county at large?— Or, in fhort, fhall there be *no* decifion, until we have inftituted a tribunal, from which no poffible abufe or inconvenience whatfoever can arife? —If I am not grofsly miftaken, thefe queftions carry a decifive anfwer along with them.

Having cleared the freedom of the prefs from

a reſtraint equally unneceſſary and illegal, I return to the uſe which has been made of it in the preſent publication.

NATIONAL reflections, I confeſs, are not juſtified in theory, nor upon any general principles. To know how well they are deſerved, and how juſtly they have been applied, we muſt have the evidence of facts before us. We muſt be converſant with the *Scots* in private life, and obſerve their principles of acting to *us*, and to each other;—the characteriſtic prudence, the ſelfiſh nationality, the indefatigable ſmile, the perſevering aſſiduity, the everlaſting profeſſion of a diſcreet and moderate reſentment.—If the inſtance were not too important for an experiment, it might not be amiſs to confide a little in their integrity.—Without any abſtract reaſoning upon cauſes and effects, we ſhall ſoon be convinced by *experience*, that the *Scots*, tranſplanted from their own country, are always a diſtinct and ſeparate body from the people who receive them. In other ſettlements, they only love themſelves;—in *England*, they cordially love themſelves, and as cordially hate their neighbours. For the remainder of their good qualities, I muſt appeal to the reader's obſervation, unleſs he will accept of *my Lord Barrington*'s authority. In a letter to the late *Lord Melcombe*, publiſhed by *Mr Lee*, he expreſſes himſelf with a truth and accuracy not very common in his Lordſhip's lucubrations;—" And Cockburn, *like moſt of his coun-* " *trymen*, is as abject to thoſe above him, as he " is inſolent to thoſe below him."——I am far from meaning to impeach the articles of the union. If the true ſpirit of thoſe articles were religiouſly adhered to, we ſhould not ſee ſuch a multitude of Scotch commoners in the lower-houſe, as repreſentatives of Engliſh boroughs,

roughs, while not a single Scotch borough is ever represented by an Englishman. We should not see English peerages given to Scotch ladies, or to the elder sons of Scotch peers, and the number of *sixteen* doubled and trebled by a scandalous evasion of the act of union.—If it should ever be thought advisable to dissolve an act, the violation or observance of which is invariably directed by the advantage and interest of the *Scots*, I shall say, very sincerely, with Sir Edward Coke, * " When ". poor England stood alone, and had not the ac-" cess of another kingdom, and yet had more and " as potent enemies as it now hath, yet the King " of England prevailed."

SOME opinion may now be expected from me, upon a point of equal delicacy to the writer, and hazard to the printer. When the character of the chief magistrate is in question, more must be understood than may safely be expressed. If it be really a part of our constitution, and not a mere *dictum* of the law, *that the King can do no wrong,* it is not the only instance, in the wisest of human institutions, where theory is at variance with practice.—That the sovereign of this country is not amenable to any form of trial known to the laws, is unquestionable. But exemption from punishment is a singular privilege annexed to the royal character, and no way excludes the possibility of deserving it. How long, and to what extent, a King of *England* may be protected by the forms, when he violates the spirit of the constitution, deserves to be considered. A mistake in this matter proved fatal to *Charles* and his son.—For my own part, far from thinking that the King can do no wrong, far from suffering myself to be deterred or imposed upon by the language of forms

in

* Parliamentary History, V. vii. p. 406.

in opposition to the substantial evidence of truth,
if it were my misfortune to live under the inau-
spicious reign of a prince, whose whole life was
employed in one base contemptible struggle with
the free spirit of his people, or in the detestable
endeavour to corrupt their moral principles, I
would not scruple to declare to him,—" Sir, You
" alone are the author of the greatest wrong to
" your subjects and to yourself. Instead of reign-
" ing in the hearts of your people, instead of
" commanding their lives and fortunes thro' the
" medium of their affections; has not the strength
" of the crown, whether influence or prerogative,
" been uniformly exerted, for eleven years to-
" gether, to support a narrow pitiful system of
" government, which defeats itself, and answers
" no one purpose of real power, profit, or per-
" sonal satisfaction to You?—With the greatest
" unappropriated revenue of any prince in Eu-
" rope, have we not seen You reduced to such
" vile and sordid distresses, as would have con-
" ducted any other man to a prison?—With a
" great military, and the greatest naval power in
" the known world, have not foreign nations re-
" peatedly insulted You with impunity?—Is it
" not notorious, that the vast revenues, extorted
" from the labour and industry of your subjects,
" and given You to do honour to Yourself and
" to the nation, are dissipated in corrupting their
" representatives?———Are You a prince of the
" house of Hanover, and do You exclude all the
" leading Whig families from your councils?—
" Do You profess to govern according to Law;
" and is it consistent with that profession, to im-
" part your confidence and affection to those
" men only, who, though now perhaps detached
" from the desperate cause of the Pretender, are
" marked in this country by an hereditary attach-
" ment to high and arbitrary principles of go-
                  C                " vernment?

" vernment?—Are You so infatuated as to take
" the sense of your people from the representa-
" tion of ministers, or from the shouts of a mob,
" notoriously hired to surround your coach, or
" stationed at a theatre?—And if You are, in
" reality, that public man, that King, that Ma-
" giftrate, which these questions suppose You to
" be, is it any answer to your people, to say, That
" among yonr domestics You are good-humoured;
" —that to one lady You are faithful;—that to
" your children you are indulgent?——Sir, the
" man who addresses You in these terms is your
" best friend. He would willingly hazard his
" life in defence of your title to the crown; and,
" if *power* be your object, would still show You
" how possible it is for a King of England, by the
" noblest means, to be the most absolute prince
" in Europe. You have no enemies, Sir, but
" those who persuade You to aim at power with-
" out right, and who think it flattery to tell You,
" that the character of King dissolves the natural
" relation between guilt and punishment."

I cannot conceive that there is a heart so
callous, or an understanding so depraved, as to
attend to a discourse of this nature, and not to
feel the force of it. But where is the man,
among those who have access to the closet, reso-
lute and honest enough to deliver it? The liberty
of the press is our only resource. It will command
an audience, when every honest man in the kingdom is excluded. This glorious privilege may be
a security to the King, as well as a resource to his
people. Had there been no star-chamber, there
would have been no rebellion against Charles the
first. The constant censure and admonition of the
press would have corrected his conduct, prevented
a civil war, and saved him from an ignominious
death.—I am no friend to the doctrine of prece-

dents

dents exclufive of right; though lawyers often tell us, that whatever has been once done may lawfully be done again.

I SHALL conclude this preface with a quotation applicable to the fulject, from a foreign writer *; whofe effay on the Englifh conftitution I beg leave to recommend to the public, as a performance deep, folid, and ingenious.

" IN fhort, whoever confiders what it is that
" conftitutes the moving principle of what we
" call great affairs, and the invincible fenfibility of
" man to the opinion of his fellow-creatures, will
" not hefitate to affirm, that if it were poffible for
" the liberty of the prefs to exift in a defpotic go-
" vernment, and (what is not lefs difficult) for it
" to exift without changing the conftitution, this
" liberty of the prefs would alone form a coun-
" terpoife to the power of the prince. If, for ex-
" ample, in an empire of the Eaft, a fanctuary
" could be found, which, rendered refpectable
" by the ancient religion of the people, might in-
" fure fafety to thofe who fhould bring thither
" their obfervations of any kind; and that, from
" thence, printed papers fhould iffue, which, un-
" der a certain feal, might be equally refpected;
" and which, in their daily appearance, fhould
" examine and freely difcufs the conduct of the
" Cadis, the Bafhaws, the Vizir, the Divan, and
" the Sultan himfelf; that would introduce imme-
" diately fome degree of liberty."

C 2         L E T-

---

* *Monfieur de Lolme.*

# LETTERS

## OF

# JUNIUS,

## ETC.

---

## LETTER I.

ADDRESSED TO THE PRINTER OF THE PUBLIC ADVERTISER.

SIR,　　　　　　　　　　　JANUARY 21. 1769.

THE fubmiffion of a free people to the executive authority of government is no more than a compliance with laws, which they themfelves have enacted. While the national honour is firmly maintained abroad, and while juftice is impartially adminiftered at home, the obedience of the fubject will be voluntary, cheerful, and I might almoft fay unlimited. A generous nation is grateful even for the prefervation of its rights, and willingly extends the refpect due to the Office of a good prince into an affection for his Perfon. Loyalty, in the heart and underftanding of an Englifhman, is a rational attachment to the guardian of the laws. Prejudices and paffion have fometimes carried it to a criminal length; and, whatever foreigners may imagine, we know that Englifhmen have erred as much in a miftaken zeal for particular perfons and families, as they ever did in defence of what they thought moft dear and interefting to themfelves.

It naturally fills us with refentment, to fee fuch a temper infulted and abufed. In reading the hiftory of a free people, whofe rights have

been invaded, we are interested in their caufe.
Our own feelings tell us how they ought to have
fubmitted, and at what moment it would have
been treachery to themfelves not to have refifted.
How much warmer will be our refentment, if experience fhould bring the fatal example home to
ourfelves !

The fituation of this country is alarming e-
nough to roufe the attention of every man who
pretends to a concern for the public welfare. Appearances juftify fufpicion; and when the fafety
of a nation is at ftake, fufpicion is a juft ground
of inquiry. Let us enter into it with candour
and decency. Refpect is due to the ftation of
minifters; and, if a refolution muft at laft be
taken, there is none fo likely to be fupported
with firmnefs as that which has been adopted
with moderation.

The ruin or profperity of a ftate depends fo
much upon the adminiftration of its government,
that, to be acquainted with the merit of a miniftry, we need only obferve the condition of the
people. If we fee them obedient to the laws,
profperous in their induftry, united at home, and
refpected abroad, we may reafonably prefume
that their affairs are conducted by men of experience, abilities, and virtue. If, on the contrary, we
fee an univerfal fpirit of diftruft and diffatisfaction,
a rapid decay of trade, diffenfions in all parts of the
empire, and a total lofs of refpect in the eyes of
foreign powers, we may pronounce without hefitation, that the government of that country is
weak, diftracted, and corrupt. The multitude,
in all countries, are patient to a certain point.
Ill-ufage may roufe their indignation, and hurry
them into exceffes; but the original fault is in
government. Perhaps there never was an inftance of a change, in the circumftances and
temper of a whole nation, fo fudden and extraordinary

ordinary as that which the mifconduct of minifters has, within thefe few years, produced in
Great Britain.  When our gracious fovereign afcended the throne, we were a flourifhing and a
contented people.  If the perfonal virtues of a
king could have infured the happinefs of his fubjects, the fcene could not have altered fo entirely
as it has done.  The idea of uniting all parties,
of trying all characters, and diftributing the offices of ftate by rotation, was gracious and benevolent to an extreme, though it has not yet produced the many falutary effects which were intended by it.  To fay nothing of the wifdom of
fuch a plan, it undoubtedly arofe from an un-
bounded goodnefs of heart, in which folly had no
fhare.  It was not a capricious partiality to new
faces ;—it was not a natural turn for low in-
trigue ;—nor was it the treacherous amufement of
double and triple negotiations.  No, Sir; it arofe
from a continued anxiety, in the pureft of all poffible hearts, for the general welfare.  Unfortunately for us, the event has not been anfwerable
to the defign.  After a rapid fucceffion of changes,
we are reduced to that ftate, which hardly any
change can mend.  Yet there is no extremity of
diftrefs, which of itfelf ought to reduce a great
nation to defpair.  It is not the diforder, but the
phyfician ;—it is not a cafual concurrence of ca-
lamitous circumftances ;—it is the pernicious hand
of government, which alone can make a whole
people defperate.

Without much political fagacity, or any extraordinary depth of obfervation, we need only mark
how the principal departments of the ftate are
beftowed, and look no farther for the true caufe
of every mifchief that befals us.

† The finances of a nation, finking under its
debts

---

† The Duke of Grafton took the office of Secretary of State,
with an engagement to fupport the Marquis of Rockingham's
admini-

debts and expences, are committed to a young nobleman already ruined by play. Introduced to act under the auspices of Lord Chatham, and left at the head of affairs by that nobleman's retreat, he became minister by accident; but deserting the principles and professions which gave him a moment's popularity, we see him, from every honourable engagement to the public, an apostate by design. As for business, the world yet knows nothing of his talents or resolution; unless a wayward, wavering inconsistency be a mark of genius, and caprice a demonstration of spirit. It may be said, perhaps, that it is his Grace's province, as surely it is his passion, rather to distribute than to save the public money; and that while Lord North is Chancellor of the Exchequer, the First Lord of the Treasury may be as thoughtless and extravagant as he pleases. I hope, however, he will not rely too much on the fertility of Lord North's genius for finance. His Lordship is yet to give us the first proof of his abilities: It may be candid to suppose that he has hitherto voluntarily concealed his talents; intending perhaps to astonish the world, when we least expect it, with a knowledge of trade, a choice of expedients, and a depth of resources, equal to the necessities, and far beyond the hopes, of his country. He must now exert the whole power of his capacity, if he would wish us to forget, that, since he has been in office, no plan has been formed, no system adhered to, nor any one important measure adopted for the relief of public credit. If his plan for the service of the current year be not irrevocably fixed on, let me warn him to think seriously

administration. He resigned, however, in a little time, under pretence that he could not act without Lord Chatham, nor bear to see Mr Wilkes abandoned; but that under Lord Chatham he would act in *any* office. This was the signal of Lord Rockingham's dismission. When Lord Chatham came in, the Duke got possession of the Treasury. Reader, mark the consequence!

riouíly of confequences before he ventures to increafe the public debt.  Outraged and oppreffed
as we are, this nation will not bear, after a fix
years peace, to fee new millions borrowed, without an eventual diminution of debt, or reduction
of intereft.  The attempt might roufe a fpirit of
refentment, which might reach beyond the facrifice of a minifter.  As to the debt upon the civil
lift, the people of England expect that it will not
be paid without a ftrict inquiry how it was incurred.  If it muft be paid by parliament, let me
advife the Chancellor of the Exchequer to think
of fome better expedient than a lottery.  To
fupport an expenfive war, or in circumftances of
abfolute neceffity, a lottery may perhaps be al-
lowable; but, befides that it is at all times the
very worft way of raifing money upon the people,
I think it ill becomes the Royal dignity to have
the debts of a King provided for, like the repairs
of a country bridge, or a decayed hofpital.  The
management of the King's affairs in the Houfe
of Commons cannot be more difgraced than it
has been.  * A leading minifter repeatedly called
down for abfolute ignorance ;—ridiculous motions ridiculoufly withdrawn ;—deliberate plans
difconcerted, and a week's preparation of graceful oratory loft in a moment, give us fome
though not adequate idea of Lord North's parliamentary abilities and influence.  Yet before he
had the misfortune of being Chancellor of the Exchequer, he was neither an object of derifion to his
enemies, nor of melancholy pity to his friends.

A feries of inconfiftent meafures has alienated
the colonies from their duty as fubjects, and from
their natural affection to their common country.
When Mr Grenville was placed at the head of
the Treafury, he felt the impoffibility of Great
Britain's fupporting fuch an eftablifhment as her
former

* This happened frequently to poor Lord North.

former fucceffes had made indifpenfable, and at the fame time of giving any fenfible relief to foreign trade, and to the weight of the public debt. He thought it equitable that thofe parts of the empire which had benefited moft by the expences of the war, fhould contribute fomething to the expences of the peace, and he had no doubt of the conftitutional right vefted in parliament to raife the contribution. But, unfortunately for this country, Mr Grenville was at any rate to be diftreffed becaufe he was minifter, and Mr Pitt * and Lord Camden were to be the patrons of America becaufe they were in oppofition. Their declaration gave fpirit and argument to the colonies; and while perhaps they meant no more than the ruin of a minifter, they in effect divided one half of the empire from the other.

Under one adminiftration the ftamp-act is made; under the fecond it is repealed; under the third, in fpite of all experience, a new mode of taxing the colonies is invented, and a queftion revived which ought to have been buried in oblivion. In thefe circumftances a new office is eftablifhed for the bufinefs of the plantations, and the Earl of Hilfborough called forth, at a moft critical feafon, to govern America. The choice at leaft announced to us a man of fuperior capacity and knowledge. Whether he be fo or not, let his difpatches as far as they have appeared, let his meafures as far as they have operated, determine for him. In the former, we have feen ftrong affertions without proof, declamation without argument, and violent cenfures without dignity or moderation; but neither correctnefs in the compofition, nor judgment in the defign. As for his meafures, let it be remembered, that he was called upon to conciliate and unite; and that when he entered into office, the moft refractory

of

---

* Yet *Junius* has been called the partizan of Lord Chatham?

of the colonies were ſtill diſpoſed to proceed by
the conſtitutional methods of petition and remonſtrance. Since that period they have been
driven into exceſſes little ſhort of rebellion. Petitions have been hindered from reaching the
throne; and the continuance of one of the principal aſſemblies reſted upon an arbitrary condition*; which, conſidering the temper they were
in, it was impoſſible they ſhould comply with,
and which would have availed nothing as to the
general queſtion if it had been complied with.
So violent, and I believe I may call it ſo unconſtitutional, an exertion of the prerogative, to ſay
nothing of the weak injudicious terms in which
it was conveyed, gives us as humble an opinion
of his lordſhip's capacity as it does of his temper
and moderation.   While we are at peace with
other nations, our military force may perhaps be
ſpared to ſupport the Earl of Hilſborough's meaſures in America.   Whenever that force ſhall be
neceſſarily withdrawn or diminiſhed, the diſmiſ-
ſion of ſuch a miniſter will neither conſole us for
his imprudence, nor remove the ſettled reſentment of a people, who, complaining of an act of
the legiſlature, are outraged by an unwarrantable
ſtretch of prerogative, and, ſupporting their claims
by argument, are inſulted with declamation.

Drawing lots would be a prudent and reaſonable method of appointing the officers of ſtate,
compared to a late diſpoſition of the ſecretary's
office. Lord Rochford was acquainted with the
affairs and temper of the ſouthern courts: Lord
Weymouth was equally qualified for either de-
partment†. By what unaccountable caprice has
it

* That they ſhould retract one of their reſolutions, and eraſe
the entry of it.

† It was pretended that the Earl of Rochford, while ambaſſador
in France, had quarrelled with the Duke of Choiſeuïl; and that
therefore he was appointed to the Northern department, out of
compliment to the French miniſter.

it happened, that the latter, who pretends to no experience whatſoever, is removed to the moſt important of the two departments, and the former by preference placed in an office where his experience can be of no uſe to him ? Lord Weymouth had diſtinguiſhed himſelf in his firſt employment by a ſpirited if not judicious conduct. He had animated the civil magiſtrate beyond the tone of civil authority, and had directed the operations of the army to more than military execution. Recovered from the errors of his youth, from the diſtraction of play, and the bewitching ſmiles of Burgundy, behold him exerting the whole ſtrength of his clear unclouded faculties, in the ſervice of the crown. It was not the heat of midnight exceſſes, nor ignorance of the laws, nor the furious ſpirit of the houſe of Bedford : No, Sir, when this reſpectable miniſter interpoſed his authority between the magiſtrate and the people, and ſigned the mandate, on which, for aught he knew, the lives of thouſands depended, he did it from the deliberate motion of his heart ſupported by the beſt of his judgment.

It has lately been a faſhion to pay a compliment to the bravery and generoſity of the commander in chief† at the expence of his underſtanding. They who love him leaſt make no queſtion of his courage, while his friends dwell chiefly on the facility of his diſpoſition. Admitting him to be as brave as a total abſence of all feeling and reflection can make him, let us ſee what ſort of merit he derives from the remainder of his character. If it be generoſity to accumulate in his own perſon and family a number of lucrative employments; to provide, at the public expence, for every creature that bears the name of Manners; and, neglecting the merit and ſervices of the reſt of the army, to heap promotions
upon

---

† The late Lord Granby.

upon his favourites and dependants; the present commander in chief is the most generous man alive. Nature has been sparing of her gifts to this noble lord; but where birth and fortune are united, we expect the noble pride and independance of a man of spirit, not the servile humiliating complaisance of a courtier. As to the goodness of his heart, if a proof of it be taken from the facility of never refusing, what conclusion shall we draw from the indecency of never performing? And if the discipline of the army be in any degree preserved, what thanks are due to a man, whose cares, notoriously confined to filling up vacancies, have degraded the office of commander in chief into a broker of commissions?

With respect to the navy, I shall only say, that this country is so highly indebted to Sir Edward Hawke, that no expence should be spared to secure to him an honourable and affluent retreat.

The pure and impartial administration of justice is perhaps the firmest bond to secure a cheerful submission of the people, and to engage their affections to government. It is not sufficient that questions of private right or wrong are justly decided, nor that judges are superior to the vileness of pecuniary corruption. Jefferies himself, when the court had no interest, was an upright judge. A court of justice may be subject to another sort of bias more important and pernicious, as it reaches beyond the interest of individuals, and affects the whole community. A judge, under the influence of government, may be honest enough in the decision of private causes, yet a traitor to the public. When a victim is marked out by the ministry, this judge will offer himself to perform the sacrifice. He will not scruple to prostitute his dignity, and betray the sanctity of his office, whenever an arbitrary point is to be

D

carried

carried for government, or the refentment of a
court to be gratified.

These principles and proceedings, odious and
contemptible as they are, in effect are no lefs injudicious. A wife and generous people are roufed by every appearance of oppreffive, unconftitutional meafures, whether thofe meafures are
fupported only by the power of government, or
mafked under the forms of a court of juftice.
Prudence and felf-prefervation will oblige the
moft moderate difpofitions to make common caufe,
even with a man whofe conduct they cenfure, if
they fee him perfecuted in a way which the real
fpirit of the laws will not juftify. The facts, on
which thefe remarks are founded, are too notorious
to require an application.

This, Sir, is the detail. In one view, behold a
nation overwhelmed with debt; her revenues
wafted; her trade declining; the affections of her
colonies alienated; the duty of the magiftrate
transferred to the foldiery; a gallant army, which
never fought unwillingly but againft their fellow-
fubjects, mouldering away for want of the direction of a man of common abilities and fpirit;
and in the laft inftance, the adminiftration of
juftice become odious and fufpected to the whole
body of the people. This dpelorable fcene admits of but one addition—that we are governed
by counfels, from which a reafonable man can expect no remedy but poifon, no relief but death.

If, by the immediate interpofition of Providence, it were poffible for us to efcape a crifis fo
full of terror and defpair, pofterity will not believe the hiftory of the prefent times. They
will either conclude that our diftreffes were imaginary, or that we had the good fortune to be
governed by men of acknowledged integrity and
wifdom: they will not believe it poffible that
their anceftors could have furvived or recovered

from

from fo defperate a condition, while a Duke of
Grafton was Prime Minifter, a Lord North Chan-
cellor of the Exchequer, a Weymouth and a
Hilfborough Secretaries of State, a Granby Com-
mander in Chief, and Mansfield chief criminal
Judge of the kingdom.

J U N I U S.

## LETTER II.

### TO THE PRINTER OF THE PUBLIC AD-VERTISER.

S I R,                          JAN. 26. 1769.

THE kingdom fwarms with fuch numbers of fe-
lonious robbers of private character and virtue,
that no honeft or good man is fafe; efpecially as
thefe cowardly bafe affaffins ftab in the dark, without having the courage to fign their real names
to their malevolent and wicked productions.  A
writer, who figns himfelf *Junius*, in the Public
Advertifer of the 21ft inftant, opens the delorable
fituation of his country in a very affecting manner; with a pompous parade of his candour and
decency, he tells us, that we fee diffenfions in
all parts of the empire, an univerfal fpirit of diftruft and diffatisfaction, and a total lofs of refpect
towards us in the eyes of foreign powers.  But
this writer, with all his boafted candour, has not
told us the real caufe of the evils he fo patheti-
cally enumerates.  I fhall take the liberty to explain the caufe for him.  Junius and fuch writers as himfelf occafion all the mifchief complained of, by falfely and malicioufly traducing
the beft characters in the kingdom.  For when
our deluded people at home, and foreigners
abroad, read the poifonous and inflammatory
libels that are daily publifhed with impunity, to
vilify thofe who are any way diftinguifhed by
D 2 their

their good qualities and eminent virtues; when they find no notice taken of, or reply given to, these slanderous tongues and pens; their conclusion is, that both the ministers and the nation have been fairly described; and they act accordingly. I think it therefore the duty of every good citizen to stand forth, and endeavour to undeceive the public, when the vilest arts are made use of to defame and blacken the brightest characters among us. An eminent author affirms it to be almost as criminal to hear a worthy man traduced, without attempting his justification, as to be the author of the calumny against him. For my own part, I think it a sort of misprision of treason against society. No man, therefore, who knows Lord Granby, can possibly hear so good and great a character most vilely abused, without a warm and just indignation against this Junius, this high-priest of envy, malice, and all uncharitableness, who has endeavoured to sacrifice our beloved commander in chief at the altars of his horrid deities. Nor is the injury done to his lordship alone, but to the whole nation, which may too soon feel the contempt, and consequently the attacks of our late enemies, if they can be induced to believe that the person, on whom the safety of these kingdoms so much depends, is unequal to his high station, and destitute of those qualities which form a good general. One would have thought that his lordship's services in the cause of his country, from the battle of Culloden to his most glorious conclusion of the late war, might have intitled him to common respect and decency at least: but this uncandid indecent writer has gone so far as to turn one of the most amiable men of the age into a stupid, unfeeling, and senseless being; possessed indeed of a personal courage, but void of those

essential

effential qualities which diftinguifh the commander from the common foldier.

A very long, uninterrupted, impartial, I will
add, a moft difinterefted, friendfhip with Lord
Granby, gives me the right to affirm, that all
Junius's affertions are falfe and fcandalous. Lord
Granby's courage, though of the brighteft and
moft ardent kind, is among the loweft of his numerous good qualities; he was formed to excel
in war by nature's liberality to his mind as well
as perfon. Educated and inftructed by his moft
noble father, and a moft fpirited as well as excellent fcholar, the prefent Bifhop of Bangor, he
was trained to the niceft fenfe of honour, and to
the trueft and nobleft fort of pride, that of never
doing or fuffering a mean action. A fincere love
and attachment to his king and country, and to
their glory, firft impelled him to the field, where
be never gained aught but honour. He impaired,
through his bounty, his own fortune: for his
bounty, which this writer would in vain depre-
ciate, is founded upon the nobleft of the human
affections; it flows from a heart melting to goodnefs from the moft refined humanity. Can a man,
who is defcribed as unfeeling and void of reflection, be conftantly employed in feeking proper
objects on whom to exercife thofe glorious virtues of compaffion and generofity? The diftreffed
officer, the foldier, the widow, the orphan, and a
long lift befides, know that vanity has no fhare
in his frequent donations; he gives, becaufe he
feels their diftreffes. Nor has he ever been ra-
pacious with one hand, to be bountiful with the
other: yet this uncandid Junius would infinuate,
that the dignity of the commander in chief is depraved into the bafe office of commiffion broker;
that is, Lord Granby bargains for the fale of commiffions; for it muft have this meaning, if it has
any at all. But where is the man living who can

juftly charge his lordſhip with ſuch mean practices? Why does not Junius produce him? Junius
knows that he has no other means of wounding
this hero, than from ſome miſſile weapon, ſhot
from an obſcure corner: He ſeeks, as all defama-
tory writers do,

> ———ſpargere voces
> In Vulgum ambiguas———

to raiſe a ſuſpicion in the minds of the people.
But I hope that my countrymen will be no longer
impoſed upon by artful and defigning men, or by
wretches, who, bankrupts in buſineſs, in fame,
and in fortune, mean nothing more than to involve this country in the ſame common ruin with
themſelves. Hence it is, that they are conſtantly
aiming their dark and too often fatal weapons
againſt thoſe who ſtand forth as the bulwark of
our national ſafety. Lord Granby was too conſpicuous a mark not to be their object. He is
next attacked for being unfaithful to his promiſes
and engagements: Where are Junius's proofs?
Although I could give ſome inſtances, where a
breach of promiſe would be a virtue, eſpecially
in the caſe of thoſe who would pervert the open,
unſuſpecting moments of convivial mirth, into ſly,
inſidious applications for preferment or party-
fyſtems, and would endeavour to ſurpriſe a good
man, who cannot bear to ſee any one leave him
diſſatisfied, into unguarded promiſes. Lord Granby's attention to his own family and relations is
called ſelfiſh. Had he not attended to them,
when fair and juſt opportunities preſented themſelves, I ſhould have thought him unfeeling, and
void of reflection indeed. How are any man's
friends or relations to be provided for, but from
the influence and protection of the patron? It is
unfair to ſuppoſe that Lord Granby's friends have
not as much merit as the friends of any other

great

great man: If he is generous at the public expence, as Junius invidiously calls it; the public is
at no more expence for his lordship's friends, than
it would be if any other set of men possessed those
offices.  The charge is ridiculous!

. The last charge against Lord Granby is of a
most serious and alarming nature indeed.  Junius asserts, that the army is mouldering away
for want of the direction of a man of common
abilities and spirit.  The present condition of the
army gives the directest lie to his assertions.  It
was never upon a more respectable footing with
regard to discipline, and all the essentials that can
form  good  soldiers.  Lord  Ligonier  delivered
a firm and noble palladium of our safeties into
Lord Granby's hands, who has kept it in the
same good order in which he received it.  The
strictest care has been taken to fill up the vacant
commissions, with such gentlemen as have the
glory of their ancestors to support, as well as their
own, and are doubly bound to the cause of their
king and country, from motives of private property, as well as public spirit.  The adjutant-
general, who has the immediate care of the
troops after Lord Granby, is an officer that would
do great honour to any service in Europe, for his
correct arrangements, good sense and discernment
upon all occasions, and for a punctuality and pre-
cision which give the most entire satisfaction to
all who are obliged to consult him.  The reviewing generals, who inspect the army twice a-year,
have been selected with the greatest care, and
have answered the important trust reposed in
them in the most laudable manner.  Their reports of the condition of the army are much more
to be credited than those of Junius, whom I do
advise to atone, for his shameful aspersions, by
asking pardon of Lord Granby and the whole
kingdom, whom he has offended by his abomi-
nable

nable fcandals. In fhort, to turn Junius's own battery againft him, I muft affert, in his own words, "that has given ftrong affertions without proof, declamation without argument, and violent cenfures without dignity or moderation."

WILLIAM DRAPER.

---

## LETTER III.

### TO SIR WILLIAM DRAPER, KNIGHT OF THE BATH.

S I R,                       Feb. 7. 1769.

YOUR defence of Lord Granby does honour to the goodnefs of your heart. You feel, as you ought to do, for the reputation of your friend, and you exprefs yourfelf in the warmeft language of your paffions. In any other caufe, I doubt not, you would have cautioufly weighed the confequences of committing your name to the licentious difcourfes and malignant opinions of the world. But here, I prefume, you thought it would be a breach of friendfhip to lofe one moment in confulting your underftanding; as if an appeal to the public were no more than a military *coup de main*, where a brave man has no rules to follow but the dictates of his courage. Touched with your generofity, I freely forgive the exceffes into which it has led you: and, far from refenting thofe terms of reproach, which, confidering that you are an advocate for decorum, you have heaped upon me rather too liberally, I place them to the account of an honeft unreflecting indignation, in which your cooler judgment and natural politenefs had no concern. I approve of the fpirit with which you have given your name to the public; and, if it were a proof of any thing but fpirit, I fhould have thought myfelf bound to follow your example. I fhould have hoped that even

*my*

*my* name might have carried some authority with it, if I had not seen how very little weight or consideration a printed paper receives even from the respectable signature of Sir William Draper.

You begin with a general assertion, that writers, such as I am, are the real cause of all the public evils we complain of. And do you really think, Sir William, that the licentious pen of a political writer is able to produce such important effects? A little calm reflection might have shown you, that national calamities do not arise from the description, but from the real character and conduct, of ministers. To have supported your assertion, you should have proved that the present ministry are unquestionably the *best and brightest* characters of the kingdom; and that, if the affections of the colonies have been alienated, if Corsica has been shamefully abandoned, if commerce languishes, if public credit is threatened with a new debt, and your own Manilla ransom most dishonourably given up, it has all been owing to the malice of political writers, who will not suffer the best and brightest characters (meaning still the present ministry) to take a single right step for the honour or interest of the nation. But it seems you were a little tender of coming to particulars. Your conscience insinuated to you, that it would be prudent to leave the characters of Grafton, North, Hilsborough, Weymouth, and Mansfield, to shift for themselves; and truly, Sir William, the part you have undertaken is at least as much as you are equal to.

Without disputing Lord Granby's courage, we are yet to learn in what articles of military knowledge nature has been so very liberal to his mind. If you have served with him, you ought to have pointed out some instances of able disposition and well-concerted enterprize, which might fairly be attributed to his capacity as a general. It is you,

Sir

Sir William, who make your friend appear aukward and ridiculous, by giving him a laced suit of
tawdry qualifications, which nature never intended
him to wear.

You say, he has acquired nothing but honour
in the field.   Is the Ordinance nothing?   Are the
Blues nothing?  Is the command of the army, with
all the patronage annexed to it, nothing?  Where
he got thefe *nothings*, I know not; but you at
leaft ought to have told us where he deferved
them.

As to his bounty, compaffion, &c. it would
have been but little to the purpofe, though you
had proved all that you have afferted.  I meddle
with nothing but his character as commander in
chief: and, though I acquit him of the bafenefs
of felling commiffions, I ftill affert that his military cares have never extended beyond the difpofal of vacancies; and I am juftified by the complaints of the whole army, when I fay, that in
this diftribution he confults nothing but parliamentary intereft, or the gratification of his immediate dependants.  As to his fervile fubmiffion
to the reigning miniftry, let me afk, whether he
did not defert the caufe of the whole army when
he fuffered Sir Jeffery Amherft to be facrificed,
and what fhare he had in recalling that officer to
the fervice?  Did he not betray the juft intereft of
the army, in permitting Lord Percy to have a regiment?  And does he not at this moment give up
all character and dignity as a gentleman, in reced-
ing from his own repeated declarations in favour
of Mr Wilkes?

In the two next articles I think we are agreed.
You candidly admit, that he often makes fuch
promifes as it is a virtue in him to violate, and
that no man is more affiduous to provide for his
relations at the public expence.  I did not urge
the laft as an abfolute vice in his difpofition,

but

but to prove that a *carele*ſ*s di*ſ*intere*ſ*ted* ſ*pirit* is no part of his character; and as to the other, I deſire it may be remembered, that I never deſcended to the indecency of inquiring into his *convivial hours.* It is you, Sir William Draper, who have taken care to repreſent your friend in the character of a drunken landlord, who deals out his promiſes as liberally as his liquor, and will ſuffer no man to leave his table either ſorrowful or ſober. None but an intimate friend, who muſt frequently have ſeen him in theſe unhappy, diſgraceful moments, could have deſcribed him ſo well.

The laſt charge, of the neglect of the army, is indeed the moſt material of all. I am ſorry to tell you, Sir William, that, in this article, your firſt fact is falſe; and as there is nothing more painful to me than to give a direct contradiction to a gentleman of your appearance, I could wiſh that, in your future publications, you would pay a greater attention to the truth of your premiſes, before you ſuffer your genius to hurry you to a concluſion. Lord Ligonier *did not* deliver the army (which you, in claſſical language, are pleaſed to call a palladium) into Lord Granby's hands. It was taken from him much againſt his inclination, ſome two or three years before Lord Granby was commander in chief. As to the ſtate of the army, I ſhould be glad to know where you have received your intelligence. Was it in the rooms at Bath, or at your retreat at Clifton? The reports of reviewing generals comprehend only a few regiments in England, which, as they are immediately under the royal inſpection, are perhaps in ſome tolerable order. But do you know any thing of the troops in the Weſt-Indies, the Mediterranean, and North-America, to ſay nothing of a whole army abſolutely ruined in Ireland? Inquire a little into facts, Sir William,

before

before you publish your next panegyric upon Lord Granby; and believe me, you will find there is a fault at head-quarters, which even the acknowledged care and abilities of the adjutant-general cannot correct.

Permit me now, Sir William, to address myself personally to you, by way of thanks for the honour of your correspondence. You are by no means undeserving of notice; and it may be of consequence even to Lord Granby to have it determined, whether or no the man, who has praised him so lavishly, be himself deserving of praise. When you returned to Europe, you zealously undertook the cause of that gallant army, by whose bravery at Manilla your own fortune had been established. You complained, you threatened, you even appealed to the public in print. By what accident did it happen, that in the midst of all this bustle, and all these clamours for justice to your injured troops, the name of the Manilla ransom was suddenly buried in a profound, and, since that time, an uninterrupted silence? Did the ministry suggest any motives to you, strong enough to tempt a man of honour to desert and betray the cause of his fellow-soldiers? Was it that blushing riband, which is now the perpetual ornament of your person? Or was it that regiment, which you afterwards (a thing unprecedented among soldiers) sold to colonel Gisborne? Or was it that government, the full pay of which you are contented to hold, with the half-pay of an Irish colonel? And do you now, after a retreat not very like that of Scipio, presume to intrude yourself, unthought-of, uncalled-for, upon the patience of the public? Are your flatteries of the commander in chief directed to another regiment, which you may again dispose of on the same honourable terms? We know your prudence, Sir

I

William,

William, and I fhould be forry to ftop your preferment.

J U N I U S.

---

## L E T T E R   IV.

### TO JUNIUS.

S I R,                                 FEB. 17. 1769.

I RECEIVED Junius's favour laft night: he is determined to keep his advantage by the help
of his mafk; it is an excellent protection, it has
faved many a man from an untimely end.  But
whenever he will be honeft enough to lay it a-
fide, avow himfelf, and produce the face which
has fo long lurked behind it, the world will be
able to judge of his motives for writing fuch infamous invectives.  His real name will difcover
his freedom and independency, or his fervility to
a faction.  Difappointed ambition, refentment for
defeated hopes, and defire of revenge, affume but
too often the appearance of public fpirit; but be
his defigns wicked or charitable, Junius fhould
learn, that it is poffible to condemn meafures,
without a barbarous and criminal outrage againft
men.  Junius delights to mangle carcafes with a
hatchet; his language and inftrument have a
great connection with Clare-Market, and, to do
him juftice, he handles his weapon moft admi-
rably.  One would imagine he had been taught
to throw it by the favages of America.  It is
therefore high time for me to ftep in once more
to fhield my friend from this mercilefs weapon,
although I may be wounded in the attempt.  But
I muft firft afk Junius, by what forced analogy
and conftruction the moments of convivial mirth
are made to fignify indecency, a violation of engagements, a drunken landlord, and a defire that
every one in company fhould be drunk likewife?

E

He

He muſt have culled all the flowers of St Giles's
and Billingſgate to have produced ſuch a piece
of oratory. Here the hatchet deſcends with tenfold vengeance; but, alas! it hurts no one but its
maſter! For Junius muſt not think to put words
into my mouth, that ſeem too foul even for his
own.

My friend's political engagements I know not;
ſo cannot pretend to explain them, or aſſert their
conſiſtency. I know not whether Junius be con-
ſiderable enough to belong to any party; if he
ſhould be ſo, can he affirm that he has always
adhered to one ſet of men and meaſures? Is he
ſure that he has never ſided with thoſe whom he
was firſt hired to abuſe? Has he never abuſed
thoſe he was hired to praiſe? To ſay the truth,
moſt mens politics ſits much too looſely about
them. But as my friend's military character was
the chief object that engaged me in this controverſy, to that I ſhall return.

Junius aſks, what inſtances my friend has given
of his military ſkill and capacity as a general?
When and where he gained his honour? When
he deſerved his emoluments? The united voice
of the army which ſerved under him, the glorious teſtimony of prince Ferdinand, and of van-
quiſhed enemies, all Germany will tell him.
Junius repeats the complaints of the army againſt
parliamentary influence. I love the army too well,
not to wiſh that ſuch influence were leſs. Let
Junius point out the time when it has not prevailed. It was of the leaſt force in the time
of that great man, the late duke of Cumberland,
who, as a prince of the blood, was able as well
as willing to ſtem a torrent which would have
overborne any private ſubject. In time of war
this influence is ſmall. In peace, when diſcon-
tent and faction have the ſureſt means to operate,
eſpecially in this country, and when from a
                                              ſcarcity

scarcity of public spirit the wheels of government are rarely moved but by the power and force of obligations, its weight is always too great. Yet, if this influence at present has done no greater harm than the placing Earl Percy at the head of a regiment, I do not think that either the rights or best interests of the army are sacrificed and betrayed, or the nation undone. Let me ask Junius, if he knows any one nobleman in the army, who has had a regiment by seniority? I feel myself happy in seeing young noblemen of illustrious name and great property come among us. They are an additional security to the kingdom from foreign or domestic slavery. Junius needs not be told, that should the time ever come, when this nation is to be defended only by those who have nothing more to lose than their arms and their pay, its danger will be great indeed. A happy mixture of men of quality with soldiers of fortune is always to be wished for. But the main point is still to be contended for, I mean the discipline and condition of the army; and I must still maintain, though contradicted by Junius, that it was never upon a more respectable footing, as to all the essentials that can form good soldiers, than it is at present. Junius is forced to allow, that our army at home may be in some tolerable order; yet how kindly does he invite our late enemies to the invasion of Ireland, by assuring them that the army in that kingdom is totally ruined! (The colonels of that army are much obliged to him.) I have too great an opinion of the military talents of the lord lieutenant, and of all their diligence and capacity, to believe it. If from some strange, unaccountable fatality, the people of that kingdom cannot be induced to consult their own security by such an effectual augmentation as may enable the troops there to act with power and energy, is the commander in

E 2

chief

chief here to blame.? Or is he to blame, becaufe the troops in the Mediterranean, in the Weft-Indies, in America, labour under great difficulties from the fcarcity of men, which is but too vifible all over thefe kingdoms? Many of our forces are in climates unfavourable to Britifh conftitutions; their lofs is in proportion. Britain muft recruit all thefe regiments from her own emaciated bofom, or, more precarioufly, by Catholics from Ireland. We are likewife fubject to the fatal drains to the Eaft-Indies, to Senegal, and the alarming emigrations of our people to other countries: Such depopulation can only be repaired by a long peace, or by fome fenfible bill of naturalization.

I muft now take the liberty to talk to Junius on my own account. He is pleafed to tell me that he addreffes himfelf to me *perfonally;* I fhall be glad to fee him. It is his *imperfonality* that I complain of, and his invifible attacks: for his dagger in the air is only to be regarded becaufe one cannot fee the hand which holds it; but had it not wounded other people more deeply than myfelf, I fhould not have obtruded myfelf at all on the patience of the public.

Mark how a plain tale fhall put him down, and transfufe the blufh of my riband into his own cheeks. Junius tells me, that at my return, I zealoufly undertook the caufe of the gallant army by whofe bravery at Manilla my own fortunes were eftablifhed; that I complained, that I even appealed to the public. I did fo; I glory in having done fo, as I had an undoubted right to vindicate my own character attacked by a Spanifh memorial, and to affert the rights of my brave companions. I glory likewife, that I have never taken up my pen, but to vindicate the injured. Junius afks by what accident did it happen, that in the midft of all this buftle, and all the clamours

for

for juftice to the injured troops, the Manilla ranfom was fuddenly buried in a profound, and, fince that time, an uninterrupted filence? I will explain the caufe to the public. The feveral minifters who have been employed fince that time have been very defirous to do juftice, from two moft laudable motives; a ftrong inclination to affift injured bravery, and to acquire a well deferved popularity to themfelves. Their efforts have been in vain. Some were ingenious enough to own, that they could not think of involving this diftreffed nation into another war for our private concerns. In fhort, our rights for the prefent are facrificed to national convenience; and I muft confefs, that although I may lofe five-and-twenty thoufand pounds by their acquiefcence to this breach of faith in the Spaniards, I think they are in the right to temporize, confidering the critical fituation of this country, convulfed in every part by poifon infufed by anonymous, wicked, and incendiary writers. Lord Shelburne will do me the juftice to own, that, in September laft, I waited upon him with a joint memorial from the admiral Sir S. Cornifh and myfelf, in behalf of our injured companions. His lordfhip was as frank upon the occafion as other fecretaries had been before him. He did not deceive us by giving any immediate hopes of relief.

Junius would bafely infinuate, that my filence may have been purchafed by my government, by my *blufhing* riband, by my regiment, by the fale of that regiment, and by half-pay as an Irifh colonel.

His Majefty was pleafed to give me my government for my fervice at Madras. I had my firft regiment in 1757. Upon my return from Manilla, his Majefty, by Lord Egremont, informed me that I fhould have the firft vacant red riband, as a reward for many fervices in an enterprife which I had planned as well as executed. The Duke of Bedford and Mr Grenville confirmed thofe affurances many months before the Spaniards had protefted the ranfom bills. To accommodate Lord Clive, then going upon a moft important fervice to Bengal, I waved my claim to the vacancy which then happened. As there was no other vacancy until the Duke of Grafton and Lord Rockingham were joint minifters, I was then honoured with the order: and it is furely no fmall honour to me, that in fuch a fucceffion of minifters, they were all pleafed to think that I had deferved it; in my favour they were all united. Upon the reduction of the 79th regiment, which had ferved fo glorioufly in the Eaft-Indies, his Majefty, unfolicited by me, gave me the 16th of foot as an equivalent. My motives for retiring afterwards are foreign to the purpofe : let it fuffice, that his Majefty was pleafed to approve of them; they are fuch as no man can think indecent, who knows the fhocks that repeated viciffitudes of heat and cold, of dangerous and fickly climates, will give to the beft conftitutions, in a pretty long courfe of fervice. I refigned my regiment to colonel Gifborne, a very good officer, for his half-pay, 200 l. Irifh annuity ; fo that, according to Junius, I have been bribed to fay nothing more of the Manilla ranfom, and facrifice thofe brave men, by the ftrange avarice of accepting three hundred and eighty pounds per annum, and giving up eight hundred! If this be bribery, it is not the bribery of thefe times. As to my flattery, thofe who know me will judge of it. By the afperity of Junius's ftyle, I cannot indeed call him a flatterer, unlefs he be as a cynick, or a maftiff; if he wags his tail, he will ftill growl, and long to bite. The public will now judge of the credit that ought to be given to Junius's

writings

writings, from the falſities that he has inſinuated with reſpect to myſelf.

WILLIAM DRAPER.

---

## L E T T E R   V.

### TO SIR WILLIAM DRAPER, KNIGHT OF THE BATH.

SIR,                                   Feb. 21. 1769

I ſhould juſtly be ſuſpected of acting upon mo-tives of more than common enmity to Lord Granby, if I continued to give you freſh materials or occaſion for writing in his defence. Individuals who hate, and the public who deſpiſe, have read *your* letters, Sir William, with infinitely more ſatisfaction than mine. Unfortunately ſor him, his reputation, like that unhappy country to which you refer me ſor his laſt military atchieve-ments, has ſuffered more by his friends than his enemies. In mercy to him, let us drop the ſub-ject. For my own part, I willingly leave it to the public to determine whether your vindication of your friend has been as able and judicious, as it was certainly well intended; and you, I think, may be ſatisfied with the warm acknowledg-ments he already owes you for making him the principle figure in a piece, in which, but for your amicable aſſiſtance, he might have paſſed without prrticular notice or diſtinction.

In juſtice to your friends, let your future la-bours be confined to the care of your own repu-tation. Your declaration, that you are happy in ſeeing young noblemen *come among us*, is liable to two objections. With reſpect to Lord Percy, it means nothing, for he was already in the army. He was aid-de-camp to the King, and had the rank of colonel. A regiment therefore could not make him a more military man, though it made

him

him richer, and probably at the expence of some brave, deferving, friendlefs officer.—The other concerns yourfelf.—After felling the companions of your victory in one inftance, and after felling your profeffion in the other, by what authority do you prefume to call yourfelf a foldier? The plain evidence of facts is fuperior to all declarations. Before you were appointed to the 16th regiment, your complaints were a diftrefs to government;—from that moment you were filent. The conclufion is inevitable. You infinuate to us that your ill ftate of health obliged you to quit the fervice. The retirement neceffary to repair a broken conftitution would have been as good a reafon for not accepting, as for refigning, the command of a regiment. There is certainly an error of the prefs, or an affected obfcurity in that paragraph, where you fpeak of your bargain with colonel Gifborne. Inftead of attempting to anfwer what I do not really underftand, permit me to explain to the public what I really know. In exchange for your regiment, you accepted of a colonel's half-pay (at leaft 220 l. a-year) and an annuity of 200 l. for your own and lady Draper's life jointly.——And is this the lofing bargain, which you would reprefent to us, as if you had given up an income of 800 l. a-year for 380 l.? Was it decent, was it honourable, in a man who pretends to love the army, and calls himfelf a foldier, to make a traffic of the royal favour, and turn the higheft honour of an active profeffion into a fordid provifion for himfelf and his family? It were unworthy of me to prefs you farther. The contempt with which the whole army heard of the manner of your retreat, affures me, that as your conduct was not juftified by precedent, it will never be thought an example for imitation.

The laft and moft important queftion remains. When you receive your half pay, do you, or do you

you not, take a folemn oath, or fign a declaration upon your honour, to the following effect? *That you do not actually hold any place of profit, civil or military, under his Majefty.* The charge which the queftion plainly conveys againft you, is of fo fhocking a complexion, that I fincerely wifh you may be able to anfwer it well, not merely for the colour of your reputation, but for your own peace of mind.　　　　　JUNIUS.

---

## LETTER VI.

### TO JUNIUS.

SIR,　　　　　　　　　　FEB. 27. 1769.

I HAVE a very fhort anfwer for Junius's important queftion; I do not either take an oath, or declare upon honour, that I have no *place* of profit, *civil* or military, when I receive the half-pay as an Irifh colonel. My moft gracious Sovereign gives it me as a penfion; he was pleafed to think I deferved it. The annuity of 200 l. Irifh, and the equivalent for the half-pay, together, produce no more than 380 l. per annum, clear of fees and perquifites of office. I receive 167 l. from my government of Yarmouth. Total 547 l. per annum. My confcience is much at eafe in thefe particulars; my friends need not blufh for me.

Junius makes much and frequent ufe of interrogations: they are arms that may be eafily turned againft himfelf. I could, by malicious interrogation, difturb the peace of the moft virtuous man in the kingdom. I could take the decalogue, and fay to one man, Did you never fteal? To the next, Did you never commit murder? And to Junius himfelf, who is putting my life and conduct to the rack, Did you never bear falfe witnefs againft thy neighbour? Junius muft

eafily

eafily fee, that unlefs he affirms to the contrary in his real name, fome people who may be as ignorant of him as I am, will be apt to fufpect him of having deviated a little from the truth : therefore let Junius afk no more queftions. You bite againft a file : ceafe, viper.     W. D.

---

## L E T T E R  VII.

TO SIR WILLIAM DRAPER, KNIGHT OF THE BATH.

S I R,        MARCH 3. 1769.

AN academical education has given you an unlimited command over the moft beautiful figures of fpeech. Mafks, hatchets, racks, and vipers, dance through your lettters in all the mazes of metaphorical confufion. Thefe are the gloomy companions of a difturbed imagination ; the melancholy madnefs of poetry, without the infpiration. I will not contend with you in point of compofition. You are a fcholar, Sir William; and, if I am truly informed, you write Latin with almoft as much purity as Englifh. Suffer me then, for I am a plain unlettered man, to continue that ftyle of interrogation, which fuits my capacity, and to which, confidering the readinefs of your anfwers, you ought to have no objection. Even * Mr Bingly promifes to anfwer, if put to the torture.

Do you then really think, that, if I were to afk a *moft virtuous man* whether he ever committed theft, or murder, it would difturb his peace of mind ? Such a queftion might perhaps difcompofe the gravity of his mufcles, but I believe it would little affect the tranquillity of his confci- ence.

* Th's man, being committed to the court of King's Bench for contempt, voluntarily made oath, that he would never anfwer interrogatories, unlefs he fhould be put to the torture.

ence. Examine your own breaft, Sir William, and you will difcover, that reproaches and inquiries have no power to afflict either the man of unblemifhed integrity, or the abandoned profligate. It is the middle compound character which alone is vulnerable; the man, who, without firmnefs enough to avoid a difhonourable action, has feeling enough to be afhamed of it.

I thank you for the hint of the decalogue, and fhall take an opportunity of applying it to fome of your moft virtuous friends in both houfes of parliament.

You feem to have dropped the affair of your regiment; fo let it reft. When you are appointed to another, I dare fay you will not fell it either for a grofs fum, or for an annuity upon lives.

I am truly glad (for really, Sir William, I am not your enemy, nor did I begin this conteft with you) that you have been able to clear yourfelf of a crime, though at the expence of the higheft indifcretion. You fay that your half-pay was given you by way of penfion. I will not dwell upon the fingularity of uniting in your own perfon two forts of provifion, which in their own nature, and in all military and parliamentary views, are incompatible; but I call upon you to juftify that declaration, wherein you charge your Sovereign with having done an act in your favour notorioufly againft law. The half-pay, both in Ireland and England, is appropriated by Parliament; and if it be given to perfons who, like you, are legally incapable of holding it, it is a breach of law. It would have been more decent in you to have called this difhonourable tranfaction by its true name; a job to accommodate two perfons, by particular intereft and management at the caftle. What fenfe muft government have had of your fervices, when the rewards they have given you are only a difgrace to you!

And now, Sir William, I fhall take my leave

of you for ever. Motives very different from any apprehenfion of your refentment, make it impoffible you fhould ever know me. In truth, you have fome reafon to hold yourfelf indebted to me. From the leffons I have given you, you may collect a profitable inftruction for your future life. They will either teach you fo to regulate your conduct, as to be able to fet the moft malicious inquiries at defiance; or, if that be a loft hope, they will teach you prudence enough not to attract the public attention to a character, which will only pafs without cenfure, when it paffes without obfervation. JUNIUS.

It has been faid, I believe truly, that it was fignified to Sir William Draper as the requeft of Lord Granby, that he fhould defift from writing in his Lordfhip's defence. Sir Willirm Draper certainly drew *Junius* forward to fay more of Lord Granby's character than he originally intended. He was reduced to the dilemma of either being totally filenced, or of fupporting his firft letter. Whether Sir William had a right to reduce him to this dilemma, or to call upon him for his name, after a voluntary attack on *his* fide, are queftions fubmitted to the candor of the public.—The death of Lord Granby was lamented by *Junius*. He undoubtedly owed fome compenfations to the public, and feemed determined to acquit himfelf of them. In private life, he was unqueftionably that good man, who, for the intereft of his country, ought to have been a great one. *Bonum virum facile dixeris ;—magnum libenter.* I fpeak of him now without partiality :—I never fpoke of him with refentment. His miftakes, in public conduct, did not arife either from want of fentiment, or want of judgment, but in general from the difficulty of faying NO to the bad people who furrounded him.

As for the reft, the friends of Lord Granby fhould remember, that he himfelf thought proper to condemn, retract, and difavow, by a moft folemn declaration in the houfe of Commons, that very fyftem of political conduct which *Junius* had held forth to the difapprobation of the public.

---

## LETTER VIII.

### TO THE DUKE OF GRAFTON.

MY LORD,                    MARCH 18. 1769.

BEFORE you were placed at the head of affairs, it had been a maxim of the Englifh government, not unwillingly admitted by the people, that every ungracious or fevere exertion of the prerogative fhould be placed to the account of the Minifter; but that, whenever an act of grace or benevolence was to be performed, the whole merit of it fhould be attributed to the Sovereign himfelf *. It was a wife doctrine, my Lord, and equally advantageous to the King and his fubject; for while it preferved that fufpicious attention, with which the people ought always to examine the conduct of minifters, it tended at the fame time rather to increafe than diminifh their attachment to the perfon of their Sovereign. If there be not a fatality attending every meafure you are concerned in, by what treachery, or by what excefs of folly, has it happened, that thofe ungracious acts which have diftinguifhed your adminiftration, and which I doubt not were entirely your own, fhould carry with them a ftrong appearance of perfonal intereft, and even of perfonal enmity, in a quarter where no fuch intereft or enmity can be fuppofed to exift without the higheft injuftice and the higheft difhonour? On the other hand, by what injudicious management have you contrived it, that the only act of mercy, to which you have ever advifed your Sovereign, far from adding to the luftre of a character truly gracious and benevolent, fhould be received with univerfal difapprobation and difguft? I fhall confider it as a minifterial meafure, becaufe it is an odious one; and as your meafure, my Lord Duke, becaufe you are the minifter.

As long as the trial of this chairman was depending, it was natural enough that government fhould give him every poffible encouragement and fupport. The honourable fervice for which he was hired, and the fpirit with which he performed it, made a common caufe between your Grace and

F

him.

---

* Les rois ne fe font refervé que les graces. Ils renvoient les condamnations vers leurs officiers.     *Montefquieu.*

him. The minister, who by secret corruption invades the freedom of elections, and the ruffian, who by open violence destroys that freedom, are embarked in the same bottom. They have the same interests, and mutually feel for each other. To do justice to your Grace's humanity, you felt for M'Quirk as you ought to do; and if you had been contented to assist him indirectly, without a notorious denial of justice, or openly insulting the sense of the nation, you might have satisfied every duty of political friendship, without commuting the honour of your Sovereign, or hazarding the reputation of his government. But when this unhappy man had been solemnly tried, convicted, and condemned;—when it appeared that he had been frequently employed in the same services, and that no excuse for him could be drawn either from the innocence of his former life, or the simplicity of his character; was it not hazarding too much to interpose the strength of the prerogative between this felon and the justice of his country*? You ought to have known that an example

* *Whitehall, March* 11, 1769. His Majesty has been graciously pleased to extend his royal mercy to Edward M'Quirk, found guilty of the murder of George Clarke, as appears by his royal warrant to the tenor following.

GEORGE R.

WHEREAS a doubt had arisen in Our Royal breast concerning the evidence of the death of George Clarke, from the representations of William Broomfield, Esq; surgeon, and Solomon Starling, apothecary; both of whom, as has been represented to Us, attended the deceased before his death, and expressed their opinions that he did not die of the blow he received at Brentford : And whereas it appears to Us, that neither of the said persons were produced as witnesses upon the trial, though the said Solomon Starling had been examined before the Coroner ; and the only person called to prove that the death of the said George Clarke was occasioned by the said blow, was John Foot, surgeon, who never saw the deceased till after his death: We thought fit thereupon to refer the said representations, together with the report of the Recorder of Our city of London, of the evidence given by Richard and William Beale, and the said John Foot, on the trial of Edward Quirk, otherwise called Edward Kirk, otherwise called Edward M'Quirk, for the murder of the said Clarke, to the master, wardens, and the rest of the court

of

ample of this fort was never fo neceffary.as at prefent; and certainly you muft have known that the lot could not have fallen upon a more guilty object. What fyftem of government is this? You are perpetually complaining of the riotous difpofition of the lower clafs of people; yet when the laws have given you the means of making an example in every fenfe unexceptionable, and by far the moft likely to awe the multitude, you pardon the offence, and are not afhamed to give the fanction of government to the riots you complain of, and even to future murders. You are partial perhaps to the military mode of execution; and had rather fee a fcore of thefe wretches butchered by the guards, than one of them fuffer death by regular courfe of law. How does it happen, my Lord,

F 2

that,

of examiners of the Surgeons company, commanding them likewife to take fuch further examination of the faid perfons fo reprefenting, and of faid John Foot, as they might think neceffary, together with the premiffes above mentioned, to form and report to Us their opinion, " Whether it did or did not appear to them, that the faid " George Clarke died in confequence of the blow he received in the " riot at Brentford on the 8th of December laft." And the faid court of examiners of the Surgeons company having thereupon reported to Us their opinion, " That it did not appear to them that " he did;" We have thought proper to extend Our royal mercy to him the faid Edward Quirk, otherwife Edward Kirk, otherwife called Edward M'Quirk, and to grant him Our free pardon for the murder of the faid George Clarke, of which he has been found guilty. Our will and pleafure therefore is, That he the faid Edward Quirk, otherwife called Kirk, otherwife called Edward M Quirk, be inferted for the faid murder, in Our firft and next general pardon that fhall come out for the poor convicts of Newgate, without any condition whatfoever; and that in the mean time you take bail for his appearance, in order to plead Our faid pardon. And for fo doing this fhall be your warrant.

Given at Our court at St. James's the 10th day of March 1769, in the ninth year of Our reign.

By his Majefty's command,

ROCHFORD.

To our trufty and well beloved James
    Eyre, Efq; Recorder of Our city of
    London, the Sheriffs of our faid city
    and county of Middlefex, and all
    others whom it may concern.

that, in *your* hands, even the mercy of the prerogative is cruelty and oppreſſion to the ſubjeĉt?

The meaſure, it ſeems, was ſo extraordinary, that you thought it neceſſary to give ſome reaſons for it to the public. Let them be fairly examined.

1. You ſay *that Meſſrs Bromfield and Starling were not examined at M'Quirk's trial.* I will tell your Grace why they were not. They muſt have been examined upon oath; and it was foreſeen, that their evidence would either not benefit, or might be prejudiĉial to the priſoner. Otherwiſe, is it conceivable that his counſel ſhould negleĉt to call in ſuch material evidence?

You ſay that *Mr Foot did not ſee the deceaſed until after his death.* A ſurgeon, my Lord, muſt know very little of his profeſſion, if upon examining a wound or a contuſion, he cannot determine whether it was mortal or not.—While the party is alive, a ſurgeon will be cautious of pronouncing; whereas by the death of the patient, ·he is enabled to conſider both cauſe and eſſeĉt in one view, and to ſpeak with a certainty confirmed by experience.

Yet we are to thank your Grace for the eſtabliſhment of a new tribunal. Your *inquiſitio poſt mortem* is unknown to the laws of England, and does honour to your invention. The only material objeĉtion to it is, that if Mr Foot's evidence was inſufficient, becauſe he did not examine the wound till after the death of the party, much leſs can a negative opinion, given by gentlemen who never ſaw the body of Mr Clarke, either before or after his deceaſe, authoriſe you to ſuperſede the verdiĉt of a jury, and the ſentence of the law.

Now, my Lord, let me aſk you, Has it never occurred to your Grace, while you were withdrawing this deſperate wretch from that juſtice which the laws had awarded, and which the whole
people

people of England demanded againſt him, that there is another man, who is the favourite of his country, whoſe pardon would have been accepted with gratitude, whoſe pardon would have healed all our diviſions? Have you quite forgotten that this man was once your Grace's friend; Or is it to murderers only that you will extend the mercy of the crown?

Theſe are queſtions you will not anſwer, nor is it neceſſary. The character of your private life, and the tenour of your public conduct, is an anſwer to them all.    J U N I U S.

---

## LETTER IX.

TO HIS GRACE THE DUKE OF GRAFTON.

My Lord,       April 10. 1769.

I Have ſo good an opinion of your Grace's diſcernment, that when the author of the vindication of your conduct aſſures us, that he writes from his own mere motion, without the leaſt authority from your Grace, I ſhould be ready enough to believe him but for one fatal mark, which ſeems to be fixed upon every meaſure in which either your perſonal or your political character is concerned.—Your firſt attempt to ſupport Sir William Proctor ended in the election of Mr Wilkes; the ſecond enſured ſucceſs to Mr Glynn. The extraordinary ſtep you took to make Sir James Lowther lord paramount of Cumberland, has ruined his intereſt in that country for ever. The Houſe Liſt of Directors was curſed with the concurrence of government; and even the miſerable * Dingley could not eſcape the miſ-

F 3      fortune

---

* This unfortunate perſon had been perſuaded by the Duke of Grafton to ſet up for Middleſex, his Grace being determined to ſeat him in the Houſe of Commons if he had but a ſingle vote. It happened unluckily that he could not prevail upon any one freeholder to put him in nomination.

fortune of your Grace's protection. With this
uniform experience before us, we are authorifed
to fufpect, that when a pretended vindication of
your principles and conduct in reality contains
the bittereft reflections upon both, it could not
have been written without your immediate direction and affiftance. The author indeed calls God
to witnefs for him, with all the fincerity and in
the very terms of an Irifh evidence, *to the beft of
his knowledge and belief.* My Lord, you fhould
not encourage thefe appeals to heaven. The pious Prince from whom you are fuppofed to defcend, made fuch frequent ufe of them in his
public declarations, that at laft the people alfo
found it neceffary to appeal to heaven in their
turn. Your adminiftration has driven us into
circumftances of equal diftrefs; beware at leaft
how you remind us of the remedy.

You have already much to anfwer for. You
have provoked this unhappy gentleman to play
the fool once more in public life, in fpite of his
years and infirmities; and to fhow us, that, as you
yourfelf are a fingular inftance of youth without fpirit, the man who defends you is a no lefs remarkable
example of age without the benefits of experience.
To follow fuch a writer minutely would, like his
own periods, be a labour without end. The fubject too has been already difcuffed, and is fufficiently underftood. I cannot help obferving,
however, that, when the pardon of M'Quirk
was the principal charge againft you, it would
have been but a decent compliment to your
Grace's underftanding, to have defended you upon
your own principles. What credit does a man
deferve, who tells us plainly, that the facts fet
forth in the King's proclamation were not the
true motives on which the pardon was granted;
and that he wifhes that thofe chirurgical reports,
which firft gave occafion to certain doubts in the
royal

royal breaft, had not been laid before his Majefty. You fee, my Lord, that even your friends cannot defend your actions, without changing your principles; nor juftify a deliberate meafure of government, without contradicting the main affertion on which it was founded.

The conviction of M'Quirk had reduced you to a dilemma, in which it was hardly poffible for you to reconcile your political intereft with your duty. You were obliged either to abandon an active ufeful partifan, or to protect a felon from public juftice. With your ufual fpirit, you preferred your intereft to every other confideration; and with your ufual judgment, you founded your determination upon the only motives which fhould not have been given to the public.

I have frequently cenfured Mr Wilkes's conduct, yet your advocate reproaches me with having devoted myfelf to the fervice of fedition. Your Grace can beft inform us, for which of Mr Wilkes's good qualities you firft honoured him with your friendfhip, or how long it was before you difcovered thofe bad ones in him at which, it feems, your delicacy was offended. Remember, my Lord, that you continued your connection with Mr Wilkes long after he had been convicted of thofe crimes which you have fince taken pains to reprefent in the blackeft colours of blafphemy and treafon. How unlucky is it that the firft inftance you have given us of a fcrupulous regard to decorum is united with the breach of a moral obligation! For my own part, my Lord, I am proud to affirm, that if I had been weak enough to form fuch a friendfhip, I would never have been bafe enough to betray it. But, let Mr Wilkes's character be what it may, this at leaft is certain, that, circumftanced as he is with regard to the public, even his vices plead for him. The people of England have too much difcern-

ment

ment to fuffer your Grace to take advantage of
the failings of a private character, to eftablifh a
precedent by which the public liberty is affected,
and which you may hereafter, with equal eafe
and fatisfaction, employ to the ruin of the beft
men in the kingdom.——Content yourfelf, my
Lord, with the many advantages which the un-
fullied purity of your own character has given you
over your unhappy deferted friend.　Avail yourfelf of all the unforgiving piety of the court you
live in, and blefs God that you " are not as
" other men are; extortioners, unjuft, adulterers,
" or even as this publican."　In a heart void of
feeling, the laws of honour and good faith may
be violated with impunity, and there you may
fafely indulge your genius.　But the laws of England fhall not be violated, even by your holy zeal
to opprefs a finner; and though you have fucceeded in making him a tool, you fhall not make
him the victim of your ambition.　　JUNIUS.

---

## LETTER X.

### TO MR EDWARD WESTON.

S I R,　　　　　　　　　　　APRIL 21. 1769.

I SAID you were an old man without the benefit
of experience　It feems you are alfo a volunteer with the ftipend of twenty commiffions;
and, at a period when all profpects are at an end,
you are ftill looking forward to rewards which
you cannot enjoy.　No man is better acquainted
with the bounty of government than you are.

　　　——ton impudence,
*Temeraire vieillard, aura fa recompenfe.*

But I will not defcend to an altercation either
with the impotence of your age, or the peevifh-
nefs of your difeafes.　Your pamphlet, ingenious

as

as it is, has been fo little read, that the public cannot know how far you have a right to give me the lie, without the following citation of your own words.

Page 6—' 1. That he is perfuaded that the mo-
' tives, which he (Mr Welton) has alleged, muft
' appear fully fufficient, with or without the opi-
' nions of the furgeons.

' 2. That thofe very motives MUST HAVE
' BEEN the foundation on which the Earl of
' Rochford thought proper, &c.

' 3. That he CANNOT BUT REGRET that the
' Earl of Rochford feems to have thought proper
' to lay the chirurgical reports before the king,
' in preference to all the other fufficient mo-
' tives,' &c.

Let the public determine whether this be defending government on their principles or your own.

The ftyle and language you have adopted are, I confefs, not ill fuited to the elegance of your own manners, or to the dignity of the caufe you have undertaken. Every common dauber writes rafcal and villain under his pictures, becaufe the pictures themfelves have neither character nor refemblance. But the works of a mafter require no index. His features and colouring are taken from nature. The impreffion they make is immediate and uniform ; nor is it poffible to miftake his characters, whether they reprefent the treachery of a minifter, or the abufed fimplicity of a king.

J U N I U S.

# LETTER XI.



My Lord,                                    April 24. 1769.

THE fyftem you feemed to have adopted, when Lord Chatham unexpectedly left you at the head of affairs, gave us no promife of that uncommon exertion of vigour, which has fince illuftrated your character and diftinguifhed your adminiftration. Far from difcovering a fpirit bold enough to invade the firft rights of the people and the firft principles of the conftitution, you were fcrupulous of exercifing even thofe powers with which the executive branch of the legiflature is legally invefted. We have not yet forgotten how long Mr Wilkes was fuffered to appear at large, nor how long he was at liberty to canvafs for the city and county, with all the terrors of an outlawry hanging over him. Our Gracious Sovereign has not yet forgotten the extraordinary care you took of his dignity and of the fafety of his perfon, when, at a crifis which courtiers affected to call alarming, you left the metropolis expofed for two nights together, to every fpecies of riot and diforder. The fecurity of the Royal refidence from infult was then fufficiently provided for in Mr Conway's firmnefs, and Lord Weymouth's difcretion; while the prime minifter of Great Britain, in a rural retirement, and in the arms of faded beauty, had loft all memory of his Sovereign, his country, and himfelf. In thefe inftances you might have acted with vigour, for you would have had the fanction of the laws to fupport you. The friends of government might have defended you without fhame; and moderate men, who wifh well to the peace and good order of fociety, might have had a pretence for applauding your conduct. But thefe, it feems, were not occafions

fions worthy of your Grace's interpofition.　You
referved the proofs of your intrepid fpirit for trials
of greater hazard and importance; and now, as
if the moft difgraceful relaxation of the executive authority had given you a claim of credit to
indulge in exceffes ftill more dangerous, you feem
determined to compenfate amply for your former
negligence, and to balance the non-execution of
the laws with a breach of the conftitution. From
one extreme you fuddenly ftart to the other, without leaving, between the weaknefs and the fury
of the paffions, one moment's interval for the firmnefs of the underftanding.

Thefe obfervations, general as they are, might
eafily be extended into a faithful hiftory of your
Grace's adminiftration, and perhaps may be the
employment of a future hour.　But the bufinefs of
the prefent moment will not fuffer me to look back
to a feries of events, which ceafe to be interefting or important, becaufe they are fucceeded by a
meafure fo fingularly daring, that it excites all
our attention, and engroffes all our refentment.

·　Your patronage of Mr Luttrell has been crowned
with fuccefs. With this precedent before you, with
the principles on which it was eftablifhed, and
with a future houfe of commons, perhaps lefs
virtuous than the prefent, every county in England, under the aufpices of the treafury, may be
reprefented as completely as the county of Middlefex.　Pofterity will be indebted to your Grace
for not contenting yourfelf with a temporary expedient, but entailing upon them the immediate
bleffings of your adminiftration.　Boroughs were
already too much at the mercy of government.
Counties could neither be purchafed nor intimidated.　But their folemn determined election may
be rejected, and the man they deteft may be appointed, by another choice, to reprefent them in parliament.　Yet it is admitted, that the Sheriffs obeyed

the laws and performed their duty *. The return
they made muft have been legal and valid, or undoubtedly they would have been cenfured for making it. With every good-natured allowance for
your Grace's youth and inexperience, there are
fome things which you cannot but know. You
cannot but know that the right of the freeholders
to adhere to their choice (even fuppofing it improperly exerted) was as clear and indifputable as
that of the houfe of commons to exclude one of
their own members?—Nor is it poffible for you
not to fee the wide diftance there is between the
negative power of rejecting one man, and the pofitive power of appointing another. The right of
expulfion, in the moft favourable fenfe, is no more
than the cuftom of parliament. The right of e-
lection is the very effence of the conftitution. To
violate that right, and much more to transfer it
to any other fet of men, is a ftep leading immediately to the diffolution of all government. So
far forth as it operates, it conftitutes a houfe of
commons which *does not* reprefent the people. A
houfe of commons fo formed would involve a contradiction and the groffeft confufion of ideas; but
there are fome minifters, my Lord, whofe views
can only be anfwered by reconciling abfurdities,
and making the fame propofition, which is falfe
and abfurd in argument, true in fact.

This meafure, my Lord, is however attended
with one confequence favourable to the people,
which I am perfuaded you did not forefee †.
While the conteft lay between the miniftry and
Mr Wilkes, his fituation and private character
gave you advantages over him, which common
candour, if not the memory of your former friendfhip, fhould have forbidden you to make ufe of.

To

---

* Sir Fletcher Norton, when it was propofed to punifh the fheriffs,
declared in the houfe of commons that they, in returning Mr Wilkes,
had done no more than their duty.

† The reader is defired to mark this prophecy. .

'To religious men, you had an opportunity of exaggerating the irregularities of his past life;—to moderate men, you held forth the pernicious consequences of faction.  Men, who with this character looked no farther than to the object before them, were not dissatisfied at seeing Mr Wilkes excluded from parliament.  You have now taken care to shift the question; or rather, you have created a new one, in which Mr Wilkes is no more concerned than any other English gentleman.  You have united this country against you on one grand constitutional point, on the decision of which our existence, as a free people, absolutely depends. You have asserted, not in words but in fact, that the representation in parliament does not depend upon the choice of the freeholders.  If such a case can possibly happen once, it may happen frequently; it may happen always:—and if three hundred votes, by any mode of reasoning whatsoever, can prevail against twelve hundred, the same reasoning would equally have given Mr Luttrell his seat with ten votes, or even with one.  The consequences of this attack upon the constitution are too plain and palpable not to alarm the dullest apprehension. I trust you will find, that the people of England are neither deficient in spirit nor understanding, though you have treated them as if they had neither sense to feel, nor spirit to resent.  We have reason to thank God and our ancestors, that there never yet was a minister in this country, who could stand the issue of such a conflict; and with every prejudice in favour of your intentions, I see no such abilities in your Grace, as should intitle you to succeed in an enterprize, in which the ablest and basest of your predecessors have found their destruction.  You may continue to deceive your gracious master with false representations of the temper and condition of his subjects.  You may command a venal vote, because it is the common

G                           esta-

eftablifhed appendage of your office. But never hope that the freeholders will make a tame furrender of their rights, or that an Englifh army will join with you in overturning the liberties of their country. They know that their firft duty as citizens, is paramount to all fubfequent engagements; nor will they prefer the difcipline or even the honours of their profeffion to thofe facred original rights, which belonged to them before they were foldiers, and which they claim and poffefs as the birth-right of Englifhmen.

Return, my Lord, before it be too late, to that eafy infipid fyftem which you firft fet out with. Take back your * miftrefs; —the name of friend may be fatal to her, for it leads to treachery and perfecution. Indulge the people. Attend Newmarket. Mr Luttrell may again vacate his feat; and Mr Wilkes, if not perfecuted, will foon be forgotten. To be weak and inactive, is fafer than to be daring and criminal; and wide is the diftance between a riot of the populace and a convulfion of the whole kingdom. You may live to make the experiment, but no honeft man can wifh you fhould furvive it. J U N I U S.

---

## LETTER XII.

TO HIS GRACE THE DUKE OF GRAFTON.

My Lord, May 30. 1769.

IF the meafures in which you have been moft fuccefsful, had been fupported by any tolerable appearance of argument, I fhould have thought my time not ill employed, in continuing to examine your conduct as a minifter, and ftating it fairly to the public. But when I fee queftions of the higheft

* The Duke, about this time, had feparated himfelf from Ann Parfons; but propofed to continue united with her, on fome platonic terms of friendfhip, which fhe rejected with contempt. His bafenefs to this woman is beyond defcription or belief.

higheſt national importance carried as they have
been, and the firſt principles of the conſtitution openly violated, without argument or decency, I confeſs
I give up the cauſe in deſpair.  The meaneſt of your
predeceſſors had abilities ſufficient to give a colour
to their meaſures.  If they invaded the rights of
the people, they did not dare to offer a direct inſult to their underſtanding; and in former times,
the moſt venal parliaments made it a condition, in
their bargain with the miniſter, that he ſhould
furniſh them with ſome plauſible pretences for ſell-
ing their country and themſelves.  You have had
the merit of introducing a more compendious ſyſtem of government and logic.  You neither addreſs
yourſelf to the paſſions, nor to the underſtanding,
but ſimply to the touch.  You apply yourſelf immediately to the feelings of your friends; who,
contrary to the forms of parliament, never enter
heartily into a debate, until they have divided.

Relinquiſhing, therefore, all idle views of amendment to your Grace, or of benefit to the public,
let me be permitted to conſider your character and
conduct merely as a ſubject of curious ſpeculation.
—There is ſomething in both, which diſtinguiſhes
you not only from all other miniſters, but all other
men; it is not that you do wrong by deſign, but
that you ſhould never do right by miſtake.  It is
not that your indolence and your activity have been
equally miſapplied; but that the firſt uniform principle, or if I may call it the genius of your life,
ſhould have carried you through every poſſible
change and contradiction of conduct, without the
momentary imputation or colour of a virtue; and
that the wildeſt ſpirit of inconſiſtency ſhould never
once have betrayed you into a wiſe or honourable
action.  This I own gives an air of ſingularity to
your fortune as well as to your diſpoſition.  Let us
look back together to a ſcene in which a mind like
yours will find nothing to repent of.  Let us try,

my Lord, how well you have fupported the various relations in which you ftood, to your fovereign, your country, your friends, and yourfelf. Give us, if it be poffible, fome excufe to pofterity, and to ourfelves, for fubmitting to your adminiftration. If not the abilities of a great minifter, if not the integrity of a patriot, or the fidelity of a friend, fhow us at leaft the firmnefs of a man.—For the fake of your miftrefs, the lover fhall be fpared. I will not lead her into public, as you have done, nor will I infult the memory of departed beauty. Her fex, which alone made her amiable in your eyes, makes her refpectable in mine.

The character of the reputed anceftors of fome men, has made it poffible for their defcendents to be vicious in the extreme, without being degenerate. Thofe of your Grace, for inftance, left no diftreffing 'examples of virtue even to their legitimate pofterity; and you may look back with pleafure to an illuftrious pedigree, in which heraldry has not left a fingle good quality upon record to infult or upbraid you. You have better proofs of your defcent, my Lord, than the regifter of a marriage, or any troublefome inheritance of reputation. There are fome hereditary ftrokes of character, by which a family may be as clearly diftinguifhed as by the blackeft features of the human face. Charles the Firft lived and died a hypocrite. Charles the Second was a hypocrite of another fort, and fhould have died upon the fame fcaffold. At the diftance of a century, we fee their different characters happily revived and blended in your Grace. Sullen and fevere without religion, profligate without gaiety, you live like Charles the Second, without being an amiable companion; and, for aught I know, may die as his father did, without the reputation of a martyr.

You had already taken your degrees with credit in thofe fchools in which the Englifh nobility are

formed

formed to virtue, when you were introduced to
Lord Chatham's protection *.  From Newmarket,
White's, and the oppofition, he gave you to the
world with an air of popularity, which young
men ufually fet out with, and feldom preferve :—
grave and plaufible enough to be thought fit for
bufinefs; too young for treachery; and, in fhort,
a patriot of no unpromifing expectations.  Lord
Chatham was the earlieft object of your political
wonder and attachment; yet you deferted him,
upon the firft hopes that offered of an equal fhare
of power with Lord Rockingham.  When the
Duke of Cumberland's firft negociation failed, and
when the favourite was pufhed to the laft extremity, you faved him by joining with an adminiftration in which Lord Chatham had refufed to
engage.  Still, however, he was your friend: and
you are yet to explain to the world, why you con-
fented to act without him ; or why, after uniting
with Lord Rockingham, you deferted and betrayed him.  You complained that no meafures were
taken to fatisfy your patron; and that your friend
Mr Wilkes, who had fuffered fo much for the
party, had been abandoned to his fate.  They
have fince contributed, not a little, to your prefent plenitude of power: yet, I think, Lord Chatham has lefs reafon than ever to be fatisfied; and
as for Mr Wilkes, it is, perhaps, the greateft
misfortune of his life that you fhould have fo
many compenfations to make in the clofet for
your former friendfhip with him.  Your gracious
mafter underftands your character; and makes you
a perfecutor, becaufe you have been a friend.

Lord Chatham formed his laft adminiftration
upon principles which you certainly concurred in,
or you could never have been placed at the head
of the treafury.  By deferting thofe principles, and

G 3

by

---

* To underftand thefe paffages, the reader is referred to a noted
pamphlet, called, *The Hiftory of the minority.*

by acting in direct contradiction to them, in which
he found you were secretly supported in the
closet, you soon forced him to leave you to yourself, and to withdraw his name from an administration which had been formed on the credit of
it.   You had then a prospect of friendships better
suited to your genius, and more likely to fix your
disposition.  Marriage is the point on which every
rake is stationary at last: and truly, my Lord, you
may well be weary of the circuit you have taken;
for you have now fairly travelled through every
sign in the political zodiac, from the Scorpion, in
which you stung Lord Chatham, to the hopes of
a Virgin * in the house of Bloomsbury.  One would
think that you had had sufficient experience of
the frailty of nuptial engagements, or, at least,
that such a friendship as the Duke of Bedford's
might have been secured to you by the auspicious
marriage of your late Duchess with † his nephew.
But ties of this tender nature cannot be drawn
too close; and it may possibly be a part of the
Duke of Bedford's ambition, after making *her* an
honest woman, to work a miracle of the same sort
upon your Grace.   This worthy nobleman has
long dealt in virtue.  There has been a large con-
sumption of it in his own family; and, in the way
of traffic, I dare say, he has bought and sold more
than half the representative integrity of the nation.

In a political view, this union is not imprudent.
The favour of princes is a perishable commodity.
You have now a strength sufficient to command
the closet; and if it be necessary to betray one
friendship more, you may set even Lord Bute at
defiance.   Mr Stuart Mackenzie may possibly
remember what use the Duke of Bedford usually
makes

* His Grace had lately married Miss Wrottesly, niece of the *Good
Gertrude, Duchess of Bedford.*

† Miss Liddel, after her divorce from the Duke, married Lord
Upper Ossory.

makes of his power; and our gracious Sovereign, I doubt not, rejoices at this firſt appearance of union among his ſervants.  His late Majeſty, under the happy influence of a family connexion between his miniſters, was relieved from the cares of the government.  A more active prince may perhaps obſerve, with ſuſpicion, by what degrees an artful ſervant grows upon his maſter, from the firſt unlimited profeſſions of duty and attachment, to the painful repreſentation of the neceſſity of the royal ſervice, and ſoon, in regular progreſſion, to the humble inſolence of dictating in all the obſequious forms of peremptory ſubmiſſion.  The interval is carefully employed in forming connexions, creating intereſts, collecting a party, and laying the foundation of double marriages; until the deluded prince, who thought he had found a creature proſtituted to his ſervice, and inſignificant enough to be always dependent upon his pleaſure, finds him at laſt too ſtrong to be commanded, and too formidable to be removed.

Your Grace's public conduct, as a miniſter, is but the counter part of your private hiſtory;—the ſame inconſiſtency, the ſame contradictions.  In America we trace you, from the firſt oppoſition to the Stamp Act, on principles of convenience, to Mr Pitt's ſurrender of the right: then forward to Lord Rockingham's ſurrender of the fact; then back again to Lord Rockingham's declaration of the right; then forward to taxation with Mr Townſhend; and in the laſt inſtance, from the gentle Conway's undetermined diſcretion, to blood and compulſion with the Duke of Bedford: Yet, if we may believe the ſimplicity of Lord North's eloquence, at the opening of next ſeſſions you are once more to be the patron of America. Is this the wiſdom of a great miniſter? or is it the ominous vibration of a pendulum? Had you no opinion of your own, my Lord? or was it

the

the gratification of betraying every party with which you have been united, and of deserting every political principle in which you had concurred?

Your enemies may turn their eyes without regret from this admirable system of provincial government. They will find gratification enough in the survey of your domestic and foreign policy.

If, instead of disowning Lord Shelburne, the British court had interposed with dignity and firmness, you know, my Lord, that Corsica would never have been invaded. The French saw the weakness of a distracted ministry, and were justified in treating you with contempt. They would probably have yielded in the first instance, rather than hazard a rupture with this country; but, being once engaged, they cannot retreat, without dishonour. Common sense foresees consequences, which have escaped your Grace's penetration. Either we suffer the French to make an acquisition, the importance of which you have probably no conception of; or we oppose them by an underhand management, which only disgraces us in the eyes of Europe, without answering any purpose of policy or prudence. From secret, indirect assistance, a transition to some more open decisive measures becomes unavoidable; till at last we find ourselves principal in the war, and are obliged to hazard every thing for an object which might have originally been obtained without expence or danger. I am not versed in the politics of the north; but this I believe is certain, that half the money you have distributed to carry the expulsion of Mr Wilkes, or even your secretary's share in the last subscription, would have kept the Turks at your devotion. Was it œconomy, my Lord? or did the coy resistance you have constantly met with in the British senate, make you despair of corrupting the Divan? Your friends indeed have

the

the firſt claim upon your bounty; but if five hun‑
dred pounds a-year can be ſpared in penſion to
Sir John Moore, it would not have diſgraced you
to have allowed ſomething to the ſecret ſervice of
the public.

You will ſay perhaps, that the ſituation of affairs
at home demanded and engroſſed the whole of your
attention. Here, I confeſs, you have been active.
An amiable, accompliſhed prince aſcends the
throne under the happieſt of all auſpices, the ac‑
clamations and united affections of his ſubjects.
The firſt meaſures of his reign, and even the odium
of a favourite, were not able to ſhake their attach‑
ment. *Your* ſervices, my Lord, have been more
ſucceſsful. Since you were permitted to take the
lead, we have ſeen the natural effects of a ſyſtem
of government at once both odious and contemp‑
tible. We have ſeen the laws ſometimes ſcanda‑
louſly relaxed, ſometimes violently ſtretched be‑
yond their tone. We have ſeen the perſon of the
Sovereign inſulted; and in profound peace, and
with an undiſputed title, the fidelity of his ſubjects
brought by his own ſervants into public queſtion *.
Without abilities, reſolution, or intereſt, you have
done more than Lord Bute could accompliſh with
all Scotland at his heels.

Your Grace, little anxious perhaps either for
preſent or future reputation, will not deſire to be
handed down in theſe colours to poſterity. You
have reaſon to flatter yourſelf that the memory of
your adminiſtration will ſurvive even the forms of
a conſtitution, which our anceſtors vainly hoped
would be immortal: and as for your perſonal cha‑
racter, I will not, for the honour of human nature,
ſuppoſe that you can wiſh to have it remembered.
The condition of the preſent times is deſperate in‑
deed:

* The wiſe Duke, about this time, exerted all the influence of
government to procure addreſſes to ſatisfy the King of the fidelity
of his ſubjects. They came in very thick from *Scotland*; but, after
the appearance of this letter, we heard no more of them.

deed: but there is a debt due to thofe who come after us; and it is the hiftorian's office to punifh, though he cannot correct. I do not give you to pofterity as a pattern to imitate, but as an example to deter; and as your conduct comprehends every thing that a wife or honeft minifter fhould avoid, I mean to make you a negative inftruction to your fucceflors for ever.

JUNIUS.

---

## LETTER XIII.

### ADDRESSED TO THE PRINTER OF THE PUBLIC ADVERTISER.

S I R,　　　　　　　　　　JUNE 12. 1769.

THE Duke of Grafton's friends, not finding it convenient to enter into a conteft with *Junius*, are now reduced to the laft melancholy refource of defeated argument, the flat general charge of fcurrility and falfehood. As for his ftyle, I fhall leave it to the critics. The truth of his facts is of more importance to the public. They are of fuch a nature, that I think a bare contradiction will have no weight with any man who judges for himfelf. Let us take them in the order in which they appear in his laft letter.

1. Have not the firft rights of the people, and the firft principles of the conftitution, been openly invaded, and the very name of an election made ridiculous, by the arbitrary appointment of Mr Luttrell?

2. Did not the Duke of Grafton frequently lead his miftrefs into public, and even place her at the head of his table, as if he had pulled down an ancient temple of Venus, and could bury all decency and fhame under the ruins?—Is this the man who dares to talk of Mr Wilkes's morals?

3. Is not the character of his prefumptive an-

ceftors

ceftors as ftrongly marked in him as if he had defcended from them in a direct legitimate line? The idea of his death is only prophetic; and what is prophecy but a narrative preceding the fact!

4. Was not Lord Chatham the firft who raifed him to the rank and poft of a minifter, and the firft whom he abandoned?

5. Did he not join with Lord Rockingham, and betray him?

6. Was he not the bofom friend of Mr Wilkes, whom he now purfues to deftruction?

7. Did he not take his degrees with credit at Newmarket, White's, and the oppofition?

8. After deferting Lord Chatham's principles, and facrificing his friendfhip, is he not now clofely united with a fet of men, who, tbo' they have occafionally joined with all parties, have in every different fituation, and at all times, been equally and conftantly detefted by this country?

9. Has not Sir John Moore a penfion of five hundred pounds a-year?—This may probably be an acquittance of favours upon the turf; but is it poffible for a minifter to offer a groffer outrage to a nation, which has fo very lately cleared away the beggary of the civil lift at the expence of more than half a million.?

10. Is there any one mode of thinking or acting with refpect to America, which the Duke of Grafton has not fucceffively adopted and abandoned?

11. Is there not a fingular mark of fhame fet upon this man, who has fo little delicacy and feeling as to fubmit to the opprobrium of marrying a near relation of one who had debauched his wife? —In the name of decency, how are thefe amiable coufins to meet at their uncle's table?—It will be a fcene in Oedipus, without the diftrefs.—Is it wealth, or wit, or beauty—or is the amorous youth in love?

The reft is notorious. That Corfica has been

facri-

facrificed to the French: that in fome inftances
the laws have been fcandaloufly relaxed, and in
others daringly violated; and that the King's fubjects have been called upon to affure him of their
fidelity, in fpite of the meafures of his fervants.

A writer, who builds his arguments upon facts
fuch as thefe, is not eafily to be confuted. He is
not to be anfwered by general affertions, or general reproaches. He may want eloquence to amufe
and perfuade; but, fpeaking truth, he muft always convince.　　　　　　　　PHILO JUNIUS.

----

## LETTER XIV.

### ADDRESSED TO THE PRINTER OF THE PUBLIC ADVERTISER.

S I R,　　　　　　　　　　　　JUNE 22. 1769.

THE name of *Old Noll* is deftined to be the ruin
of the houfe of Stuart. There is an ominous fatality in it, which even the fpurious de-
fcendants of the family cannot efcape. Oliver
Cromwell had the merit of conducting Charles
the Firft to the block. Your correfpondent OLD
NOLL appears to have the fame defign upon the
Duke of Grafton. His arguments confift better
with the title he has affumed, than with the principles he profeffes; for though he pretends to be
an advocate for the Duke, he takes care to give us
the beft reafons why his patron fhould regularly
follow the fate of his prefumptive anceftor.——
Through the whole courfe of the Duke of Grafton's
life, I fee a ftrange endeavour to unite contradictions, which cannot be reconciled. He marries,
to be divorced; he keeps a miftrefs, to remind
him of conjugal endearments; and he choofes fuch
friends, as it is virtue in him to defert. If it were
poffible for the genius of that accomplifhed prefident who pronounced fentence upon Charles the

1　　　　　　　　　　　　　　　　　　　　Firft,

Firſt, to be revived in ſome modern ſycophant *, his Grace, I doubt not, would by ſympathy diſcover him among the dregs of mankind, and take him for a guide in thoſe paths which naturally conduct a miniſter to the ſcaffold.

The aſſertion that two-thirds of the nation approve of the *acceptance* of Mr Luttrell (for even *Old Noll* is too modeſt to call it an election) can neither be maintained nor confuted by argument. It is a point of fact, on which every Engliſh gentleman will determine for himſelf. As to lawyers, their profeſſion is ſupported by the indiſcriminate defence of right and wrong; and I confeſs I have not that opinion of their knowledge or integrity, to think it neceſſary that they ſhould decide for me upon a plain conſtitutional queſtion. With reſpect to the appointment of Mr Luttrell, the chancellor has never yet given any authentic opinion. Sir Fletcher Norton is indeed an honeſt, a very honeſt man; and the Attorney General is *ex officio* the guardian of liberty, to take care, I preſume, that it ſhall never break out into a criminal exceſs. Doctor Blackſtone is Solicitor to the Queen. The Doctor recollected that he had a place to preſerve, though he forgot that he had a reputation to loſe. We have now the good fortune to underſtand the Doctor's principles, as well as writings. For the defence of truth, of law, and reaſon, the Doctor's book may be ſafely conſulted; but whoever wiſhes to cheat a neighbour of his eſtate, or to rob a country of its rights, need make no ſcruple of conſulting the Doctor himſelf.

The example of the Engliſh nobility may, for aught I know, ſufficiently juſtify the Duke of Grafton, when he indulges his genius in all the faſhionable exceſſes of the age; yet, conſidering his rank and ſtation, I think it would do him more

3       H      ho-

* It is hardly neceſſary to remind the reader of the name of *Bradſhaw*.

honour to be able to deny the fact, than to defend
it by such authority.   But if vice itself could be
excused, there is yet a certain display of it, a certain outrage to decency, and violation of public
decorum, which, for the benefit of society, should
never be forgiven. It is not that he kept a mistress
at home, but that he constantly attended her a-
broad.——It is not the private indulgence, but the
public insult, of which I complain.   The name of
Miss Parsons would hardly have been known, if
the First Lord of the Treasury had not led her in
triumph through the Opera House, even in the
presence of the Queen.   When we see a man act
in this maaner, we may admit the shameless depravity of his heart, but what are we to think of his
understanding?

His Grace, it seems, is now to be a regular domestic man; and as an omen of the future delicacy
and correctness of his conduct, he marries a first
cousin of the man who had fixed that mark and
title of infamy upon him, which, at the same
moment, makes a husband unhappy and ridiculous.
The ties of consanguinity may possibly preserve
him from the same fate a second time; and as to
the distress of meeting, I take for granted the venerable uncle of these common cousins has settled
the etiquette in such a manner, that if a mistake
should happen, it may reach no farther than from
*Madame ma femme* to *Madame ma cousine*.

The Duke of Grafton has always some excellent
reason for deserting his friends—The age and incapacity of Lord Chatham—the debility of Lord
Rockingham—or the infamy of Mr Wilkes.
There was a time, indeed, when he did not appear
to be quite so well acquainted, or so violently offended, with the infirmities of his friends.   But
now I confess they are not ill exchanged for the
youthful, vigorous virtue of the Duke of Bedford;
—the firmness of General Conway;—the blunt,

or

or if I may call it the aukward, integrity of Mr Rigby;—and the fpotlefs morality of Lord Sandwich.

If a late penfion to a * broken gambler be an act worthy of commendation, the Duke of Grafton's connexions will furnifh him with many opportunities of doing praife-worthy actions; and as he himfelf bears no part of the expence, the generofity of diftributing the public money for the fupport of virtuous families in diftrefs will be an unqueftionable proof of his Grace's humanity.

As to the public affairs, *Old Noll* is a little tender of defcending to particulars. He does not deny that Corfica has been facrificed to France; and he confeffes, that, with regard to America, his patron's meafures have been fubject to fome variation; but then he promifes wonders of ftability and firmnefs for the future. Thefe are myfteries, of which we muft not pretend to judge by experience; and truly, I fear we fhall perifh in the Defart, before we arrive at the Land of Promife. In the regular courfe of things, the period of the Duke of Grafton's minifterial manhood fhould now be approaching. The imbecillity of his infant-ftate was committed to Lord Chatham. Charles Townfhend took fome care of his education at that ambiguous age, which lies between the follies of political childhood and the vices of puberty. The empire of the paffions foon fucceeded. His earlieft principles and connexions were of courfe forgotten or defpifed. The company he has lately kept has been of no fervice to his morals; and, in the conduct of public affairs, we fee the character of his time of life ftrongly diftinguifhed. And obftinate ungovernable felf-fufficiency plainly points out to us that ftate of imperfect maturity, at which the graceful levity of youth is loft, and the folidity of experience not yet acquired. It is

H 2

poffible

* Sir John Moore.

poſſible the young man may in time grow wiſer, and reform ; but, if I underſtand his diſpoſition, it is not of ſuch corrigible ſtuff, that we ſhould hope for any amendment in him, before he has accompliſhed the deſtruction of this country. Like other rakes, he may perhaps live to ſee his error, but not until he has ruined his eſtate.

PHILO JUNIUS.

---

## LETTER XV.

TO HIS GRACE THE DUKE OF GRAFTON.

MY LORD,                              JULY 8. 1769.

IF nature had given you an underſtanding qualified to keep pace with the wiſhes and principles of your heart, ſhe would have made you, perhaps, the moſt formidable miniſter that ever was
employed, under a limited monarch, to accompliſh
the ruin of a free people. When neither the feelings of ſhame, the reproaches of conſcience, nor
the dread of puniſhment, form any bar to the deſigns of a miniſter, the people would have too
much reaſon to lament their condition, if they did
not find ſome reſource in the weakneſs of his underſtanding. We owe it to the bounty of providence, that the completeſt depravity of the heart
is ſometimes ſtrangely united with a confuſion of
the mind, which counteracts the moſt favourite
principles, and makes the ſame man treacherous
without art, and a hypocrite without deceiving.
The meaſures, for inſtance, in which your Grace's
activity has been chiefly exerted, as they were adopted without ſkill, ſhould have been conducted with
more than common dexterity. But truly, my Lord,
the execution has been as groſs as the deſign. By
one deciſive ſtep, you have defeated all the arts of
writing. You have fairly confounded the intrigues
of oppoſition, and ſilenced the clamours of faction.

A

A dark, ambiguous fyftem might require and furnifh the materials of ingenious illuftration; and in doubtful meafures, the virulent exaggeration of party muft be employed, to roufe and engage the paffions of the people. You have now brought the merits of your adminiftration to an iffue, on which every Englifhman, of the narroweft capacity, may determine for himfelf. It is not an alarm to the paffions, but a calm appeal to the judgment of the people, upon their own moft effential interefts. A more experienced minifter would not have hazarded a direct invafion of the firft principles of the conftitution, before he had made fome progrefs in fubduing the fpirit of the people. With fuch a caufe as your's, my Lord, it is not fufficient that you have the court at your devotion, unlefs you can find means to corrupt or intimidate the jury. The collective body of the people form that jury, and from *their* decifion there is but one appeal.

Whether you have talents to fupport you, at a crifis of fuch difficulty and danger, fhould long fince have been confidered. Judging truly of your difpofition, you have perhaps miftaken the extent of your capacity. Good-faith and folly have fo long been received as fynonimous terms, that the reverfe propofition has grown into credit, and every villain fancies himfelf a man of abilities. It is the apprehenfion of your friends, my Lord, that you have drawn fome hafty conclufion of this fort, and that a partial reliance upon your moral character has betrayed you beyond the depth of your under-ftanding. You have now carried things too far to -retreat. You have plainly declared to the people what they are to expect from the continuance of your adminiftration. It is time for your Grace to confider what you alfo may expect in return from *their* fpirit and *their* refentment.

Since the acceffion of our moft gracious Sove-



reign

reign to the throne, we have feen a fyftem of government which may well be called a reign of experiments. Parties of all denominations have been employed and difmiffed. The advice of the ableft men in this country has been repeatedly called for and rejected; and when the Royal difpleafure has been fignified to a minifter, the marks of it have ufually been proportioned to his abilities and integrity. The fpirit of the FAVOURITE had fome apparent influence upon every adminiftration; and every fet of minifters preferved an appearance of duration, as long as they fubmitted to that influence. But there were certain fervices to be performed for the favourite's fecurity, or to gratify his refentments, which your predeceffors in office had the wifdom or the virtue not to undertake. The moment this refractory fpirit was difcovered, their difgrace was determined. Lord Chatham, Mr Grenville, and Lord Rockingham, have fuccefsively had the honour to be difmiffed for preferring their duty, as fervants of the public, to thofe compliances, which were expected from their ftation. A fubmiffive adminiftration was at laft gradually collected from the deferters of all parties, interefts, and connexions; and nothing remained but to find a leader for thefe gallant well-difciplined troops. Stand forth, my Lord, for thou art the man. Lord Bute found no refource of dependence or fecurity in the proud impofing fuperiority of Lord Chatham's abilities, the fhrewd inflexible judgment of Mr Grenville, nor in the mild but determined integrity of Lord Rockingham. His views and fituation required a creature void of all thefe properties; and he was forced to go through every divifion, refolution, compofition, and refinement of political chemiftry, before he happily arrived at the caput mortuum of vitriol in your Grace. Flat and infipid in your retired ftate, but brought into action you become vitriol again. Such are the ex-

tremes

tremes of alternate indolence or fury which have governed your whole administration. Your circumstances with regard to the people soon becoming desperate, like other honest servants you determined to involve the best of masters in the same difficulties with yourself. We owe it to your Grace's well-directed labours, that your Sovereign has been persuaded to doubt of the affections of his subjects, and the people to suspect the virtues of their Soevreign, at a time when both were unquestionable. You have degraded the Royal dignity into a base and dishonourable competition with Mr Wilkes; nor had you abilities to carry even the last contemptible triumph over a private man, without the grossest violation of the fundamental laws of the constitution and rights of the people. But these are rights, my Lord, which you can no more annihilate, than you can the foil to which they are annexed. The question no longer turns upon points of national honour and security abroad, or on the degrees of expedience and propriety of measures at home. It was not inconsistent that you should abandon the cause of liberty in another country, which you had persecuted in your own; and in the common arts of domestic corruption, we miss no part of Sir Robert Walpole's system except his abilities. In this humble imitative line, you might long have proceeded, safe and contemptible. You might probably never have risen to the dignity of being hated, and even have been despised with moderation. But it seems you meant to be distinguished; and, to a mind like your's, there was no other road to fame but by the destruction of a noble fabric, which you thought had been too long the admiration of mankind. The use you have made of the military force introduced an alarming change in the mode of executing the laws. The arbitrary appointment of Mr Luttrell invades the foundation of the laws themselves, felves, as it manifestly transfers the right of legiflation from thofe whom the people have chofen, to thofe whom they have rejected. With a fucceffion of fuch appointments, we may foon fee a houfe of commons collected, in the choice of which the other towns and counties of England will have as little fhare as the devoted county of Middlefex.

Yet I truft that your Grace will find that the people of this country are neither to be intimidated by violent meafures, nor deceived by refinements. When they fee Mr Luttrell feated in the houfe of commons by mere dint of power, and in direct oppofition to the choice of a whole county, they will not liften to thofe fubtleties by which every arbitrary exertion of authority is explained into the law and privilege of parliament. It requires no perfuafion of argument, but fimply the evidence of the fenfes, to convince them, that to transfer the right of election from the collective to the reprefentative body of the people, contradicts all thofe ideas of a Houfe of Commons, which they have received from their forefathers, and which they had already, though vainly perhaps, delivered to their children. The principles on which this violent meafure has been defended, have added fcorn to injury; and forced us to feel, that we are not only oppreffed, but infulted.

With what force, my Lord, with what protection, are you prepared to meet the united deteftation of the people of England? The city of London has given a generous example to the kingdom, in what manner a king of this country ought to be addreffed; and I fancy, my Lord, it is not yet in your courage to ftand between your Sovereign and the addreffes of his fubjects. The injuries you have done this country are fuch as demand not only redrefs, but vengeance. In vain fhall you look for protection to that venal vote,

which

which you have already paid for—Another muft
be purchafed ; and to fave a minifter, the houfe
of commons muft declare themfelves not only independent of their conftituents, but the determined enemies of the conftitution.  Confider, my
Lord, whether this be an extremity to which their
fears will permit them to advance ; or, if *their*
protection fhould fail you, how far you are authorifed to rely upon the fincerity of thofe fmiles
which a pious Court lavifhes without reluctance
upon a libertine by profeffion.  It is not indeed
the leaft of the thoufand contradictions which attend you, that a man, marked to the world by
the groffeft violation of all ceremony and decorum,
fhould be the firft fervant of a Court, in which
prayers are morality, and kneeling is religion.
Truft not too far to appearances, by which your
predeceffors have been deceived, though they have
not been injured.  Even the beft of princes may
at laft difcover, that this is a contention, in which
every thing may be loft, but nothing can be gained ;
and as you became minifter by accident, were
adopted without choice, trufted without confidence, and continued without favour, be affured,
that, whenever an occafion preffes, you will be
difcarded without even the forms of regret.  You
will then have reafon to be thankful, if you are
permitted to retire to that feat of learning, which,
in contemplation of the fyftem of your life, the
comparative purity of your manners with thofe of
their high fteward, and a thoufand other recommending circumftances, has chofen you to encourage the growing virtue of their youth, and to
prefide over their education.  Whenever the fpirit of diftributing prebends and bifhopricks fhall
have departed from you, you will find that learned feminary perfectly recovered from the delirium
of an inftallation, and, what in truth it ought to
be, once more a peaceful fcene of flumber and
thought.

thoughtlefs meditation. The venerable tutors of the univerfity will no longer diftrefs your modefty, by propofing you for a pattern to their pupils. The learned dulnefs of declamation will be filent; and even the venal mufe, though happieft in fiction, will forget your virtues. Yet, for the benefit of the fucceeding age, I could wifh that your retreat might be deferred, until your morals fhall happily be ripened to that maturity of corruption, at which the worft examples ceafe to be contagious.                                              JUNIUS.

---

## LETTER XVI.

### TO THE PRINTER OF THE PUBLIC ADVERTISER.

SIR,                                                    July 19. 1769.

A GREAT deal of ufelefs argument might have been faved, in the political conteft, which has arifen from the expulfion of Mr Wilkes, and the fubfequent appointment of Mr Luttrell, if the queftion had been once ftated with precifion, to the fatisfaction of each party, and clearly underftood by them both. But in this, as in almoft every other difpute, it ufually happens, that much time is loft in referring to a multitude of cafes and precedents, which prove nothing to the purpofe; or in maintaining propofitions, which are either not difputed, or, whether they be admitted or denied, are entirely indifferent as to the matter in debate; until at laft the mind, perplexed and confounded with the endlefs fubtleties of controverfy, lofes fight of the main queftion, and never arrives at truth. Both parties in the difpute are apt enough to practife thefe difhoneft artifices. The man who is confcious of the weaknefs of his caufe, is interefted in concealing it: and on the other fide, it is not uncommon to fee

a

a good caufe mangled by advocates who do not
know the real ftrength of it.

I fhould be glad to know, for inftance, to what
purpofe, in the prefent cafe, fo many precedents
have been produced to prove, That the houfe of
commons have a right to expel one of their own
members; that it belongs to them to judge of the
validity of elections; or that the law of parliament
is part of the law of the land *? After all thefe
propofitions are admitted, Mr Luttrell's right to his
feat will continue to be juft as difputable as it was
before. Not one of them is at prefent in agitation.
Let it be admitted that the houfe of commons were
authorifed to expel Mr Wilkes, that they are the
proper court to judge of elections, and that the
law of parliament is binding upon the people; ftill
it remains to be inquired, whether the houfe, by
their refolution in favour of Mr Luttrell, have or
have not truly declared that law. To facilitate this
inquiry, I would have the queftion cleared of all
foreign or indifferent matter. The following ftate
of it will probably be thought a fair one by both
parties; and then I imagine there is no gentleman
in this country, who will not be capable of forming a judicious and true opinion upon it. I take
the queftion to be ftrictly this : " Whether or not
" it be the known, eftablifhed law of parliament,
" that the expulfion of a member of the houfe of
" commons of itfelf creates in him fuch an inca-
" pacity to be re-elected, that, at a fubfequent
" election, any votes given to him are null and
" void; and that any other candidate, who, except
" the perfon expelled, has the greateft number of
" votes, ought to be the fitting member?"

To prove that the affirmative is the law of parliament, I apprehend it is not fufficient for the prefent houfe of commons to declare it to be fo. We
may

------

* The reader will obferve, that thefe admiffions are made, not as
of truths unqueftionable, but for the fake of argument, and in order to bring the real queftion to iffue.

may shut our eyes indeed to the dangerous conse-quences of suffering one branch of the legiflature to declare new laws, without argument or example, and it may perhaps be prudent enough to submit to authority; but a mere affertion will never con-vince, much lefs will it be thought reafonable to prove the right by the fact itfelf. The miniftry have not yet pretended to fuch a tyranny over our minds. To fupport the affirmative fairly, it will either be neceffary to produce fome ftatute, in which that pofitive provifion fhall have been made, that fpecific difability clearly created, and the con-fequences of it declared : or, if there be no fuch ftatute, the cuftom of parliament muft then be re-ferred to ; and fome cafe or cafes *, ftrictly in point, muft be produced, with the decifion of the court upon them ; for I readily admit, that the cuftom of parliament, once clearly proved, is equally binding with the common and ftatute law.

The confideration of what may be reafonable or unreafonable makes no part of this queftion. We are inquiring what the law is, not what it ought to be. Reafon may be applied to fhow the impro-priety or expedience of a law, but we muft have either ftatute or precedent to prove the exiftence of it. At the fame time I do not mean to admit that the late refolution of the houfe of commons is defenfible on general principles of reafon, any more than in law. This is not the hinge on which the debate turns.

Suppofing therefore that I have laid down an ac-curate ftate of the queftion, I will venture to affirm, 1ft, That there is no ftatute exifting, by which that fpecific difability which we fpeak of is created. If there be, let it be produced. The argument will then be at an end.

2dly, That there is no precedent, in all the pro-

ceedings

* Precedents, in oppofition to principles, have little weight with *Junius ;* but he thought it neceffary to meet the miniftry upon their own ground.

ceedings of the houfe of commons, which comes entirely home to the prefent cafe, viz. " where " an expelled member has been returned again, " and another candidate, with an inferior number " of votes, has been declared the fitting member." If there be fuch a precedent, let it be given to us plainly, and I am fure it will have more weight than all the cunning arguments which have been drawn from inferences and probabilities.

The miniftry, in that laborious pamphlet which I prefume contains the whole ftrength of the party, have declared *, " that Mr Walpole's was the firft " and only inftance in which the electors of any " county or borough had returned a perfon expelled " to ferve in the fame parliament." It is not pof- -fible to conceive a cafe more exactly in point. Mr Walpole was expelled ; and, having a majority of votes at the next election, was returned again. The friends of Mr Taylor, a candidate fet up by the miniftry, petitioned the houfe that he might be the fittingmember. Thus far the circumftan- ces tally exactly, except that our houfe of com- mons faved Mr Luttrell the trouble of petitioning. The point of law, however, was the fame. It came regularly before the houfe, and it was their bufi- nefs to determine upon, it. They did determine it, for they declared Mr Taylor *not duly elected*. If it be faid that they meant this refolution as matter of favour and indulgence to the borough, which had retorted Mr Walpole upon them, in order that the burgeffes, knowing what the law was, might correct their error, I anfwer,

I. That it is a ftrange way of arguing, to oppofe a fuppofition, which no man can prove, to a fact which proves itfelf.

II. That if this were the intention of the houfe of commons, it muft have defeated itfelf. The burgeffes of Lynn could never have known their

I

error,

* *Cafe of the Middlefex election confidered*, page 38.

error, much lefs could they have corrected it by any inftruction they received from the proceedings of the houfe of commons. They might perhaps have forefeen, that, if they returned Mr Walpole again, he would again be rejected; but they never could infer, from a refolution by which the candidate with the feweft votes was declared *not duly elected*, that, at a future election, and in fimilar circumftances, the houfe of commons would reverfe their refolution, and receive the fame candidate as duly elected, whom they had before rejected.

This indeed would have been a moft extraordinary way of declaring the law of parliament, and what I prefume no man, whofe underftanding is not at crofs-purpofes with itfelf, could poffibly underftand.

If, in a cafe of this importance, I thought myfelf at liberty to argue from fuppofitions rather than from facts, I think the probabilty, in this inftance, is directly the reverfe of what the miniftry affirm; and that it is much more likely that the houfe of commons at that time would rather have ftrained a point in favour of Mr Taylor, than that they would have violated the law of parliament, and robbed Mr Taylor of a right legally vefted in him, to gratify a refractory borough, which, in defiance of them, had returned a perfon branded with the ftrongeft mark of the difpleafure of the houfe.

But really, Sir, this way of talking, for I cannot call it argument, is a mockery of the common underftanding of the nation, too grofs to be endured. Our deareft interefts are at ftake. An attempt had been made, not merely to rob a fingle county of its rights, but, by inevitable confequence, to alter the conftitution of the houfe of commons. This fatal attempt has fucceeded, and ftands as a precedent recorded for ever. If the
mini-

minſtry are unable to defend their cauſe by fair argument founded on facts, let them ſpare us at leaſt
the mortification of being amuſed and deluded like
children.  I believe there is yet a ſpirit of reſiſtance
in this country, which will not ſubmit to be op-
preſſed; but I am ſure there is a fund of good ſenſe
in this country, which cannot be deceived.

J U N I U S.

---

## LETTER XVII.

### TO THE PRINTER OF THE PUBLIC ADVER-TISER.

S I R,                              Aug. 1. 1769.

IT will not be neceſſary for *Junius* to take the
trouble of anſwering your correſpondent G. A.
or the quotation from a ſpeech without doors,
publiſhed in your paper of the 28th of laſt month.
The ſpeech appeared before *Junius's* letter; and as
the author ſeems to conſider the great propoſition,
on which all his argument depends, viz. *that Mr
Wilkes was under that known legal incapacity of
which Junius ſpeaks,* as a point granted, his ſpeech
is in no ſhape an anſwer to *Junius,* for this is the
very queſtion in debate.

As to G. A. I obſerve, firſt, that if he did not
admit *Junius's* ſtate of the queſtion, he ſhould
have ſhown the fallacy of it, or given us a more
exact one;——ſecondly, that, conſidering the
many hours and days which the miniſtry and their
advocates have waſted, in public debate, in com-
piling large quartos, and collecting innumerable
precedents, expreſsly to prove that the late proceedings of the houſe of commons are warranted
by the law, cuſtom, and practice of parliament, it
is rather an extraordinary ſuppoſition, to be made by
one of their own party even for the ſake of argument, *that no ſuch ſtatute, no ſuch cuſtom of parlia-*

I 2

*ment,*

*ment, no such case in point, can be produced.* G. A.
may however make the suppofition with fafety. It
contains nothing, but literally the fact, except that
there is a cafe exactly in point, with a decifion of
the houfe diametrically oppofite to that which the
prefent houfe of commons came to in favour of Mr
Luttrel.

The miniftry now begin to be afhamed of the
weaknefs of their caufe ; and, as it ufually happens
with falfhood, are driven to the neceffity of fhift-
ing their ground, and changing their whole defence.
At firft we were told, that nothing could be clearer
than that the proceedings of the houfe of commons
were juftified by the known law and uniform cuftom of parliament. But now it feems, if there be
no law, the houfe of commons have a right to
make one ; and if there be no precedent, they have
a right to create the firft :—for this I prefume is
the amount of the queftions propofed to *Junius.*
If your correfpondent had been at all verfed in the
law of parliament, or generally in the laws of this
country, he would have feen that this defence is
as weak and falfe as the former.

The privileges of either houfe of parliament, it
is true, are indefinite, that is, they have not been
defcribed or laid down in any one code or declaration whatfoever ; but whenever a queftion of privilege has arifen, it has invariably been difputed
or maintained upon the footing of precedents a-
lone *. In the courfe of the proceedings upon the
Aylfbury election, the houfe of lords refolved,
" That neither houfe of parliament had any power,
" by any vote or declaration, to create to themfelves
" any new privilege that was not warranted by the
" known laws and cuftoms of parliament." And
to this rule the houfe of commons, though otherwife they had acted in a very arbitrary manner,

gave

---

* This is ftill meeting the miniftry upon their own ground; for,
in truth, no precedents will fupport either natural injuftice, or violation of pofitive right.

gave their affent; for they affirmed that they had guided themfelves by it, in afferting their privileges.—Now, Sir, if this be true with refpect to matters of privilege, in which the houfe of commons, individually and as a body, are principally concerned, how much more ftrongly will it hold againft any pretended power in that houfe to create or declare a new law, by which not only the rights of the houfe over their own member, and thofe of the member himfelf, are included, but alfo thofe of a third and feparate party, I mean the freeholders of the kingdom. To do juftice to the miniftry, they have not yet pretended that any one or any two of the three eftates have power to make a new law, without the concurrence of the third. They know that a man who maintains fuch a doctrine, is liable, by ftatute, to the heavieft penalties. They do not acknowledge that the houfe of commons have affumed a *new* privilege, or declared a *new* law.—On the contrary, they affirm that their proceedings have been ftrictly conformable to and founded upon the ancient law and cuftom of parliament. Thus therefore the queftion returns to the point at which *Junius* had fixed it, viz. *Whether or no this be the law of parliament ?* If it be not, the houfe of commons had no legal authority to eftablifh the precedent ; and the precedent itfelf is a mere fact, without any proof of right whatfoever.

Your correfpondent concludes with a queftion of the fimpleft nature, *Muft a thing be wrong becaufe it has never been done before ?* No. But admitting it were proper to be done, that alone does not convey any authority to do it. As to the prefent cafe, I hope, I fhall never fee the time, when not only a fingle perfon, but a whole county, and in effect the entire collective body of the people, may again be robbed of their birth-right by a vote of the houfe of commons. But if, for reafons



which

which I am unable to comprehend, it be neceſſary
to truſt that houſe with a power ſo exorbitant and
ſo unconſtitutional, at leaſt let it be given to them
by an act of the legiſlature.

PHILO JUNIUS.

---

## LETTER XVIII.

### TO SIR WILLIAM BLACKSTONE, SOLICITOR GENERAL TO HER MAJESTY.

S I R,                                   JULY 29. 1769.

I SHALL make you no apology for conſidering a
certain pamphlet, in which your late conduct
is defended, as written by yourſelf.  The perſonal
intereſts, the perſonal reſentments, and, above all,
that wounded ſpirit, unaccuſtomed to reproach, and
I hope not frequently conſcious of deſerving it, are
ſignals which betray the author to us as plainly as
if your name were in the title-page.  You appeal
to the public in defence of your reputation.  We
hold it, Sir, that an injury offered to an individual
is intereſting to ſociety.  On this principle the
people of England made common cauſe with Mr
Wilkes.  On this principle, if *you* are injured, they
will join in your reſentment.  I ſhall not follow
you through the inſipid form of a third perſon, but
addreſs myſelf to you directly.

You ſeem to think the channel of a pamphlet
more reſpectable and better ſuited to the dignity
of your cauſe, than that of a newſpaper.  Be it ſo.
Yet if newſpapers are ſcurrilous, you muſt confeſs they are impartial.  They give us, without any
apparent preference, the wit and argument of the
miniſtry, as well as the abuſive dulneſs of the oppoſition.  The ſcales are equally poiſed.  It is
not the printer's fault if the greater weight in-
clines the balance.

Your pamphlet then is divided into an attack
upon

'upon Mr Grenville's character, and a defence of your own. It would have been more confiftent perhaps with your profeffed intention, to have confined yourfelf to the laft. But anger has fome claim to indulgence, and railing is ufually a relief to the mind. I hope you have found benefit from the experiment. It is not my defign to enter into a formal vindication of Mr Grenville, upon his own principles. I have neither the honour of being perfonally known to him, nor do I pretend to be completely mafter of all the facts. I need not run the rifk of doing an injuftice to his opinions or to his conduct, when your pamphlet alone carries, upon the face of it, a full vindication of both.

Your firft reflection, is, that Mr Grenville * was, of all men, the perfon who fhould not have complained of inconfiftence with regard to Mr Wilkes. This, Sir, is either an unmeaning fneer, a peevifh expreffion of refentment, or, if it means any thing, you plainly beg the queftion; for whether his parliamentary conduct with regard to Mr Wilkes has or has not been inconfiftent, remains yet to be proved. But it feems he received upon the fpot a fufficient chaftifement for exercifing *fo unfairly* his talents of mifreprefentation. You are a lawyer, Sir, and know better than I do, upon what particular occafions a talent for mifreprefentation may be *fairly* exerted; but to punifh a man a fecond time, when he has been once fufficiently chaftifed, is rather too fevere. It is not in the laws of England; it is not in your own commentaries; nor is it yet, I believe, in the new law you have revealed to the houfe of commons. I hope this doctrine has no exiftence but in your own heart. After all, Sir, if you had confulted that fober difcretion, which you feem to oppofe with triumph to the honeft

* Mr Grenville had quoted a paffage from the Doctor's excellent commentaries, which directly contradicted the doctrine maintained by the Doctor in the houfe of commons.

neft jollity of a tavern, it might occurred to you, that, although you could have fucceeded in fixing a charge of inconfiftence upon Mr Grenville, it would not have tended in any fhape to exculpate yourfelf.

Your next infinuation, that Sir William Meredith had haftily adopted the falfe gloffes of his new ally, is of the fame fort with the firft. It conveys a fneer as little worthy of the gravity of your character, as it is ufelefs to your defence. It is of little moment to the public to inquire, by whom the charge was conceived, or by whom it was adopted. The only queftion we afk is, whether or no it be true? The remainder of your reflections upon Mr Grenville's conduct deftroy themfelves. He could not poffibly come prepared to traduce your integrity to the houfe. He could not forefee that you would even fpeak upon the queftion; much lefs would he forefee that you could maintain a direct contradiction of that doctrine, which you had folemnly, difintereftedly, and upon fobereft reflection, delivered to the public. He came armed indeed with what he thought a refpectable authority, to fupport what he was convinced was the caufe of truth; and I doubt not he intended to give you, in the courfe of the debate, an honourable and public teftimony of his efteem. Thinking highly of his abilities, I cannot however allow him the gift of divination. As to what you are pleafed to call a plan coolly formed to impofe upon the houfe of commons, and his producing it without provocation at midnight, I confider it as the language of pique and invective, therefore unworthy of regard. But, Sir, I am fenfible I have followed your example too long, and wandered from the point.

The quotation from your commentaries is matter of record. It can neither be *altered* by your friends, nor mifreprefented by your enemies; and I am willing to take your own word for what you

have

have faid in the houfe of commons.   If there be a
real difference between what you have written and
what you have fpoken, you confefs that your book
ought to be the ftandard.   Now, Sir, if words
mean any thing, I apprehend, that, when a long
enumeration of difqualifications, (whether by ftatute or the cuftom of parliament) concludes with
thefe general comprehenfive words, " But, fubject
" to thefe reftrictions and difqualifications, *every*
" fubject of the realm is eligible of common
" right," a reader of plain underftanding muft of
courfe reft fatisfied that no fpecies of difqualification
whatfoever had been omitted.   The known character of the author, and the apparent accuracy
with which the whole work is compiled, would
confirm him in his opinion ; nor could he poffibly
form any other judgment, without looking upon
your commentaries in the fame light in which you
confider thofe penal laws which, though not repealed, are fallen into difufe, and are now in effect
A SNARE TO THE UNWARY *.

You tell us indeed, that it was not part of your
plan to fpecify any temporary incapacity ; and that
you could not, without a fpirit of prophecy, have
fpecified the difability of a private individual, fubfequent to the period at which you wrote.   What
your plan was, I know not ; but what it fhould have
been, in order to complete the work you have given
us, is by no means difficult to determine.   The incapacity, which you call temporary, may continue
feven years ; and though you might not have forefeen the particular cafe of Mr Wilkes, you might
and fhould have forefeen the poffibility of *fuch* a
cafe, and told us how far the houfe of commons
were authorifed to proceed in it by the law and
cuftom of parliament. The freeholders of Middlefex

* If, in ftating the law upon any point, a judge deliberately affirms that he has included *every* cafe, and it fhould appear that he
has purpofely omitted a material cafe, he does in effect lay a fnare
for the unwary.

sex would then have known what they had to trust to, and would never have returned Mr Wilkes, when Colonel Luttrell was a candidate against him. They would have chosen some indifferent person, rather than submit to be represented by the object of their contempt and detestation.

Your attempt to distinguish between disabilities which affect whole classes of men, and those which affect individuals only, is really unworthy of your understanding. Your commentaries had taught me, that, although the instance in which a penal law is exerted be particular, the laws themselves are general. They are made for the benefit and instruction of the public, though the penalty falls only upon an individual. You cannot but know, Sir, that what was Mr Wilkes's case yesterday, may be yours or mine to-morrow, and that consequently the common right of every subject of the realm is invaded by it. Professing therefore to treat of the constitution of the house of commons, and of the laws and customs relative to that constitution, you certainly were guilty of a most unpardonable omission in taking no notice of a right and privilege of the house, more extraordinary and more arbitrary than all the others they possess put together. If the expulsion of a member, not under any legal disability, of itself creates in him an incapacity to be elected, I see a ready way marked out, by which the majority may at any time remove the honestest and ablest men who happen to be in opposition to them. To say that they *will not* make this extravagant use of their power, would be a language unfit for a man so learned in the laws as you are. By your doctrine, Sir, they *have* the power; and laws, you know, are intended to guard against what men *may* do, not to trust to what they *will* do.

Upon the whole, Sir, the charge against you is of a plain, simple nature: It appears even upon the face of your own pamphlet. On the contrary,

your

your juſtification of yourſelf is full of ſubtlety and refinement, and in ſome places not very intelligible. If I were perſonally your enemy, I ſhould dwell, with a malignant pleaſure, upon thoſe great and uſeful qualifications which you certainly poſſeſs, and by which you once acquired, though they could not preſerve to you, the reſpect and eſteem of your country. I ſhould enumerate the honours you have loſt, and the virtues you have diſgraced: but having no private reſentments to gratify, I think it ſufficient to have given my opinion of your public conduct, leaving the puniſhment it deſerves to your cloſet and to yourſelf. JUNIUS.

---

## LETTER XIX.

### ADDRESSED TO THE PRINTER OF THE PUBLIC ADVERTISER.

S I R,                                 AUGUST 14. 1769.

A CORRESPONDENT of the St James's Evening Poſt firſt wilfully miſunderſtands Junius, then cenſures him for a bad reaſoner. Junius does not ſay that it was incumbent upon Doctor Blackſtone to foreſee and ſtate the crimes for which Mr Wilkes was expelled. If, by a ſpirit of prophecy, he had even done ſo, it would have been nothing to the purpoſe. The queſtion is, not for what particular offences a perſon may be expelled, but generally whether by the law of parliament expulſion alone creates a diſqualification. If the affirmative be the law of parliament, Doctor Blackſtone might and ſhould have told us ſo. The queſtion is not confined to this or that particular perſon, but forms one great general branch of diſqualification, too important in itſelf, and too extenſive in its conſequence, to be omitted in an accurate work expreſsly treating of the law of parliament.

The truth of the matter is evidently this. Dr Black-

Blackstone, while he was speaking in the house of commons, never once thought of his Commentaries, until the contradiction was unexpectedly urged, and stared him in the face. Instead of defending himself upon the spot, he sunk under the charge in an agony of confusion and despair. It is well known that there was a pause of some minutes in the house, from a general expectation that the Doctor would say something in his own defence; but it seems his faculties were too much overpowered to think of those subtleties and refinements which have since occurred to him. It was then Mr Grenville received the severe chastisement, which the Doctor mentions with so much triumph: *I wish the honourable gentleman, instead of shaking his head, would shake a good argument out of it.* If to the elegance, novelty, and bitterness of this ingenious sarcasm, we add the natural melody of the amiable Sir Fletcher Norton's pipe, we shall not be surprised that Mr Grenville was unable to make him any reply.

As to the Doctor, I would recommend it to him to be quiet. If not, he may perhaps hear again from Junius himself.          PHILO JUNIUS.


Postscript to a pamphlet intitled, ‘ An Answer to ‘ the question stated.’ Supposed to be written by Dr Blackstone, Solicitor to the Queen, in answer to Junius's Letter.


SINCE these papers were sent to the press, a writer in the public papers, who subscribes himself Junius, has made a feint of bringing this question to a short issue. Though the foregoing observations contain, in my opinion at least, a full refutation of all that this writer has offered, I shall, however, bestow a very few words upon him. It will cost me very little trouble to unravel and expose the sophistry of this argument.

' I take the queftion (fays he) to be ftrictly this:
' Whether or no it be the known eftablifhed law
' of parliament, that the expulfion of a member
' of the houfe of commons of itfelf creates in him
' fuch an incapacity to be re-elected, that, at a
' fubfequent election, any votes given to him are
' null and void; and that any other candidate, who,
' except the perfon expelled, has the greateft num-
' ber of votes, ought to be the fitting member.'

Waving for the prefent any objection I may have
to this ftate of the queftion, I fhall venture to
meet our champion upon his own ground; and
attempt to fupport the affirmative of it, in one of
the two ways by which he fays it can be alone
fairely fupported. ' If there be no ftatute (fays he)
' in which the fpecific difability is clearly created,
' &c. (and we acknowledge there is none), the
' cuftom of parliament muft then be referred to,
' and fome cafe, or cafes, ftrictly in point, muft be
' produced, with the decifion of the court upon
' them.' Now I affert, that this has been done.
Mr Walpole's cafe is ftrictly in point, to prove
that expulfion creates abfolute incapacity of being
re-elected. This was the clear decifion of the houfe
upon it; and was a full declaration, that incapacity was the neceffary confequence of expulfion.
The law was as clearly and firmly fixed by this refolution, and is as binding in every fubfequent
cafe of expulfion, as if it had been declared by an
exprefs ftatute, " that a member expelled by a re-
" folution of the houfe of commons fhall be deemed
" incapable of being re-elected." Whatever doubt
then there might have been of the law before Mr
Walpole's cafe, with refpect to the full operation
of a vote of expulfion, there can be none now.
The decifion of the houfe upon this cafe is ftrictly
in point to prove, that expulfion creates abfolute
incapacity in law of being re-elected.

But incapacity in law in this inftance muft have

K

the

the same operation and effect with incapacity in law in every other instance. Now, incapacity of being re-elected implies in its very terms, that any votes given to the incapable person, at a subsequent election, are null and void. This is its necessary operation, or it has no operation at all : It is *vox et praterea nihil.* We can no more be called upon to prove this proposition, than we can to prove that a dead man is not alive, or that twice two are four. When the terms are understood, the proposition is self-evident.

Lastly, it is, in all cases of election, the known and established law of the land, grounded upon the clearest principles of reason and common sense, that if the votes given to one candidate are null and void, they cannot be opposed to the votes given to another candidate. They cannot affect the votes of such candidate at all. As they have on the one hand no positive quality to add or establish, so they have on the other hand no negative one to substract or destroy. They are, in a word, a mere nonentity. Such was the determination of the house of commons in the Malden and Bedford elections; cases strictly in point to the present question, as far as they are meant to be in point. And to say, that they are not in point in all circumstances, in those particularly which are independent of the proposition which they are quoted to prove, is to say no more than that Malden is not Middlesex, nor Serjeant Comyns Mr Wilkes.

Let us see then how our proof stands. Expulsion creates incapacity, incapacity annihilates any votes given to the incapable person; the votes given to the qualified candidate, stand upon their own bottom, firm and untouched, and can alone have effect. This, one would think, would be sufficient. But we are stopped short, and told, that none of our precedents come home to the present case; and are challenged to produce " a precedent in all the

pro-

" proceedings of the houfe of commons that does
" come home to it, viz. *where an expelled member*
" *has been returned again; and another candidate,*
" *with an inferior number of votes, has been declared*
" *the fitting member.*"

Inftead of a precedent, I will beg leave to put a cafe; which, I fancy, will be quite as decifive to the prefent point. Suppofe another Sacheverel (and every party muft have its Sachaverel) fhould at fome future election take it into his head to offer himfelf a candidate for the county of Middle-fex. He is oppofed by a candidate, whofe coat is of a different colour; but, however, of a very good colour. The divine has an indifputable majority; nay, the poor layman is abfolutely diftanced. The fheriff, after having had his confcience well informed by the reverend cafuift, returns him, as he fuppofes, duly elected. The whole houfe is in an uproar, at the apprehenfion of fo ftrange an appearance amongft them. A motion, however, is at length made, that the perfon was incapable of being elected, that his election therefore is null and void, and that his competitor ought to have been returned. No, fays a great orator; firft, fhow me your law for this proceeding. " Either pro-
" duce me a ftatute, in which the fpecific difabi-
" lity of a clergyman is created; or, produce me
" a precedent *where a clergyman has been returned,*
" *and another candidate, with an inferior number of*
" *votes, has been declared the fitting member.*" No fuch ftatute, no fuch precedent, to be found. What anfwer then is to be given to this demand? The very fame anfwer which I will give to that of Junius: That there is no more than one precedent in the proceedings of the houfe—" where an in-
" capable perfon has been returned, and another
" candidate, with an inferior number of votes,
" has been declared the fitting member; and that
" this is the known and eftablifhed law, in all



" cafes

" cafes of incapacity, from whatever caufe it may
" arife."

I fhall now therefore beg leave to make a flight
amendment to Junius's ftate of the queftion, the
affirmative of which will then ftand thus:

" It is the known and eftablifhed law of parlia-
" ment, that the expulfion of any member of the
" houfe of commons creates in him an incapacity
" of being re-elected; that any votes given to him
" at a fubfeqnent election are, in confequence of
" fuch incapacity, null and void; and that any
" other candidate, who, except the perfon ren-
" dered incapable, has the greateft number of
" votes, ought to be the fitting member."

But our bufinefs is not yet quite finifhed. Mr
Walpole's cafe muft have a re-hearing. " It is
" not poffible (fays this writer) to conceive a cafe
" more exactly in point. Mr Walpole was ex-
" pelled; and, having a majority of votes at the
" next election, was returned again. The friends
" of Mr Taylor, a candidate fet up by the mini-
" ftry, petitioned the houfe that he might be the
" fitting member. Thus far the circumftances
" tally exactly, except that our houfe of com-
" mons faved Mr Luttrell the trouble of petition-
" ing. The point of law, however, was the fame.
" It came regularly before the houfe, and it was
" their bufinefs to determine upon it. They did
" determine it; for they declared Mr Taylor *not*
" *duly elected*."

Inftead of examining the juftnefs of this reprefentation, I fhall beg leave to oppofe againft it my
own view of this cafe, in as plain a manner and
as few words as I am able.

It was the known and eftablifhed law of parliament, when the charge againft Mr Walpole came
before the houfe of commons, that they had power
to expel, to difable, and to render incapable for offences. In virtue of this power, they expelled him.

Had

Had they, in the very vote of expulfion, ad-
judged him, in terms, to be incapable of being
re-elected, there muft have been at once an end
with him.  But though the right of the houfe,
both to expel, and adjudge incapable, was clear
and indubitable, it does not appear to me, that
the full operation and effect of a vote of expulfion
fingly was fo.  The law in this cafe had never
been exprefsly declared.  There had been no event
to call up fuch a declaration.  I trouble not myfelf with the grammatical meaning of the word
expulfion.  I regard only its legal meaning.  This
was not, as I think, precifely fixed.  The houfe
thought proper to fix it, and explicitly to declare
the full confequences of their former vote, before
they fuffered thefe confequences to take effect.
And in this proceeding they acted upon the moft
liberal and folid principles of equity, juftice, and
law.  What then did the burgefles of Lynn collect
from the fecond vote ?  Their fubfequent conduct
will tell us : it will with certainty tell us, that
they confidered it as decifive againft Mr Walpole;
it will alfo, with equal certainty, tell us, that,
upon fuppofition that the law of election ftood
then, as it does now, and that they knew it to
ftand thus, they inferred, " that at a future elec-
" tion, and in cafe of a fimilar return, the houfe
" would receive the fame candidate, as duly elec-
" ted, whom they had before rejected."  They
could infer nothing but this.

It is needlefs to repeat the circumftance of dif-
fimilarity in the prefent cafe.  It will be fufficient
to obferve, that as the law of parliament, upon
which the houfe of commons grounded every ftep
of their proceedings, was clear beyond the reach
of doubt, fo neither could the freeholders of
Middlefex be at a lofs to forefee what muft be
the inevitable confequence of their proceedings in
oppofition to it.  For upon every return of Mr

Wilkes, the houfe made inquiry whether any votes were given to any other candidate.

But I could venture, for the experiment's fake, even to give this writer the utmoft he afks; to allow the moft perfect fimilarity throughout in thefe two cafes; to allow, that the law of expulfion was quite as clear to the burgeffes of Lynn, as to the freeholders of Middlefex. It will, I am confident, avail his caufe but little. It will only prove, that the law of election at that time was different from the prefent law. It will prove, that, in all cafes of an incapable candidate returned, the law then was, that the whole election fhould be void. But now we know that this is not law. The cafes of Malden and Bedford were, as has been feen, determined upon other and more juft principles. And thefe determinations are, I imagine, admitted on all fides to be law.

I would willingly draw a veil over the remaining part of this paper. It is aftonifhing, it is painful, to fee men of parts and ability, giving into the moft unworthy artifices, and defcending fo much below their true line of character. But if they are not the dupes of their fophiftry (which is hardly to be conceived), let them confider that they are fomething much worfe.

The deareft interefts of this country are its laws and its conftitution. Againft every attack upon thefe, there will, I hope, be always found amongft us the firmeft *fpirit of refiftance;* fuperior to the united efforts of faction and ambition. For ambition, though it does not always take the lead of faction, will be fure in the end to make the moft fatal advantage of it, and draw it to its own purpofes. But, I truft, our day of trial is yet far off; and there is a *fund of good fenfe in this country, which cannot long be deceived* by the arts either of falfe reafoning or falfe patriotifm.

L E T-

## LETTER XX.

TO THE PRINTER OF THE PUBLIC ADVER-
TISER.

SIR,                                       Aug 8. 1769.

THE gentleman who has publifhed an anfwer
to Sir William Meredith's pamphlet, having
honoured me with a poftfcript of fix quarto pages,
which he moderately calls beftowing a *very few*
words upon me, I cannot, in common politenefs,
refufe him a reply. The form and magnitude of
a quarto impofes upon the mind; and men, who
are unequal to the labour of difcuffing an intricate
argument, or wifh to avoid it, are willing enough
to fuppofe, that much has been proved, becaufe
much has been faid. Mine, I confefs, are humble
labours. I do not prefume to inftruct the learned,
but fimply to inform the body of the people; and
I prefer that channel of conveyance, which is
likely to fpread fartheft among them. The advocates of the miniftry feem to me to write for fame,
and to flatter themfelves, that the fize of their
works will make them immortal. They pile up
reluctant quarto upon folid folio, as if their labours, becaufe they are gigantic, could contend
with truth and heaven.

The writer of the volume in queftion, meets
me upon my own ground. He acknowledges
there is no ftatute, by which the fpecific difability
we fpeak of is created: but he affirms, that the
cuftom of parliament has been referred to; and that
a cafe ftrictly in point has been produced, with
the decifion of the court upon it.——I thank him
for coming fo fairly to the point. He afferts, that
the cafe of Mr Walpole is ftrictly in point to prove
that expulfion creates an abfolute incapacity of
being re-elected; and for this purpofe he refers
gene-

generally to the firſt vote of the houſe upon that occaſion, without venturing to recite the vote itſelf. The unfair, diſingenuous artifice of adopting that part of a precedent which ſeems to ſuit his purpoſe, and omitting the remainder, deſerve ſome pity, but cannot excite my reſentment. He takes advantage eagerly of the firſt reſolution, by which Mr Walpole's incapacity is declared; but as to the two following, by which the candidate with the feweſt votes was declared " not duly elected," and the election itſelf vacated, I dare ſay he would be well ſatisfied if they were for ever blotted out of the journals of the houſe of commons. In fair argument, no part of a precedent ſholud be admitted, unleſs the whole of it be given to us together. The author has divided his precedent; for he knew, that, taken together, it produced a conſequence directly the reverſe of that which he endeavours to draw from a vote of expulſion. But what will this honeſt perſon ſay, if I take him at his word, and demonſtrate to him, that the houſe of commons never meant to found Mr Walpole's incapacity upon his expulſion only? What ſubter-fuge will then remain?

Let it be remembered that we are ſpeaking of the intention of men who lived more than half a century ago, and that ſuch intention can only be collected from their words and actions as they are delivered to us upon record. To prove their deſigns by a ſuppoſition of what they would have done, oppoſed to what they actually did, is mere trifling and impertinence. The vote, by which Mr Walpole's incapacity was declared, is thus expreſſed: " That Robert Walpole, Eſq; having " been this ſeſſion of parliament committed a pri- " ſoner to the Tower, and expelled this houſe for " a breach of truſt in the execution of his office, " and notorious corruption when ſecretary at war, " was and is incapable of being elected a member

" to

" to ferve in this prefent parliament *." Now, Sir, to my underftanding, no propofition of this kind can be more evident, than that the houfe of commons, by this very vote, themfelves underftood, and meant to declare, that Mr Walpole's incapacity arofe from the crimes he had committed, not from the punifhment the houfe annexed to them. The high breach of truft, the notorious corruption, are ftated in the ftrougeft terms. They do not tell us that he was incapable becaufe he was expelled, but becaufe he had been guilty of fuch offences as juftly rendered him unworthy of a feat in parliament. If they had intended to fix the difability upon his expulfion alone, the mention of his crimes in the fame vote would have been highly improper. It could only perplex the minds of the electors, who, if they collected any thing from fo confufed a declaration of the law of parliament, muft have concluded that their reprefentative had been declared incapable, becaufe he was highly guilty, not becaufe he had been punifhed. But even admitting them to have underftood it in the other fenfe, they muft then, from the very terms of the vote, have united the idea of his being fent to the Tower with that of his expulfion, and confidered his incapacity as the joint effect of both †.

I

* It is well worth remarking, that the compiler of a certain quarto, called *The cafe of the laft election for the county of Middlefex confidered*, has the impudence to recite this very vote, in the following terms, vide page 11. " Refolved, that Robert Walpole, Efq; " having been that feffion of parliament expelled the houfe, was " and is incapable of being elected a member to ferve in the pre- " fent parliament." There cannot be a ftronger pofitive proof of the treachery of the compiler, nor a ftronger prefumptive proof that he was convinced that the vote, if truly recited, would overturn his whole argument.

† ADDRESSED TO THE PRINTER OF THE PUBLIC ADVERTISER.

SIR, MAY 22. 1777.

VERY early in the debate upon the decifion of the Middlefex election, it was obferved by Junius, that the houfe of commons

I do not mean to give an opinion upon the juftice of the proceedings of the houfe of commons
with regard to Mr Walpole; but certainly, if I
admitted their cenfure to be well founded, I could
no

mons had not only exceeded their hoafted precedent of the expulfion and fubfequent incapacitation of Mr Walpole, but that they
had not even adhered to it ftrictly as far as it went. After convicting Mr Dyfon of giving a falfe quotation from the Journals,
and having explained the purpofe which that contemptible fraud
was intended to anfwer, he proceeds to ftate the vote itfelf by which
Mr Walpole's fuppofed incapacity was declared, viz.—" Refolved,
" That Robert Walpole, Efq; having been this feffion of parli-
" ment committed a prifoner to the Tower, and expelled this
" houfe for a high breach of truft in the execution of his office, and
" notorious corruption when fecretary at war, was and is incapable
" of being elected a member to ferve in the prefent parliament :"
—and then obferves that, from the terms of the vote, we have no
right to annex the incapacitation to the *expulfion* only; for that, as
the propofition ftands, it muft arife equally from the expulfion and
the committment to the Tower. I believe, Sir, no man, who
knows any thing of Dialectics, or who underftands Englifh, will
difpute the truth and fairnefs of this conftruction. But Junius has
a great authority to fupport him, which, to fpeak with the Duke
of Grafton, I accidently met with this morning in the courfe of
my reading. It contains an admonition, which cannot be repeated
too often. Lord Sommers, in his excellent tract upon the rights
of the people, after reciting the votes of the convention of the 28th
of January 1789, viz.—" That King James the Second, having en-
" deavoured to fubvert the conftitution of this kingdom by break-
" ing the original contract between King and people, and by the
" advice of Jefuits and other wicked perfons having violated the
" fundamental laws, and having withdrawn himfelf out of this
" kingdom, hath abdicated the government, &c."—makes this
obfervation upon it : " The word *abdicated* relates to *all* the claufes
" aforegoing, as well as to his deferting the kingdom, or elfe they
" would have been wholly in vain." And that there might be no
pretence for confining the *abdication* merely to the *withdrawing*,
Lord Sommers farther obferves, *that King James, by refufing to govern us according to that law by which he held the crown, implicitely
renounced his title to it.*

If Junius's conftruction of the vote againft Mr Walpole be now
admitted (and indeed I cannot comprehend how it can honeftly be
difputed), the advocates of the houfe of commons muft either give
up their precedent entirely, or be reduced to the neceffity of maintaining one of the groffeft abfurdities imaginable, viz. " That a
" committment to the Tower is a conftituent part of, and contri-
" butes half at leaft to, the incapacitation of the perfon who fuffers
" it."

I need not make you any excufe for endeavouring to keep alive
the

no way avoid agreeing with them in the confequence they drew from it.   I could never have a
doubt in law or reafon, that a man convicted of a
high breach of truft, and of a notorious corruption,
in the execution of a public office, was and ought
to be incapable of fitting in the fame parliament.
Far from attempting to invalidate that vote, I
fhould have wifhed that the incapacity declared by
it could legally have been continued for ever.

Now, Sir, obferve how forcibly the argument
returns.   The houfe of commons, upon the face
of their proceedings, had the ftrongeft motives to
declare Mr Walpole incapable of being re-elected.
They thought fuch a man unworthy to fit among
them.  To that point they proceeded, and no farther;
for they refpected the rights of the people, while
they afferted their own.   They did not infer, from
Mr Walpole's incapacity, that his opponent was
duly elected; on the contrary they declared Mr Taylor "Not duly elected," and the election itfelf void.

Such, however, is the precedent which my
honeft

the attention of the public to the decifion of the Middlefex election.
The more I confider it, the more I am convinced, that, as a *fact*, it
is indeed highly injurious to the rights of the people; but that, as a
*precedent*, it is one of the moft dangerous that ever was eftablifhed
againft thofe who are to come after us.   Yet I am fo far a moderate man, that I verily believe the majority of the houfe of commons,
when they paffed this dangerous vote, neither underftood the
queftion, nor knew the confequence of what they were doing.
Their motives were rather defpicable, than criminal, in the extreme.   One effect they certainly did not forefee.   They are now
reduced to fuch a fituation, that if a member of the prefent houfe of
commons were to conduct himfelf ever fo improperly, and in reality
deferve to be fent back to his conftituents with a mark of difgrace,
they would not dare to expel him; becaufe they know that the
people, in order to try again the great queftion of right, or to
thwart an odious houfe of commons, would probably overlook his
immediate unworthinefs, and return the fame perfon to parliament.
—But, in time, the precedent will gain ftrength.   A future houfe
of commons will have no fuch apprehenfions; confequently will
not fcruple to follow a precedent, which they did not eftablifh.
The mifer himfelf feldom lives to enjoy the fruit of his extortion;
but his heir fucceeds him of courfe, and takes poffeffion without
cenfure.   No man expects him to make reftitution; and no matter for his title, he lives quietly upon the eftate.   PHILO JUNIUS.

honeſt friend aſſures us is ſtrictly in point to prove, that expulſion of itſelf creates an incapacity of being elected.　If it had been ſo, the preſent houſe of commons ſhould at leaſt have followed ſtrictly the example before them, and ſhould have ſtated to us in the ſame vote the crimes for which they expelled Mr Wilkes;　whereas they reſolve ſimply, that, " having been expelled, he was, and " is incapable."　In this proceeding I am authoriſed to affirm, they have neither ſtatute, nor cuſtom, nor reaſon, nor one ſingle precedent to ſupport them.　On the other ſide, there is indeed a precedent ſo ſtrongly in point, that all the enchanted caſtles of miniſterial magic fall before it.　In the year 1698 (a period which the rankeſt Tory dare not except againſt), Mr Wollaſton was expelled, re-elected, and admitted to take his ſeat in the ſame parliament.　The miniſtry have precluded themſelves from all objections drawn from the cauſe of his expulſion;　for they affirm abſolutely, that expulſion of itſelf creates the diſability.　Now, Sir, let ſophiſtry evade, let falſehood aſſert, and impudence deny—here ſtands the precedent, a land-mark to direct us through a troubled ſea of controverſy, conſpicuous and unremoved.

I have dwelt the longer upon the diſcuſſion of this point, becauſe, in *my* opinion, it comprehends the whole queſtion.　The reſt is unworthy of notice.　We are inquiring whether incapacity be or be not created by expulſion.　In the caſes of Bedford and Malden, the incapacity of the perſons returned was matter of public notoriety, for it was created by act of parliament.　But really, Sir, my honeſt friend's ſuppoſitions are as unfavourable to him as his facts.　He well knows that the clergy, beſides that they are repreſented in common with their fellow-ſubjects, have alſo a ſeparate parliament of their own:——that their incapacity to ſit in the houſe of commons has been



con-

confirmed by repeated decifions of the houfe; and that the law of parliament declared by thofe decifions, has been for above two centuries notorious and undifputed. The author is certainly at liberty to fancy cafes, and make whatever comparifons he thinks proper; his fuppofitions ftill continue as diftant from fact, as his wild difcourfes are from folid argument.

The conclufion of his book is candid to extreme. He offers to grant me all I defire. He thinks he may fafely admit that the cafe of Mr Walpole makes directly againft him, for it feems he has one grand folution *in petto* for all difficulties. *If,* fays he, *I were to allow all this, it will only prove, that the law of election was different in Queen Anne's time from what it is at prefent.*

This indeed is more than I expected. The principle, I know, has been maintained in fact; but I never expected to fee it fo formally declared. What can he mean? Does he affume this language to fatisfy the doubts of the people; or does he mean to roufe their indignation? Are the miniftry daring enough to affirm, that the houfe of commons have a right to make and unmake the law of parliament at their pleafure?—Does the law of parliament, which we are fo often told is the law of the land; —does the common right of every fubject of the realm, depend upon an arbitrary capricious vote of one branch of the legiflature?—The voice of truth and reafon muft be filent.

The miniftry tell us plainly, that this is no longer a queftion of right, but of power and force alone. What was law yefterday is not law to-day: and now it feems we have no better rule to live by, than the temporary difcretion and fluctuating integrity of the houfe of commons.

Profeffions of patriotifm are become ftale and ridiculous. For my own part, I claim no merit from endeavouring to do a fervice to my fellow-fub-
L
jects.

jects. I have done it to the best of my understanding; and without looking for the approbation of
other men, my conscience is satisfied. What remains to be done concerns the collective body of
the people. They are now to determine for themselves, whether they will firmly and constitution-
ally affert their rights; or make an humble, slavish
surrender of them at the feet of the ministry. To
a generous mind there cannot be a doubt. We
owe it to our ancestors to preserve entire these
rights which they have delivered to our care: we
owe it to our posterity, not to suffer their dearest
inheritance to be destroyed. But if it were possible
for us to be insensible of these sacred claims, there
is yet an obligation binding upon ourselves, from
which nothing can acquit us;—a personal interest,
which we cannot surrender. To alienate even
our own rights, would be a crime as much more
enormous than suicide, as a life of civil security
and freedom is superior to a bare existence; and
if life be the bounty of heaven, we scornfully reject the noblest part of the gift, if we consent to
surrender that certain rule of living, without which
the condition of human nature is not only miserable, but contemptible. JUNIUS.

---

## LETTER XXI.

TO THE PRINTER OF THE PUBLIC ADVER-
TISER.

S I R,                              Aug. 22. 1769.

I MUST beg of you to print a few lines, in explanation of some passages in my last letter, which
I see have been misunderstood.

1. When I said, that the house of commons
never meant to found Mr Walpole's incapacity on
his expulsion *only*, I meant no more than to deny
the general proposition that expulsion *alone* creates
K                        the

the incapacity.   If their be any thing ambiguous
in the expreſſion, I beg leave to explain it by ſaying, that, in my opinion, expulſion neither creates,
nor in any part contributes to create, the incapacity
in queſtion..

2. I carefully avoided entering into the merits
of Mr Walpole's caſe.   I did not inquire, whether
the houſe of commons acted juſtly, or whether they
truly declared the law of parliament.  My remarks
went only to their apparent meaning and intention, as it ſtands declared in their own reſolution.

3. I never meant to affirm, that a commitment
to the tower created a diſqualification.   On the
contrary, I conſidered that idea as an abſurdity,
into which the miniſtry muſt inevitably fall, if
they reaſoned right upon their own principles.

The caſe of Mr Wollaſton ſpeaks for itſelf.  The
miniſtry aſſert that *expulſion alone* creates an abſolute complete incapacity to be re-elected to ſit in
the ſame parliament.  This propoſition they have
uniformly maintained, without any condition or
modification whatſoever.  Mr Wollaſton was expelled, re-elected, and admitted to take his ſeat
in the ſame parliament.—I leave it to the public
to determine, whether this be a plain matter of
fact, or mere nonſenſe or declamation.

J U N I U S.

---

## L E T T E R  XXII.

TO THE PRINTER OF THE PUBLIC ADVER-
TISER.

SEPT. 4. 1769.

ARGUMENT againſt FACT; or, A new ſyſtem of
political Logic, by which the miniſtry have de-
monſtrated, to the ſatisfaction of their friends,
that expulſion alone creates a complete incapacity to be re-elected; *alias*, that a ſubject of

L 2

this

this realm may be robbed of his common right by a vote of the houfe of commons.

### First Fact.

M^R *Wollafton, in 1698, was expelled, re-elected, and admitted to take his feat.*

### Argument.

As this cannot conveniently be reconcilied wit^h our general propofition, it may be neceffary to fhift our ground, and look back to the *caufe* of Mr Wollafton's expulfion. From thence it will appear clearly, that, " although he was expelled, he had " not rendered himfelf a culprit too ignominious " to fit in parliament; and that having refigned " his employment, he was no longer incapacitated " by law." *Vide Serious Confiderations*, page 23. Or thus, " The houfe, fomewhat *inaccurately,* " ufed the word EXPELLED; they fhould have " called it A MOTION." *Vide Mungo's cafe confidered*, page 11. Or in fhort, if thefe arguments fhould be thought infufficient, we may fairly deny the fact. For example: " I affirm that he was " not re-elected. The fame Mr Wollafton, who " was expelled, was not again elected. The fame " individual, if you pleafe, walked into the houfe, " and took his feat there; but the fame perfon in " law was not admitted a member of that parlia- " ment, from which he had been difcarded." *Vide Letter to Junius*, page 12.

### Second Fact.

*Mr Walpole having been committed to the Tower, and expelled for a high breach of truft and notorious corruption in a public office, was declared incapable,* &c.

### Argument.

From the terms of this vote, nothing can be

more

more evident, than that the houfe of commons
m*ant to fix the incapacity upon the punifhment,
and not upon the crime; but left it fhould appear
in a different light to weak, uninformed perfons,
it may be advifable to gut the refolution, and give
it to the public, with all poffible folemnity, in the
following terms, viz. " Refolved, that Robert
" Walpole, Efq; having been that feffion of par-
" liament expelled the houfe, was and is incapa-
" ble of being elected member to ferve in that
" prefent parliament."   *Vide Mungo on the ufe of
quotations*, page 11.

   N. B. The author of the anfwer to Sir William
Meredith feems to have made ufe of Mungo's quotation; for in page 18, he affures us, " That the
" declaratory vote of the 17th of February 1769,
" was indeed a literal copy of the refolution of
" the houfe in Mr Walpole's cafe."

## THIRD FACT.

*His opponent, Mr Taylor, having the fmalleft num-
ber of votes at the next election, was declared* NOT
DULY ELCETED.

## ARGUMENT.

This fact we confider as directly in point to
prove that Mr Luttrell ought to be the fitting
member, for the following reafons.  " The bur-
" geffes of Lynn could draw no other inference
" from this refolution, but this, that at a future
" election, and in cafe of a fimilar return, the
" houfe would receive the fame candidate as duly
" elected, whom they had before rejected."  *Vide
Poftfcript to Junius*, p. 37.  Or thus: " This their
" refolution leaves no room to doubt what part
" they *would* have taken, if, upon a fubfequent re-
" election of Mr Walpole, there had been any
" other candidate in competition with him.  For,
" by their vote, they could have no other inten-
" tion than to admit fuch other candidate."  *Vide
Mungo's*

*Mungo's case considered,* p. 39. Or take it in this light :—The burgesses of Lynn having, in defiance of the house, retorted upon them a person, whom they had branded with the most ignominious marks of their displeasure, were thereby so well intitled to favour and indulgence, that the house could do no less than rob Mr Taylor of a right legally vested in him, in order that the burgesses might be apprised of the law of parliament; which law the house took a very direct way of explaining to them, by resolving that the candidate with the fewest votes was not duly elected :—" And was not this much " more equitable, more in the spirit of that equal " and substantial justice, which is the end of all " law, than if they had violently adhered to the strict " maxims of law ?" *Vide Serious Considerations,* p. 33 and 34. " And if the present house of com- " mons had chosen to follow the spirit of this re- " solution, they would have received and esta- " blished the candidate with the fewest votes." *Vide Answer to Sir W. M.* p. 18.

Permit me now, Sir, to show you, that the worthy Dr Blackstone sometimes contradicts the ministry as well as himself. The Speech without doors asserts, page 9. " That the legal effect of an " incapacity, founded on a judicial determination " of a complete court, is precisely the same as that " of an incapacity created by act of parliament." Now for the Doctor.—*The law and the opinion of the judge are not always convertible terms, or one and the same thing ; since it sometimes may happen that the judge may mistake the law.* Commentaries, Vol. I. p. 71.

The answer to Sir W. M. asserts, page 23. " That " the returning officer is not a judicial, but a purely " ministerial officer. His return is no judicial act." —At 'em again, Doctor. *The Sheriff in his judicial capacity is to hear and determine causes of forty shillings value and under in his county court. He*

has

*has also a judicial power in divers other civil cases.*
*He is likewise to decide the elections of Knights of the*
*shire ( subject to the controul of the house of commons ),*
*to judge of the qualification of voters, and to return*
*such as he shall* DETERMINE *to be duly elected.*
*Vide* Commentaries, Vol. I. page 332.

What conclusion shall we draw from such facts,
and such arguments, such contradictions? I cannot express my opinion of the present ministry
more exactly than in the words of Sir Richard
Steele : "That we are governed by a set of drivel-
" lers, whose folly takes away all dignity from
" distress, and makes even calamity ridiculous."

PHILO JUNIUS.

---

### LETTER XXIII.

TO HIS GRACE THE DUKE OF BEDFORD.

MY LORD,                          SEPT 19. 1769.

YOU are so little accustomed to receive any
marks of respect or esteem from the public,
that if, in the following lines, a compliment or
expression of applause should escape me, I fear you
would consider it as a mockery of your established
character, and perhaps an insult to your understanding. You have nice feelings, my Lord, if
we may judge from your resentments. Cautious,
therefore of giving offence, where you have so little
deserved it, I shall leave the illustration of your
virtues to other hands. Your friends have a privilege to play upon the easiness of your temper, or
possibly they are better acquainted with your good
qualities than I am. You have done good by
stealth. The rest is upon record. You have still
left ample room for speculation, when panegyric
is exhausted.

You are indeed a very considerable man. The
highest rank ;—a splendid fortune ;—and a name,

glorious

glorious till it was your's,—were fufficient to have fupported you with meaner abilities than I think you poffefs. From the firft, you derive a conftitutional claim to refpect; from the fecond, a natural extenfive authority;—the laft created a partial expectation of hereditary virtues. The ufe you have made of thefe uncommon advantages might have been more honourable to yourfelf, but could not be more inftructive to mankind. We may trace it in the veneration of your country, the choice of your friends, and in the accomplifhment of every fanguine hope which the public might have conceived from the illuftrious name of Ruffel.

The eminence of your ftation gave you a commanding profpect of your duty. The road, which led to honour, was open to your view. You could not lofe it by miftake, and you had no temptation to depart from it by defign. Compare the natural dignity and importance of the richeft peer of England;—the noble independence which he might have maintained in parliament, and the real intereft and refpect which he might have acquired, not only in parliament, but through the whole kingdom:—compare thefe glorious diftinctions with the ambition of holding a fhare in government, the emoluments of a place, the fale of a borough, or the purchafe of a corporation; and though you may not regret the virtues which create refpect, you may fee with anguifh how much real importance and authority you have loft. Confider the character of an independent virtuous Duke of Bedford; imagine what he might be in this country, then reflect one moment upon what you are. If it be poffible for me to withdraw my attention from the fact, I will tell you in the theory what fuch a man might be.

Confcious of his own weight and importance, his conduct in parliament would be directed by nothing but the conftitutional duty of a peer. He

would

would confider himfelf as a guardian of the laws·
Willing to fupport the juft meafures of government·
but determined to obferve the conduct of the minifter with fufpicion, he would oppofe the violence
of faction with as much firmnefs as the encroach-
ments of prerogative. He would be as little capable of bargaining with the minifter for places for
himfelf or his dependants, as of defcending to mix
himfelf in the intrigues of oppofition. Whenever
an important queftion called for his opinion in parliament, he would be heard, by the moft profligate minifter, with deference and refpect. His
authority would either fanctify or difgrace the
meafures of government.—The people would look
up to him as their protector; and a virtuous prince
would have one honeft man in his dominions, in
whofe integrity and judgment he might fafely confide. If it fhould be the will of Providence to
afflict him with a domeftic misfortune *, he would
fubmit to the ftroke, with feeling, but not without
dignity. He would confider the people as his children, and receive a generous heart-felt confolation
in the fympathifing tears and bleffings of his
country.

Your *Grace* may probably difcover fomething
more intelligible in the negative part of this illuftrious character. The man I have defcribed would
never proftitute his dignity in parliament by an indecent violence either in oppofing or defending a
minifter. He would not at one moment ranco-
roufly perfecute, at another bafely cringe to the
favourite of his Sovereign. After outraging the
royal dignity with preremptory conditions little
fhort of menace and hoftility, he would never defcend to the humility of foliciting an interview †
with

---

* The Duke lately loft his ony fon, by a fall from his horfe.

† At this interview, which paffed at the houfe of the late Lord
Eglingtoun, Lord Bute told the Duke that he was determined never
to have any connexion with a man who had fo bafely betrayed
him.

with the favourite, and of offering to recover at any price the honour of his friendship. Though deceived perhaps in his youth, he would not, through the course of a long life, have invariably chosen his friends from among the most profligate of mankind. His own honour would have forbidden him from mixing his private pleasures or conversation with jockeys, gamesters, blasphemers, gladiators, or buffoons. He would then have never felt, much less would he have submitted to, the dishonest necessity of engaging in the interests and intrigues of his dependants; of supplying their vices, or relieving their beggary, at the expence of his country. He would not have betrayed such ignorance, or such contempt, of the constitution, as openly to avow, in a court of justice, the * purchase and sale of a borough. He would not have thought it consistent with his rank in the state, or even with his personal importance, to be the little tyrant of a little corporation †. He would never have been insulted with virtues, which he had laboured to extinguish; nor suffered the disgrace of a mortifying defeat, which has made him ridiculous and contemptible, even to the few by whom he was not detested.—I reverence the afflictions of a good man,—his sorrows are sacred. But how can we take part in the distresses of a man, whom we can neither love nor esteem; or feel for a calamity, of which he himself is insensible? Where was the father's heart, when he could look for, or find, an immediate consolation for the loss of an only son, in consultations and bargains for a place

at

---

* In an answer in Chancery, in a suit against him to recover a large sum paid him by a person whom he had undertaken to return to parliament, for one of his Grace's boroughs. He was compelled to repay the money.

† Of Bedford; where the tyrant was held in such contempt and detestation, that, in order to deliver themselves from him, they admitted a great number of strangers to the freedom. To make his defeat truly ridiculous, he tried his whole strength again Mr. *Horne*, and was beaten upon his own ground.

at court, and even in the mifery of balloting at the
India houfe!

Admitting then that you have miftaken or deferted thofe honourable principles which ought to
have directed your conduct ; admitting that you
have as little claim to private affection as to public
efteem ; let us fee with what abilities, with what
degree of judgment, you have carried your own
fyftem into execution.   A great man, in the fuccefs
and even in the magnitude of his crimes, finds a
refcue from contempt.   Your Grace is every way
unfortunate.   Yet I will not look back to thofe
ridiculous fcenes, by which in your earlier days
you thought it an honour to be diftinguifhed*.;
—the recorded ftripes, the public infamy, your
own fufferings, or Mr Rigby's fortitude.   Thefe
events undoubtedly left an impreffion, though not
upon your mind.   To fuch a mind it may perhaps
be a pleafure to reflect, that there is hardly a corner of any of his Majefty's kingdoms except France,
in which, at one end or another, your valuable
life has not been in danger.   Amiable man! we
fee and acknowledge the protection of Providence,
by which you have fo often efcaped the perfonal
deteftation of your fellow-fubjects, and are ftill
referved for the public juftice of your country.

Your hiftory begins to be important at that au-
fpicious period, at which you were deputed to reprefent the Earl of Bute at the court of Verfailles.
It was an honourable office, and executed with the
fame fpirit with which it was accepted.   Your
                                              patrons

* Mr Hefton Homphrey, a country Attorney, horfewhipped the
Duke, with equal juftice, feverity, and perfeverance, on the Courfe
at Litchfield.  *Rigby* and Lord *Trentham* were alfo cudgelled in a
moft examplary manner.  This gave rife to the following ftory :
" When the late King heard that Sir Edward Hawke had given the
" French a *drubbing*, his Majefty, who had never received that
" kind of chaftifenent, was pleafed to afk Lord Chefterfield the
" meaning of the word ——Sir, fays Lord Chefterfield, the mean-
" ing of the word—but here comes the Duke of Bedford, who is
" better able to explain it to your majefty than I am."

patrons wanted an ambaſſador, who would ſubmit to make conceſſions without daring to inſiſt upon any honourable condition for his Sovereign. Their buſineſs required a man who had as little feeling for his own dignity as for the welfare of his country ; and they found him in the firſt rank of the nobility.　Belleiſle, Goree, Guadeloupe, St. Lucia, Martinique, the Fiſhery, and the Havannah, are glorious monuments of your Grace's talents for negociation.　My Lord, we are too well acquainted with your pecuniary character, to think it poſſible that ſo many public ſacrifices ſhould have been made without ſome private compenſations.　Your conduct carries with it an internal evidence, beyond all the legal proofs of a court of juſtice. Even the callous pride of Lord Egremont was alarmed *.　He ſaw and felt his own diſhonour in correſponding with you; and there certainly was a moment, at which he meant to have reſiſted, had not a fatal lethargy prevailed over his faculties, and carried all ſenſe and memory away with it.

I will not pretend to ſpecify the ſecret terms on which you were invited to ſupport an † adminiſtration which Lord Bute pretended to leave in full poſſeſſion of their miniſteral authority, and perfectly maſters of themſelves.　He was not of a temper to relinquiſh power, though he retired from employment.　Stipulations were certainly made between your Grace and him, and certainly violated.　After two years ſubmiſſion, you thought you had collected a ſtrength ſufficient to controul his influence; and that it was your turn to be a tyrant, becauſe you had been a ſlave.　When you found yourſelf miſtaken in your opinion of your gracious Maſter's firmneſs, diſappointment got the

better

---

* This man, notwithſtanding his pride and Tory principles, had ſome Engliſh ſtuff in him.　Upon an official letter he wrote to the Duke of Bedford, the Duke deſired to be recalled, and it was with the utmoſt difficulty that Lord Bute could appeaſe him.

† Mr Grenville, Lord Halifax, and Lord Egremont.

better of all your humble difcretion, and carried you to an excefs of outrage to his perfon, as diftant from true fpirit, as from all decency and refpect *. After robbing him of the rights of a King, you would not permit him to preferve the honour of a gentleman. It was then Lord Weymouth was nominated to Ireland, and difpatched (we well remember with what indecent hurry) to plunder the treafury of the firft fruits of an employment which you well know he was never to execute †.

This fudden declaration of war againft the favourite might have given you a momentary merit with the public, if it had either been adopted upon principle, or maintained with refolution. Without looking back to all your former fervility, we need only obferve your fubfequent conduct, to fee upon what motives you acted. Apparently united with Mr Grenville, you waited until Lord Rockingham's feeble adminiftration fhould diffolve in its own weaknefs.—The moment their difmiffion was fufpected, the moment you perceived that another fyftem was adopted in the clofet, you thought it no difgrace to return to your former dependence, and folicit once more the friendfhip of Lord Bute. You begged an interview, at which he had fpirit enough to treat you with contempt.

It would be now of little ufe to point out, by what a train of weak, injudicious meafures, it became neceffary, or was thought fo, to call you back to a fhare in the adminiftration ‡. The friends

M

whom

---

* The miniftry having endeavoured to exclude the Dowager out of the regency bill, the Earl of Bute determined to difmifs them. Upon this the Duke of Bedford demanded an audience of the——; reproached him in plain terms with his duplicity, bafenefs, falfehood, treachery, and hypocrify—repeatedly gave him the lie, and left him in convulfions.

† He received three thoufand pounds for plate and equipage money.

‡ When Earl Gower was appointed Prefident of the council, the King with his ufual fincerity affured him, that he had not had one happy moment fince the Duke of Bedford left him.

whom you did not in the laſt inſtance deſert, were not of a character to add ſtrength or credit to government; and at that time your alliance with the Duke of Grafton was, I preſume, hardly foreſeen. We muſt look for other ſtipulations, to account for that ſudden reſolution of the cloſet, by which three of your dependants * (whoſe characters, I think, cannot be leſs reſpected than they are) were advanced to offices, through which you might again controul the miniſter, and probably engroſs the whole direction of affairs.

The poſſeſſion of abſolute power is now once more within your reach. The meaſures you have taken to obtain and confirm it, are too groſs to eſcape the eyes of a diſcerning judicious prince. His palace is beſieged; the lines of circumvallation are drawing round him; and unleſs he finds a reſource in his own activity, or in the attachment of the real friends of his family, the beſt of princes muſt ſubmit to the confinement of a ſtate-priſoner, until your Grace's death, or ſome leſs fortunate event, ſhall raiſe the ſiege. For the preſent, you may ſafely reſume that ſtyle of inſult and menace, which even a private gentleman cannot ſubmit to hear without being contemptible. Mr Mackenzie's hiſtory is not yet forgotten; and you may find precedents enough of the mode, in which an imperious ſubject may ſignify his pleaſure to his Sovereign. Where will this gracious monarch look for aſſiſtance, when the wretched Grafton could forget his obligations to his maſter, and deſert him for a hollow alliance with *ſuch* a man as the Duke of Bedford!

Let us conſider you, then, as arrived at the ſummit of worldly greatneſs; let us ſuppoſe, that all your plans of avarice and ambition are accompliſhed, and your moſt ſanguine wiſhes gratified in the fear as well as the hatred of the people:

Can

* Lords Gower, Weymouth, and Sandwich.

Can age itfelf forget that you are in the laft act of life? Can gray hairs make folly venerable? and is there no period to be referved for meditation and retirement? For fhame! my Lord: let it not be recorded of you, that the lateft moments of your life were dedicated to the fame unworthy purfuits, the fame bufy agitations, in which your youth and manhood were exhaufted. Confider, that although you cannot difgrace your former life, you are violating the character of age, and expofing the impotent imbecillity after you have loft the vigour of the paffions.

Your friends will afk, perhaps, Whither fhall this unhappy old man retire? Can he remain in the metropolis, where his life has been fo often threatened, and his palace fo often attacked? If he returns to Wooburn, fcorn and mokery await him. He muft create a folitude round his eftate, if he would avoid the face of reproach and derifion. At Plymouth, his deftruction would be more than probable; at Exeter, inevitable. No honeft Englifhman will ever forget his attachment, nor any honeft Scotchman forgive his treachery, to Lord Bute. At every town he enters, he muft change his liveries and name. Whichever way he flies, the *Hue and Cry* of the country purfues him.

In another kingdom, indeed, the bleffings of his adminiftration have been more fenfibly felt; his virtues better underftood; or at worft they will not, for him alone, forget their hofpitality.—As well might VERRES have returned to Sicily. You have twice efcaped, my Lord; beware of a third experiment. The indignation of a whole people, plundered, infulted, and oppreffed as they have been, will not always be difappointed.

It is in vain therefore to fhift the fcene. You can no more fly from your enemies than from yourfelf. Perfecuted abroad, you look into your own heart for consolation, and find nothing but reproaches and despair. But, my Lord, you may quit the field of business, though not the field of danger; and though you cannot be safe, you may cease to be ridiculous. I fear you have listened too long to the advice of those pernicious friends, with whose interests you have sordidly united your own, and for whom you have sacrificed every thing that ought to be dear to a man of honour. They are still base enough to encourage the follies of your age, as they once did the vices of your youth. As little acquainted with the rules of decorum as with the laws of morality, they will not suffer you to profit by experience, nor even to consult the propriety of a bad character. Even now they tell you, that life is no more than a dramatic scene, in which the hero should preserve his consistency to the last; and that as you lived without virtue, you should die without repentance. JUNIUS.

---

## LETTER XXIV.

### TO JUNIUS.

SIR, SEPT. 14. 1769.

HAVING accidentally seen a *republication* of your letters, wherein you have been pleased to *assert*, that I had *sold* the companions of my success; I am again obliged to declare the said assertion to be a most *infamous* and *malicious falsehood;* and I *again* call upon you to stand forth, avow yourself, and *prove* the charge. If you can make it out to the satisfaction of any one man in the kingdom, I will be content to be thought the worst man in it; if you do not, what must the nation think of you? *Party* has nothing to do in this affair: you have made a personal attack upon my honour, defamed me by a most vile calumny, which might possibly have sunk into oblivion, had

not

not such uncommon pains been taken to renew and perpetuate this scandal, chiefly because it has been told in good language: for I give you full credit for your elegant diction, well-turned periods, and Attic wit: but wit is oftentimes false, though it may appear brilliant; which is exactly the case of your *whole performance*. But, Sir, I am obliged in the most *serious* manner to accuse you of being guilty of *falsities*. You have said the thing that is *not*. To support your story, you have recourse to the following *irresistible* argument: " You *sold* the " companions of your victory, because when the " 16th regiment was given to *you*, you was *silent*. " The conclusion is inevitable." I believe that such *deep* and *acute reasoning* could only come from such an extraordinary writer as *Junius*. But unfortunately for you, the *premises* as well as the *conclusion* are absolutely *false*. Many applications have been made to the ministry on the subject of the Manilla Ransom *since* the time of my being colonel of that regiment. As I have for some years quitted London, I was obliged to have recourse to the honourable Colonel Monson and Sir Samuel Cornish to *negotiate* for me; in the last autumn, I personally delivered a memorial to the Earl of Shelburn at his seat in Wiltshire. As you have told us of your importance, that you are a person of *rank* and *fortune*, and above a *common* bribe, you may in all probability be not *unknown* to his Lordship, who can satisfy you of the truth of what I say. But I shall now take the liberty, Sir, to seize your battery, and turn it against yourself. If your puerile and tinsel logic could carry the least weight or conviction with it, how must you stand affected by the *inevitable conclusion*, as you are pleased to term it? According to *Junius*, *Silence* is *Guilt*. In many of the public papers, you have been called in the most direct and offensive terms a *liar*, and a *coward*. When did you reply to these



foul

foul accusations ? You have been quite *silent;* quite chop-fallen : therefore, *because* you was *silent,* the nation has a right to pronounce you to be both a liar and a coward from your own argument. But, Sir, I will give you fair play ; I will afford you an opportunity to wipe off the first appellation, by desiring the proofs of your charge against me. Produce them! To wipe off the last, produce *your-self.* People cannot bear any longer your *Lion's skin,* and the despicable *imposture* of the *old Roman name* which you have *affected.* For the future assume the name of some *modern* * bravo and dark assassin : let your appellation have some affinity to your practice. But if I must *perish,* *Junius,* let me *perish* in the face of day ; be for *once* a generous and open enemy. I allow that Gothic *appeals* to cold iron are no better proof of a man's honesty and veracity, than hot iron and burning plough-shares are of *female chastity:* but a soldier's honour is as delicate as a woman's ; it must not be suspected ; you have dared to throw more than a suspicion upon mine : you cannot but know the consequences, which even the meekness of Christianity would pardon me for, after the injury you have done me.                    WILLIAM DRAPER.

---

## LETTER XXV.

*Haret lateri lethalis arundo.*

TO SIR WILLIAM DRAPER, K. B.

SIR,                                            SEPT. 25. 1769.

AFTER so long an interval, I did not expect to see the debate revived between us. My answer to your last letter shall be short ; for I write to you with reluctance, and I hope we shall now conclude our correspondence for ever.

                                                        Had

---

* Was *Brutus* an *ancient* bravo and dark assassin? or does Sir W. D. think it criminal to stab a tyrant to the heart ?

Had you been originally and without provocation attacked by an anonymous writer, you would have some right to demand his name. But in this cause you are a volunteer. You engaged in it with the unpremeditated gallantry of a soldier. You were content to set your name in opposition to a man who would probably continue in concealment. You understood the terms upon which we were to correspond, and gave at least a tacit assent to them. After voluntarily attacking me under the character of Junius, what possible right have you to know me under any other? Will you forgive me if I insinuate to you, that you foresaw some honour in the apparent spirit of coming forward in person, and that you were not quite indifferent to the display of your literary qualifications?

You cannot but know, that the republication of my letters was no more than a catchpenny contrivance of a printer, in which it was impossible I should be concerned, and for which I am no way answerable. At the same time I wish you to understand, that if I do not take the trouble of reprinting these papers, it is not from any fear of giving offence to Sir William Draper.

Your remarks upon a signature adopted merely for distinction, are unworthy of notice: but when you tell me I have submitted to be called a liar and a coward, I must ask you in my turn, Whether you think seriously it any way incumbent upon me to take notice of the silly invectives of every simpleton who writes in a newspaper; and what opinion you would have conceived of my discretion, if I had suffered myself to be the dupe of so shallow an artifice?

Your appeal to the sword, though consistent enough with your late profession, will neither prove your innocence, nor clear you from suspicion.——Your complaints with regard to the Manilla

nilla ranfom were for a confiderable time a diftrefs to government. You were appointed (greatly out of your turn) to the command of a regiment, and *during that adminiftration* we heard no
more of Sir William Draper. The facts of which
I fpeak may indeed be varioufly accounted for,
but they are too notorious to be denied: and I
think you might have learnt at the univerfity, that
a falfe conclufion is an error in argument, not a
breach of veracity. Your folicitations, I doubt
not, were renewed under *another* adminiftration.
Admitting the fact, I fear an indifferent perfon
would only infer from it, that experience had
made you acquainted with the benefits of complaining. Remember, Sir, that you have yourfelf confeffed, that, *confidering the critical fituation
of this country, the miniftry are in the right to tem-
porife with Spain.* This confeffion reduces you to
an unfortunate dilemma. By renewing your folicitations, you muft either mean to force your
country into a war at a moft unfeafonable junc-
ture; or, having no view or expectation of that
kind, that you look for nothing but a private compenfation to yourfelf.

As to me, it is by no means neceffary that I
fhould be expofed to the refentment of the worft
and the moft powerful men in this country, tho'
I may be indifferent about your's. Though *you*
would fight, there are others who would affaffi-
nate.

But after all, Sir, where is the injury? You
affure me, that my logic is puerile and tinfel; that
it carries not the leaft weight or conviction; that
my premifes are falfe, and my conclufions abfurd.
If this be a juft defcription of me, how is it poffible for fuch a writer to difturb your peace of
mind, or to injure a character fo well eftablifhed
as yours? Take care, Sir William, how you indulge this unruly temper, left the world fhould
fufpect

fufpect that confcience has fome fhare in your refentments. You have more to fear from the treachery of your own paffions, than from any malevolence of mine.

I believe, Sir, you will never know me. A confiderable time muft certainly elapfe before we are perfonally acquainted. You need not, however, regret the delay, or fuffer an apprehenfion that any length of time can reftore you to the Chriftian meeknefs of your temper, and difappoint your prefent indignation. If I underftand your character, there is in your own breaft a repofitory, in which your refentments may be fafely laid up for future occafions, and preferved without the hazard of diminution. The *Odia in longum jaciens, quæ reconderet, auctaque promeret*, I thought had only belonged to the worft character of antiquity. The text is in Tacitus;—you know beft where to look for the commentary.          JUNIUS.

---

## · L E T T E R  XXVI.

### A WORD AT PARTING TO JUNIUS.

* S I R,                              Oct. 7. 1769.

AS you have not favoured me with either of the *explanations* demanded of you, I can have nothing more to fay to you upon my *own* account.
Your

* *Meafures and not men* is the common cant of affected moderation;—a bafe, counterfeit language, fabricated by knaves, and made current among fools. Such gentle cenfure is not fitted to the prefent degenerate ftate of fociety. What does it avail to expofe the abfurd contrivance or pernicious tendency of meafures, if the man who advifes or executes, fhall be fuffered not only to efcape with impunity, but even to preferve his power, and infult us with the favour of his Sovereign! I would recommend to the reader the whole of Mr Pope's letter to Doctor Arbuthnot, dated July 16. 1734, from which the following is an extract. "To reform and "not to chaftife, I am afraid is impoffible; and that the beft pre-"cepts, as well as the beft laws, would prove of fmall ufe, if "there were no examples to enforce them. To attack vices in the "abftract, without touching, perfons, may be fafe fighting indeed,
" but

Your mercy to me, or tenderneſs for yourſelf, has been very great. The public will judge of your *motives.* If your exceſs of modeſty forbids you to produce either the proofs, or yourſelf, I will excuſe it. Take courage; I have not the temper of Tiberius, any more than the rank or power. You, indeed, are a tyrant of another ſort; and upon your political bed of torture can excruciate any ſubject, from a firſt miniſter down to ſuch a grub or butterfly as myſelf; like another deteſted tyrant of antiquity, can make the wretched ſufferer fit the bed, if the bed will not fit the ſufferer, by disjointing or tearing the trembling limbs until they are ſtretched to its extremity. But courage, conſtancy, and patience, under torments, have ſometimes cauſed the moſt hardened monſters to relent, and forgive the object of their cruelty. You, Sir, are determined to try all that human nature can endure, until ſhe expires: elſe, was it poſſible that you could be the author of that moſt inhuman letter to the Duke of Bedford, I have read with aſtoniſhment and horror? Where, Sir, where were the feelings of your own heart, when you could upbraid a moſt affectionate father with the loſs of his only and moſt amiable ſon? Read over again thoſe cruel lines of yours, and let them wring your very ſoul. Cannot political queſtions be diſcuſſed without deſcending to the moſt odious perſonalities? Muſt you go wantonly out of your way to torment declining age, becauſe the Duke of Bedford may have quarrelled with thoſe whoſe cauſe and politics you eſpouſe? For ſhame! for ſhame! As you have *ſpoke daggers* to him, you may juſtly dread the *uſe* of them againſt your own breaſt, did a want of courage, or of noble ſentiments, ſtimulate him to ſuch mean revenge. He

is

" but it is fighting with ſhadows. My greateſt comfort and en-
" couragement to proceed has been to ſee, that thoſe who have no
" ſhame, and not fear of any thing elſe, have appeared touched
"by my ſatires."

is above it ; he is brave. Do you fancy that your own bafe arts have infected our whole ifland ? But your own reflections, your own confcience, muft and will, if you have any fpark of humanity remaining, give him moft ample vengeance. Not all the power of words with which you are fo graced, will ever wafh out, or even palliate, this foul blot in your character. I have not time at prefent to diffect your letter fo minutely as I could wifh ; but I will be bold enough to fay, that it is (as to reafon and argument) the moft extraordinary piece of *florid impotence* that was ever impofed upon the eyes and ears of the too credulous and deluded mob. It accufes the Duke of Bedford of, high treafon. Upon what foundation ? You tell us, " that the Duke's *pecuniary character* makes it " more than *probable*, that he could not have made " fuch facrifices at the peace, without *fome private* " *compenfations:* that his conduct carried with it " an interior evidence, beyond all the legal proofs " of a court of juftice."

My academical education, Sir, bids me tell you, that it is neceffary to eftablifh the truth of your firft propofition, before you prefume to draw inferences from it. Firft prove the avarice, before you make the rafh, hafty, and moft wicked conclufion. This father, *Junius*, whom you call avaricious, allowed that fon eight thoufand pounds a year. Upon his moft unfortunate death, which your ufual good-nature took care to remind him of, he greatly increafed the jointure of the afflicted lady his widow. Is this avarice ? Is this doing good by *ftealth ?* It is upon record.

If exact order, method, and true œconomy, as a mafter of a family ; if fplendor and juft magnificence, without wild wafte and thoughtlefs extravagance, may conftitute the character of an avaricious man, the Duke is guilty. But for a moment let us admit that an ambaffador may love
money

money too much; what proof do you give that he has taken any to betray his country? Is it hearsay, or the evidence of letters, or ocular; or the evidence of those concerned in this black affair? Produce your authorities to the public. It is an impudent kind of sorcery, to attempt to blind us with the smoke, without convincing us that the fire has existed. You first brand him with a vice that he is free from, to render him odious and suspected. Suspicion is the foul weapon with which you make all your chief attacks; with that you stab. But shall one of the first subjects of the realm be ruined in his fame; shall even his life be in constant danger, from a charge built upon such sandy foundations? must his house be besieged by lawless ruffians, his journey impeded, and even the asylum of an altar be insecure from assertions so base and false? Potent as he is, the Duke is amenable to justice; if guilty, punishable. The parliament is the high and solemn tribunal for matters of such great moment. To that be they submitted. But I hope also that some notice will be taken of, and some punishment inflicted upon, false accusers; especially upon such, *Junius*, who are *wilfully false*. In any truth I will agree even with *Junius*; will agree with him that it is highly unbecoming the dignity of peers to tamper with boroughs. Aristocracy is as fatal as democracy. Our constitution admits of neither. It loves a King, Lords, and Commons, really chosen by the unbought suffrages of a free people. But if corruption only shifts hands; if the wealthy commoner gives the bribe, instead of the potent peer, is the state better served by this exchange? Is the real emancipation of the borough effected, because new parchment bonds may possibly supersede the old? To say the truth, wherever such practices prevail, they are equally criminal to and destructive of our freedom.



The

The rest of your declamation is scarce worth considering, excepting for the elegance of the language. Like Hamlet in the play, you produce two pictures; you tell us, that one is not like the Duke of Bedford; then you bring a most hideous caricatura, and tell us of the resemblance; but *multum abludit imago.*

All your long tedious accounts of the ministerial quarrels, and the intrigues of the cabinet, are reducible to a few short lines; and to convince you, Sir, that I do not mean to flatter any minister, either past or present, these are my thoughts: They seem to have acted like lovers, or children; have * pouted, quarrelled, cried, kissed, and been friends again, as the objects of desire, the ministerial rattles, have been put into their hands. But such proceedings are very unworthy of the gravity and dignity of a great nation. We do not want men of abilities; but we have wanted steadiness; we want unanimity: your letters, *Junius,* will not contribute thereto. You may one day expire by a flame of your own kindling. But it is my humble opinion, that lenity and moderation, pardon and oblivion, will disappoint the efforts of all the seditious in the land, and extinguish their wide spreading fires. I have lived with this sentiment; with this I shall die.

WILLIAM DRAPER.

---

L E T T E R   XXVII.



S I R,                              Oct. 13. 1769.

IF Sir William Draper's bed be a bed of torture, he has made it for himself. I shall never interrupt his repose. Having changed the subject, there

N

are

---

* Sir William gives us a pleasant account of men, who, in *his* opinion at least, are the best qualified to govern an empire.

are parts of his laſt letter not undeſerving of a reply. Leaving his private character and conduct out of the queſtion, I ſhall conſider him merely in the capacity of an author, whoſe labours certainly do no diſcredit to a newſpaper.

We ſay, in common diſcourſe, that a man may be his own enemy; and the frequency of the fact makes the expreſſion intelligible. But that a man ſhould be the bittereſt enemy of his friends, implies a contradiction of a peculiar nature. There is ſomething in it, which cannot be conceived without a confuſion of ideas, nor expreſſed without a ſoleciſm in language. Sir William Draper is ſtill that fatal friend Lord Granby found him. Yet I am ready to do juſtice to his generoſity; if indeed it be not ſomething more than generous, to be the voluntary advocate of men who think themſelves injured by his aſſiſtance, and to conſider nothing in the cauſe he adopts but the difficulty of defending it. I thought however he had been better read in the hiſtory of the human heart, than to compare or confound the tortures of the body with thoſe of the mind. He ought to have known, though perhaps it might not be his intereſt to confeſs, that no outward tyranny can reach the mind. If conſcience plays the tyrant, it would be greatly for the benefit of the world that ſhe were more arbitrary, and far leſs placable, than ſome men find her.

But it ſeems I have outraged the feelings of a father's heart.—Am I indeed ſo injudicious? Does Sir William Draper think I would have hazarded my credit with a generous nation, by ſo groſs a violation of the laws of humanity? Does he think I am ſo little acquainted with the firſt and nobleſt characteriſtic of Engliſhmen? Or how will he reconcile ſuch folly with an underſtanding ſo full of artifice as mine? Had *he* been a father, he would have been but little offended with the ſe-

verity

verity of the reproach, for his mind would have been filled with the justice of it. He would have seen that I did not insult the feelings of a father, but the father who felt nothing. He would have trusted to the evidence of his own paternal heart; and boldly denied the possibility of the fact, instead of defending it. Against whom then will his honest indignation be directed, when I assure him, that this whole town beheld the Duke of Bedford's conduct, upon the death of his son, with horror and astonishment. Sir William Draper does himself but little honour in opposing the general sense of his country. The people are seldom wrong in their opinions,—in their sentiments they are never mistaken. There may be a vanity perhaps in a singular way of thinking;—but when a man professes a want of those feelings which do honour to the multitude, he hazards something infinitely more important than the character of his understanding. After all, as Sir William may possibly be in earnest in his anxiety for the Duke of Bedford, I should be glad to relieve him from it. He may rest assured this worthy nobleman laughs, with equal indifference, at my reproaches, and Sir William's distress about him. But here let it stop. Even the Duke of Bedford, insensible as he is, will consult the tranquility of his life, in not provoking the moderation of my temper. If, from the profoundest contempt, I should ever rise into anger, he should soon find, that all I have already said of him was lenity and compassion.

Out of a long catalogue, Sir William Draper has confined himself to the refutation of two charges only. The rest he had not time to discuss; and indeed it would have been a laborious undertaking. To draw up a defence of such a series of enormities, would have required a life at least as long as that which has been uniformly employed in the practice of them. The public opinion of the Duke of Bedford's extreme œconomy is, it seems, entirely without foundation. Though not very prodigal abroad, in his own family at least he is regular and magnificent. He pays his debts, abhors a beggar, and makes a handsome provision for his son. His charity has improved upon the proverb, and ended where it began. Admitting the whole force of this single instance of his domestic generosity (wonderful indeed, considering the narrowness of his fortune, and the little merit of his only son), the public may still perhaps be dissatisfied, and demand some other less equivocal proofs of his munificence. Sir William Draper should have entered boldly into the detail—of indigence relieved—of arts encouraged—of science patronized, men of learning protected, and works of genius rewarded ;—in short, had there been a single instance, besides Mr Rigby *, of blushing merit brought forward by the Duke for the service of the public, it should not have been omitted.

I wish it were possible to establish my inference with the same certainty, on which I believe the principle is founded. My conclusion, however, was not drawn from the principle alone. I am not so unjust as to reason from one crime to another ; though I think, that, of all the vices, avarice is most apt to taint and corrupt the heart. I combined the known temper of the man with the extravagant concessions made by the ambassador ; and though I doubt not sufficient care was taken to leave no document of any treasonable negociation, I still maintain that the conduct † of this

mini-

* This gentleman is supposed to have the same idea of *blushing*, that a man blind from his birth has of scarlet or sky-blue.

† If Sir W. D. will take the trouble of looking into Torcy's Memoirs, he will see with what little ceremony a bribe may be offered to a Duke, and with what little ceremony it was *only not accepted.*

minifter carries with it an internal and convincing evidence againſt him. Sir William Draper ſeems not to knov the value or force of ſuch a proof. He will not permit us to judge of the motives of men, by the manifeſt tendency of their actions, nor by the notorious character of their minds. He calls for papers and witneſſes, with a triumphant ſecurity; as if nothing could be true, but what could be proved in a court of juſtice. Yet a religious man might have remembered, upon what foundation ſome truths, moſt intereſting to mankind, have been received and eſtabliſhed. If it were not for the internal evidence, which the pureſt of religions carries with it, what would have become of his once well-quoted decalogue, and of the meeknefs of his Chriſtianity?

The generous warmth of his reſentment makes him confound the order of events. He forgets that the inſults and diſtreſſes which the Duke of Bedford has ſuffered, and which Sir William has lamented with many delicate touches of the true pathetic, were only recorded in my letter to his Grace, not occaſioned by it. It was a ſimple candid narrative of facts; though, for aught I know, it may carry with it ſomething prophetic. His Grace undoubtedly has received ſeveral ominous hints; and I think, in certain circumſtances, a wife man would do well to prepare himſelf for the event.

But I have a charge of a heavier nature againſt Sir William Draper. He tells us that the Duke of Bedford is amenable to juſtice; that parliament is a high and ſolemn tribunal; and that, if guilty, he may be puniſhed by due courſe of law: and all this he ſays with as much gravity as if he believed one word of the matter. I hope, indeed, the day of impeachments will arrive, before this nobleman eſcapes out of life;—but to refer us to that mode of proceeding now, with ſuch a mini-

N 3

ſtry,

ftry, and fuch a houfe of commons as the prefent, what is it, but an indecent mockery of the common fenfe of the nation? I think he might have contented himfelf with defending the greateft enemy, without infulting the diftreffes, of his country.

His concluding declaration of his opinion, with refpect to the prefent condition of affairs, is too loofe and undetermined to be of any fervice to the public. How ftrange is it that this gentleman fhould dedicate fo much time and argument to the defence of worthlefs or indifferent characters, while he gives but feven folitary lines to the only fubject which can deferve his attention, or do credit to his abilities.　　JUNIUS.

---

## LETTER XXVIII.

TO THE PRINTER OF THE PUBLIC ADVERTISER.

SIR,　　　　　　　　　　Oct. 20. 1769.

I VERY fincerely applaud the fpirit with which a lady has paid the debt of gratitude to her benefactor. Though I think fhe has miftaken the point, fhe fhows a virtue which makes her refpectable. The queftion turned upon the perfonal generofity or avarice of a man, whofe private fortune is immenfe. The proofs of his munificence muft be drawn from the ufes to which he has applied that fortune. I was not fpeaking of a Lord Lieutenant of Ireland, but of a rich Englifh duke, whofe wealth gave him the means of doing as much good in this country, as he derived from his power in another. I am far from wifhing to leffen the merit of this fingle benevolent action; —perhaps it is the more confpicuous from ftanding alone. All I mean to fay is, that it proves nothing in the prefent argument.　　JUNIUS.

LET-

## L E T T E R   XXIX.

### ADDRESSED TO THE PRINTER OF THE PUBLIC ADVERTISER.

S I R,                                     Oct. 19. 1769.

I AM well affured that *Junius* will never defcend to a difpute with fuch a writer as *Modeftus* (whofe letter appeared in the Gazetteer of Monday) efpecially as the difpute muft be chiefly about words. Notwithftanding the partiality of the Public, it does not appear that *Junius* values himfelf upon any fuperior fkill in compofition; and I hope his time will always be more ufefully employed than in the trifling refinements of verbal criticifm. *Modeftus*, however, fhall have no reafon to triumph in the filence and moderation of *Junius*. If he knew as much of the propriety of language, as I believes he does of the facts in queftion, he would have been as cautious of attacking *Junius* upon his compofition, as he feems to be of entering into the fubject of it; yet after all, the laft is the only article of any importance to the public.

I do not wonder at the unremitted rancour with which the Duke of Bedford and his adherents invariably fpeak of a nation, which we well know has been too much injured to be eafily forgiven. But why muft *Junius* be an Irifhman?—*The abfurdity of his writings betrays him.*—Waving all confideration of the infult offered by *Modeftus* to the declared judgment of the people (they may well bear this among the reft), let us follow the feveral inftances, and try whether the charge be fairly fupported.

Firft then—The leaving a man to enjoy fuch repofe as he can find upon a bed of torture, is fevere indeed; perhaps too much fo, when applied to fuch a trifler as Sir William Draper; but there is

nothing

nothing abfurd either in the idea or expreffion. *Modeftus* cannot diftinguifh between a farcafm and a contradiction.

2. I affirm with *Junius,* that it is the *frequency* of the fact, which alone can make us comprehend how a man can be his own enemy. We fhould never arrive at the complex idea conveyed by thofe words, if we had only feen one or two inftances of a man acting to his own prejudice. Offer the propofition to a child, or a man unufed to compound his ideas, and you will foon fee how little either of them underftand you. It is not a fimple idea arifing from a fingle fact; but a very complex idea arifing from many facts well obferved, and accurately compared.

3. Modeftus could not, without great affectation, miftake the meaning of *Junius* when he fpeaks of a man who is the bittereft enemy of his friends. He could not but know, that *Junius* fpoke, not of a falfe or hollow friendfhip, but of a real intention to ferve, and that intention producing the worft effects of enmity. Whether the defcription be ftrictly applicable to Sir William Draper, is another queftion. *Junius* does not fay that it is more *criminal* for a man to be the enemy of his friends than his own, though he might have affirmed it with truth. In a moral light, a man may certainly take greater liberties with himfelf than with another. To facrifice ourfelves merely, is a weaknefs we may indulge in, if we think proper; for we do it at our own hazard and expence: but, under the pretence of friendfhip, to fport with the reputation, or facrifice the honour, of another, is fomething worfe than weaknefs; and if, in favour of the foolifh intention, we do not call it a crime, we muft allow at leaft that it arifes from an overweening, bufy, meddling impudence.——*Junius* fays only, and he fays truly, that it is more extraordinary, that it involves a greater contradiction, than the

other;

other; and is it not a maxim received in life, that in general we can determine more wisely for others than for ourselves? The reason of it is so clear in argument, that it hardly wants the confirmation of experience. Sir William Draper, I confess, is an exception to the general rule, though not much to his credit.

4. If this gentleman will go back to his Ethicks, he may perhaps discover the truth of what *Junius* says, *that no outward tyranny can reach the mind.* The tortures of the body may be introduced by way of ornament or illustration to represent those of the mind, but strictly there is no similitude between them. They are totally different both in their cause and operation. The wretch who suffers upon the rack, is merely passive; but when the mind is tortured, it is not at the command of any outward power. It is the sense of guilt which constitutes the punishment, and creates that torture with which the guilty mind acts upon itself.

5. He misquotes what *Junius* says of conscience; and makes the sentence ridiculous, by making it his own.

So much for composition. ·Now for fact.—*Junius*, it seems, has mistaken the Duke of Bedford. His Grace had all the proper feelings of a father, though he took care to suppress the appearance of them. Yet it was an occasion, one would think, on which he need not have been ashamed of his grief;—on which less fortitude would have done him more honour. I can conceive indeed a benevolent motive for his endeavouring to assume an air of tranquillity in his own family; and I wish I could discover any thing, in the rest of his character, to justify my assigning that motive to his behaviour. But is there no medium? Was it necessary to appear abroad, to ballot at the India-house, and make a public display, tho' it were only of an apparent insensibility?—I know we are treading on

tender

tender ground, and *Junius*, I am convinced, does not wish to argue this question farther. Let the friends of the Duke of Bedford observe that humble silence which becomes their situation. They should recollect that there are still some facts in store, at which human nature would shudder. I shall be understood by those whom it concerns, when I say that these facts go farther than to the Duke *.

It is not inconsistent to suppose that a man may be quite indifferent about one part of a charge, yet severely stung with another ; and though he feels no remorse, that he may wish to be revenged. The charge of insensibility carries a reproach indeed, but no danger with it.——*Junius* had said, *there are others who would assassinate*. *Modestus*, knowing his man, will not suffer the insinuation to be divided, but fixes it all upon the Duke of Bedford.

Without determining upon what evidence *Junius* would *choose to be condemned*, I will venture to maintain, in opposition to *Modestus*, or to Mr Rigby (who is certainly not *Modestus*), or any other of the Bloomsbury gang, that the evidence against the Duke of Bedford is as strong as any presumptive evidence can be. It depends upon a combination of facts and reasoning, which require no confirmation from the anecdote of the Duke of Marlborough.

* Within a fortnight after Lord Tavistock's death, the venerable Gertrude had a route at Bedford-house. The good Duke (who had only sixty thousand pounds a-year) ordered an inventory to be taken of his son's wearing apparel, down to his slippers, sold them all, and put the money in his pocket. The amiable Marchioness, shocked at such brutal, unfeeling avarice, gave the value of the cloaths to the Marquis's servant, out of her own purse. That incomparable woman did not long survive her husband. When she died, the Duchess of Bedford treated her as the Duke had treated his only son. She ordered every gown and trinket to be sold, and pocketed the money.——These are the monsters whom Sir William Draper comes forward to defend——May God protect me from doing any thing that may require such defence, or to deserve such friendship!

borough. This anecdote was referred to merely to fhow how ready a great man may be to receive a great bribe ; and if *Modeſtus* could read the original, he would fee that the expreffion, *only not accepted,* was probably the, only one in our language that exactly fitted the cafe : The bribe, offered to the Duke of Marlborough, was not refufed.

I cannot conclude without taking notice of this honeſt gentleman's learning, and wifhing he had given us a little more of it. When he accidentally found himfelf fo near fpeaking truth, it was rather unfair of him to leave out the *non potuiſſe refelli.* As it ftands, the *pudet hæc opprobria* may be divided equally between Mr Rigby and the Duke of Bedford. Mr Rigby, I take for granted, will affert his natural right to the modeſty of the quotation, and leave all the opprobrium to his Grace.

PHILO JUNIUS.

---

## LETTER XXX.



SIR,             Oct. 17. 1769.

IT is not wonderful that the great caufe, in which this country is engaged, fhould have roufed and engroffed the whole attention of the people. I rather admire the generous fpirit with which they feel and affert their intereſt in this important queſtion, than blame them for their indifference about any other. When the conſtitution is openly invaded, when the firſt original right of the people, from which all laws derive their authority, is directly attacked, inferior grievances naturally lofe their force, and are fuffered to pafs by without punifhment or obfervation. The prefent miniſtry are as fingularly marked by their fortune as by their crimes. Inſtead of atoning for their

former

former conduct by any wife or popular meafure, they have found, in the enormity of one fact, a cover and defence for a feries of meafures, which muſt have been fatal to any other adminiſtration. I fear we are too remifs in obferving the whole of their proceedings. Struck with the principal figure, we do not fufficiently mark in what manner the canvafs is filled up. Yet furely it is not a lefs crime, nor lefs fatal in its confequences, to encourage a flagrant breach of the law by a military force, than to make ufe of the forms of parliament to deſtroy the conſtitution.—The miniſtry feem determined to give us a choice of difficulties, and, if poffible, to perplex us with the multitude of their offences. The expedient is worthy of the Duke of Grafton. But though, he has preferved a gradation and variety in his meafures, we fhould remember that the principle is uniform. Dictated by the fame fpirit, they deferve the fame attention. The following fact, though of the moſt alarming nature, has not yet been clearly ſtated to the public; nor have the confequences of it been fufficiently underſtood. Had I taken it up at an earlier period, I fhould have been accufed of an uncandid, malignant precipitation, as if I watched for an unfair advantage againſt the miniſtry, and would not allow them a reafonable time to do their duty. They now ſtand without excufe. Inſtead of employing the leifure they have had in a ſtrict examination of the offence, and punifhing the offenders, they feem to have confidered *that* indulgence as a fecurity to them; that, with a little time and management, the whole affair might be buried in filence, and utterly forgotten.

A major-general* of the army is arreſted by the fheriff's officers for a confiderable debt. He perfuades them to conduct him to the Tilt-yard in

4　　　　　　　　　　　　　　　St

* Major General Ganfel.

St James's Park, under some pretence of business,
which it imported him to settle before he was
confined.  He applies to a serjeant, not immediately on duty, to assist with some of his companions in favouring his escape.  He attempts it.
A bustle ensues.  The bailiffs claim their prisoner.
An officer of the guards *, not then on duty,
takes part in the affair, applies to the lieutenant †
commanding the Tilt-yard guard, and urges him
to turn out his guard to relieve a general officer.
The lieutenant declines interfering in person; but
stands at a distance, and suffers the business to be
done.  The officer takes upon himself to order
out the guard.  In a moment they are in arms,
quit their guard, march, rescue the general, and
drive away the sheriff's officers ; who in vain represent their right to the prisoner, and the nature
of the arrest.  The soldiers first conduct the general into the guard-room; then escort him to a
place of safety, with bayonets fixed, and in all the
forms of military triumph.  I will not enlarge
upon the various circumstances which attended
this atrocious proceeding.  The personal injury
received by the officers of the law in the execution of their duty, may perhaps be atoned for by
some private compensation.  I consider nothing
but the wound which has been given to the law
itself, to which no remedy has been applied, no
satisfaction made.  Neither is it my design to dwell
upon the misconduct of the parties concerned, any
farther than is necessary to show the behaviour of
the ministry in its true light. I would make every
compassionate allowance for the infatuation of the
prisoner, the false and criminal discretion of one
officer, and the madness of another.  I would
leave the ignorant soldiers entirely out of the question.  They are certainly the least guilty, though
they are the only persons who have yet suffered,

O

even

---

* Lieutenant Dodd.          † Lieutenant Garth.

even in the appearance of punifhment*. The faƈt itfelf, however atrocious, is not the principal point to be confidered.  It might have happened under a more regular government, and with guards better difciplined than ours.  The main queftion is, In what manner have the miniftry aƈted on this extraordinary occafion?  A general officer calls upon the king's own guard, then aƈtually on duty, to refcue him from the laws of his country; yet at this moment he is in a fituation no worfe, than if he had not committed an offence, equally enormous in a civil and military view.— A lieutenant upon duty defignedly quits his guard, and fuffers it to be drawn out by another officer, for a purpofe which he well knew (as we may colleƈt from an appearance of caution, which only makes his behaviour the more criminal) to be in the higheft degree illegal.  Has this gentleman been called to a court-martial to anfwer for his conduƈt?  No.  Has it been cenfured?  No.  Has it been in any fhape inquired into?  No,—Another lieutenant, not upon duty, nor even in his regimentals, is daring enough to order out the king's guard, over which he had properly no command, and engages them in a violation of the laws of his country, perhaps the moft fingular and extravagant that ever was attempted.—What punifhment has *he* fuffered?  Literally none.  Suppofing he fhould be profecuted at common law for the refcue, will that circumftance, from which the miniftry can derive no merit, excufe or juftify their fuffering fo flagrant a breach of military difcipline to pafs by unpunifhed and unnoticed?  Are they aware of the outrage offered to their fovereign, when his own proper guard is ordered out to ftop by main force the execution of his laws?  What are we to conclude from fo fcandalous a negleƈt of their duty, but that they have other views

which

---

* A few of them were confined.

which can only be anfwered by fecuring the attachment of the guards? The minifter would
hardly be fo cautious of offending them, if he did
not mean, in due time, to call for their affiftance.

With refpect to the parties themfelves, let it
be obferved, that thefe gentlemen are neither
young officers, nor very young men. Had they
belonged to the unfledged race of enfigns, who
infeft our ftreets, and difhonour our public places,
it might perhaps be fufficient to fend them back
to that difcipline, from which their parents, judging lightly from the maturity of their vices, had
removed them too foon. In this cafe, I am forry
to fee, not fo much the folly of youth, as the fpirit of the corps, and the connivance of government. I do not queftion that there are many
brave and worthy officers in the regiments of
guards. But confidering them as a corps, I fear
it will be found that they are neither good foldiers
nor good fubjects. Far be it from me to infinuate
the moft diftant reflection upon the army. On
the contrary, I honour and efteem the profeffion;
and if thefe gentlemen were better foldiers, I am
fure they would be better fubjects. It is not that
there is any internal vice or defect in the profeffion itfelf as regulated in this country, but that
it is the fpirit of this particular corps to defpife
their profeffion; and that, while they vainly affume the lead of the army, they make it matter
of impertinent comparifon, and triumph over the
braveft troops in the world (I mean our marching
regiments), that *they* indeed ftand upon higher
ground, and are privileged to neglect the laborious forms of military difcipline and duty. Without dwelling longer upon a moft invidious fubject,
I fhall leave it to military men, who have feen a
fervice more active than the parade, to determine
whether or no I fpeak truth.

How far this dangerous fpirit has been encouraged by government, and to what pernicious pur-pofes it may be applied hereafter, well deferves our moft ferious confideration. I know, indeed, that when this affair happened, an affectation of alarm ran through the miniftry. Something muft be done to fave appearances. The cafe was too flagrant to be paffed by abfolutely without notice. But how have they acted? Inftead of ordering the officers concerned, (and who, ftrictly fpeak-ing, are alone guilty), to be put under arreft, and brought to trial, they would have it underftood, that they did their duty completely, in confining a ferjeant and four private foldiers, until they fhould be demanded by the civil power; fo that while the officers, who ordered or permitted the poor men who obeyed thofe orders, who in a mi-litary view are no way refponfible for what they did, and who for that reafon have been difcharged by the civil magiftrates, are the only objects whom the miniftry have thought proper to expofe to pu-nifhment. They did not venture to bring even thefe men to a court-martial, becaufe they knew their evidence would be fatal to fome perfons, whom they were determined to protect. Other-wife, I doubt not, the lives of thefe unhappy, friendlefs foldiers, would long fince have been fa-crificed without fcruple to the fecurity of their guilty officers.

I have been accufed of endeavouring to inflame the paffions of the people.—Let me now appeal to their underftanding. If there be any tool of adminiftration daring enough to deny thefe facts; or fhamelefs enough to defend the conduct of the miniftry, let him come forward. I care not un-der what title he appears. He fhall find me ready to maintain the truth of my narrative, and the juftice of my obfervations upon it, at the hazard of my utmoft credit with the public.

Under

Under the moſt arbitrary governments, the common adminiſtration of juſtice is ſuffered to take its courſe. The ſubject, though robbed of his ſhare in the legiſlature, is ſtill protected by the laws. The political freedom of the Engliſh conſtitution was once the pride and honour of an Engliſhman. The civil equality of the laws preſerved the property, and defended the ſafety, of the ſubject. Are theſe glorious privileges the birthright of the people; or are we only tenants at the will of the miniſtry?—But that I know there is a ſpirit of reſiſtance in the hearts of my countrymen; that they value life, not by its conveniences, but by the independence and dignity of their condition; I ſhould, at this moment, appeal only to their diſcretion. I ſhould perſuade them to baniſh from their minds all memory of what we were; I ſhould tell them this is not a time to remember that we were Engliſhmen; and give it as my laſt advice, to make ſome early agreement with the miniſter, that, ſince it has pleaſed him to rob us of thoſe political rights which once diſtinguiſhed the inhabitants of a country where honour was happineſs, he would leave us at leaſt the humble obedient ſecurity of citizens, and graciouſly condeſcend to protect us in our ſubmiſſion.                    JUNIUS.

---

## LETTER XXXI.



SIR,                                        Nov. 14. 1769.

THE variety of remarks which have been made upon the laſt letter of *Junius*, and my own opinion of the writer, who, whatever may be his faults, is certainly not a weak man, have induced me to examine, with ſome attention, the ſubject of that letter. I could not perſuade myſelf, that,



while

while he had plenty of important materials, he would have taken up a light or trifling occafion to attack the miniftry; much lefs could I conceive that it was his intention to ruin the officers concerned in the refcue of General Ganfel, or to injure the General himfelf. Thefe are little objects, and can no way contribute to the great purpofes he feems to have in view by addreffing himfelf to the public.——Without confidering the ornamented ftyle he has adopted, I determined to look farther into the matter, before I decided upon the merits of his letter. The firft ftep I took was to inquire into the truth of the facts; for if thefe were either falfe or mifreprefented, the moft artful exertion of his underftanding, in reafoning upon them, would only be a difgrace to him.—Now, Sir, I have found every circumftance ftated by *Junius* to be literally true. General Ganfel perfuaded the bailiffs to conduct him to the parade, and certainly folicited a corporal and other foldiers to affift him in making his efcape. Captain Dodd did certainly apply to Captain Garth for the affiftance of his guard. Captain Garth declined appearing himfelf; but ftood aloof, while the other took upon him to order out the King's guard, and by main force refcued the General. It is alfo ftrictly true, that the General was efcorted by a file of mufqueteers to a place of fecurity.—Thefe are facts, Mr Woodfall, which I promife you no gentleman in the guards will deny. If all or any of them are falfe, why are they not contradicted by the parties themfelves? However fecure againft military cenfure, they have yet a character to lofe; and furely, if they are innocent, it is not beneath them to pay fome attention to the opinion of the public.

The force of *Junius*'s obfervations upon thefe facts cannot be better marked, than by ftating and refuting the objections which have been made

to

to them.   One writer fays, " Admitting the of-
" ficers have offended, they are punifhable at com-
" mon law, and will you have a Britifh fubject
" punifhed twice for the fame offence ?"—I anfwer, that they have committed two offences, both
very enormous, and violated two laws.  The refcue is one offence, the flagrant breach of difcipline
another; and hitherto it does not appear that they
have been punifhed, or even cenfured, for either.
Another gentleman lays much ftrefs upon the calamity of the cafe; and inftead of difproving facts,
appeals at once to the compaffion of the public.
This idea, as well as the infinuation that *depriving
the parties of their commiffions would be an injury
to their creditors*, can only refer to General Ganfel.  The other officers are in no diftrefs, therefore have no claim to compaffion; nor does
it appear, that their creditors, if they have any,
are more likely to be fatisfied by their continuing
in the guards.  But this fort of plea will not hold
in any fhape.  Compaffion to an offender, who
has grofsly violated the laws, is in effect a cruelty
to the peaceable fubject who has obferved them;
and, even admitting the force of any alleviating
circumftances, it is neverthelefs true, that, in
this inftance, the royal compaffion has interpofed
too foon.  The legal and proper mercy of a King
of England may remit the punifhment, but ought
not to ftop the trial.

Befides thefe particular objections, there has
been a cry raifed againft *Junius* for his malice and
injuftice in attacking the miniftry upon an event
which they could neither hinder nor forefee.  This,
I muft affirm, is a falfe reprefentation of his argument.  He lays no ftrefs upon the event itfelf
as a ground of accufation againft the miniftry,
but dwells entirely upon their fubfequent conduct.
He does not fay that they are anfwerable for the
offence; but for the fcandalous neglect of their

duty,

duty, in suffering an offence, so flagrant, to pass by without notice or inquiry. Supposing them ever so regardless of what they owe to the public, and as indifferent about the opinion as they are about the interests of their country, what answer, as officers of the crown, will they give to *Junius*, when he asks them, *Are they aware of the outrage offered to their Sovereign, when his own proper guard is ordered out to stop by main force the execution of his laws?*——And when we see a ministry giving such a strange unaccountable protection to the officers of the guards, is it unfair to suspect, that they have some secret and unwarrantable motives for their conduct? If they feel themselves injured by such a suspicion, why do they not immediately clear themselves from it, by doing their duty? For the honour of the guards, I cannot help expressing another suspicion, that, if the commanding officer had not received a secret injunction to the contrary, he would, in the ordinary course of his business, have applied for a court-martial to try the two subalterns; the one for quitting his guard; the other for taking upon him the command of the guard, and employing it in the manner he did. I do not mean to enter into or defend the severity with which *Junius* treats the guards. On the contrary, I will suppose, for a moment, that they deserve a very different character. If this be true, in what light will they consider the conduct of two subalterns, but as a general reproach and disgrace to the whole corps? And will they not wish to see them censured in a military way, if it were only for the credit and discipline of the regiment?

Upon the whole, Sir, the ministry seem to me to have taken a very improper advantage of the good-nature of the public, whose humanity, they found, considered nothing in this affair, but the distress of General Gansel. They would persuade us, that it was only a common rescue by a few dis-

orderly

orderly foldiers, and not the formal deliberate act of the king's guard headed by an officer; and the public has fallen into the deception. I think, therefore, we are obliged to *Junius* for the care he has taken to inquire into the facts, and for the juft commentary with which he has given them to the world.—For my own part, I am as unwilling as any man to load the unfortunate; but, really, Sir, the precedent, with refpect to the guards, is of a moft important nature, and alarming enough (confidering the confequences with which it may be attended) to deferve a parliamentary inquiry: when the guards are daring enough, not only to violate their own difcipline, but publicly and with the moft atrocious violence to ftop the execution of the laws, and when fuch extraordinary offences pafs with impunity, believe me, Sir, the precedent ftrikes deep.                    PHILO JUNIUS.

---

## LETTER XXXII.

### TO THE PRINTER OF THE PUBLIC ADVER-
### TISER.

S I R,                                   Nov. 15. 1769.

I ADMIT the claim of a gentleman who publifhes in the Gazetteer under the name of *Modeftus*. He has fome right to expect an anfwer from me; though, I think, not fo much from the merit or importance of his objections, as from my own voluntary engagement. I had a reafon for not taking notice of him fooner, which, as he is a candid perfon, I believe he will think fufficient. In my firft letter, I took for granted, from the time which had elapfed, that there was no intention to cenfure, nor even to try, the perfons concerned in the refcue of General Ganfel; but *Modeftus* having fince either affirmed, or ftrongly infinuated, that the of-

fenders

fenders might ftill be brought to a legal trial, any attempt to prejudge the caufe, or to prejudice the minds of a jury or a court-martial, would be highly improper.

A man, more hoftile to the miniftry than I am, would not fo often remind them of their duty. If the Duke of Grafton will not perform the duty of his ftation, why is he minifter?—I will not defcend to a fcurrilous altercation with any man; but this is a fubject too important to be paffed over with filent indifference. If the gentlemen, whofe conduct is in queftion, are not brought to a trial, the Duke of Grafton fhall hear from me again.

The motives on which I am fuppofed to have taken up this caufe, are of little importance, compared with the facts themfelves, and the obfervations I have made upon them. Without a vain profeffion of integrity, which in thefe times might juftly be fufpected, I fhall fhow myfelf in effect a friend to the interefts of my countrymen, and leave it to them to determine, whether I am moved by a perfonal malevolence to three private gentlemen, or merely by a hope of perplexing the miniftry; or whether I am animated by a juft and honourable purpofe of obtaining a fatisfaction to the laws of this country, equal, if poffible, to the violation they have fuffered.                    JUNIUS.

---

## LETTER XXXIII.

### TO HIS GRACE THE DUKE OF GRAFTON.

My Lord,                    Nov. 29. 1769.

THOUGH my opinion of your Grace's integrity was but little affected by the coynefs with which you received Mr Vaughan's propofals, I confefs I give you fome credit for your difcretion. You had a fair opportunity of difplaying a certain delicacy, of which you had not been fufpected; and

                    and

and you were in the right to make ufe of it.   By laying in a moderate ftock of reputation, you undoubtedly meant to provide for the future neceffities of your charaĉter, that, with an honourable refiftance upon record, you may fafely indulge your genius, and yield to a favourite inclination with fecurity.   But you have difcovered your purpofes too foon; and, inftead of the modeft referve of virtue, have fhown us the termagant chaftity of a prude, who gratifies her paffions with diftinĉtion, and profecutes one lover for a rape, while fhe folicits the lewd embraces of another.

Your cheek turns pale; for a guilty confcience tells you, you are undone.—Come forward, thou virtuous minifter, and tell the world by what intereft Mr Hine has been recommended to fo extraordinary a mark of his Majefty's favour; what was the price of the patent he has bought, and to what honourable purpofe the purchafe-money has been applied. Nothing lefs than many thoufands could pay Colonel Burgoyne's expences at Prefton.   Do you dare to profecute fuch a creature as Vaughan, while you are bafely fetting up the Royal Patronage to auĉtion? Do you dare to complain of an attack upon your own honour, while you are felling the favours of the Crown, to raife a fund for corrupting the morals of the people? And, do you think it is poffible fuch enormities fhould efcape without impeachment? It is indeed highly your intereft to maintain the prefent houfe of commons.   Having fold the nation to you in grofs, they will undoubtedly proteĉt you in the detail; for while they patronize your crimes, they feel for their own.          J U N I U S.

## LETTER XXXIV.

### TO HIS GRACE THE DUKE OF GRAFTON.

My Lord,                          Dec. 12. 1769.

I FIND with some surprise, that you are not supported as you deserve. Your most determined
advocates have scruples about them, which you
are unacquainted with ; and though there be nothing too hazardous for your Grace to engage in,
there are some things too infamous for the vilest
prostitute of a newspaper to defend *. In what
other manner shall we account for the profound,
submissive silence, which you and your friends have
observed upon a charge, which called immediately
for the clearest refutation; and would have justified the severest measures of resentment ? I did
not attempt to blast your character by an indirect,
ambiguous insinuation; but candidly stated to you
a plain fact, which struck directly at the integrity
of a privy-counsellor, of a first commissioner of the
treasury, and of a leading minister, who is supposed
to enjoy the first share in his Majesty's confidence †.
In every one of these capacities, I employed the
most moderate terms to charge you with treachery
to your Sovereign, and breach of trust in your office. I accused you of having sold a patent place
in the collection of the customs at Exeter, to one
Mr Hine, who, unable or unwilling to deposit the
whole purchase-money himself, raised part of it by
contribution, and has now a certain Doctor Brooke
quartered upon the salary for one hundred pounds
a-year.—No sale by the candle was ever conducted
with greater formality.—I affirm, that the price at
which

---

* From the publication of the preceding to this date, not one
word was said in defence of the infamous duke of Grafton. But
vice and impudence soon recovered themselves, and the sale of the
royal favour was openly avowed and defended  We acknowledge
the piety of St James's; but what is become of *his* morality ?

† And by the same means preserves it to this hour.

which the place was knocked down (and which, I have good reason to think, was not less than three thousand five hundred pounds) was, with your connivance and consent, paid to Colonel Burgoyne, to reward him, I presume, for the decency of his deportment at Preston; or to reimburse him, perhaps, for the fine of one thousand pounds, which, for that very deportment, the court of King's Bench thought proper to set upon him.—It is not often that the chief justice and the prime minister are so strangely at variance in their opinions of men and things.

I thank God, there is not in human nature a degree of impudence daring enough to deny the charge I have fixed upon you. Your courteous secretary *, your confidential architect †, are silent as the grave. Even Mr Rigby's countenance fails him. He violates his second nature, and blushes whenever he speaks of you.—Perhaps the noble colonel himself will relieve you. No man is more tender of his reputation. He is not only nice, but perfectly sore in every thing that touches his honour. If any man, for example, were to accuse him of taking his stand at a gaming table, and watching, with the soberest attention, for a fair opportunity of engaging a drunken young nobleman at piquet, he would undoubtedly consider it as an infamous aspersion upon his character, and resent it like a man of honour.—Acquitting him therefore of drawing a regular and splendid subsistence from any unworthy practices either in his own house or elsewhere, let me ask your Grace, for what military merits you have been pleased to reward him with military government? He had a regiment of dragoons, which one would imagine was at least an equivalent for any services he ever performed. Besides, he is but a young officer considering

P

dering

dering his preferment, and, except in his activity at Preston, not very conspicuous in his profession. But it seems the sale of a civil employment was not sufficient; and military governments, which were intended for the support of worn-out veterans, must be thrown into the scale, to defray the extensive bribery of a contested election. Are these the steps you take to secure to your Sovereign the attachment of his army? With what countenance dare you appear in the royal presence, branded as you are with the infamy of a notorious breach of trust? With what countenance can you take your seat at the treasury-board or in council, when you feel that every circulating whisper is at your expence alone, and stabs you to the heart? Have you a single friend in parliament so shameless, so thoroughly abandoned, as to undertake your defence? You know, my Lord, that there is not a man in either house, whose character, however flagitious, would not be ruined by mixing his reputation with yours; and does not your heart inform you, that you are degraded below the condition of a man, when you are obliged to hear these insults with submission, and even to thank me for my moderation?

We are told, by the highest judicial authority, that Mr Vaughan's offer to purchase the reversion of a patent place in Jamaica (which he was otherwise sufficiently intitled to) amounted to a high misdemeanour. Be it so; and if he deserves it, let him be punished. But the learned judge might have had a fairer opportunity of displaying the powers of his eloquence. Having delivered himself with so much energy upon the criminal nature and dangerous consequences of any attempt to corrupt a man in your Grace's station, what would he have said to the minister himself, to that very privy counsellor, to that first commissioner of the treasury, who does not wait for, but impatiently solicits the touch of
corruption;

corruption; who employs the meaneſt of his crea-
tures in theſe honourable ſervices, and, forgetting
the genius and fidelity of his ſecretary, deſcends
to apply to his houſe-builder for aſſiſtance?

This affair, my Lord, will do infinite credit to
government, if, to clear your character, you ſhould
think proper to bring it into the houſe of Lords, or
into the court of King's Bench.———But, my Lord,
you dare not do either.          JUNIUS.

A little before the publication of this and the preceding letter,
the chaſte Duke of Grafton had commenced a perſecution againſt
Mr Samuel Vaughan, for endeavouring to corrupt his integrity by
an offer of five thouſand pounds for a patent place in Jamaica. A
rule to ſhow cauſe why an information ſhould not be exhibited
againſt Vaughan for certain miſdemeanours being granted by the
Court of King's Bench, the matter was ſolemnly argued on the 27th
of November 1769, and, by the unanimous opinion of the four
judges, the rule was made abſolute. The pleadings and ſpeeches
were accurately taken in ſhort-hand, and publiſhed. The whole of
Lord Mansfield's ſpeech, and particularly the following extracts
from it, deſerve the reader's attention. " A practice of the kind
" complained of here is certainly diſhonourable and ſcandalous.——
" If a man, ſtanding under the relation of an officer under the King,
" or of a perſon in whom the King puts confidence, or of a mini-
" ſter, takes money for the uſe of that confidence the King puts in
" him, he baſely betrays the King,——he baſely betrays his truſt.
" ——If the King ſold the office, it would be acting contrary to
" the truſt the conſtitution hath repoſed in him. The conſtitution
" does not intend the crown ſhould ſell thoſe offices, to raiſe a revenue
" out of them.——Is it poſſible to heſitate, whether this would not
" be criminal in the Duke of Grafton——contrary to his duty as
" a privy counſellor——contrary to his duty as a miniſter——
" contrary to his duty as a ſubject?——His advice ſhould be free
" according to his judgment——It is the duty of his office;——
" he hath ſworn to it."——Notwithſtanding all this, the chaſte
Duke of Grafton certainly ſold a patent place to Mr Hine for three
thouſand five hundred pounds; and, for ſo doing, is now Lord
Privy Seal to the chaſte George, with whoſe piety we are perpetually
deafened. If the houſe of commons had done their duty, and impeached the black Duke for this moſt infamous breach of truſt, how
wofully muſt poor, honeſt Mansfield have been puzzled! His em-
barraſſment would have afforded the moſt ridiculous ſcene that ever
was exhibited. To ſave the worthy judge from this perplexity,
and the no leſs worthy Duke from impeachment, the proſecution
againſt *Vaughan* was immediately dropped upon my diſcovery and
publication of the Duke's treachery. The ſuffering this charge to
paſs, without any inquiry, fixes ſhameleſs proſtitution upon the face
of the houſe of commons, more ſtrongly than even the Middleſex
election.——Yet the licentiouſneſs of the preſs is complained of!

# LETTER XXXV.



Dec. 19. 1769.

When the complaints of a brave and powerful people are obferved to increafe in proportion to the wrongs they have fuffered; when, inftead of finking into fubmiffion, they are roufed to refiftance; the time will foon arrive at which every inferior confideration muft yield to the fecurity of the Sovereign, and to the general fafety of the ftate. There is a moment of difficulty and danger, at which flattery and falfehood can no longer deceive, and fimplicity itfelf can no longer be mifled. Let us fuppofe it arrived. Let us fuppofe a gracious, well-intentioned prince, made fenfible at laft of the great duty he owes to his people, and of his own difgraceful fituation; that he looks round him for affiftance, and afks for no advice but how to gratify the wifhes and fecure the happinefs of his fubjects. In thefe circumftances, it may be matter of curious SPECULATION to confider, if an honeft man were permitted to approach a King, in what terms he would addrefs himfelf to his Sovereign. Let it be imagined, no matter how improbable, that the firft prejudice againft his character is removed, that the ceremonious difficulties of an audience are furmounted, that he feels himfelf animated by the pureft and moft honourable affection to his King and country, and that the great perfon whom he addreffes has fpirit enough to bid him fpeak freely, and underftanding enough to liften to him with attention. Unacquainted with the vain impertinence of forms, he would deliver his fentiments with dignity and firmnefs, but not without refpect.

SIR,

S I R,

IT is the misfortune of your life, and originally
the cause of every reproach and diftrefs which
has attended your government, that you fhould
never have been acquainted with the language of
truth, until you heard it in the complaints of your
people. It is not, however, too late to correct
the error of your education. We are ftill inclined
to make an indulgent allowance for the pernicious
leffons you received in your youth, and to form
the moft fanguine hopes from the natural benevolence of your difpofition *. We are far from thinking you capable of a direct, deliberate purpofe to
invade thofe original rights of your fubjects, on
which all their civil and political liberties depend.
Had it been poffible for us to entertain a fufpicion
fo difhonourable to your character, we fhould long
fince have adopted a ftyle of remonftrance very
diftant from the humility of complaint. The doctrine inculcated by our laws, *That the King can do
no wrong*, is admitted without reluctance. We

P. 3

feparate

* The plan of tutelage and future dominion over the heir-apparent, laid many years ago at Carlton-houfe between the Princefs
Dowager and her favourite the Earl of Bute, was as grofs and palpable, as that which was concerted between Anne of Auftria and
Cardinal Mazarin to govern Lewis the Fourteenth, and in effect
to prolong his minority until the end of their lives. That prince
had ftrong natural parts, and ufed frequently to blufh for his own
ignorance and want of education, which had been wilfully neglected
by his mother and her minion. A little experience however foon
fhowed him how fhamefully he had been treated, and for what infamous purpofes he had been kept in ignorance. Our great Edward
too, at an early period, had fenfe enough to underftand the nature
of the connection between his abandoned mother and the detefted
Mortimer. But, fince that time, human nature, we may obferve,
is greatly altered for the better. Dowagers may be chafte, and minions may be honeft. When it was propofed to fettle the prefent
King's houfehold as Prince of Wales, it is well known that the
Earl of Bute was forced into it, in direct contradiction to the late
King's inclination. That was the falient point, from which all the
mifchiefs and difgraces of the prefent reign took life and motion.
From that moment, Lord Bute never fuffered the Prince of Wales
to be an inftant out of his fight.—We need not look farther.

separate the amiable, good-natured prince from the folly and treachery of his servants, and the private virtues of the man from the vices of his government. Were it not for this just distinction, I know not whether your Majesty's condition, or that of the English nation, would deserve most to be lamented. I would prepare your mind for a favourable reception of truth, by removing every painful, offensive idea of personal reproach. Your subjects, Sir, wish for nothing but that, as *they* are reasonable and affectionate enough to separate your person from your government, so *you*, in your turn, should distinguish between the conduct which becomes the permanent dignity of a King, and that which serves only to promote the temporary interest and miserable ambition of a minister.

You ascended the throne with a declared, and, I doubt not, a sincere resolution of giving universal satisfaction to your subjects. You found them pleased with the novelty of a young prince, whose countenance promised even more than his words; and loyal to you, not only from principle, but passion. It was not a cold profession of allegiance to the first magistrate; but a partial, animated attachment to a favourite prince, the native of their country. They did not wait to examine your conduct, nor to be determined by experience; but gave you a generous credit for the future blessings of your reign, and paid you in advance the dearest tribute of their affections. Such, Sir, was once the disposition of a people, who now surround your throne with reproaches and complaints. Do justice to yourself. Banish from your mind those unworthy opinions, with which some interested persons have laboured to possess you.—Distrust the men who tell you that the English are naturally light and inconstant—that they complain without a cause. Withdraw your confidence equally from all parties; from ministers, favourites, and relations;

tions; and let there be one moment in your life, in which you have confulted your own underftanding.

When you affectedly renounced the name of Englifhman, believe me, Sir, you were perfuaded to pay a very ill-judged compliment to one part of your fubjects, at the expence of another. While the natives of Scotland are not in actual rebellion, they are undoubtedly intitled to protection; nor do I mean to condemn the policy of giving fome encouragement to the novelty of their affections for the houfe of Hanover. I am ready to hope for every thing from their new-born zeal, and from the future fteadinefs of their allegiance. But hitherto they have no claim to your favour. To honour them with a determined predilection and confidence, in exclufion of your Englifh fubjects, who placed your family, and in fpite of treachery and rebellion have fupported it upon the throne, is a miftake too grofs even for the unfufpecting generofity of youth. In this error we fee a capital violation of the moft obvious rules of policy and prudence. We trace it, however, to an original bias in your education, and are ready to allow for your inexperience.

To the fame early influence we attribute it, that you have defcended to take a fhare not only in the narrow views and interefts of particular perfons, but in the fatal malignity of their paffions. At your acceffion to the throne, the whole fyftem of government was altered, not from wifdom or deliberation, but becaufe it had been adopted by your predeceffor. A little perfonal motive of pique and refentment was fufficient to remove the ableft fervants of the crown *; but it is not in this country, Sir, that fuch men can be difhonoured by the frowns of a King. They were difmiffed, but could

not

<hr>

* One of the firft acts of the prefent reign was to difmifs Mr Legge, becaufe he had fome years before refufed to yield his intereft in Hampfhire to a Scotchman recommended by Lord Bute. This was the reafon publicly affigned by his Lordfhip.

not be difgraced. Without entering into a minuter difcuffion of the merits of the peace, we
may obferve, in the imprudent hurry with which
the firft overtures from France were accepted, in
the conduct of the negotiation and terms of the
treaty, the ftrongeft marks of that precipitate fpirit
of conceffion with which a certain part of your
fubjects have been at all times ready to purchafe a
peace with the natural enemies of this country.
On *your* part we are fatisfied that every thing was
honourable and fincere; and if England was fold
to France, we doubt not that your Majefty was
equally betrayed. The conditions of the peace were
matter of grief and furprife to your fubjects; but not
the immediate caufe of their prefent difcontent.

Hitherto, Sir, you had been facrificed to the prejudices and paffions of others. With what firmnefs will you bear the mention of your own?

A man,-not very honourably diftinguifhed in
the world, commences a formal attack upon your
favourite, confidering nothing but how he might
beft expofe his perfon and principles to deteftation,
and the national character of his countrymen to
contempt. The natives of that country, Sir, are
as much diftinguifhed by a peculiar character, as
by your Majefty's favour. Like another chofen
people, they have been conducted into the land of
plenty, where they find themfelves effectually
marked, and divided from mankind. There is
hardly a period at which the moft irregular character may not be redeemed. The miftakes of one
fex find a retreat in patriotifm, thofe of the other
in devotion. Mr Wilkes brought with him into
politics the fame liberal fentiments by which his
private conduct had been directed; and feemed to
think, that, as there are few exceffes in which an
Englifh gentleman may not be permitted to indulge, the fame latitude was allowed him in the
choice of his political principles, and in the fpirit

of

of maintaining them.—I mean to ſtate, not entirely to defend, his conduct. In the earneſtneſs of his zeal, he ſuffered ſome unwarrantable inſinuations to eſcape him. He ſaid more than moderate men would juſtify; but not enough to intitle him to the honour of your Majeſty's perſonal reſentment. The rays of Royal indignation, collected upon him, ſerved only to illuminate, and could not conſume. Animated by the favour of the people on the one ſide, and heated by perſecution on the other, his views and ſentiments changed with his ſituation. Hardly ſerious at firſt, he is now an enthuſiaſt. The coldeſt bodies warm with oppoſition, the hardeſt ſparkle in colliſion. There is a holy miſtaken zeal in politics as well as religion. By perſuading others, we convince ourſelves. The paſſions are engaged, and create a maternal affection in the mind, which forces us to love the cauſe for which we ſuffer.—Is this a contention worthy of a King? Are you not ſenſible how much the meanneſs of the cauſe gives an air of ridicule to the ſerious difficulties into which you have been betrayed? The deſtruction of one man has been now for many years the ſole object of your government; and if there can be any thing ſtill more diſgraceful, we have ſeen, for ſuch an object, the utmoſt influence of the executive power, and every miniſterial artifice, exerted without ſucceſs. Nor can you ever ſucceed, unleſs *he* ſhould be imprudent enough to forfeit the protection of thoſe laws to which you owe your crown, or unleſs your miniſters ſhould perſuade you to make it a queſtion of force alone, and try the whole ſtrength of government in oppoſition to the people. The leſſons *he* has received from experience, will probably guard him from ſuch exceſs of folly; and in your Majeſty's virtues we find an unqueſtionable aſſurance that no illegal violence will be attempted.

Far·

Far from fufpecting you of fo horrible a defign, we would attribute the continued violation of the laws, and even this laft enormous attack upon the vital principles of the conftitution, to an ill-advifed, unworthy, perfonal refentment. From one falfe ftep you have been betrayed into another; and as the caufe was unworthy of you, your minifters were determined that the prudence of the execution fhould correfpond with the wifdom and dignity of the defign. They have reduced you to the neceffity of choofing out of a variety of difficulties; —to a fituation fo unhappy, that you can neither do wrong without ruin, nor right without affliction. Thefe worthy fervants have undoubtedly given you many fingular proofs of their abilities. Not contented with making Mr Wilkes a man of importance, they have judicioufly transferred the queftion, from the rights and interefts of one man, to the moft important rights and interefts of the people; and forced your fubjects, from wifhing well to the caufe of an individual, to unite with him in their own. Let them proceed as they have begun, and your Majefty need not doubt that the cataftrophe will do no difhonour to the conduct of the piece.

The circumftances to which you are reduced, will not admit of a compromife with the Englifh nation. Undecifive qualifying meafures will difgrace your government ftill more than open violence, and, without fatisfying the people, will excite their contempt. They have too much underftanding and fpirit to accept of an indirect fatisfaction for a direct injury. Nothing lefs than a repeal, as formal as the refolution itfelf, can heal the wound which has been given to the conftitution, nor will any thing lefs be accepted. I can readily believe that there is an influence fufficient to recal that pernicious vote. The houfe of commons undoubtedly confider their duty to the crown

as

as paramount to all other obligations. To *us* they are only indebted for an accidental exiſtence, and have juſtly transferred their gratitude from their parents to their benefactors;—from thoſe who gave them birth, to the miniſter, from whoſe benevolence they derive the comforts and pleaſures of their political life—who has taken the tendereſt care of their infancy, and relieves their neceſſities without offending their delicacy. But if it were poſſible for their integrity to be degraded to a condition ſo vile and abject, that, compared with it, the preſent eſtimation they ſtand in is a ſtate of honour and reſpect, conſider, Sir, in what manner you will afterwards proceed. Can you conceive that the people of this country will long ſubmit to be governed by ſo flexible a houſe of commons? It is not in the nature of human ſociety, that any form of government, in ſuch circumſtances, can long be preſerved. In ours, the general contempt of the people is as fatal as their deteſtation. Such, I am perſuaded, would be the neceſſary effect of any baſe conceſſion made by the preſent houſe of commons, and, as a qualifying meaſure would not be accepted, it remains for you to decide whether you will, at any hazard, ſupport a ſet of men who have reduced you to this unhappy dilemma, or whether you will gratify the united wiſhes of the whole people of England by diſſolving the parliament.

Taking it for granted, as I do very ſincerely, that you have perſonally no deſign againſt the conſtitution, or any view inconſiſtent with the good of your ſubjects, I think you cannot heſitate long upon the choice which it equally concerns your intereſt and your honour to adopt. On one ſide, you hazard the affections of all your Engliſh ſubjects, you relinquiſh every hope of repoſe to yourſelf, and you endanger the eſtabliſhment of your family for ever. All this you venture for no object whatſoever, or for ſuch an object as it would be an affront to you



to

to came.   Men of fenfe will examine your conduct
with fufpicion ;   while thofe who are incapable of
comprehending to what degree they are injured,
afflict you with clamours equally infolent and unmeaning. Suppofing it poffible that no fatal ftruggle
fhould enfue, you determine at once to be unhappy,
without the hope of a compenfation either from
intereft or ambition.   If an Englifh King be hated
or defpifed, he *muft* be unhappy; and this perhaps
is the only political truth which he ought to be
convinced of without experiment.   But if the
Englifh people fhould no longer confine their refentment to a fubmiffive reprefentation of their
wrongs ;   if, following the glorious example of
their anceftors, they fhould no longer appeal to
the creature of the conftitution, but to that high
Being who gave them the rights of humanity,
whofe gifts it were facrilege to furrender; let me
afk you, Sir, upon what part of your fubjects
would you rely for affiftance ?

The people of Ireland have been uniformly plundered and oppreffed.   In return, they give you e-
very day frefh marks of their refentment.   They
defpife the miferable governor you have fent them*,
becaufe he is the creature of Lord Bute; nor is it
from any natural confufion in their ideas that they
are fo ready to confound the original of a King
with the difgraceful reprefentation of him.

The diftance of the Colonies would make it impoffible for them to take an active concern in your
affairs, if they were as well affected to your government as they once pretended to be to your perfon.
They were ready enough to diftinguifh between
*you* and your minifters.   They complained of an
act of the legiflature, but traced the origin of it no
higher than to the fervants of the crown : They
pleafed

----

* Vifcount Townfhend, fent over on the plan of being refident
governor.   The hiftory of his ridiculous adminiftration fhall not
be loft to the public.

pleafed themfelves with the hope that their Sovereign, if not favourable to their caufe, at leaft was
impartial. The decifive perfonal part you took
againft them, has effectually banifhed that firft
diftinction from their minds*. They confider you
as united with your fervants againft America;
and know how to diftinguifh the Sovereign and a
venal parliament on one fide, from the real fentiments of the Englifh people on the other. Looking forward to independence, they might poffibly
receive you for their King; but, if ever you retire
to America, be affured they will give you fuch a
covenant to digeft, as the Prefbytery of Scotland
would have been afhamed to offer to Charles II.
They left their native land in fearch of freedom,
and found it in a defart. Divided as they are into
a thoufand forms of policy and religion, there is
one point in which they all agree:—they equally
deteft the pageantry of a King, and the fupercilious
hypocrify of a bifhop.

It is not then from the alienated affections of
Ireland or America that you can reafonably look
for affiftance; ftill lefs from the people of England,
who are actually contending for their rights, and
in this great queftion are parties againft you. You
are not however deftitute of every appearance of
fupport: You have all the Jacobites, Nonjurors,
Roman Catholics, and Tories of this country, and
all Scotland without exception. Confidering from
what family you are defcended, the choice of your
friends has been fingularly directed; and truly, Sir, if you had not loft the whig intereft of

Q      England,

---

* In the King's fpeech of 8th November 1768, it was declared,
" That the fpirit of faction had broken out afrefh in fome of the
" colonies, and, in one of them, proceeded to acts of violence and
" refiftance to the execution of the laws;—that Bofton was in a
" ftate of difobedience to all law and government, and had pro-
" ceeded to meafures fubverfive of the conftitution, and attended
" with circumftances that manifefted a difpofition to throw off
" their dependence on Great Britain."

England, I should admire your dexterity in turning the hearts of your enemies. Is it possible for you to place any confidence in men, who, before they are faithful to you, must renounce every opinion, and betray every principle, both in church and state, which they inherit from their ancestors, and are confirmed in by their education? whose numbers are so inconsiderable, that they have long since been obliged to give up the principles and language which distinguish them as a party, and to fight under the banners of their enemies? Their zeal begins with hypocrisy, and must conclude in treachery. At first they deceive; at last they betray.

As to the Scotch, I must suppose your heart and understanding so biassed, from your earliest infancy, in their favour, that nothing less than *your own* misfortunes can undeceive you. You will not accept of the uniform experience of your ancestors; and, when once a man is determined to believe, the very absurdity of the doctrine confirms him in his faith. A bigotted understanding can draw a proof of attachment to the house of Hanover from a notorious zeal for the house of Stuart, and find an earnest of future loyalty in former rebellions. Appearances are, however, in their favour; so strongly indeed, that one would think they had forgotten that you are their lawful King, and had mistaken you for a pretender to the crown. Let it be admitted then that the Scotch are as sincere in their present professions, as if you were in reality not an Englishman, but a Briton of the North. You would not be the first prince, of their native country, against whom they have rebelled, nor the first whom they have basely betrayed. Have you forgotten, Sir, or has your favourite concealed from you that part of our history, when the unhappy Charles (and he too had private virtues) fled from the open, avowed indignation

nation

nation of his Englifh fubjects, and furrendered
himfelf at difcretion to the good faith of his own
countrymen.   Without looking for fupport in
their affections as fubjects, he applied only to their
honour as gentlemen for protection.   They received him as they would your Majefty, with bows,
and fmiles, and falfehood, and kept him until they
had fettled their bargain with the Englifh parliament ; then bafely fold their native king to the
vengeance of his enemies.   This, Sir, was not the
act of a few traitors ; but the deliberate treachery
of a Scotch parliament, reprefenting the nation.
A wife prince might draw from it two leffons of
equal utility to himfelf.   On one fide he might
learn to dread the undifguifed refentment of a generous people, who dare openly affert their rights,
and who in a juft caufe are ready to meet their
Sovereign in the field.   On the other fide, he would
be taught to apprehend fomething far more formidable ;—a fawning treachery, againft which no
prudence can guard, no courage can defend.   The
infidious fmile upon the cheek would warn him of
the canker in the heart.

From the ufes to which one part of the army
has been too frequently applied, you have fome
reafon to expect that there are no fervices they
would refufe.   Here too we trace the partiality of
your underftanding.   You take the fenfe of the
army from the conduct of the guards, with the
fame juftice with which you collect the fenfe of
the people from the reprefentations of the miniftry.
Your marching regiments, Sir, will not make the
guards their example either as foldiers or fubjects.
They feel and refent, as they ought to do, that invariable, undiftinguifhing favour with which the
guards are treated * ; while thofe gallant troops,

Q 2

by

* The number of commiffioned officers in the guards are to the
marching regiments as *one* to eleven ;—the number of regiments
given to the guards, compared with thofe given to the line, is above
three

by whom every hazardous, every laborious fervice
is performed, are left to perifh in garrifons abroad,
or pine in quarters at home, neglected and forgotten. If they had no fenfe of the great original duty they owe their country, their refentment
would operate like patriotifm, and leave your caufe
to be defended by thofe to whom you have lavifhed
the rewards and honours of their profeffion. The
Prætorian Bands, enervated and debauched as they
were, had ftill ftrength enough to awe the Roman
populace : but when the diftant legions took the
alarm, they marched to Rome, and gave away the
empire.

On this fide then, whichever way you turn your
eyes, you fee nothing but perplexity and diftrefs.
You may determine to fupport the very miniftry
who have reduced your affairs to this deplorable
fituation: you may fhelter yourfelf under the forms
of a parliament, and fet your people at defiance.
But be affured, Sir, that fuch a refolution would
be as imprudent as it would be odious. If it did
not immediately fhake your eftablifhment, it would
rob you of your peace of mind for ever.

On the other, how different is the profpect!
How eafy, how fafe and honourable, is the path
before you! The Englifh nation declare they are
grofsly injured by their reprefentatives, and folicit
your Majefty to exert your lawful prerogative, and
give them an opportunity of recalling a truft which
they find has been fcandaloufly abufed. You are
not to be told that the power of the houfe of commons is not original, but delegated to them for the
welfare of the people, from whom they received
it.

three to one, at a moderate computation; confequently the partiality
in favour of the guards is as thirty-three to one.—So much for the
officers.—The private men have four-pence a day to fubfift on, and
five hundred lafhes if they defert. Under this punifhment, they
frequently expire. With thefe encouragements, it is fuppofed,
they may be depended upon, whenever a certain perfon thinks it
neceffary to butcher his *fellow-fubjects*.

it. A queſtion of right ariſes between the conſti-
tuent and the repreſentative body. By what authority ſhall it be decided? Will your Majeſty interfere in a queſtion in which you have properly
no immediate concern.——It would be a ſtep equally
odious and unneceſſary. Shall the lords be called
upon to determine the rights and privileges of the
commons?——They cannot do it without a flagrant
breach of the conſtitution. Or will you refer it to
the judges?——They have often told your anceſtors,
that the law of parliament is above them. What
part then remains, but to leave it to the people
to determine for themſelves? They alone are injured; and ſince there is no ſuperior power to
which the cauſe can be referred, they alone ought
to determine.

I do not mean to perplex you with a tedious argument upon a ſubject already ſo diſcuſſed, that
inſpiration could hardly throw a new light upon it.
There are, however, two points of view in which
it particularly imports your Majeſty to conſider
the late proceedings of the houſe of commons.
By depriving a ſubject of his birthright, they have
attributed to their own vote an authority equal to
an act of the whole legiſlature; and, tho' perhaps
not with the ſame motives, have ſtrictly followed the
example of the long parliament, which firſt declared
the regal office uſeleſs, and ſoon after with as little
ceremony diſſolved the houſe of lords. The ſame
pretended power, which robs an Engliſh ſubject of
his birth-right, may rob an Engliſh King of his
crown. In another view, the reſolution of the
houſe of commons, apparently not ſo dangerous
to your Majeſty, is ſtill more alarming to your
people. Not contented with diveſting one man of
his right, they have arbitrarily conveyed that right
to another. They have ſet aſide a return as illegal,
without daring to cenſure thoſe officers, who were
particularly appriſed of Mr Wilkes's incapacity,

Q 3 not

not only by the declaration of the houfe, but ex-prefsly by the writ directed to them, and who ne-verthelefs returned him as duly elected. They have rejected the majority of votes, the only cri-terion by which our laws judge of the fenfe of the people; they have transferred the right of election from the collective to the reprefentative body; and by thefe acts, taken feparately or together, they have effentially altered the conftitution of the houfe of commons. Verfed, as your Majefty un-doubtedly is, in the Englifh hiftory, it cannot eafily efcape you, how much it is your intereft, as well your duty, to prevent one of the three eftates from encroaching upon the province of the other two, or affuming the authority of them all. When once they have departed from the great conftitu-tional line, by which all their proceedings fhould be directed, who will anfwer for their future mo-deration ? Or what affurance will they give you, that, when they have trampled upon their equals, they will fubmit to a fuperior ? Your Majefty may learn hereafter, how nearly the flave and tyrant are allied.

, Some of your council, more candid than the reft, admit the abandoned profligacy of the prefent houfe of commons, but oppofe their diffolution upon an opinion, I confefs, not very unwarrantable, that their fucceffors would be equally at the difpofal of the treafury. I cannot perfuade myfelf that the nation will have profited fo little by experience. But if that opinion were well founded, you might then gratify our wifhes at an eafy rate, and appeafe the prefent clamour againft your government, with-out offering any material injury to the favourite caufe of corruption.

You have ftill an honourable part to act. The affections of your fubjects may ftill be recovered. But before you fubdue *their* hearts, you muft gain a noble victory over your own. Difcard thofe little,

perfonal

perſonal reſentments, which have too long directed your public conduct. Pardon this man the remainder of his puniſhment; and if reſentment ſtill prevails, make it, what it ſhould have been long ſince, an act, not of mercy, but of contempt. He will ſoon fall back into his natural ſtation,—a ſilent ſenator, and hardly ſupporting the weekly eloquence of a newſpaper. The gentle breath of peace would leave him on the ſurface, neglected and unremoved. It is only the tempeſt that lifts him from his place.

Without conſulting your miniſter, call together your whole council. Let it appear to the public, that you can determine and act for yourſelf. Come forward to your people. Lay aſide the wretched formalities of a King; and ſpeak to your ſubjects with the ſpirit of a man, and in the language of a gentleman. Tell them you have been fatally deceived. The acknowledgement will be no diſgrace, but rather an honour, to your underſtanding. Tell them you are determined to remove every cauſe of complaint againſt your government; that you will give your confidence to no man, who does not poſſeſs the confidence of your ſubjects; and leave it to themſelves to determine, by their conduct at a future election, whether or no it be in reality the general ſenſe of the nation, that their rights have been arbitrarily invaded by the preſent houſe of commons, and the conſtitution betrayed. They will then do juſtice to their repreſentatives and to themſelves.

Theſe ſentiments, Sir, and the ſtyle they are conveyed in, may be offenſive, perhaps, becauſe they are new to you. Accuſtomed to the language of courtiers, you meaſure their affections by the vehemence of their expreſſions; and when they only praiſe you indirectly, you admire their ſincerity. But this is not a time to trifle with your fortune. They deceive you, Sir, who tell you that

you

you have many friends whose affections are founded upon a principle of personal attachment. The first foundation of friendship is not the power of conferring benefits, but the equality with which they are received and *may be* returned. The fortune, which made you a King, forbad you to have a friend. It is a law of nature which cannot be violated with impunity. The mistaken prince, who looks for friendship, will find a favourite, and in that favourite the ruin of his affairs.

The people of England are loyal to the house of Hanover, not from a vain preference of one family to another, but from a conviction that the establishment of that family was necessary to the support of their civil and religious liberties. This, Sir, is a principle of allegiance equally solid and rational;—fit for Englishmen to adopt, and well worthy of your Majesty's encouragement. We cannot long be deluded by nominal distinctions. The name of Stuart, of itself is only contemptible;—armed with the Sovereign authority, their principles are formidable. The Prince, who imitates their conduct, should be warned by their example; and, while he plumes himself upon the security of his title to the crown, should remember, that, as it was acquired by one revolution, it may be lost by another. JUNIUS.

---

## LETTER XXXVI.

### TO HIS GRACE THE DUKE OF GRAFTON.

My Lord,        Feb. 14. 1770.

IF I were personally your enemy, I might pity and forgive you. You have every claim to compassion, that can arise from misery and distress. The condition you are reduced to would disarm a private enemy of his resentment, and leave no consolation to the most vindictive spirit, but that such

an

an object as you are would difgrace the dignity
of revenge.  But in the relation you have borne to
this country, you have no title to indulgence; and
if I had followed the dictates of my own opinion,
I never fhould have allowed you the refpite of a
moment.  In your public chafacter, you have injured every fubject of the empire; and though an
individual is not authorifed to forgive the injuries
done to fociety, he is called upon to affert his feparate fhare in the public refentment.  I fubmitted however to the judgment of men, more moderate, perhaps more candid, than myfelf.  For my
own part, I do not pretend to underftand thofe
prudent forms of decorum, thofe gentle rules of
difcretion, which fome men endeavour to unite
with the conduct of the greateft and moft hazardous affairs.  Engaged in the defence of an honourable caufe, I would take a decifive part.—I
fhould fcorn to provide for a future retreat, or to
keep terms with a man who preferves no meafures
with the public.  Neither the abject fubmiffion of
deferting his poft in the hour of danger, nor even
the * facred fhield of cowardice, fhould protect
him.  I would purfue him through life, and try the
laft exertion of my abilities to preferve the perifhable infamy of his name, and make it immortal.

What then, my Lord, is this the event of all the
facrifices you have made to Lord Bute's patronage,
and to your own unfortunate ambition?  Was it
for this you abandoned your earlieft friendfhips,
—the warmeft connections of your youth, and all
thofe honourable engagements, by which you once
folicited, and might have acquired, the efteem of
your country?  Have you fecured no recompence
for fuch a wafte of honour?—Unhappy man! what
party will receive the common deferter of all parties? Without a client to flatter, without a friend

to

<hr>

* ———Sacro tremuere timore.  Every coward pretends to be
planet-ftruck.

to confole you, and with only one companion from
the honeft houfe of Bloomfbury, you muft now
retire into a dreadful folitude.   At the moft active period of life, you muft quit the bufy fcene,
and conceal yourfelf from the world, if you would
hope to fave the wretched remains of a ruined reputation.   The vices operate like age,—bring on
difeafe before its time, and in the prime of youth
leave the character broken and exhaufted.

Yet your conduct has been myfterious, as well
as contemptible.   Where is now that firmnefs, or
obftinacy, fo long boafted of by your friends, and
acknowledged by your enemies? We were taught
to expect, that you would not leave the ruin of
this country to be completed by other hands, but
were determined either to gain a decifive victory
over the conftitution, or to perifh bravely at leaft
behind the laft dike of the prerogative. You knew
the danger, and might have been provided for it.
You took fufficient time to prepare for a meeting
with your parliament, to confirm the mercenary
fidelity of your dependants, and to fuggeft to your
Sovereign a language fuited to his dignity at leaft,
if not to his benevolence and wifdom.   Yet, while
the whole kingdom was agitated with anxious expectation upon one great point, you meanly evaded
the queftion, and, inftead of the explicit firmnefs
and decifion of a King, gave us nothing but the
mifery of a ruined * grazier, and the whining piety
of a Methodift.   We had reafon to expect, that
notice would have been taken of the petitions
which the King had received from the Englifh nation; and although I can conceive fome perfonal
motives for not yielding to them, I can find none,
in common prudence or decency, for treating them
with contempt.   Be affured, my Lord, the Englifh
people will not tamely fubmit to this unworthy
treatment:

---

* There was fomething wonderfully pathetic in the mention of
the horned cattle.

treatment:—they had a right to be heard; and their petitions, if not granted, deserved to be confidered. Whatever be the real views and doctrine of a court, the Sovereign should be taught to preferve fome forms of attention to his fubjects; and, if he will not redrefs their grievances, not to make them a topic of jeft and mockery among lords and ladies of the bedchamber. Injuries may be atoned for, and forgiven; but infults admit of no compenfation. They degrade the mind in its own efteem, and force it to recover its level by revenge. This neglect of the petitions was however a part of your original plan of government; nor will any confequences it has produced account for your deferting your Sovereign, in the midft of that diftrefs in which you and your * new friends had involved him. One would think, my Lord, you might have taken this fpirited refolution before you had diffolved the laft of thofe early connections, which once, even in your own opinion, did honour to your youth;—before you had obliged Lord Granby to quit a fervice he was attached to;—before you had difcarded one chancellor, and killed another. To what an abject condition have you laboured to reduce the beft of princes, when the unhappy man, who yields at laft to fuch perfonal inftance and folicitation as never can be fairly employed againft a fubject, feels himfelf degraded by his compliance, and is unable to furvive the difgraceful honours which his gracious Sovereign had compelled him to accept. He was a man of fpirit, for he had a quick fenfe of fhame, and death has redeemed his character. I know your Grace too well to appeal to your feelings upon this event; but there is another heart not yet, I hope, quite callous to the touch of humanity, to which it ought to be a dreadful lefson for ever †.

Now,

* The Bedford party.

† The moft fecret particulars of this deteftable tranfaction fhall,

in

Now, my Lord, let us confider the fituation to which you have conducted, and in which you have thought it advifeable to abandon, your royal mafter. Whenever the people have complained, and nothing better could be faid in defence of the meafures of government, it has been the fafhion to anfwer us, though not very fairly, with an appeal to the private virtues of your Sovereign. "Has " he not, to relieve the people, furrendered a " confiderable part of his revenue ?—Has he not " made the judges independent, by fixing them " in their places for life ?"—My Lord, we acknowledge the gracious principle which gave birth to thefe conceffions, and have nothing to regret but that it has never been adhered to. At the end of feven years, we are loaded with a debt of above five hundred thoufand pounds upon the civil lift; and we now fee the Chancellor of Great Britain tyrannically forced out of his office, not for want of abilities, not for want of integrity, or of attention to his duty, but for delivering his honeft opinion in parliament, upon the greateft conftitutional queftion that has arifen fince the revolution.—We care not to whofe private virtues you appeal :—the theory of fuch a government is falfehood and mockery ; the practice is oppreffion. You have laboured then (though I confefs to no purpofe) to rob your mafter of the only plaufible anfwer that ever was given in defence of his government,—of the opinion which the people had conceived of his perfonal honour and integrity.— The Duke of Bedford was more moderate than your Grace. He only forced his mafter to violate a folemn promife made to an individual *. But you, my Lord, have fuccefsfully extended your advice to every political, every moral engagement,

I                                     that

in due time, be given to the public. The people fhall know what kind of man they have to deal with.
    * Mr Stuart Mackenzie.

that could bind either the magiftrate or the man.
The condition of a King is often miferable, but it
required your Grace's abilities to make it contemptible.——You will fay perhaps, that the faithful
fervants, in whofe hands you have left him, are
able to retrieve his honour, and to fupport his government.  You have publicly declared, even fince
your refignation, that you approved of their meafures, and admired their conduct, particularly that
of the Earl of Sandwich.  What a pity it is, that,
with all this appearance, you fhould think it neceffary to feparate yourfelf from fuch amiable companions!  You forget, my Lord, that while you
are lavifh in the praife of men whom you defert,
you are publicly oppofing your conduct to your
opinions, and depriving yourfelf of the only plaufible pretence you had for leaving your Sovereign
overwhelmed with diftrefs: I call it plaufible; for,
in truth, there is no reafon whatfoever, lefs than
the frowns of your mafter, that could juftify a
man of fpirit for abandoning his poft at a moment
fo critical and important.  It is in vain to evade
the queftion.  If you will not fpeak out, the public have a right to judge from appearances.  We
are authorifed to conclude, that you either differ-
ed from your colleagues, whofe meafures you ftill
affect to defend, or that you thought the adminiftration of the King's affairs no longer tenible.
You are at liberty to choofe between the hypocrite
and the coward.  Your beft friends are in doubt
which way they fhall incline.  Your country u-
nites the characters, and gives you credit for them
both.  For my own part, I fee nothing inconfiftent in your conduct.  You begin with betraying
the people,——you conclude with betraying the
King.

In your treatment of particular perfons, you
have preferved the uniformity of your character.
Even Mr Bradfhaw declares, that no man was ever

so ill used as himself. As to the provision * you have made for his family, he was intitled to it by the house he lives in. The successor of one Chancellor might well pretend to be the rival of another. It is the breach of private friendship which touches Mr Bradshaw; and to say the truth, when a man of his rank and abilities had taken so active a part in your affairs, he ought not to have been let down at last with a miserable pension of fifteen hundred pounds a-year. Colonel Luttrell, Mr Onslow, and Governor Burgoyne, were equally engaged with you, and have rather more reason to complain than Mr Bradshaw. These are men, my Lord, whose friendship you should have adhered to on the same principle on which you deserted Lord Rockingham, Lord Chatham, Lord Camden, and the Duke of Portland. We can easily account for your violating your engagements with men of honour, but why should you betray your natural connections? Why separate yourself from Lord Sandwich, Lord Gower, and Mr Rigby, or leave the three worthy gentlemen abovementioned to shift for themselves? With all the fashionable indulgence of the times, this country does not abound in characters like theirs; and you may find it a very difficult matter to recruit the black catalogue of your friends.

The recollection of the royal patent you sold to Mr Hine, obliges me to say a word in defence of

a

---

* A pension of 1500 l. per annum, insured upon the 4 1-half per cents, (he was too cunning to trust to Irish security), for the lives of himself and all his sons. This gentleman, who a very few years ago was clerk to a contractor for forage, and afterwards exalted to a petty post in the war-office, thought it necessary (as soon as he was appointed Secretary to the Treasury) to take that great house in Lincoln's-Inn-Fields, in which the Earl of Northington had resided while he was Lord High Chancellor of Great Britain. As to the pension, Lord North very solemnly assured the house of commons, that no pension was ever so well deserved as Mr Bradshaw's.—N. B. Lord Camden and Sir Jeffery Amherst are not near so well provided for; and Sir Edward Hawke, who saved the state, retires with two thousand pounds a-year on the Irish establishment, from which he in fact receives less than Mr Bradshaw's pension.

a man whom you have taken the moſt diſhonourable means to injure. I do not refer to the ſham
proſecution which you affected to carry on againſt
him. On that ground, I doubt not, he is prepared
to meet you with tenfold recrimination, and ſet
you at defiance. The injury you had done him
affects his moral character. You knew that the
offer to purchaſe the reverſion of a place, which
has heretofore been ſold under a decree of the
court of Chancery, however imprudent in his ſituation, would no way tend to cover him with that
ſort of guilt which you wiſhed to fix upon him in
the eyes of the world. You laboured then, by
every ſpecies of falſe ſuggeſtion, and even by pub-
liſhing counterfeit letters, to have it underſtood
that he had propoſed terms of accommodation to
you, and had offered to abandon his principles,
his party, and his friends. You conſulted your
own breaſt for a character of conſummate treachery, and gave it to the public for that of Mr
Vaughan. I think myſelf obliged to do this juſtice
to an injured man, becauſe I was deceived by the
appearances thrown out by your Grace, and have
frequently ſpoken of his conduct with indignation.
If he really be, what I think him, honeſt, though
miſtaken, he will be happy in recovering his reputation, though at the expence of his underſtanding. Here, I ſee, the matter is likely to reſt.
Your Grace is afraid to carry on the proſecution.
Mr Hine keeps quiet poſſeſſion of his purchaſe;
and Governor Burgoyne, relieved from the apprehenſion of refunding the money, ſits down, for
the remainder of his life, INFAMOUS AND CON-
TENTED.

I believe, my Lord, I may now take my leave
of you for ever. You are no longer that reſolute
miniſter, who had ſpirit to ſupport the moſt violent meaſures; who compenſated for the want of
good and great qualities, by a brave determination

                      (which

(which some people admired and relied on) to maintain himself without them. The reputation of obstinacy and perseverance might have supplied the place of all the absent virtues. You have now added the last negative to your character, and meanly confessed that you are destitute of the common spirit of a man. Retire then, my Lord, and hide your blushes from the world; for, with such a load of shame, even BLACK may change its colour. A mind such as yours, in the solitary hours of domestic enjoyment, may still find topics of consolation. You may find it in the memory of violated friendship; in the afflictions of an accomplished prince, whom you have disgraced and deserted; and, in the agitations of a great country, driven, by your counsels, to the brink of destruction.

The palm of ministerial firmness is now transferred to Lord North. He tells us so himself, with the plenitude of the *ore rotundo* *; and I am ready enough to believe, that, while he can keep his place, he will not easily be persuaded to resign it. Your Grace was the firm minister of yesterday; Lord North is the firm minister of to-day. To-morrow, perhaps, his Majesty, in his wisdom, may give us a rival for you both. You are too well acquainted with the temper of your late allies, to think it possible that Lord North should be permitted to govern this country. If we may believe common fame, they have shown him their superiority already. His Majesty is indeed too gracious to insult his subjects, by choosing his first minister from among the domestics of the Duke of Bedford. That would have been too gross an outrage to the three kingdoms. Their purpose, however, is equally answered by pushing forward this unhappy figure, and forcing it to bear the odium of measures

* 'This eloquent person has got as far as the *discipline* of Demosthenes. He constantly speaks with pebbles in his mouth, to improve his articulation.

fures which they in reality direct.  Without immediately appearing to govern, they poffefs the
power and diftribute the emoluments of government as they think proper.  They ftill adhere to
the fpirit of that calculation which made Mr Luttrell reprefentative of Middlefex.  Far from regretting your retreat, they affure us very gravely, that
it increafes the real ftrength of the miniftry.  According to this way of reafoning, they will probably grow ftronger, and more flourifhing, every
hour they exift ; for I think there is hardly a day
paffes in which fome one or other of his Majefty's
fervants does not leave them to improve by the lofs
of his affiftance.  But, alas! their countenances
fpeak a different language.  When the members
drop off, the main body cannot be infenfible of
its approaching diffolution.  Even the violence of
their proceedings is a fignal of defpair.  Like broken tenants, who have had warning to quit the
premiffes, they curfe their landlord, deftroy the
fixtures, throw every thing into confufion, and care
not what mifchief they do the eftate.

---

## LETTER XXXVII.

TO THE PRINTER OF THE PUBLIC ADVERTISER.

S I R,                              MARCH 19. 1770.
I BELIEVE there is no man, however indifferent
  about the interefts of this country, who will
not readily confefs that the fituation to which we
are now reduced, whether it has arifen from the
violence of faction, or from an arbitrary fyftem
of government, juftifies the moft melancholy apprehenfions, and calls for the exertion of whatever
wifdom or vigour is left among us.  The King's
anfwer to the remonftrance of the city of London,
and the meafures fince adopted by the miniftry,
amount to a plain declaration, that the principle,
R 3
on

on which Mr Luttrell was seated in the house of commons, is to be supported in all its consequences, and carried to its utmost extent. The same spirit, which violated the freedom of election, now invades the declaration and bills of rights, and threatens to punish the subject for exercising a privilege, hitherto undisputed, of petitioning the crown. The grievances of the people are aggravated by insults; their complaints not merely disregarded, but checked by authority; and every one of those acts, against which they remonstrated, confirmed by the King's decisive approbation. At such a moment, no honest man will remain silent or inactive. However distinguished by rank or property, in the rights of freedom we are all equal. As we are Englishmen, the least considerable man among us has an interest equal to the proudest nobleman, in the laws and constitution of this country, and is equally called upon to make a generous contribution in support of them;—whether it be the heart to conceive, the understanding to direct, or the hand to execute. It is a common cause, in which we are all interested, in which we should all be engaged. The man who deserts it at this alarming crisis, is an enemy to his country, and, what I think of infinitely less importance, a traitor to his Sovereign. The subject, who is truly loyal to the chief magistrate, will neither advise nor submit to arbitrary measures. The city of London hath given an example, which, I doubt not, will be followed by the whole kingdom. The noble spirit of the metropolis is the life-blood of the state, collected at the heart: from that point it circulates, with health and vigour, through every artery of the constitution. The time is come, when the body of the English people must assert their own cause: conscious of their strength, and animated by a sense of their duty, they will not surrender their birthright to ministers, parliaments, or kings.

The

The city of London have expreſſed their ſentiments with freedom and firmneſs; they have ſpoken truth boldly; and, in whatever light their remonſtrance may be repreſented by courtiers, I defy the moſt ſubtle lawyer in this country to point
out a ſingle inſtance in which they have exceeded
the truth. Even that aſſertion, which we are told
is moſt offenſive to parliament, in the theory of
the Engliſh conſtitution, is ſtrictly true. If any
part of the repreſentative body be not choſen by
the people, that part vitiates and corrupts the
whole. If there be a defect in the repreſentation
of the people, that power, which alone is equal
to the making of the laws in this country, is not
complete, and the acts of parliament under that
circumſtance are not the acts of a pure and entire
legiſlature. I ſpeak of the theory of our conſtitution; and whatever difficulties or inconveniences may attend the practice, I am ready to maintain, that as far as the fact deviates from the principle, ſo far the practice is vitious and corrupt.
I have not heard a queſtion raiſed upon any other
part of the remonſtrance. That the principle on
which the Middleſex election was determined, is
more pernicious in its effects than either the le-
vying of ſhip-money by Charles I. or the ſuſpend-
ing power aſſumed by his ſon, will hardly be diſputed by any man who underſtands or wiſhes well
to the Engliſh conſtitution. It is not an act of o-
pen violence done by the King, or any direct or palpable breach of the laws attempted by his miniſter,
that can ever endanger the liberties of this country.
Againſt ſuch a King or miniſter the people would
immediately take the alarm, and all the parties unite
to oppoſe him. The laws may be groſsly violated
in particular inſtances, without any direct attack
upon the whole ſyſtem. Facts of that kind ſtand
alone; they are attributed to neceſſity, not defended
by principle. We can never be really in danger,

until

until the forms of parliament are made use of to
deftroy the fubftance of our civil and political liberties;—until parliament itfelf betrays its truft, by
contributing to eftablifh new principles of government, and employing the very weapons committed
to it by the collective body, to ftab the conftitution.

As for the terms of the remonftrance, I prefume
it will not be affirmed, by any perfon lefs polifhed
than a gentleman-ufher, that this is a feafon for
compliments. Our gracious King indeed is abundantly civil to himfelf. Inftead of an anfwer to a
petition, his Majefty very gracioufly pronounces
his own panegyric ; and I confefs, that, as far as
his perfonal behaviour, or the royal purity of his
intentions, is concerned, the truth of thofe declarations, which the minifter has drawn up for his
mafter, cannot decently be difputed. In every o-
ther refpect, I affirm, that they are abfolutely un-
fupported either in argument or fact. I muft add
too, that fuppofing the fpeech were otherwife unexceptionable, it is not a direct anfwer to the petition of the city. His Majefty is pleafed to fay,
that he is always ready to receive the requefts of
his fubjects : yet the fheriffs were twice fent back
with an excufe, and it was certainly debated in
council, whether or no the magiftrates of the city
of London fhould be admitted to an audience.
Whether the remonftrance be or be not injurious
to parliament, is the very queftion between the
parliament and the people; and fuch a queftion as
cannot be decided by the affertion of a third party,
however refpectable. That the petitioning for a
diffolution of parliament is irreconcileable with the
principles of the conftitution, is a new doctrine.
His Majefty perhaps has not been informed, that
the houfe of commons themfelves have, by a formal refolution, admitted it to be the right of the
fubject. His Majefty proceeds to affure us, that
he has made the laws the rule of his conduct.—

Was

Was it in ordering or permitting his minifters to apprehend Mr Wilkes by a general warrant ?— Was it in fuffering his minifters to revive the obfolete maxim of *nullum tempus* to rob the Duke of Portland of his property, and thereby give a decifive turn to a county election ?—Was it in erecting a chamber confultation of furgeons, with authority to examine into and fuperfede the legal verdict of a jury ? Or did his Majefty confult the laws of this country, when he permitted his fecretary of ftate to declare, that, whenever the civil magiftrate is trifled with, a military force muft be fent for, *without the delay of a moment*, and effectually employed ? or was it in the barbarous exactnefs with which this illegal, inhuman doctrine was carried into execution ?—If his Majefty had recollected thefe facts, I think he would never have faid, at leaft with any reference to the meafures of his government, that he had made the laws the rule of his conduct. To talk of preferving the affections, or relying on the fupport, of his fubjects, while he continues to act upon thefe principles, is indeed paying a compliment to their loyalty, which I hope they have too much fpirit and underftanding to deferve.

His Majefty, we are told, is not only punctual in the performance of his own duty, but careful not to affume any of thofe powers which the conftitution has placed in other hands. Admitting this laft affertion to be ftrictly true, it is no way to the purpofe. The city of London have not defired the King to affume a power placed in other hands. If they had, I fhould hope to fee the perfon, who dared to prefent fuch a petition, immediately impeached. They folicit their Sovereign to exert that conftitutional authority, which the laws have vefted in him, for the benefit of his fubjects. They call upon him to make ufe of his lawful prerogative in a cafe, which our laws evident-

ly

ly fuppofed might happen, fince they have provided for it by trufting the Sovereign with a difcretionary power to diffolve the parliament. This requeft will, I am confident, be fuppolked by remonftrances from all parts of the kingdom. His Majefty will find at laft, that this is the fenfe of his people; and that it is not his intereft to fupport either miniftry or parliament, at the hazard of a breach with the collective body of his fubjects.—That he is the King of a free people, is indeed his greateft glory. That he may long continue the King of a free people, is the fecond wifh that animates my heart. The firft is, THAT THE PEOPLE MAY BE FREE *.                    JUNIUS.

---

## L E T T E R   XXXVIII.

TO THE PRINTER OF THE PUBLIC ADVERTISER.

S I R,                                APRIL 3. 1770.

IN my laft letter, I offered you my opinion of the truth and propriety of his Majefty's anfwer to the city of London, confidering it merely as the fpeech of a minifter, drawn up in his own defence, and delivered, as ufual, by the chief magiftrate. I would feparate, as much as poffible, the King's perfonal character and behaviour from the acts of the prefent government. I wifh it to be underftood that his Majefty had in effect no more concern in the fubftance of what he faid, than Sir James Hodges had in the remonftrance; and that as Sir James, in virtue of his office, was obliged to fpeak the fentiments of the people, his Majefty might think himfelf bound, by the fame official obligation, to give a graceful utterance to the fentiments of his minifter. The cold formality of a well-repeated
lefton

* When his Majefty had done reading his fpeech, the Lord Mayer, &c. had the honour of kiffing his Majefty's hand; after which, as they were withdrawing, his Majefty inftantly turned round to his courtiers, *and burft out a laughing.*

*Nero fiddled, while Rome was burning.*     JOHN HORNE.

leſſon is widely diſtant from the animated expreſſion of the heart.

This diſtinction, however, is only true with reſpect to the meaſure itſelf. The conſequences of
it reach beyond the miniſter, and materially affect
his Majeſty's honour. In their own nature they
are formidable enough to alarm a man of prudence,
and diſgraceful enough to afflict a man of ſpirit.
A ſubject, whoſe ſincere attachment to his Majeſty's perſon and family is founded upon rational
principles, will not, in the preſent conjuncture, be
ſcrupulous of alarming, or even of afflicting, his
Sovereign. I know there is another ſort of loyalty, of which his Majeſty has had plentiful experience. When the loyalty of Tories, Jacobites,
and Scotchmen, has once taken poſſeſſion of an
unhappy Prince, it ſeldom leaves him without ac-
compliſhing his deſtruction. When the poiſon of
their doctrines have tainted the natural benevolence of his diſpoſition, when their inſidious coun-
ſels have corrupted the *ſtamina* of his government,
what antidote can reſtore him to his political
health and honour, but the firm ſincerity of his
Engliſh ſubjects?

It has not been uſual in this country, at leaſt
ſince the days of Charles I. to ſee the Sovereign
perſonally at variance or engaged in a direct altercation with his ſubjects. Acts of grace and indulgence are wiſely appropriated to him, and
ſhould conſtantly be performed by himſelf. He
never ſhould appear but in an amiable light to his
ſubjects. Even in France, as long as any ideas of
a limited monarchy were thought worth preſer-
ving, it was a maxim, that no man ſhould leave
the royal preſence diſcontented. They have loſt
or renounced the moderate principles of their government ; and now when their parliaments venture to remonſtrate, the tyrant comes forward and
anſwers abſolutely for himſelf. The ſpirit of their
- preſent

prefent conftitution requires that the King fhould
be feared; and the principle, I believe, is tolerably fupported by the fact. But, in our political
fyftem, the theory is at variance with the practice;
for the King fhould be beloved. Meafures of
greater feverity may, indeed, in fome circumftances, be neceffary; but the minifter who advifes,
fhould take the execution and odium of them entirely upon himfelf. He not only betrays his mafter, but violates the fpirit of the Englifh conftitution, when he expofes the chief magiftrate to
the perfonal hatred or contempt of his fubjects.
When we fpeak of the firmnefs of government,
we mean an uniform fyftem of meafures, deliberately adopted, and refolutely maintained by the
fervants of the crown; not a peevifh afperity in the
language or behaviour of the Sovereign. The government of a weak irrefolute monarch may be
wife, moderate, and firm; that of an obftinate capricious prince, on the contrary, may be feeble,
undetermined, and relaxed. The reputation of
public meafures depends upon the minifter, who
is refponfible; not upon the King, whofe private
opinions are not fuppofed to have any weight a-
gainft the advice of his counfel, and whofe perfonal authority fhould therefore never be interpofed
in public affairs.—This I believe is true conftitutional doctrine. But for a moment let us fuppofe
it falfe. Let it be taken for granted, that an occafion may arife in which a King of England fhall
be compelled to take upon himfelf the ungrateful
office of rejecting the petitions and cenfuring the
conduct of his fubjects; and let the City remonftrance be fuppofed to have created fo extraordinary an occafion. On this principle, which I prefume no friend of adminiftration will difpute, let
the wifdom and fpirit of the miniftry be examined. They advife the King to hazard his dignity, by a pofitive declaration of his own fenti-

ments.—They fuggeft to him a language full of feverity and reproach. What follows? When his Majefty had taken fo decifive a part in fupport of his miniftry and parliament, he had a right to expect from them a reciprocal demonftration of firmnefs in their own caufe, and of their zeal for his honour. He had reafon to expect (and fuch, I doubt not, were the bluftering promifes of Lord North), that the perfons, whom he had been advifed to charge with having failed in their refpect to him, with having injured parliament and violated the principles of the conftitution, fhould not have been permitted to efcape without fome fevere marks of the difpleafure and vengeance of parliament. As the matter ftands, the minifter, after placing his Sovereign in the moft unfavourable light to his fubjects, and after attempting to fix the ridicule and odium of his own precipitate meafures upon the royal character, leaves him a folitary figure upon the fcene, to recal, if he can, or to compenfate, by future compliances, for one unhappy demonftration of ill-fupported firmnefs and ineffectual refentment. As a man of fpirit, his Majefty cannot but be fenfible, that the lofty terms in which he was perfuaded to reprimand the city, when united with the filly conclufion of the bufinefs, refemble the pomp of a mock-tragedy, where the moft pathetic fentiments, and even the fufferings of the hero, are calculated for derifion.

Such has been the boafted firmnefs and confiftency of a minifter *, whofe appearance in the houfe of commons was thought effential to the King's fervice;—whofe prefence was to influence every divifion;—who had a voice to perfuade, an eye to penetrate, a gefture to command. The re-

S

putation

---

* This graceful minifter is oddly conftructed. His tongue is a little too big for his mouth, and his eyes a great deal too big for their fockets. Every part of his perfon fets natural proportion at defiance. At this prefent writing, his head is fuppofed to be much too heavy for his fhoulders.

reputation of thefe great qualities has been fatal to his friends. The little dignity of Mr Ellis has been committed. The mine was funk;—combuftibles were provided; and Welbore Ellis, the Guy Faux of the fable, waited only for the fignal of command. All of a fudden the country gentlemen difcover how grofsly they have been deceived:—the minifter's heart fails him; the grand plot is defeated in a moment; and poor Mr Ellis and his motion taken into cuftody. From the event of Friday laft, one would imagine that fome fatality hung over this gentleman. Whether he makes or fuppreffes a motion, he is equally fure of his difgrace. But the complexion of the times will fuffer no man to be vice-treafurer of Ireland with impunity *.

I do not mean to exprefs the fmalleft anxiety for the minifter's reputation. He acts feparately for himfelf, and the moft fhameful inconfiftency may perhaps be no difgrace to him. But when the Sovereign, who reprefents the majefty of the ftate, appears in perfon, his dignity fhould be fupported. The occafion fhould be important;—the plan well confidered;—the execution fteady and confiftent. My zeal for his Majefty's real honour compels me to affert, that it has been too much the fyftem of the prefent reign, to introduce

duce

---

*' About this time, the courtiers talked of nothing but a bill of pains and penalties againft the Lord Mayor and Sheriffs, or impeachment at the leaft. Little *Mannikin Ellis* told the King, that, if the bufinefs were left to his management, he would engage to do wonders. It was thought very odd, that a motion of fo much importance fhould be intrufted to the moft contemptible little piece of machinery in the whole kingdom. His honeft zeal however was difappointed. The minifter took fright; and, at the very inftant that little Ellis was going to open, fent him an order to fit down. All their magnanimous threats ended in a ridiculous vote of cenfure, and a ftill more ridiculous addrefs to the King. This fhameful defertion fo afflicted the generous mind of George the Third, that he was obliged to live upon potatoes for three weeks, to keep off a malignant fever.——Poor man!——*Quis talid fando temperet a lacrymis!*

duce him perſonally, either to act for, or to defend his ſervants. They perſuade him to do what
is properly *their* buſineſs, and deſert him in the
midſt of it*. Yet this is an inconvenience to
which he muſt be for ever expoſed, while he adheres to a miniſtry divided among themſelves, or
unequal in credit and ability to the great taſk they
have undertaken. Inſtead of reſerving the inter-
poſition of the royal perſonage as the laſt reſource
of government, their weakneſs obliges them to
apply it to every ordinary occaſion, and to render it cheap and common in the opinion of the
people. Inſtead of ſupporting their maſter, they
look to *him* for ſupport ; and, for the emoluments
of remaining one day more in office, care not how
much his ſacred character is proſtituted and diſ-
honoured.

If I thought it poſſible for this paper to reach
the cloſet, I would venture to appeal at once to
his Majeſty's judgment. I would aſk him, but in
the moſt reſpectful terms, " As you are a young
" man, Sir, who ought to have a life of happi-
" neſs in proſpect ;—as you are a huſband ;—as
" you are a father, [your filial duties, I own, have
" been religiouſly performed]; is it *bona fide* for
" your intereſt or your honour, to ſacrifice your
" domeſtic tranquillity, and to live in a perpetual
" diſagreement with your people, merely to pre-
" ſerve ſuch a chain of beings as North, Barring-
" ton, Weymouth, Gower, Ellis, Onſlow, Rigby,
" Jerry Dyſon, and Sandwich ? Their very names
" are a ſatire upon all government, and I defy the
" graveſt of your chaplains to read the catalogue
" without laughing."

For my own part, Sir, I have always conſidered
addreſſes from parliament, as a faſhionable, un-

S 2

meaning

* After a certain perſon had ſucceeded in cajolling Mr Yorke, he
told the Duke of Grafton, with a witty ſmile, " My Lord, you
" may kill the next Percy yourſelf."——N. B. He had but that
inſtant wiped the tears away which overcame Mr York.

meaning formality. Usurpers, idiots, and tyrants, have been succeffively complimented with almoft the fame profeffions of duty and affection. But let us fuppofe them to mean exactly what they profefs. The confequences deferve to be confidered. Either the fovereign is a man of high fpirit and dangerous ambition, ready to take advantage of the treachery of his parliament, ready to accept of the furrender they make him of the public liberty;—or he is a mild, undefigning prince, who, provided they indulge him with a little ftate and pageantry, would of himfelf intend no mifchief. On the firft fuppofition, it muft foon be decided by the fword, whether the conftitution fhould be loft or preferved. On the fecond, a prince no way qualified for the execution of a great and hazardous enterprize, and without any determined object in view, may neverthelefs be driven into fuch defperate meafures, as may lead directly to his ruin, or difgrace himfelf by a fhameful fluctuation between the extremes of violence at one moment, and timidity at another. The minifter, perhaps, may have reafon to be fatisfied with the fuccefs of the prefent hour, and with the profits of his employment. He is the tenant of the day, and has no intereft in the inheritance. The fovereign himfelf is bound by other obligations; and ought to look forward to a fuperior, a permanent intereft. His paternal tendernefs fhould remind him, how many hoftages he has given to fociety. The ties of nature come powerfully in aid of oaths and proteftations. The father, who confiders his own precarious ftate of health, and the poffible hazard of a long minority, will wifh to fee the family-eftate free and unencumbered *. What is the dignity of the crown, though it were really maintained;—what is the honour of parliament,

fup-

---

* Every true friend of the houfe of Brunfwick fees with affliction, how rapidly fome of the principal branches of the family have dropped off.

fuppofing it could exift without any foundation of
integrity and juftice ;—or what is the vain reputation of firmnefs, even if the fcheme of the government were uniform and confiftent, compared
with the heart-felt affections of the people, with
the happinefs and fecurity of the royal family, or
even with the grateful acclamations of the populace ? Whatever ftyle of contempt may be adopted by minifters or parliaments, no man fincerely
defpifes the voice of the Englifh nation. The
houfe of commons are only interpreters, whofe
duty it is to convey the fenfe of the people faithfully to the crown. If the interpretation be falfe
or imperfect, the conftituent powers are called upon to deliver their own fentiments. Their fpeech
is rude, but intelligible ;—their geftures fierce, but
full of explanation. Perplexed by fophiftries, their
honeft eloquence rifes into action. Their firft appeal was to the integrity of their reprefentatives ;
—the fecond, to the King's juftice ;—the laft argument of the people, whenever they have re-
courfe to it, will carry more perhaps than perfuafion to parliament, or fupplication to the throne.

J U N I U S.

---

## L E T T E R  XXXIX.

**TO THE PRINTER OF THE PUBLIC ADVER-
TISER.**

S I R,                              MAY 28. 1770.

WHILE parliament was fitting, it would neither have been fafe, nor perhaps quite regular, to offer any opinion to the public, upon the
juftice or wifdom of their proceedings. To pronounce fairly upon their conduct, it was neceffary
to wait until we could confider, in one view, the
beginning, progrefs, and conclufion of their deli-
berations. The caufe of the public was under-

S 3

taken

taken and supported by men, whose abilities and united authority, to say nothing of the advantageous ground they stood on, might well be thought sufficient to determine a popular question in favour of the people. Neither was the house of commons so absolutely engaged in defence of the ministry or even of their own resolutions, but that *they* might have paid some decent regard to the known disposition of their constituents; and, without any dishonour to their firmness, might have retracted an opinion too hastily adopted, when they saw the alarm it had created, and how strongly it was opposed by the general sense of the nation. The ministry too would have consulted their own immediate interest, in making some concession satisfactory to the moderate part of the people. Without touching the fact, they might have consented to guard against or give up the dangerous principle on which it was established. In this state of things, I think it was highly improbable at the beginning of the session, that the complaints of the people upon a matter which, in *their* apprehension at least, immediately affected the life of the constitution, would be treated with as much contempt by their own representatives, and by the house of lords, as they had been by the other branch of the legislature. Despairing of their integrity, we had a right to expect something from their prudence, and something from their fears. The Duke of Grafton certainly did not foresee to what an extent the corruption of a parliament might be carried. He thought, perhaps, that there was still some portion of shame or virtue left in the majority of the house of commons, or that there was a line in public prostitution beyond which they would scruple to proceed. Had the young man been a little more practised in the world, or had he ventured to mea-

sure

fure the characters of other men by his own, he would not have been fo eafily difcouraged.

The prorogation of parliament naturally calls upon us to review their proceedings, and to confider the condition in which they have left the kingdom.  I do not queftion but they have done what is ufually called the King's bufinefs, much to his Majefty's fatisfaction.  We have only to lament, that, in confequence of a fyftem introduced or revived in the prefent reign, this kind of merit fhould be very confiftent with the neglect of every duty they owe to the nation.  The interval between the opening of the laft and clofe of the former feffion was longer than ufual.  Whatever were the views of the minifter in deferring the meeting of parliament, fufficient time was certainly given to every member of the houfe of commons, to look back upon the fteps he had taken, and the confequences they had produced.  The zeal of party, the violence of perfonal animofities, and the heat of contention, had leifure to fubfide.- From that period, whatever refolution they took was deliberate and prepenfe.  In the preceding feffion, the dependants of the miniftry had affected to believe,. that the final determination of the queftion would have fatisfied the nation, or at leaft put a ftop to their complaints; as if the certainty of an evil could diminifh the fenfe of it, or the nature of injuftice could be altered by decifion.  But they found the people of England were in a temper very diftant from fubmiffion; and, although it was contended that the houfe of commons could not themfelves reverfe a refolution, which had the force and effect of a judicial fentence, there were other conftitutional expedients, which would have given a fecurity againft any fimilar attempts for the future.  The general propofition, in which the whole country had an intereft, might have been reduced to a particular fact, in which Mr Wilkes

and

and Mr Luttrel would alone have been concerned. The houfe of lords might interpofe;—the King might diffolve the parliament;—or, if every other refource failed, there ftill lay a grand conftitutional writ of error, in behalf of the people, from the decifion of one court to the wifdom of the whole legiflature. Every one of thefe remedies has been fucceffively attempted. The people performed *their* part with dignity, fpirit, and perfeverance. For many months his Majefty heard nothing from his people but the language of complaint and refentment;—unhappily for this country, it was the daily triumph of his courtiers that he heard it with an indifference approaching to contempt.

The houfe of commons having affumed a power unknown to the conftitution, were determined not merely to fupport it in the fingle inftance in queftion, but to maintain the doctrine in its utmoft extent, and to eftablifh the fact as a precedent in law, to be applied in whatever manner his Majefty's fervants fhould hereafter think fit. Their proceedings upon this occafion are a ftrong proof that a decifion, in the firft inftance illegal and unjuft, can only be fupported by a continuation of falfehood and injuftice. To fupport their former refolutions, they were obliged to violate fome of the beft known and eftablifhed rules of the houfe. In one inftance, they went fo far as to declare, in open defiance of truth and common fenfe, that it was not the rule of the houfe to divide a complicated queftion, at the requeft of a member *. But after trampling upon the laws of the land, it was not wonderful that they fhould treat the private regulations of their own affembly with equal difregard. The fpeaker, being young in office, began with pretended ignorance, and ended with deciding

ding

* This extravagant refolution appears in the Votes of the houfe; but, in the minutes of the committees, the inftances of refolutions contrary to law and truth, or of refufals to acknowledge law and truth when propofed to them, are innumerable.

ding for the miniftry. We are not furprifed at the
decifion ; but he hefitated and blufhed at his own
bafenefs, and every man was aftonifhed*.

The intereft of the public was vigoroufly fupported in the houfe of lords. Their right to defend the conftitution againft an encroachment of
the other eftates, and the neceffity of exerting it at
this period, was urged to them with every argument that could be fuppofed to influence the heart
or the underftanding. But it foon appeared, that
they had already taken their part, and were determined to fupport the houfe of commons, not only
at the expence of truth and decency, but even by
a furrender of their own moft important rights.
Inftead of performing that duty which the conftitution expected from them, in return for the dignity and independence of their ftation, in return
for the hereditary fhare it has given, them in the
legiflature, the majority of them made common
caufe with the other houfe in oppreffing the people,
and eftablifhed another doctrine as falfe in itfelf,
and if poffible more pernicious to the conftitution,
than that on which the Middlefex election was
determined. By refolving, " that they had no
" right to impeach a judgment of the houfe of
" commons in any cafe whatfoever where that
" houfe has a competent jurifdiction," they in effect gave up that conftitutional check and reciprocal controul of one branch of the legiflature over
the other, which is perhaps the greateft and moft
important

---

* When the King firft made it a meafure of his government to
deftroy Mr Wilkes, and when for this purpofe it was neceffary to
run down privilege, Sir Fletcher Norton, with his ufual proftituted
effrontery, affured the houfe of commons, that he fhould regard
one of their votes no more than a refolution of fo many drunken
porters. This is the very Lawyer whom Ben Johnfton defcribes
in the following lines :

  " Gives forked counfel ; takes provoking gold,
  " *On either hand*, and puts it up.
  " So wife, fo grave, of fo perplex'd a tongue,
  " And *loud* withal, that would not wag nor fcarce
  " Lie ftill without *a fee*."

important object provided for by the division of the whole legiflative power into three eftates : and now, let the judicial decifions of the houfe of commons be ever fo extravagant, let their declarations of the law be ever fo flagrantly falfe, arbitrary, and oppreffive to the fubject, the houfe of lords have impofed a flavifh filence upon themfelves;—they cannot interpofe,—they cannot protect the fubject, —they cannot defend the laws of their country. A conceffion fo extraordinary in itfelf, fo contradictory to the principles of their own inftitution, cannot but alarm the moft unfufpecting mind. We may well conclude, that the lords would hardly have yielded fo much to the other houfe, without the certainty of a compenfation, which can only be made to them at the expence of the people *. The arbitrary power they have affumed of impofing fines, and committing during pleafure, will now be exercifed in its full extent. The houfe of commons are too much in their debt to queftion or interrupt their proceedings. The Crown too, we may be well affured, will lofe nothing in this new diftribution of power. After declaring, that to petition for a diffolution of parliament is irreconcileable with the principles of the conftitution, his Majefty has reafon to expect that fome extraordinary compliment will be returned to the Royal prerogative. The three branches of the legiflature feem to treat their feparate rights and intereft as the Roman Triumvirs did their friends. They reciprocally facrifice them to the animofities of each other, and eftablifh a deteftable union among themfelves, upon the ruin of the laws and liberty of the commonwealth.

Through the whole proceedings of the houfe of commons

---

* The man who refifts and overcomes this iniquitous power affumed by the lords, muft be fupported by the whole people. We have the laws on our fide, and want nothing but an intrepid leader. When fuch a man ftands forth, let the nation look to it. It is not *his* caufe, but our own.

commons in this session, there is an apparent, a palpable consciousness of guilt, which has prevented their daring to assert their own dignity, where it has been immediately and grossly attacked. In the course of Doctor Musgrave's examination, he said every thing that can be conceived mortifying to individuals, or offensive to the house. They voted his information frivolous; but they were awed by his firmness and integrity, and sunk under it *. The terms, in which the sale of a patent to Mr Hine were communicated to the public, naturally called for a parliamentary inquiry. The integrity of the house of commons was directly impeached; but they had not courage to move in their own vindication, because the inquiry would have been fatal to Colonel Burgoyne and the Duke of Grafton. When Sir George Savile branded them with the name of traitors to their constituents; when the Lord Mayor, the Sheriffs, and Mr Trecothick, expressly avowed and maintained every part of the city remonstrance; why did they tamely submit to be insulted? Why did they not immediately expell those refractory members? Conscious of the motives on which they had acted, they prudently preferred infamy to danger; and were better prepared to meet the contempt, than to rouse the indignation, of the whole people. Had they expelled those five members, the consequences of the new doctrine of incapacitation would have come immediately home to every man. The truth of it would then have been fairly tried, without any reference to Mr Wilkes's private character, or the dignity of the house, or the obstinacy of one particular county. These topics, I know, have had their

weight

---

* The examination of this firm, honest man, is printed for *Almon.* The reader will find it a most curious and a most interesting tract. Doctor Musgrave, with no other support but truth and his own firmness, resisted and overcame the whole house of commons.

weight with men, who, affecting a character of moderation, in reality confult nothing but their own immediate eafe;—who are weak enough to acquiefce under a flagrant violation of the laws, when it does not directly touch themfelves; and care not what injuftice is practifed upon a man, whofe moral character they pioufly think themfelves obliged to condemn. In any other circumftances, the houfe of commons muft have forfeited all credit and dignity, if, after fuch grofs provocation, they had permitted thofe five gentlemen to fit any longer among them. We fhould then have feen and felt the operation of a precedent, which is reprefented to be perfectly barren and harmlefs. But there is a fet of men in this country, whofe underftandings meafure the violation of law by the magnitude of the inftance, not by the important confequences which flow directly from the principle; and the minifter, I prefume, did not think it fafe to quicken their apprehenfions too foon. Had Mr Hampden reafoned and acted like the moderate men of thefe days, inftead of hazarding his whole fortune in a law-fuit with the crown, he would have quietly paid the twenty fhillings demanded of him;—the Stuart family would probably have continued upon the throne, and at this moment the impofition of fhip-money would have been an acknowledged prerogative of the crown.

What then has been the bufinefs of the feffion, after voting the fupplies, and confirming the determination of the Middlefex election? The extraordinary prorogation of the Irifh parliament, and the juft difcontents of that kingdom, have been paffed by without notice. Neither the general fituation of our colonies, nor that particular diftrefs which forced the inhabitants of Bofton to take up arms in their defence, have been thought worthy of a moment's confideration. In the re-



peal

peal of thofe acts which were moft offenfive to America, the parliament have done every thing but remove the offence. They have relinquifhed the revenue, but judicioufly taken care to preferve the contention. It is not pretended that the continuation of the tea-duty is to produce any direct benefit whatfoever to the mother-country. What is it then but an odious unprofitable exertion of a fpeculative right, and fixing a badge of flavery upon the Americans, without fervice to their mafters? But it has pleafed God to give us a miniftry and a parliament, who are neither to be perfuaded by argument, nor inftructed by experience.

Lord North, I prefume, will not claim an extraordinary merit from any thing he has done this year in the improvement or application of the revenue. A great operation, directed to an important object, though it fhould fail of fuccefs, marks the genius and elevates the character of a minifter. A poor contracted underftanding deals in little fchemes, which difhonour him if they fail, and do him no credit when they fucceed. Lord North had fortunately the means in his poffeffion of reducing all the four *per cents* at once. The failure of his firft enterprife in finance, is not half fo difgraceful to his reputation as a minifter, as the enterprife itfelf is injurious to the public. Inftead of ftriking one decifive blow, which would have cleared the market at once, upon terms proportioned to the price of the four *per cents* fix weeks ago, he has tampered with a pitiful portion of a commodity, which ought never to have been touched but in grofs:—he has given notice to the holders of that ftock, of a defign formed by government to prevail upon them to furrender it by degrees, confequently has warned them to hold up and enhance the price:—fo that the plan of reducing the four *per cents* muft either be dropped



entirely,

entirely, or continued with an increaſing diſad-
vantage to the public. The miniſter's ſagacity
has ſerved to raiſe the value of the thing he means
to purchaſe, and to ſink that of the three *per cents,*
which it is his purpoſe to ſell. In effect, he has
contrived to make it the intereſt of the proprietor
of four *per cents* to ſell out, and buy three *per
cents* in the market, rather than ſubſcribe his ſtock
upon any terms that can poſſibly be offered by
overnment.

The ſtate of the nation leads us naturally to conſider the ſituation of the King. The prorogation
of parliament has the effect of a temporary diſſolution. The odium of meaſures adopted by the
collective body ſits lightly upon the ſeparate members who compoſe it. They retire into ſummer-
quarters, and reſt from the diſgraceful labours of
the campaign. But as for the Sovereign, *it is not
ſo with him.* He has a permanent exiſtence in this
country; he cannot withdraw himſelf from the
complaints, the diſcontents, the reproaches, of his
ſubjects. They purſue him to his retirement, and
invade his domeſtic happineſs, when no addreſs
can be obtained from an obſequious parliament
to encourage or conſole him. In other times, the
intereſt of the King and people of England was,
as it ought to be, entirely the ſame. A new ſyſtem has not only been adopted in fact, but pro-
feſſed upon principle. Miniſters are no longer
the public ſervants of the ſtate, but the private
domeſtics of the Sovereign. One particular claſs
of men are permitted to call themſelves the King's
friends *, as if the body of the people were the
King's enemies; or as if his Majeſty looked for a
reſource or conſolation in the attachment of a few
favourites, againſt the general contempt and deteſtation

* "An ignorant, mercenary, and ſervile crew; unanimous in
" evil, diligent in miſchief, variable in principles, conſtant to flat-
" tery, talkers for liberty, but ſlaves to power;—ſtyling themſelves
" the court party, and the prince's only friends." *Davenant.*

teftation of his fubjects.  Edward, and Richard
the fecond, made the fame diftinction between
the collective body of the people, and a contemptible party who furrounded the throne.  The e-
vent of their miftaken conduct might have been
a warning to their fucceffors.  Yet the errors of
thofe princes were not without excufe.  They had
as many falfe friends as our prefent gracious Sovereign, and infinitely greater temptations to fe-
duce them.  They were neither fober, religious, nor
demure.  Intoxicated with pleafure, they wafted
their inheritance in purfuit of it.  Their lives were
like a rapid torrent, brilliant in profpect, though
ufelefs or dangerous in its courfe.  In the dull,
unanimated exiftence of other princes, we fee nothing but a fickly ftagnant water, which taints the
atmofphere without fertilizing the foil.—The morality of a king is not to be meafured by vulgar
rules.  His fituation is fingular.  There are faults
which do him honour, and virtues that difgrace
him.  A faultlefs infipid equality in his character,
is neither capable of vice nor virtue in the extreme ; but it fecures his fubmiffion to thofe perfons whom he has been accuftomed to refpect, and
makes him a dangerous inftrument of *their* ambition.  Secluded from the world, attached from his
infancy to one fet of perfons and one fet of ideas,
he can neither open his heart to new connections,
nor his mind to better information.  A character
of this fort is the foil fitteft to produce that obftinate bigotry in politics and religion, which begins
with a meritorious facrifice of the underftanding,
and finally conducts the monarch and the martyr
to the block.

At any other period, I doubt not, the fcandalous diforders which have been introduced into the
government of all the dependencies in the empire,
would have roufed the attention of the public.
The odious abufe and proftitution of the preroga-

tive at home,—the unconftitutional employment of the military,—the arbitrary fines and commitments by the houfe of lords, and court of King's-bench ;—the mercy of a chafte and pious prince, extended cheerfully to a wilful murderer, becaufe that murderer is the brother of a common proftitute *, would, I think, at any other time, have excited univerfal indignation. But the daring attack upon the conftitution, in the Middlefex election, makes us callous and indifferent to inferior grievances. No man regards an eruption upon the furface, when the noble parts are invaded, and he feels a mortification approaching to his heart. The free election of our reprefentatives in parliament comprehends, becaufe it is, the fource and fecurity of every right and privilege of the Englifh nation. The miniftry have realifed the compendious ideas of Caligula. They know that the liberty, the laws, and property of an Englifhman, have in truth but one neck ; and that to violate the freedom of election, ftrikes deeply at them all.

J U N I U S.

---

# LETTER XL.

### TO LORD NORTH.

MY LORD,       AUG. 22. 1770.

MR Luttrel's fervices were the chief fupport and ornament of the Duke of Grafton's adminiftration. The honour of rewarding them was referved for your Lordfhip. The Duke, it feems, had contracted an obligation he was afhamed to acknowledge, and unable to acquit. You, my Lord, had no fcruples. You accepted the fucceffion with all its encumbrances; and have paid Mr Luttrel his legacy, at the hazard of ruining the eftate.

When

* Mifs Kennedy.

When this accomplished youth declared himself the champion of government, the world was busy in inquiring what honours or emoluments could be a sufficient recompence to a young man of his rank and fortune, for submitting to mark his entrance into life with the universal contempt and detestation of his country.—His noble father had not been so precipitate.—To vacate his seat in parliament,—to intrude upon a county in which he had no interest or connection,—to possess himself of another man's right, and to maintain it in defiance of public shame as well as justice, bespoke a degree of zeal, or of depravity, which all the favour of a pious Prince could hardly requite. I protest, my Lord, there is in this young man's conduct, a strain of prostitution, which, for its singularity, I cannot but admire. He has discovered a new line in the human character;—he has degraded even the name of Luttrel, and gratified his father's most sanguine expectations.

The Duke of Grafton, with every possible disposition to patronise this kind of merit, was contented with pronouncing Colonel Luttrel's panegyric. The gallant spirit, the disinterested zeal of the young adventurer, were echoed through the house of lords. His Grace repeatedly pledged himself to the house, as an evidence of the purity of his friend Mr Luttrel's intentions;—that he had engaged without any prospect of personal benefit, and that the idea of compensation would mortally offend him *. The noble Duke could hardly be in earnest; but he had lately quitted his employment, and began to think it necessary to take some care of his reputation. At that very moment the Irish negociation was probably begun. —Come forward, thou worthy representative of Lord Bute, and tell this insulted country, Who

T 3

advised

---

* He now says that his great object is the rank of colonel, and that he *will* have it.

advised the King to appoint Mr Luttrel Adju-
tant General to the army in Ireland? By
what management was Colonel Cuninghame prevailed on to resign his employment, and the ob-
sequious Gisborne to accept of a pension for the
government of Kinsale *? Was it an original sti-
pulation with the Princess of Wales, or does he
owe his preferment to your Lordship's partiality,
or to the Duke of Bedford's friendship? My Lord,
though it may not be possible to trace this measure to its source, we can follow the stream, and
warn the country of its approaching destruction.
The English nation must be roused, and put upon its guard. Mr Luttrel has already shown us
how far he may be trusted, whenever an open
attack is to be made upon the liberties of this
country. I do not doubt that there is a deliberate
plan formed.——Your Lordship best knows by
whom;—the corruption of the legislative body on
this side—a military force on the other—and then
*Farewell to England!* It is impossible that any minister shall dare to advise the King to place such
a man as Luttrel in the confidential post of Adjutant-general, if there were not some secret purpose in view, which only such a man as Luttrel is
fit to promote. The insult offered to the army
in general is as gross as the outrage intended to
the people of England. What! Lieutenant-colo-
nel Luttrel Adjutant-general of an army of sixteen

---

* This infamous transaction ought to be explained to the public.
Colonel Gisborne was quarter-master-general in Ireland. Lord
Townshend persuades him to resign to a Scotch officer, one Fraser,
and gives him the government of Kinsale.——Colonel Cuninghame
was Adjutant-general in Ireland. Lord Townshend offers him a
pension to induce him to resign to Luttrel. Cuninghame treats
the offer with contempt. What's to be done? poor Gisborne must
move once more.——He accepts of a pension of 500 l. a year, until
a government of greater value shall become vacant. Colonel
Cuninghame is made Governor of Kinsale: and Luttrel, at last,
from whom the whole machinery is put in motion, becomes adjutant-general, and in effect takes the command of the army in Ireland.

teen thousand men! One would think his Majesty's campaigns at Blackheath and Wimbleton might have taught him better.—I cannot help wishing General Harvey joy of a colleague who does so much honour to the employment.—But, my Lord, this measure is too daring to pass unnoticed, too dangerous to be received with indifference or submission. You shall not have time to new-model the Irish army. They will not submit to be garbled by Colonel Luttrel. As a mischief to the English constitution, (for he is not worth the name of enemy), they already detest him. As a boy, impudently thrust over their heads, they will receive him with indignation and contempt.—As for you, my Lord, who perhaps are no more than the blind unhappy instrument of Lord Bute and her Royal Highness the Princess of Wales, be assured, that you shall be called upon to answer for the advice which has been given, and either discover your accomplices, or fall a sacrifice to their security.　　　　　JUNIUS.

---

## LETTER XLI.

### TO THE RIGHT HONOURABLE LORD MANSFIELD.

MY LORD,　　　　　　　　　　Nov. 14. 1770.

THE appearance of this letter will attract the curiosity of the public, and command even your Lordship's attention. I am considerably in your debt ; and shall endeavour, once for all, to balance the account. Accept of this address, my Lord, as a prologue to more important scenes, in which you will probably be called upon to act or suffer.

You will not question my veracity, when I assure you, that it has not been owing to any particular respect for your person that I have abstained

from

from you fo long.  Befides the diftrefs and danger with which the prefs is threatened, when your Lordſhip is party, and the party is to be judge, I confeſs I have been deterred by the difficulty of the taſk.  Our language has no term of reproach, the mind has no i ea of deteſtation, which has not already been happily applied to you, and exhauſt-ed.—Ample juſtice has been done by abler pens than mine to the feparate merits of your life and character.  Let it be *my* humble office to collect the fcattered fweets, till their united virtue tortures the fenfe.

Permit me to begin with paying a juſt tribute to Scotch fincerity wherever I find it  I own I am not apt to confide in the profeſſions of gentle-men of that country; and when they fmile, I feel an involuntary emotion to guard myſelf againſt mifchief.  With this general opinion of an ancient nation, I always thought it much to your Lordſhip's honour, that, in your earlier days, you were but little infected with the prudence of your country. You had fome original attachments, which you took every proper opportunity to acknowledge. The liberal fpirit of youth prevailed over your na-tive difcretion.  Your zeal in the caufe of an un-happy prince was expreſſed with the fincerity of wine, and fome of the folemnities of religion*. This, I conceive, is the moſt amiable point of view in which your character has appeared.  Like an honeſt man, you took that part in politics which might have been expected from your birth, education, country, and connections.  There was fomething generous in your attachment to the ba-niſhed houfe of Stuart.  We lament the miſtakes of a good man, and do not begin to deteſt him until he affects to renounce his principles.  Why

did

---

* This man was always a rank Jacobite.  Lord Ravenſworth produced the moſt fatisfactory evidence of his having frequently drank the Pretender's health upon his knees.

did you not adhere to that loyalty you once pro-
feſſed ? Why did not you follow the example of
your worthy brother * ? With him you might have
ſhared in the honour of the Pretender's confidence
—with him you might have preſerved the integrity of your character ; and England, I think,
might have ſpared you without regret.   Your
friends will ſay, perhaps, that although you de-
ſerted the fortune of your liege Lord, you have
adhered firmly to the principles which drove his
father from the throne ;—that, without openly
ſupporting the perſon, you have done eſſential ſervice to the cauſe, and conſoled yourſelf for the
loſs of a favourite family, by reviving and eſta-
bliſhing the maxims of their government. This is
the way in which a Scotchman's underſtanding
corrects the errors of his heart.   My Lord, I acknowledge the truth of the defence, and can trace
it through all your conduct.   I ſee through your
whole life one uniform plan to enlarge the power
of the crown, at the expence of the liberty of the
ſubject.   To this object, your thoughts, words,
and actions, have been conſtantly directed.   In
contempt or ignorance of the common law of
England, you have made it your ſtudy to introduce into the court where you preſide, maxims
of juriſprudence unknown to Engliſhmen.   The
Roman code, the law of nations, and the opinion
of foreign civilians, are your perpetual theme ;—
but who ever heard you mention Magna Charta,
or the Bill of Rights, with approbation or reſpect ?
By ſuch treacherous arts, the noble ſimplicity and
free ſpirit of our Saxon laws were firſt corrupted.
The Norman conqueſt was not complete, until
Norman lawyers had introduced their laws, and
reduced ſlavery to a ſyſtem.—This one leading
principle directs your interpretation of the laws,
                                                    and

* Confidential Secretary to the late Pretender. This circumſtance
confirmed the friendſhip between the brothers.

and accounts for your treatment of juries. It is
not in political queftions only (for there the courtier might be forgiven); but let the cafe be what it
may, your underftanding is equally on the rack,
either to contract the power of the jury, or to miflead their judgment. For the truth of this affertion, I appeal to the doctrine you delivered in Lord
Grofvenor's caufe. An action for criminal converfation being brought by a peer againft a prince
of the blood, you were daring enough to tell the
jury, that, in fixing the damages, they were to
pay no regard to the quality or fortune of the parties;—that it was a trial between A and B;—that
they were to confider the offence in a moral light
only, and give no greater damages to a peer of the
realm than to the meaneft mechanic. I fhall not
attempt to refute a doctrine which, if it was meant
for law, carries falfehood and abfurdity upon the
face of it; but if it was meant for a declaration of
your political creed, is clear and confiftent. Under an arbitrary government, all ranks and diftinctions are confounded. The honour of a nobleman
is no more confidered than the reputation of a pea-
fant; for, with different liveries, they are equally
flaves.

Even in matters of private property, we fee the
fame bias and inclination to depart from the decifions of your predeceffors, which you certainly
ought to receive as evidence of the common law.
Inftead of thofe certain pofitive rules by which
the judgment of a court of law fhould invariably
be determined, you have fondly introduced your
own unfettled notions of equity and fubftantial
juftice. Decifions given upon fuch principles do
not alarm the public fo much as they ought, becaufe the confequence and tendency of each particular inftance is not obferved or regarded. In the
mean time, the practice gains ground; the Court
of King's-Bench becomes a court of equity; and

the

the judge, inftead of confulting ftrictly the law of
the land, refers only to the wifdom of the court,
and to the purity of his own confcience. The
name of Mr Juftice Yates will naturally revive in,
your mind fome of thofe emotions of fear and deteftation with which you always beheld him. That
great lawyer, that honeft man, faw your whole
conduct in the light that I do. After years of ineffectual refiftance to the pernicious principles introduced by your Lordfhip, and uniformly fupported by your *humble friends* upon the bench, he
determined to quit a court whofe proceedings and
decifions he could neither affent to with honour,
nor oppofe with fuccefs.

* The injuftice done to an individual is fometimes of fervice to the public. Facts are apt to
alarm us more than the moft dangerous principles.
The fufferings and firmnefs of a printer have roufed the public attention. You knew and felt that
your conduct would not bear a parliamentary inquiry; and you hoped to efcape it by the meaneft,
the bafeft facrifice of dignity and confiftency, that
ever was made by a great magiftrate. Where was
your firmnefs, where was that vindictive fpirit,
of which we have feen fo many examples, when
a man, fo inconfiderable as Bingley, could force
you to confefs, in the face of this country, that,
for two years together, you had illegally deprived
an Englifh fubject of his liberty, and that he had
triumphed over you at laft? Yet I own, my Lord,
that yours is not an uncommon character. Women, and men like women, are timid, vindictive,
and irrefolute. Their paffions counteract each
other; and make the fame creature, at one moment hateful, at another contemptible. I fancy,
my Lord, fome time will elapfe before you venture

to

---

* The oppreffion of an obfcure individual gave birth to the famous *Habeas Corpus* Act of 31 Car. II. which is frequently confidered as another Magna Charta of the kingdom.

*Blackftone,* iii. 135.

to commit another Englishman for refusing to answer interrogatories *.

The doctrine you have constantly delivered in
cases of libel, is another powerful evidence of a
settled plan to contract the legal power of juries,
and to draw questions, inseparable from fact, within the *arbitrium* of the court. Here, my Lord,
you have fortune on your side. When you invade
the province of the jury in matter of libel, you in
effect attack the liberty of the press, and with a
single stroke wound two of your greatest enemies.
—In some instances you have succeeded, because
jurymen are too often ignorant of their own rights,
and too apt to be awed by the authority of a chief-
justice. In other criminal prosecutions, the malice of the design is confessedly as much the subject
of consideration to a jury as the certainty of the
fact. If a different doctrine prevails in the case of
libels, why should it not extend to *all* criminal
cases?—why not to capital offences? I see no reason (and I dare say you will agree with me, that
there is no good one) why the life of the subject
should be better protected against you, than his liberty or property. Why should you enjoy the full
power of pillory, fine, and imprisonment, and not
be indulged with hanging or transportation? With
your Lordship's fertile genius and merciful disposition, I can conceive such an exercise of the power
you have, as could hardly be aggravated by that
which you have not.

But, my Lord, since you have laboured (and
not unsuccessfully) to destroy the substance *of the
trial*, why should you suffer the form of the *verdict*

I            to

* Bingley was committed for contempt in not submitting to be
examined. He lay in prison two years, until the crown thought
the matter might occasion some serious complaint; and therefore
he was let out, in the same contumelious state he had been put in,
with all his sins about him, unanointed and unanealed.—There
was much coquetry between the Court and the Attorney General,
about who should undergo the ridicule of letting him escape.——
*Vide another Letter to* ALMON, *p.* 189.

to remain? Why force twelve honeſt men, in palpable violation of their oaths, to pronounce their fellow-ſubjeſt a *guilty* man, when, almoſt at the ſame moment, you forbid their inquiring into the only circumſtance which, in the eye of law and reaſon, conſtitutes guilt—the malignity or innocence of his intentions?—But I underſtand your Lordſhip.—If you could ſucceed in making the trial by jury uſeleſs and ridiculous, you might then with greater ſafety introduce a bill into parliament for enlarging the juriſdiſtion of the court, and extending your favourite trial by interrogatories to every queſtion in which the life or liberty of an Engliſhman is concerned [*].

Your charge to the jury, in the proſecution againſt Almon and Woodfall, contradiſts the higheſt legal authorities, as well as the plaineſt diſtates of reaſon. In Miller's cauſe, and ſtill more expreſsly in that of Baldwin, you have proceeded a ſtep farther, and groſsly contradiſted yourſelf.— You may know perhaps, though I do not mean to inſult you by an appeal to your experience, that the language of truth is uniform and conſiſtent. To depart from it ſafely, requires memory and diſcretion. In the two laſt trials, your charge to the jury began as uſual, with aſſuring them that they had nothing to do with the law,—that they were to find the bare faſt, and not concern themſelves about the legal inferences drawn from it, or the degree of the defendant's guilt.—Thus far you were conſiſtent with your former praſtice.—But

U        how

---

[*] The philoſophical poet doth notably deſcribe the damnable and damned proceedings of the judge of hell.

    " Gnoſſius hæc Rhadamanthus habet duriſſima regna,

    " Caſtigatque, auditque dolos, *ſubigitque fateri.*"

Firſt he puniſheth, and *then* he heareth, and laſtly compe'leth to confeſs, and makes and mars laws at his pleaſure: like as the Centurion, in the holy hiſtory, did to St Paul; for the text ſaith, " Centurio apprehendi Paulum juſſit, et ſe catenis eligari; et *tunc* " INTERROGABAT, quis fuiſſet, et quid feciſſet." But good judges and juſtices abhor theſe courſes. *Coke, 2 Inſt. 55.*

how will you account for the conclusion? You told the jury, that " if, after all, they would take " upon themselves to determine the law, *they* " *might do it;* but they must be very sure that " they determined according to law, for it touch- " ed their consciences, and they acted at their " peril."—If I understand your first proposition, you meant to affirm, that the jury were not competent judges of the law in the criminal case of a libel;—that it did not fall within *their* jurisdiction; and that, with respect to *them,* the malice or innocence of the defendant's intentions would be a question *coram non judice.*—But the second proposition clears away your own difficulties, and restores the jury to all their judicial capacities. * You make the competence of the court to depend upon the legality of the decision. In the first instance, you deny the power absolutely. In the second, you admit the power, provided it be legally exercised. Now, my Lord, without pretending to reconcile the distinctions of Westminster-hall with the simple information of common sense or the integrity of fair argument, I shall be understood by your Lordship, when I assert, that, if a jury, or any other court of judicature, (for jurors are judges), have no right to enter into a cause or question of law, it signifies nothing whether their decision be or be not according to law. Their decision is in itself a mere nullity: the parties are not bound to submit to it: and, if the jury run any risk of punishment, it is not for pronouncing a corrupt or illegal verdict, but for the illegality of meddling with a point on which they have no legal authority to decide †.

I

* Directly the reverse of the doctrine he constantly maintained in the house of lords, and elsewhere, upon the decision of the Middlesex election. He invariably asserted, that the decision must be *legal,* because the court was *competent;* and never could be prevailed on to enter farther into the question.

† These iniquitous prosecutions cost the best of princes six thousand

I cannot quit this subject, without reminding your Lordship of the name of Mr Benson. Without offering any legal objection, you ordered a special juryman to be set aside in a cause where the King was prosecutor. The novelty of the fact required explanation. Will you condescend to tell the world, by what law or custom you were authorised to make a peremptory challenge of a juryman? The parties indeed have this power; and perhaps your Lordship, having accustomed yourself to unite the characters of judge and party, may claim it in virtue of the new capacity you have assumed, and profit by your own wrong. The time, within which you might have been punished for this daring attempt to pack a jury, is, I fear, elapsed; but no length of time shall erase the record of it.

The mischiefs you have done this country are not confined to your interpretation of the laws. You are a minister, my Lord; and, as such, have long been consulted. Let us candidly examine what use you have made of your ministerial influence. I will not descend to little matters, but come at once to those important points on which your resolution was waited for, on which the expectation of your opinion kept a great part of the nation in suspence.—A constitutional question arises upon a declaration of the law of parliament, by which the freedom of election and the birthright of the subject were supposed to have been invaded.—The King's servants are accused of violating the constitution.—The nation is in a ferment.—The ablest men of all parties engage in the question, and exert their utmost abilities in the discussion of it.—

U 2

What

fand pounds, and ended in the total defeat and disgrace of the prosecutors. In the course of one of them, Judge Aston had the unparallelled impudence to tell Mr Morris (a gentleman of unquestionable honour and integrity, and who was then giving his evidence on oath), that *he should pay very little regard to any affidavit he should make.*

What part has the honest Lord Mansfield acted? As an eminent judge of the law, his opinion would have been respected.—As a peer, he had a right to demand an audience of his Sovereign, and inform him that his ministers were pursuing unconstitutional measures.—Upon other occasions, my Lord, you have no difficulty of finding your way into the closet. The pretended neutrality of belonging to no party, will not save your reputation. In questions merely political, an honest man may stand neuter. But the laws and constitution are the general property of the subject; not to defend is to relinquish;—and who is there so senseless as to renounce his share in a common benefit, unless he hopes to profit by a new division of the spoil. As a lord of parliament, you were repeatedly called upon to condemn or defend the new law declared by the house of commons. You affected to have scruples, and every expedient was attempted to remove them.—The question was proposed and urged to you in a thousand different shapes.—Your prudence still supplied you with evasion;—your resolution was invincible. For my own part, I am not anxious to penetrate this solemn secret. I care not to whose wisdom it is intrusted, nor how soon you carry it with you to your grave*. You have betrayed your opinion by the very care you have taken to conceal it. It is not from Lord Mansfield that we expect any reserve in declaring his real sentiments in favour of government, or in opposition to the people; nor is it difficult to account for the motions of a timid, dishonest heart, which neither has virtue enough to acknowledge truth, nor courage to contradict it.—Yet you continue to support an administration which you know

is

---

* He said in the house of lords, that he believed he should carry his opinion with him to the grave. It was afterwards reported that he had intrusted it, in special confidence, to the ingenious Duke of Cumberland.

is univerfally odious, and which, on fome occafions, you yourfelf fpeak of with contempt.  You
would fain be thought to take no fhare in government; while, in reality, you are the main fpring
of the machine.—Here too we trace the *little*, prudential policy of a Scotfman.—Inftead of acting
that open, generous part, which becomes your
rank and ftation, you meanly fkulk into the clofet,
and give your Sovereign fuch advice as you have
not fpirit to avow or defend.  You fecretly en-
grofs the power, while you decline the title, of
minifter; and though you dare not be Chancellor,
you know how to fecure the emoluments of the
office.—Are the feals to be for ever in commiffion,
that you may enjoy five thoufand pounds a-year?
—I beg pardon, my Lord;—your fears have interpofed at laft, and forced you to refign.—The
odium of continuing fpeaker of the houfe of lords,
upon fuch terms, was too formidable to be refifted.  What a multitude of bad paffions are forced
to fubmit to a conftitutional infirmity!  But tho'
you have relinquifhed the falary, you ftill affume
the rights of a minifter.—Your conduct, it feems,
muft be defended in parliament.—For what other
purpofe is your wretched friend, that miferable
ferjeant, pofted to the houfe of commons?  Is it in
the abilities of Mr Leigh to defend the great Lord
Mansfield?—or is he only the Punch of the pup-
pet fhow, to fpeak as he is prompted by the CHIEF
JUGGLER behind the curtain * ?

In public affairs, my Lord, cunning, let it be
ever fo well wrought, will not conduct a man honourably through life.  Like bad money, it may be
current for a time, but it will foon be cried down.
It cannot confift with a liberal fpirit, though it be
fometimes united with extraordinary qualifications.

U 3.                      When

---

* This paragraph gagged poor *Leigh*.  I am really concerned
for the man, and wifh it were poffible to open his mouth.—He is
a very pretty crator.

When I acknowledge your abilities, you may believe I am fincere. I feel for human nature, when I fee a man, fo gifted as you are, defcend to fuch vile practices.—Yet do not fuffer your vanity to confole you too foon. Believe me, my good Lord, you are not admired in the fame degree in which you are detefted. It is only the partiality of your friends, that balances the defects of your heart with the fuperiority of your underftanding. No learned man, even among your own tribe, thinks you qualified to prefide in a court of common law. Yet it is confeffed, that, under *Juftinian,* you might have made an incomparable *Prætor.*—It is remarkable enough, but I hope not ominous, that the laws you underftand beft, and the judges you affect to admire moft, flourifhed in the decline of a great empire, and are fuppofed to have contributed to its fall.

Here, my Lord, it may be proper for us to paufe together.—It is not for my own fake that I wifh you to confider the delicacy of your fituation. Beware how you indulge the firft emotions of your refentment. This paper is delivered to the world, and cannot be recalled. The perfecution of an innocent printer cannot alter facts, nor refute arguments.—Do not furnifh me with farther materials againft yourfelf.—An honeft man, like the true religion, appeals to the underftanding, or modeftly confides in the internal evidence of his confcience. The impoftor employs force inftead of argument, impofes filence where he cannot convince, and propagates his character by the fword.

JUNIUS.

L E T-

## LETTER XLII.

TO THE PRINTER OF THE PUBLIC ADVERTISER.

SIR,                                   JAN. 30. 1771.

IF we recollect in what manner the *King's friends*
have been conftantly employed, we fhall have
no reafon to be furprifed at any condition of difgrace to which the once-refpected name of Englifhmen may be degraded. His Majefty has no
cares, but fuch as concern the laws and conftitution of this country. In his Royal breaft there is
no room left for refentment, no place for hoftile
fentiments againft the natural enemies of his crown.
The fyftem of government is uniform.—Violence
and oppreffion at home can only be fupported by
treachery and fubmiffion abroad. When the civil
rights of the people are daringly invaded on one
fide, what have we to expect, but that their political rights fhould be deferted and betrayed, in the
fame proportion, on the other? The plan of domeftic policy which has been invariably purfued
from the moment of his prefent Majefty's acceffion, engroffes all the attention of his fervants.
They know that the fecurity of their places depends upon their maintaining, at any hazard, the
fecret fyftem of the clofet. A foreign war might
embarrafs, an unfavourable event might ruin the
minifter, and defeat the deep-laid fcheme of policy to which he and his affociates owe their employments. Rather than fuffer the execution of
that fcheme to be delayed or interrupted, the King
has been advifed to make a public furrender, a folemn facrifice, in the face of all Europe, not only
of the interefts of his fubjects, but of his own perfonal reputation, and of the dignity of that crown
which his predeceffors have worn with honour.
Thefe are ftrong terms, Sir, but they are fupported by fact and argument.

The

The King of Great Britain had been for fome years in poffeffion of an ifland, to which, as the miniftry themfelves have repeatedly afferted, the Spaniards had no claim of right. The importance of the place is not in queftion. If it were, a better judgment might be formed of it from the opinion of Lord Anfon and Lord Egmont, and from the anxiety of the Spaniards, than from any fallacious infinuations thrown out by men whofe intereft it is to undervalue that property which they are determined to relinquifh. The pretenfions of Spain were a fubject of negociation between the two courts. They had been difcuffed, but not admitted. The King of Spain, in thefe circumftances, bids adieu to amicable negociation, and appeals directly to the fword. The expedition againft Port-Egmont does not appear to have been a fudden ill-concerted enterprife. It feems to have been conducted not only with the ufual military precautions, but in all the forms and ceremonies of war. A frigate was firft employed to examine the ftrength of the place. A meffage was then fent, demanding immediate poffeffion, in the Catholic King's name, and ordering our people to depart. At laft a military force appears, and compels the garrifon to furrender. A formal capitulation enfues; and his Majefty's fhip, which might at leaft have been permitted to bring home his troops immediately, is detained in port twenty days, and her rudder forcibly taken away. This train of facts carries no appearance of the rafhnefs or violence of a Spanifh governor. On the contrary, the whole plan feems to have been formed and executed, in confequence of deliberate orders and a regular inftruction from the Spanifh court. Mr Buccarelli is not a pirate, nor has he been treated as fuch by thofe who employed him. I feel for the honour of a gentleman, when I affirm, that our King owes him a fignal reparation.—

Where

Where will the humiliation of this country end ?
A King of Great Britain, not contented with placing himfelf upon a level with a Spanifh governor,
defcends fo low as to do a notorious injuftice to
that governor.   As a falvo for his own reputation,
he has been advifed to traduce the character of a
brave officer, and to treat him as a common robber, when he knew with certainty that Mr Buccarelli had acted in obedience to his orders, and
had done no more than his duty.  Thus it happens
in private life, with a man who has no fpirit nor
fenfe of honour.—One of his equals orders a fervant to ftrike him.—Inftead of returning the blow
to the mafter, his courage is contented with throw-
ing an afperfion, equally falfe and public, upon
the character of the fervant.

This fhort recapitulation was neceffary to introduce the confideration of his Majefty's fpeech of
13th November 1770, and the fubfequent meafures of government.  The exceffive caution with
which the fpeech was drawn up, had impreffed
upon me an early conviction, that no ferious refentment was thought of, and that the conclufion of the bufinefs, whenever it happened, muft
in fome degree be difhonourable to England.  There
appears through the whole fpeech a guard and
referve in the choice of expreffion, which fhows
how careful the miniftry were not to embarrafs
their future projects by any firm or fpirited declaration from the throne.  When all hopes of peace
are loft, his Majefty tells his parliament, that he
is preparing—not for barbarous war, but (with all
his mother's foftnefs) *for a different fituation.*—
An open hoftility, authorifed by the Catholic King,
is called *an act of a governor.*  This act, to avoid
the mention of a regular fiege and furrender, paffes under the piratical defcription of *feizing by
force ;* and the thing taken is defcribed, not as a
part of the King's territory or proper dominion,.

but

but merely as a *poffeffion*, a word exprefsly chofen in contradiftinction to and exclufion of the idea of *right*, and to prepare us for a future furrender both of the right and of the poffeffion. Yet this fpeech, Sir, cautious and equivocal as it is, cannot, by any fophiftry, be accommodated to the meafures which have fince been adopted. It feemed to promife, that whatever might be given up by fecret ftipulation, fome care would be taken to fave appearances to the public. The event fhows us, that to depart, in the minuteft article, from the nicety and ftrictnefs of punctilio, is as dangerous to national honour as to female virtue. The woman, who admits of one familiarity, feldom knows where to ftop, or what to refufe; and when the counfels of a great country give way in a fingle inftance,—when they once are inclined to fubmiffion, every ftep accelerates the rapidity of the defcent. The miniftry themfelves, when they framed the fpeech, did not forefee, that they fhould ever accede to fuch an accommodation as they have fince advifed their mafter to accept of.

The King fays, *The honour of my crown and the rights of my people are deeply affected.* The Spaniard, in his reply, fays, *I give you back poffeffion; but I adhere to my claim of prior right, referving the affertion of it for a more favourable opportunity.*

The fpeech fays, *I made an immediate demand of fatisfaction; and, if that fails, I am prepared to do myfelf juftice.* This immediate demand muft have been fent to Madrid on the 12th of September, or in a few days after. It was certainly refufed, or evaded, and the King has not done himfelf juftice. —When the firft magiftrate fpeaks to the nation, fome care fhould be taken of his apparent veracity.

The fpeech proceeds to fay, *I fhall not difcontinue my preparations until I have received proper reparation for the injury.* If this affurance may be

relied

relied on, what an enormous expence is entailed, *sine die*, upon this unhappy country! Restitution of a possession, and reparation of an injury, are as different in substance as they are in language. The very act of restitution may contain, as in this instance it palpably does, a shameful aggravation of the injury. A man of spirit does not measure the degree of an injury by the mere positive damage he has sustained. He considers the principle on which it is founded; he resents the superiority asserted over him; and rejects with indignation the claim of right, which his adversary endeavours to establish, and would force him to acknowledge.

The motives on which the Catholic King makes restitution are, if possible, more insolent and disgraceful to our Sovereign than even the declaratory condition annexed to it. After taking four months to consider whether the expedition was undertaken by his own orders or not, he condescends to disavow the enterprize, and to restore the island;—not from any regard to justice,—not from any regard he bears to his Britannic Majesty; but merely *from the persuasion, in which he is, of the pacific sentiments of the King of Great Britain.* —At this rate, if our King had discovered the spirit of a man,—if he had made a peremptory demand of satisfaction, the King of Spain would have given him a peremptory refusal. But why this unseasonable, this ridiculous mention of the King of Great Britain's pacific intentions? Have they ever been in question? Was *He* the aggressor? Does he attack foreign powers without provocation? Does he even resist, when he is insulted? No, Sir; if any ideas of strife or hostility have entered his royal mind, they have a very different direction. The enemies of England have nothing to fear from them.

After all, Sir, to what kind of disavowal has the King of Spain at last consented? Supposing it

made

made in proper time, it should have been accompanied with instant restitution; and, if Mr Buccarelli acted without orders, he deserved death. Now, Sir, instead of immediate restitution, we have a four month's negociation; and the officer, whose act is disavowed, returns to court, and is loaded with honours.

If the actual situation of Europe be considered, the treachery of the King's servants, particularly of Lord North, who takes the whole upon himself, will appear in the strongest colours of aggravation. Our allies were masters of the Mediterranean. The King of France's present aversion from war, and the distraction of his affairs, are notorious. He is now in a state of war with his people. In vain did the Catholic King solicit him to take part in the quarrel against us. His finances were in the last disorder, and it was probable that his troops might find sufficient employment at home. In these circumstances, we might have dictated the law to Spain. There are no terms to which she might not have been compelled to submit. At the worst, a war with Spain alone carries the fairest promise of advantage. One good effect at least would have been immediately produced by it. The desertion of France would have irritated her ally, and in all probability have dissolved the family-compact. The scene is now fatally changed. The advantage is thrown away. The most favourable opportunity is lost.—Hereafter we shall know the value of it. When the French King is reconciled to his subjects; when Spain has completed her preparations; when the collected strength of the House of Bourbon attacks us at once, the King himself will be able to determine upon the wisdom or imprudence of his present conduct. As far as the probability of argument extends, we may safely pronounce, that a conjuncture, which threatens the very being of this country, has been wilfully pre-

prepared and forwarded by our own miniſtry. How
far the people may be animated to refiſtance under the preſent adminiſtration, I know not; but
this I know with certainty, that, under the preſent adminiſtration, or if any thing like it ſhould
continue, it is of very little moment whether we
are a conquered nation or not *.

Having travelled thus far in the high road of
matter of faſt, I may now be permitted to wan-
der a little into the field of imagination.  Let us
baniſh from our minds the perſuaſion that theſe
events have really happened in the reign of the
beſt of princes.  Let us conſider them as nothing
more than the materials of a fable, in which we
may conceive the Sovereign of ſome other country to be concerned.  I mean to violate all the
laws of probability, when I ſuppoſe, that this imaginary King, after having voluntarily diſgraced
himſelf in the eyes of his ſubjeſts, might return
to a ſenſe of his diſhonour;—that he might perceive the ſnare laid for him by his miniſters, and
feel a ſpark of ſhame kindling in his breaſt.—The
part he muſt then be obliged to aſt, would over-
whelm him with confuſion.  To his parliament
he muſt ſay, *I called you together to receive your advice, and have never aſked your opinion.*—To the
merchant,—*I have diſtreſſed your commerce; I have*
X
*dragged*

* The King's acceptance of the Spaniſh Ambaſſador's declaration, is drawn up in barbarous French, and ſigned by the Earl of
Rochford.  This diplomatic Lord has ſpent his life in the ſtudy
and practice of *Etiquettes*, and is ſuppoſed to be a profound maſter
of the ceremonies.  I will not inſult him by any reference to gram-
mar or common ſenſe; If he were even acquainted with the common forms of his office, I ſhould think him as well qualified for it
as any man in his Majeſty's ſervice.—The reader is requeſted to
obſerve Lord Rochford's method of authenticating a public inſtru-
ment.  " En foi de quoi, *moi* ſouſſigné, un des principaux Secre-
" taires d' Etat S. M. B. *ai* ſigné la preſente de ma ſignature ordi-
" naire, et ici le fait appoſer le cachet de *nos* Armes."—In three
lines there are no leſs than ſeven falſe concords.  But the man does
not even know the ſtyle of his office.—If he had known it, he would
have ſaid, " *nous*, ſouſſigné Secretaire d'Etat de S. M. B. *avons*
" ſigné, &c."

*dragged your seamen out of your ships ; I have loaded you with a grievous weight of insurances.*—To the landholder,—*I told you war was too probable, when I was determined to submit to any terms of accommodation ; I extorted new taxes from you before it was possible they could be wanted,* and am now unable to account for the application of them.—To the public creditor,—*I have delivered up your fortunes a prey to foreigners and to the vilest of your fellow-subjects.* Perhaps this repenting prince might conclude with one general acknowledgment to them all :—*I have involved every rank of my subjects in anxiety and distress ; and have nothing to offer you in return, but the certainty of national dishonour, an armed truce, and peace without security.*

If these accounts were settled, there would still remain an apology to be made to his navy and to his army. To the first he would say, *You were once the terror of the world. But go back to your harbours. A man dishonoured as I am, has no use for your service.* It is not probable that he would appear again before his soldiers, even in the pacific ceremony of a review *. But wherever he appeared, the humiliating confession would be extorted from him ; *I have received a blow—and had not spirit to resent it. I demanded satisfaction ; and have accepted a declaration, in which the right to strike me again is asserted and confirmed.* His countenance at least would speak this language, and even his guards would blush for him.

But to return to our argument.—The ministry, it seems, are labouring to draw a line of distinction between the honour of the Crown and the rights of the People. This new idea has yet been only started in discourse; for in effect both objects have been equally sacrificed. I neither understand the distinction, nor what use the ministry

---

* A mistake. He appears before them every day, with the mask of a blow upon his face.—*Proh pudor !*

ftry propofe to make of it. The King's honour is
that of his people. *Their* real honour and real intereft are the fame.—I am not contending for a
vain punctilio. A clear unblemifhed character
comprehends, not only the integrity that will not
offer, but the fpirit that will not fubmit to, an injury; and whether it belongs to an individual or
to a community, it is the foundation of peace, of
independence, and of fafety. Private credit is
wealth;—public honour is fecurity.—The feather
that adorns the royal bird fupports his flight. Strip
him of his plumage, and you fix him to the earth.

JUNIUS.

---

### LETTER XLIII.

TO THE PRINTER OF THE PUBLIC ADVER-
TISER.

SIR,                   FEB. 6. 1771.

I HOPE your correfpondent *Junius* is better employed than in anfwering or reading the criti-
cifms of a newfpaper. This is a tafk from which,
if he were inclined to fubmit to it, his friends
ought to relieve him. Upon this principle I fhall
undertake to anfwer Anti-Junius; more, I believe,
to his conviction than to his fatisfaction. Not daring to attack the main body of *Junius*'s laft letter,
he triumphs in having, as he thinks, furprifed an
out-poft, and cut off a detached argument, a mere
ftraggling propofition. But even in this petty war-
fare he fhall find himfelf defeated.

Junius does not fpeak of the Spanifh *nation* as
the *natural enemies* of England. He applies that
defcription, with the ftricteft truth and juftice, to
the Spanifh *Court*. From the moment when a
Prince of the Houfe of Bourbon afcended that
throne, their whole fyftem of government was in-
verted, and became hoftile to this country. Uni-

X 2

ty

ty of poffeffion introduced a unity of politics; and Lewis the fourteenth had reafon when he faid to his grandfon, " *The Pyrenees are removed.*" The hiftory of the prefent century is one continued confirmation of the prophecy.

The affertion " *That violence and oppreffion at* " *home can only be fupported by treachery and fub-* " *miffion abroad,*" is applied to a free people whofe rights are invaded, not to the government of a country where defpotic or abfolute power is confeffedly vefted in the prince; and with this application, the affertion is true. An abfolute monarch, having no points to carry at home, will naturally maintain the honour of his crown in all his tranfactions with foreign powers: But if we could fuppofe the Sovereign of a free nation, poffeffed with a defign to make himfelf abfolute, he would be inconfiftent with himfelf, if he fuffered his projects to be interrupted or embarraffed by a foreign war, unlefs that war tended, as in fome cafes it might, to promote his principal defign. Of the three exceptions to this general rule of conduct, (quoted by Anti-Junius), that of Oliver Cromwell is the only one in point. Harry the Eighth, by the fubmiffion of his parliament, was as abfolute a prince as Lewis the Fourteenth. Queen Elifabeth's government was not oppreffive to the people; and as to her foreign wars, it ought to be confidered that they were *unavoidable.* The national honour was not in queftion: She was compelled to fight in defence of her own perfon and of her title to the crown. In the common caufe of felfifh policy, Oliver Cromwell fhould have cultivated the friendfhip of foreign powers, or at leaft have avoided difputes with them, the better to eftablifh his tyranny at home. Had he been only a bad man, he would have facrificed the honour of the nation to the fuccefs of his domeftic policy. But, with all his crimes, he had the fpirit of an

Eng-

Englishman. The conduct of such a man muſt always be an exception to vulgar rules. He had abilities ſufficient to reconcile contradictions, and to make a great nation at the ſame moment unhappy and formidable. If it were not for the reſpect I bear the miniſter, I could name a man, who, without one grain of underſtanding, can do half as much as Oliver Cromwell.

Whether or no there be a *ſecret ſyſtem* in the cloſet, and what may be the object of it, are queſtions which can only be determined by appearances, and on which every man muſt decide for himſelf.

The whole plan of *Junius*'s letter proves, that he himſelf makes no diſtinction between the real honour of the crown and the real intereſt of the people. In the climax to which your correſpondent objects, *Junius* adopts the language of the Court, and by that conformity gives ſtrength to his argument. He ſays, that " *the King has not* " *only ſacrificed the intereſts of his people, but* (what " *was likely to touch him more nearly) his perſonal* " *reputation and the dignity of his crown.*"

The queries put by *Anti-Junius* can only be anſwered by the miniſtry. Abandoned as they are, I fancy they will not confeſs that they have, for ſo many years, maintained poſſeſſion of another man's property. After admitting the aſſertion of the miniſtry—viz. *that the Spaniards had no right-ful claim*, and after juſtifying them for ſaying ſo ; —it is *his* buſineſs, not *mine*, to give us ſome good reaſon for their *ſuffering the pretenſions of Spain to be a ſubject of negociation.* He admits the facts ;— let him reconcile them if he can.

The laſt paragraph brings us back to the original queſtion, Whether the Spaniſh declaration contains ſuch a ſatisfaction as the King of Great Britain ought to have accepted. This was the field upon which he ought to have encountered

*Junius* openly and fairly. But here he leaves the argument, as no longer defensible. I shall thereforce conclude with one general admonition to my fellow-subjects :—That when they hear these matters debated, they should not suffer themselves to be misled by general declamations upon the conveniences of peace, or the miseries of war. Between peace and war, abstractedly, there is not, there cannot, be a question in the mind of a rational being. The real questions are, *Have we any security, that the peace we have so dearly purchased will last a twelvemonth?* and if not,—*Have we, or have we not, sacrificed the fairest opportunity of making war with advantage?*

PHILO JUNIUS.

---

## LETTER XLIV.

### ADDRESSED TO THE PRINTER OF THE PUBLIC ADVERTISER.

SIR, APRIL 22. 1771.

TO write for profit, without taxing the press;— to write for fame, and to be unknown ;—to support the intrigues of faction, and to be disowned, as a dangerous auxiliary, by every party in the kingdom ; are contradictions which the minister must reconcile, before I forfeit my credit with the public. I may quit the service, but it would be absurd to suspect me of desertion. The reputation of these papers is an honourable pledge for my attachment to the people. To sacrifice a respected character, and to renounce the esteem of society, requires more than Mr Wedderburne's resolution ; and though in him it was rather a profession than a desertion of his principles, (I speak tenderly of this gentleman, for when treachery is in question I think we should make allowances for a Scotchman), yet we have seen him in

the

the houfe of commons overwhelmed with confufion, and almoft bereft of his faculties.—But in
truth, Sir, I have left no room for an accommodation with the piety of St James's.   My offences
are not to be redeemed by recantation or repentance.   On one fide,. our warmeft patriots would
difclaim me as a burthen to their honeft ambition.
On the other, the vileft proftitution, if *Junius*
could defcend to it, would lofe its natural merit
and influence in the cabinet, and treachery be no
longer a recommendation to the royal favour.

The perfons who, till within thefe few years,
have been moft diftinguifhed by their zeal for high-
church and prerogative, are now, it feems, the
great affertors of the privileges of the houfe of
commons.   This fudden alteration of their fentiments or language carries with it a fufpicious appearance.   When I hear the undefined privileges
of the popular branch of the legiflature exalted by
Tories and Jacobites, at the expence of thofe ftrict
rights, which are known to the fubject, and limited by the laws, I cannot but fufpect, that fome
mifchievous fcheme is in agitation, to deftroy both
law and privilege, by oppofing them to each other.
They who have uniformly denied the power of the
whole legiflature to alter the defcent of the crown,
and whofe anceftors, in rebellion againft his Majefty's family, have defended that doctrine at the
hazard of their lives, now tell us, that privilege
of parliament is the only rule of right, and the
chief fecurity of the public freedom.—I fear, Sir,
that while forms remain, there has been fome
material change in the fubftance of our conftitution.   The opinions of thefe men were too abfurd
to be fo eafily renounced.   Liberal minds are open
to conviction.—Liberal doctrines are capable of
improvement.—There are profelytes from atheifm,
but none from fuperftition.—If their prefent profeffions were fincere, I think they could not but

be highly offended at seeing a question, concerning parliamentary privilege, unnecessarily started at a season so unfavourable to the house of commons, and by so very mean and insignificant a person as the minor *Onslow*. They knew, that the present house of commons, having commenced hostilities with the people, and degraded the authority of the laws by their own example, were likely enough to be resisted *per fas et nefas*. If they were really friends to privilege, they would have thought the question of right too dangerous to be hazarded at this season, and, without the formality of a convention, would have left it undecided.

I have been silent hitherto; though not from that shameful indifference about the interests of society which too many of us profess, and call moderation. I confess, Sir, that I felt the prejudices of my education, in favour of a house of commons, still hanging about me. I thought that a question, between law and privilege, could never be brought to a formal decision, without inconvenience to the public service, or a manifest diminution of legal liberty;—that it ought therefore to be carefully avoided: and when I saw that the violence of the house of commons had carried them too far to retreat, I determined not to deliver a hasty opinion upon a matter of so much delicacy and importance.

The state of things is much altered in this country since it was necessary to protect our representatives against the direct power of the crown. We have nothing to apprehend from prerogative, but every thing from undue influence. Formerly it was the interest of the people, that the privileges of parliament should be left unlimited and undefined. At present, it is not only their interest, but I hold it to be essentially necessary to the preservation of the constitution, that the privileges of parliament ſhould be ſtrictly aſcertained, and confined within the narroweſt bounds the nature of their inſtitution will admit of. Upon the ſame principle on which I would have reſiſted prerogative in the laſt century, I now reſiſt privilege. It is indifferent to me, whether the crown, by its own immediate act, impoſes new, and diſpenſes with old laws; or whether the ſame arbitrary power produces the ſame effects through the medium of the houſe of commons. We truſted our repreſentatives with privileges for their own defence and ours. We cannot hinder their deſertion, but we can prevent their carrying over their arms to the ſervice of the enemy. It will be ſaid, that I begin with endeavouring to reduce the argument concerning privilege to a mere queſtion of convenience;—that I deny at one moment what I would allow at another; and that to reſiſt the power of a proſtituted houſe of commons, may eſtabliſh a precedent injurious to all future parliaments.—To this I anſwer generally, that human affairs are in no inſtance governed by ſtrict poſitive right. If change of circumſtances were to have no weight in directing our conduct and opinions, the mutual intercourſe of mankind would be nothing more than a contention between poſitive and equitable right. Society would be a ſtate of war, and law itſelf would be injuſtice. On this general ground, it is highly reaſonable that the degree of our ſubmiſſion to privileges which have never been defined by any poſitive law, ſhould be conſidered as a queſtion of convenience, and proportioned to the confidence we repoſe in the integrity of our repreſentatives. As to the injury we may do to any future and more reſpectable houſe of commons, I own I am not now ſanguine enough to expect a more plentiful harveſt of parliamentary virtue in one year than another. Our political climate is ſeverely altered; and without dwelling

upon.

upon the depravity of modern times, I think no reasonable man will expect, that, as human nature is constituted, the enormous influence of the crown should cease to prevail over the virtue of individuals. The mischief lies too deep to be cured by any remedy, less than some great convulsion, which may either carry back the constitution to its original principles, or utterly destroy it. I do not doubt, that, in the first session after the next election, some popular measures may be adopted. The present house of commons have injured themselves by a too early and public profession of their principles; and if a strain of prostitution, which had no example, were within the reach of emulation, it might be imprudent to hazard the experiment too soon. But, after all, Sir, it is very immaterial whether a house of commons shall preserve their virtue for a week, a month, or a year. The influence, which makes a septennial parliament dependent upon the pleasure of the crown, has a permanent operation, and cannot fail of success.—My premisses, I know, will be denied in argument; but every man's conscience tells him they are true. It remains then to be considered, whether it be for the interest of the people, that privilege of parliament (which *, in respect to the purposes for which it has hitherto been acquiesced under, is merely nominal) should be contracted within some certain limits? or whether the subject shall be left at the mercy of a power, arbitrary

upon

---

* The necessity of securing the house of commons against the King's power, so that no interruption might be given either to the attendance of the members in parliament, or to the freedom of debate, was the foundation of parliamentary privilege; and we may observe, in all the addresses of new-appointed Speakers to the Sovereign, the utmost privilege they demand is liberty of speech and freedom from arrests. The very word *privilege* means no more than immunity, or a safeguard to the party who possesses it, and can never be construed into an active power of invading the rights of others.

upon the face of it, and notoriously under the direction of the crown.

I do not mean to decline the question of *right :* on the contrary, Sir, I join issue with the advocates for privilege; and affirm, that, "excepting " the cases wherein the house of commons are a " court of judicature, (to which, from the nature " of their office, a coercive power must belong), " and excepting such contempts as immediately " interrupt their proceedings, they have no legal " authority to imprison any man for any supposed " violation of privilege whatsoever."—It is not pretended, that privilege, as now claimed, has ever been defined or confirmed by statute; neither can it be said, with any colour of truth, to be a part of the common law of England, which had grown into prescription long before we knew any thing of the existence of a house of commons.   As for the law of parliament, it is only another name for the privilege in question; and since the power of creating new privileges has been formally renounced by both houses,—since there is no code in which we can study the law of parliament, we have but one way left to make ourselves acquainted with it,—that is, to compare the nature of the institution of a house of commons with the facts upon record.   To establish a claim of privilege in either house, and to distinguish original right from usurpation, it must appear, that it is indispensably necessary for the performance of the duty they are employed in, and also that it has been uniformly allowed.   From the first part of this description, it follows clearly, that whatever privilege does of right belong to the present house of commons, did equally belong to the first assembly of their predecessors; was as completely vested in them, and might have been exercised in the same extent. From the second, we must infer, that privileges, which for several centuries were not only never allowed,

lowed,

lowed, but never even claimed by the houfe of commons, muſt be founded upon uſurpation. The conſtitutional duties of a houſe of commons are not very complicated nor myſterious. They are to propoſe or aſſent to wholeſome laws for the bene-fit of the nation. They are to grant the neceſſary aids to the king; petition for the redreſs of grie-vances; and proſecute treaſon or high crimes a-gainſt the ſtate. If unlimited privilege be neceſ-ſary to the performance of theſe duties, we have reaſon to conclude, that, for many centuries after the inſtitution of the houſe of commons, they were never performed. I am not bound to prove a negative; but I appeal to the Engliſh hiſtory, when I affirm, that, with the exceptions already ſtated, (which yet I might ſafely relinquiſh), there is no precedent from the year 1205 to the death of Queen Elizabeth, of the houſe of commons ha-ving impriſoned any man (not a member of their houſe) for contempt or breach of privilege. In the moſt flagrant caſes, and when their acknow-ledged privileges were moſt groſsly violated, the *poor Commons*, as they then ſtyled themſelves, ne-ver took the power of puniſhment into their own hands. They either ſought redreſs by petition to the King, or, what is more remarkable, applied for juſtice to the houſe of Lords; and when ſatiſ-faction was denied them or delayed, their only re-medy was to refuſe proceeding upon the King's buſineſs. So little conception had our anceſtors of the monſtrous doctrines now maintained con-cerning privilege, that, in the reign of Elizabeth, even liberty of ſpeech, the vital principle of a de-liberative aſſembly, was reſtrained by the Queen's authority to a ſimple *aye* or *no;* and this reſtric-tion, though impoſed upon three ſucceſſive parlia-ments *, was never once diſputed by the houſe of commons.

ʋ.　　I

---

* In the year 1593—1597—and 1601.

I know there are many precedents of arbitrary commitments for contempt: but, befides that they are of too modern a date to warrant a prefumption that fuch a power was originally vefted in the houfe of commons,—*Faɛt* alone does not conftitute *Right*.—If it does, general warrants were lawful.—An ordinance of the two houfes has a force equal to law; and the criminal jurifdiɛtion affumed by the Commons in 1621, in the cafe of Edward Loyd, is a good precedent to warrant the like proceedings againft any man, who fhall unadvifedly mention the folly of a king, or the ambition of a princefs.——The truth is, Sir, that the greateft and moft exceptionable part of the privileges now contended for, were introduced and afferted by a houfe of commons which abolifhed both monarchy and peerage, and whofe proceedings, although they ended in one glorious aɛt of fubftantial juftice, could no way be reconciled to the forms of the conftitution. Their fucceffors profited by the example, and confirmed their power by a moderate or a proper ufe of it. Thus it grew by degrees, from a notorious innovation at one period, to be tacitly admitted as the privilege of parliament at another.

If, however, it could be proved, from confiderations of neceffity or convenience, that an unlimited power of commitment ought to be intrufted to the houfe of commons, and that *in faɛt* they have exercifed it without oppofition, ftill, in contemplation of law, the prefumption is ftrongly againft them. It is a leading maxim of the laws of England, (and without it all laws are nugatory), that there is no right without a remedy, nor any legal power without a legal courfe to carry it into effeɛt. Let the power now in queftion be tried by this rule. The fpeaker iffues his warrant of attachment. The party attached either refifts force with force, or appeals to a magiftrate, who de-



clares

clares the warrant illegal, and difcharges the prifoner.   Does the law provide no legal means for
enforcing a legal warrant?  Is there no regular
proceeding pointed out in our law-books to affert
and vindicate the authority of fo high a court as
the houfe of commons?  The queftion is anfwered
directly by the fact.   Their unlawful commands
are refifted, and they have no remedy.   The imprifonment of their own members is revenge indeed, but it is no affertion of the privilege they
contend for *.   Their whole proceeding ftops;
and there they ftand, afhamed to retreat, and unable to advance.   Sir, thefe ignorant men fhould
be informed, that the execution of the laws of
England is not left in this uncertain defencelefs
condition.   If the procefs of the courts of Weftminfter-hall be refifted, they have a direct courfe
fufficient to enforce fubmiffion.   The court of
King's-Bench commands the fheriff to raife the
*poffe comitatus*.   The Courts of Chancery and Exchequer iffue a *writ of rebellion;* which muft alfo
be fupported, if neceffary, by the power of the
county.—To whom will our honeft reprefentatives
direct *their* writ of rebellion?  The guards, I doubt
not, are willing enough to be employed; but they
know nothing of the doctrine of writs, and may
think it neceffary to wait for a letter from Lord
Barrington.

It may now be objected to me, that my arguments prove too much: for that certainly there
may be inftances of contempt and infult to the
houfe of commons, which do not fall within my
own exceptions; yet, in regard to the dignity of
the houfe, ought not to pafs unpunifhed.   Be it
fo.

---

* Upon their own principles, they fhould have committed Mr
Wilkes, who had been guilty of a greater offence than even the
Lord Mayor or Alderman Oliver.   But after repeatedly ordering
him to attend, they at laft adjourned beyond the day appointed
for his attendance; and by this mean, pitiful evafion, gave up the
point.——Such is the force of confcious guilt!

fo.—The courts of criminal jurifdiction are open
to profecutions, which the Attorney-General may
commence by information or indictment.  A libel,
tending to afperfe or vilify the houfe of commons,
or any of their members, may be as feverely punifhed in the court of King's-Bench as a libel upon the King.  Mr de Grey thought fo, when he
drew up the information upon my letter to his Majefty, or he had no meaning in charging it to be a
fcandalous libel upon the houfe of commons.  In
*my* opinion, they would confult their real dignity
much better, by appealing to the laws when they
are offended, than by violating the firft principle
of natural juftice, which forbids us to be judges
when we are parties to the caufe *.

I do not mean to purfue them through the remainder of their proceedings.  In their firft refolutions, it is poffible they might have been deceived by ill-confidered precedents.  For the reft,
there is no colour of palliation or excufe.  They
have advifed the King to refume a power of difpen-
fing with the laws by royal proclamation †; and
Kings, we fee, are ready enough to follow fuch
Y 2
advice.

---

* " If it be demanded, in cafe a fubject fhould be committed by
" either houfe for a matter manifeftly out of their jurifdiction,
" what remedy can he have?  I anfwer, That it cannot well be
" imagined, that the law, which favours nothing more than the
" liberty of the fubject, fhould give us a remedy againft commit-
" ments by the King himfelf, appearing to be illegal, and yet give
" us no manner of redrefs againft a commitment by our fellow-
" fubjects, equally appearing to be unwarranted.  But as this is a
" cafe which I am perfuaded will never happen, it feems needlefs
" over-nicely to examine it."——*Hawkins*, ii. 110.——*N. B.* He
was a good lawyer, but no prophet.

† That their practice might be every way conformable to their
principles, the houfe proceeded to advife the crown to publifh a
proclamation, univerfally acknowledged to be illegal.  Mr More-
ton publicly protefted againft it before it was iffued; and Lord
Mansfield, though not fcrupulous to an extreme, fpeaks of it with
horror.  It is remarkable enough, that the very men who advifed
the proclamation, and who hear it arraigned every day both within
doors and without, are not daring enough to utter one word in its
defence; nor have they ventured to take the leaft notice of Mr
Wilkes for difcharging the perfons apprehended under it.

advice.—By mere violence, and without the shadow of right, they have expunged the record of a judicial proceeding *. Nothing remained, but to attribute to their own vote a power of stopping the whole diftribution of criminal and civil juftice.

The public virtues of the chief magiftrate have long fince ceafed to be in queftion. But it is faid, that he has private good qualities; and I myfelf have been ready to acknowledge them. They are now brought to the teft. If he loves his people, he will diffolve a parliament which they can never confide in or refpect.—If he has any regard for his own honour, he will difdain to be any longer connected with fuch abandoned proftitution. But, if it were conceivable, that a King of this country had loft all fenfe of perfonal honour, and all concern for the welfare of his fubjects, I confefs, Sir, I fhould be contented to renounce the forms of the conftitution once more, if there were no other way to obtain fubftantial juftice for the people †.

J U N I U S.

* Lord Chatham very properly called this the act of a mob, not of a fenate.

† When Mr Wilkes was to be punifhed, they made no fcruple about the privileges of parliament: and although it was as well known as any matter of public record and uninterrupted cuftom could be, *that the members of either houfe are privileged, except in cafe of treafon, felony, or breach of peace*, they declared without hefitation, *that privilege of parliament did not extend to the cafe of a feditious libel*; and undoubtedly they would have done the fame if Mr Wilkes had been profecuted for any other mifdemeanour whatfoever. The miniftry are of a fudden grown wonderfully careful of privileges, which their predeceffors were as ready to invade. The known laws of the land, the rights of the fubject, the fanctity of charters, and the reverence due to our magiftrates, muft all give way, without queftion or refiftance, to a privilege of which no man knows either the origin or the extent. The houfe of commons judge of their own privileges without appeal;—they may take offence at the moft innocent action, and imprifon the perfon who offends them during their arbitrary will and pleafure. The party has no remedy;—he cannot appeal from their jurifdiction; and if he queftions the privilege which he is fuppofed to have violated, it becomes an aggravation of his offence. Surely this doctrine is not to be found in Magna Charta. If it be admitted without limitation, I affirm that there is neither law nor liberty in this king-

## L E T T E R  XLV.

TO THE PRINTER OF THE PUBLIC ADVER-
TISER.

SIR,                              MAY 1. 1771.

THEY who object to detached parts of Junius's laſt letter, either do not mean him fair-ly, or have not conſidered the general ſcope and courſe of his argument.—There are degrees in all the private vices:—Why not in public proſtitution?—The influence of the crown naturally makes a ſeptennial parliament dependent.—Does it follow that every houſe of commons will plunge at once into the *loweſt depths* of proſtitution?—Junius ſuppoſes, that the preſent houſe of commons, in going ſuch enormous lengths, have been *imprudent to themſelves*, as well as wicked to the public;—that their example is *not within the reach of emulation*;—and that, in the firſt ſeſſion after the next election, *ſome* popular meaſures may probably be adopted.  He does not expect that a diſſolution of parliament will deſtroy corruption, but that at leaſt it will be a check and terror to their ſucceſſors, who will have ſeen that, *in flagrant caſes*, their conſtituents *can* and *will* interpoſe with effect.—After all, Sir, will you not endeavour to remove or alleviate the moſt dangerous ſymptoms, becauſe you cannot eradicate the diſeaſe? Will you not puniſh *treaſon* or *parricide*, becauſe the ſight of a gibbet does not prevent highway robberies? When the main argument of Junius is admitted to be unanſwerable, I think it would become the minor critic, who hunts for blemiſhes, to be a little more diſtruſtful of his own ſagacity.—The other objection is hardly worth an anſwer.  When Junius obſerves, that Kings are ready enough to follow *ſuch* advice, he does not mean to inſinuate, that,

Y 3

if

kingdom.  We are the ſlaves of the houſe of commons; and, thro' them, we are the ſlaves of the King and his miniſters.  *Anony-mous.*

if the advice of parliament were good, the King would be fo ready to follow it.

PHILO JUNIUS.

---

# LETTER XLVI.

ADDRESSED TO THE PRINTER OF THE PUBIC ADVERTISER.

SIR,                                   MAY 22. 1771.

VERY early in the debate upon the decifion of the Middlefex election, it was well obferved by *Junius*, that the houfe of commons had not only exceeded their boafted precedent of the expulfion and fubfequent incapacitation of Mr Walpole, but that they had not even adhered to it ftrictly as far as it went. After convicting Mr Dyfon of giving a falfe quotation from the journals, and having explained the purpofe which that contemptible fraud was intended to anfwer, he proceeds to ftate the vote itfelf by which Mr Walpole's fuppofed incapacity was declared,—viz. " Refolved, That Robert Walpole, Efq; having " been this feffion of parliament committed a pri- " foner to the Tower, and expelled this houfe for " a high breach of truft in the execution of his " office, and notorious corruption when fecretary " at war, was, and is, incapable of being elected " a member to ferve in this prefent parliament :" —And then obferves, that, from the terms of the vote, we have no right to annex the incapacitation to the *expulfion* only ; for that, as the propofition ftands, it muft arife equally from the expulfion and the commitment to the Tower. I believe, Sir, no man, who knows any thing of dialectics, or who underftands Englifh, will difpute the truth and fairnefs of this conftruction. But *Junius* has a great authority to fupport him; which, to fpeak with the Duke of Grafton, I accidentally met with

this

this morning in the courfe of my reading. It contains an admonition, which cannot be repeated
too often.   Lord Sommers, in his excellent Tract
upon the Rights of the People, after reciting the
votes of the convention of the 28th of January
1689, viz.—" That King James the Second, ha-
" ving endeavoured to fubvert the conftitution of
" this kingdom, by breaking the original contract
" between King and People; and, by the advice of
" Jefuits and other wicked perfons, having violated
" the laws, and having withdrawn himfelf out of
" this kingdom, hath abdicated the government,
" &c."—makes this obfervation upon it : " The
" word *abdicated* relates to *all* the claufes aforego-
" ing, as well as to his deferting the kingdom, or
" elfe they would have been wholly in vain." And,
that there might be no pretence for confining the
*abdication* merely to the *withdrawing*, Lord Sommers farther obferves, *That King James, by refufing
to govern us according to that law by which he held
the crown, did implicitly renounce his title to it.*

If *Junius*'s conftruction of the vote againft Mr
Walpole be now admitted, (and indeed I cannot
comprehend how it can honeftly be difputed), the
advocates of the houfe of commons muft either
give up their precedent entirely, or be reduced to
the neceffity of maintaining one of the groffeft abfurdities imaginable, viz. " That a commitment to
" the Tower is a conftituent part of, and contri-
" butes half at leaft to, the incapacitation of the
" perfon who fuffers it."

I need not make you any excufe for endeavouring to keep alive the attention of the public to the
decifion of the Middlefex election.   The more I
confider it, the more I am convinced, that, as a
*fact*, it is indeed highly injurious to the rights of
the people ; but that, as a *precedent*, it is one of
the moft dangerous that ever was eftablifhed againft
thofe who are to come after us.   Yet I am fo far

a moderate man, that I verily believe the majority of the houfe of commons, when they paffed this dangerous vote, neither underftood the queftion, nor knew the confequence of what they were doing. Their motives were rather defpicable, than criminal in the extreme. One effect they certainly did not forefee. They are now reduced to fuch a fituation, that if a member of the prefent houfe of commons were to conduct himfelf ever fo improperly, and in reality deferve to be fent back to his conftituents with a mark of difgrace, they would not dare to expel him ; becaufe they know that the people, in order to try again the great queftion of right, or to thwart an odious houfe of commons, would probably overlook his immediate unworthinefs, and return the fame perfon to parliament.—But, in time, the precedent will gain ftrength. A future houfe of commons will have no fuch apprehenfions, confequently will not fcruple to follow a precedent which they did not eftablifh. The mifer himfelf feldom lives to enjoy the fruit of his extortion ; but his heir fucceeds to him of courfe, and takes poffeffion without cenfure. No man expects him to make reftitution ; and, no matter for his title, he lives quietly upon the eftate.

P H I L O   J U N I U S.

---

## LETTER XLVII.

### TO THE PRINTER OF THE PUBLIC ADVER-TISER.

SIR,                             MAY 25. 1771.

I CONFESS my partiality to *Junius*, and feel a confiderable pleafure in being able to communicate any thing to the public in fupport of his opinions. The doctrine laid down in his laft letter, concerning the power of the houfe of commons to commit for contempt, is not fo new as it

appeared

appeared to many people ; who, dazzled with the name of *privilege*, had never fuffered themfelves to examine the queftion fairly. *In the courfe of my reading this morning*, I met with the following paffage in the Journals of the Houfe of Commons, (Vol. I. page 603.) Upon occafion of a jurifdiction unlawfully affumed by the houfe in the year 1621, Mr Attorney General *Noye* gave his opinion as follows : " No doubt but, in fome cafes, this " houfe may give judgment;—in matters of re- " turns, and concerning members of our houfe, " or falling out in our view in parliament; but, " for foreign matters, knoweth not how we can " judge it.—Knoweth not that we have been ufed " to give judgment in any cafe, but thofe before- " mentioned."

Sir Edward Coke, upon the fame fubject, fays, (page 604.) " No queftion but this is a houfe of " record, and that it hath power of judicature in " fome cafes ;—have power to judge of returns " and members of our houfe ; one, no member, " offending out of the parliament, *when he came* " *hither and juftified it*, was cenfured for it."

Now, Sir, if you will compare the opinion of thefe great fages of the law with *Junius*'s doctrine, you will find they tally exactly.—He allows the power of the houfe to commit their own members; (which, however, they may grofsly abufe :) He allows their power in cafes where they are acting as a court of judicature, viz. elections, returns, &c :—And he allows it in fuch contempts as immediately interrupt their proceedings ; or, as Mr Noye expreffes it, *falling out in their view in parliament*.

They who would carry the privileges of parliament farther than *Junius*, either do not mean well to the public, or know not what they are doing. The government of England is a government of law. We betray ourfelves, we contradict the fpirit

rit of our laws, and we fhake the whole fyftem of English jurifprudence, whenever we intruft a difcretionary power over the life, liberty, or fortune of the fubject, to any man or fet of men whatfoever, upon a prefumption that it will not be abufed.

PHILO JUNIUS.

---

## LETTER XLVIII.

TO THE PRINTER OF THE PUBLIC ADVERTISER.

SIR,                                MAY 28. 1771.

ANY man, who takes the trouble of perufing the journals of the houfe of commons, will foon be convinced, that very little, if any regard at all, ought to be paid to the refolutions of one branch of the legiflature, declaratory of the law of the land, or even of what they call the law of parliament. It will appear that thefe refolutions have no one of the properties, by which, in this country particularly, *law* is diftinguifhed from mere *will* and *pleafure;* but that, on the contrary, they bear every mark of a power arbitrarily affumed, and capriciously applied:—That they are ufually made in times of conteft, and to ferve fome unworthy purpofe of paffion or party;—that the law is feldom declared until *after* the fact by which it is fuppofed to be violated;—that legiflation and jurifdiction are united in the fame perfons, and exercifed at the fame moment;—and that a court, from which there is no appeal, affumes an *original* jurifdiction in a criminal cafe: in fhort, Sir, to collect a thoufand abfurdities into one mafs, " we " have a law, which cannot be known becaufe it " is *ex poft facto*, the party is both legiflator and " judge, and the jurifdiction is without appeal." Well might the judges fay, *The law of parliament is above us.*

You

You will not wonder, Sir, that, with thefe qualifications, the declaratory refolutions of the houfe of commons fhould appear to be in perpetual contradiction, not only to common fenfe and to the laws we are acquainted with, (and which alone we can obey), but even to one another. I was led to trouble you with thefe obfervations by a paffage, which, to fpeak in luteftring, *I met with this morning in the courfe of my reading*, and upon which I mean to put a queftion to the advocates for privilege.—— On the 8th of March 1704, (*vide* Journals, Vol. XIV. p. 565.) the houfe thought proper to come to the following refolutions.—1. "That no " commoner of England, committed by the houfe " of commons for breach of privilege, or contempt " of that houfe, ought to be, by any writ of *Ha-* " *beas Corpus*, made to appear in any other place, " or before any other judicature, during that fef- " fion of parliament wherein fuch perfon was fo " committed."

2. "That the Serjeant at Arms, attending this " houfe, do make no return of or yield any obe- " dience to the faid writs of *Habeas Corpus;* and, " for fuch his refufal, that he have the protection " of the houfe of commons *."

Welbore Ellis, What fay you? Is this the law of parliament, or is it not? I am a plain man, Sir, and cannot follow you through the phlegmatic forms of an oration. Speak out, Grildrig; fay yes, or no.—If you fay *yes*, I fhall then inquire by what

autho-

---

* If there be in reality any fuch law in England as the *law of parliament*, which (under the exceptions ftated in my letter on privilege) I confefs, after long deliberation, I very much doubt, it certainly is not conftituted by, nor can it be collected from, the refolutions of either houfe, whether *enacting* or *declaratory*. I defire the reader will compare the above refolution of the year 1704, with the following of the 3d of April 1628.—"*Refolved*, That " the writ of Habeas Corpus cannot be denied, but ought to be " granted to *every* man that is committed or detained in prifon, or " otherwife reftrained, by the command of the King, the Privy " Council, *or any other*, he praying the fame."

authority Mr De Grey, the honeſt Lord Mansfield, and the Barons of the Exchequer, dared to grant a writ of *Habeas Corpus* for bringing the bodies of the Lord Mayor and Mr Oliver before them; and why the Lieutenant of the Tower made any return to a writ, which the houſe of commons had, in a ſimilar inſtance, declared to be unlawful.—If you ſay *no*, take care you do not at once give up the cauſe in ſupport of which you have ſo long and ſo laborioufly tortured your underſtanding. Take care you do not confeſs that there is no teſt by which we can diſtinguiſh,—no evidence by which we can determine, what is, and what is not, the law of parliament. The reſolutions I have quoted ſtand upon your journals, uncontroverted and unrepealed:—they contain a declaration of the law of parliament by a court competeht to the queſtion, and whoſe deciſion, as you and Lord Mansfield ſay, muſt be law, becauſe there is no appeal from it; and they were made, not haſtily, but after long deliberation upon a conſtitutional queſtion. —What farther ſanction or ſolemnity will you annex to any reſolution of the preſent houſe of commons, beyond what appears upon the face of thoſe two reſolutions, the legality of which you now deny? If you ſay that parliaments are not infallible; and that Queen Anne, in conſequence of the violent proceedings of that houſe of commons, was obliged to prorogue and diſſolve them; I ſhall agree with you very heartily, and think that the precedent ought to be followed immediately. But you, Mr Ellis, who hold this language, are inconſiſtent with your own principles. You have hitherto maintained that the houſe of commons are the ſole judges of their own privileges, and that their declaration does *ipſo faſto* conſtitute the law of parliament: yet now you confeſs that parliaments are fallible, and that their reſolutions may be illegal; conſequently that their reſolutions *do*



*net*

*not* conftitute the law of parliament. When the
King was urged to diffolve the prefent parliament,
you advifed him to tell his fubjects, that *he was
careful not to affume any of thofe powers which the
conftitution had placed in other hands,* &c. Yet
Queen Anne, it feems, was juftified in exerting
her prerogative to ftop a houfe of commons, whofe
proceedings, compared with thofe of the affembly
of which you are a moft worthy member, were the
perfection of juftice and reafon.

In what a labyrinth of nonfenfe does a man involve himfelf who labours to maintain falfehood
by argument? How much better would it become
the dignity of the houfe of commons to fpeak plainly to the people, and tell us at once, *that their will
muft be obeyed, not becaufe it is lawful and reafonable, but becaufe it is their will?* Their conftituents
would have a better opinion of their candour, and,
I promife you, not a worfe opinion of their integrity.

**PHILO JUNIUS.**

---

## LETTER XLIX.

TO HIS GRACE THE DUKE OF GRAFTON.

My Lord,                              JUNE 22. 1771.
THE profound refpect I bear to the gracious
Prince who governs this country with no lefs
honour to himfelf than fatisfaction to his fubjects,
and who reftores you to your rank under his ftandard, will fave you from a multitude of reproaches.
The attention I fhould have paid to your failings
is involuntarily attracted to the hand that rewards
them; and though I am not fo partial to the royal
judgment, as to affirm, that the favour of a King
can remove mountains of infamy, it ferves to leffen at leaft, for undoubtedly it divides, the burden.
While I remember how much is due to *his* facred

Z

cha-

character, I cannot, with any decent appearance of propriety, call you the meanest and the basest fellow in the kingdom. I protest, my Lord, I do not think you so. You will have a dangerous rival in that kind of fame to which you have hitherto so happily directed your ambition, as long as there is one man living who thinks you worthy of his confidence, and fit to be trusted with any share in his government. I confess you have great intrinsic merit; but take care you do not value it too highly. Consider how much of it would have been lost to the world, if the King had not graciously affixed his stamp, and given it currency among his subjects. If it be true that a virtuous man, struggling with adversity, be a scene worthy of the gods, the glorious contention between you and the best of Princes deserves a circle equally attentive and respectable : I think I already see other gods rising from the earth to behold it.

But this language is too mild for the occasion. The King is determined that our abilities shall not be lost to society. The perpetration and description of new crimes will find employment for us both. My Lord, if the persons who have been loudest in their professions of patriotism, had done their duty to the public with the same zeal and perseverance that I did, I will not assert that government would have recovered its dignity, but at least our gracious Sovereign must have spared his subjects this last insult *; which, if there be any feeling left among us, they will resent more than even the real injuries they received from every measure of your Grace's administration. In vain would he have looked round him for another character so consummate as yours. Lord Mansfield shrinks from his principles;—his ideas of government perhaps go farther than your own, but his heart disgraces the theory of his understanding.—
Charles

---

* The Duke was lately appointed Lord Privy Seal.

Charles Fox is yet in bloffom; and as for Mr Wedderburne, there is fomething about him which even treachery cannot truft. For the prefent, therefore, the beft of Princes muft have contented himfelf with Lord Sandwich.—You would long fince have received your final difmiffion and reward; and I, my Lord, who do not efteem you the more for the high office you poffefs, would willingly have followed you to your retirement. There is furely fomething fingularly benevolent in the character of our Sovereign. From the moment he afcended the throne, there is no crime, of which human nature is capable, (and I call upon the Recorder to witnefs it), that has not appeared venial in his fight. With any other Prince, the fhameful defertion of him in the midft of that diftrefs which you alone had created,—in the very crifis of danger, when he fancied he faw the throne already furrounded by men of virtue and abilities, would have outweighed the memory of your former fervices. But his Majefty is full of juftice, and underftands the doctrine of compenfations. He remembers with gratitude how foon you had accommodated your morals to the neceffity of his fervice;—how cheerfully you had abandoned the engagements of private friendfhip, and renounced the moft folemn profeffions to the public. The facrifice of Lord Chatham was not loft upon him. Even the cowardice and perfidy of deferting him may have done you no differvice in his efteem. The inftance was painful, but the principle might pleafe.

You did not neglect the magiftrate, while you flattered the *man*. The expulfion of Mr Wilkes, predetermined in the cabinet;—the power of depriving the fubject of his birthright, attributed to a refolution of one branch of the legiflature;—the conftitution impudently invaded by the houfe of commons;—the right of defending it treacheroufly



re-

renounced by the houfe of lords—thefe are the ftrokes, my Lord, which, in the prefent reign, recommend to office, and conftitute a minifter. They would have determined your Sovereign's judgment, if they had made no impreffion upon his heart. We need not look for any other fpecies of merit to account for his taking the earlieft opportunity to recal you to his councils. Yet you have other merit in abundance.——Mr Hine,—the Duke of Portland,—and Mr Yorke :—Breach of truft, robbery, and murder. You would think it a compliment to your gallantry, if I added rape to the catalogue ;—but the ftyle of your amours fecures you from refiftance. I know how well thefe feveral charges have been defended. In the firft inftance, the breach of truft is fuppofed to have been its own reward. Mr Bradfhaw affirms upon his honour, (and fo may the gift of fmiling never depart from him!) that you referved no part of Mr Hine's purchafe-money for your own ufe, but that every fhilling of it was fcrupuloufly paid to Governor Burgoyne.—Make hafte, my Lord ;—another patent, applied in time, may keep the OAKS* in the family.—If not, Birnham-Wood, I fear, muft come to the *Macaroni*.

The Duke of Portland was in life your earlieft friend. In defence of his property he had nothing to plead but equity againft Sir James Lowther, and prefcription againft the crown. You felt for your friend ; *but the law muft take its courfe*. Pofterity will fcarce believe that Lord Bute's fon-in-law had barely intereft enough at the treafury to get his grant completed before the general election †.

Enough

* A fuperb villa of Col. Burgoyne, about this time advertifed for fale.

† It will appear by a fubfequent letter, that the Duke's precipitation proved fatal to the grant. It looks like the hurry and confufion of a young highwayman, who takes a few fhillings, but leaves the purfe and watch behind him :—And yet the Duke was an old offender!

Enough has been said of that detestable transaction which ended in the death of Mr Yorke;
—I cannot speak of it without horror and compassion. To excuse yourself, you publicly impeach
your accomplice; and to *his* mind perhaps the accusation may be flattery. But in murder you are
both principals. It was once a question of emulation; and, if the event had not disappointed the
immediate schemes of the closet, it might still have
been a hopeful subject of jest and merriment between you.

This letter, my Lord, is only a preface to my
future correspondence. The remainder of the sum-
mer shall be dedicated to your amusement. I mean
now and then to relieve the severity of your morning studies, and to prepare you for the business of
the day. Without pretending to more than Mr
Bradshaw's sincerity, you may rely upon my attachment as long as you are in office.

Will your Grace forgive me, if I venture to express some anxiety for a man whom I know you
do not love? My Lord Weymouth has cowardice
to plead, and a desertion of a later date than your
own. You know the privy-seal was intended for
him; and, if you consider the dignity of the post
he deserted, you will hardly think it decent to quarter him on Mr Rigby. Yet he must have bread,
my Lord;—or rather he must have wine. If you
deny him the cup, there will be no keeping him
within the pale of the ministry. JUNIUS.

---

## LETTER L.

### TO HIS GRACE THE DUKE OF GRAFTON.

My Lord, July 9. 1771.

THE influence of your Grace's fortune still seems
to preside over the treasury.—The genius of



Mr

Mr Bradſhaw inſpires Mr Robinſon *. How remarkable it is, (and I ſpeak of it not as matter of reproach, but as ſomething peculiar to your character,) that you have never yet formed a friendſhip which has not been fatal to the object of it; nor adopted a cauſe, to which, one way or other, you have not done miſchief! Your attachment is infamy while it laſts; and, whichever way it turns, leaves ruin and diſgrace behind it. The deluded girl who yields to ſuch a profligate, even while he is conſtant, forfeits her reputation as well as her innocence, and finds herſelf abandoned at laſt to miſery and ſhame.—Thus it happened with the beſt of Princes. Poor Dingley too!—I proteſt I hardly know which of them we ought moſt to lament;—the unhappy man who ſinks under the ſenſe of his diſhonour, or him who ſurvives it. Characters, ſo finiſhed, are placed beyond the reach of panegyric. Death has fixed his ſeal upon Dingley; and you, my Lord, have ſet your mark upon the other.

The only letter I ever addreſſed to the King was ſo unkindly received, that I believe I ſhall never preſume to trouble his Majeſty in that way again. But my zeal for his ſervice is ſuperior to neglect; and, like Mr Wilkes's patriotiſm, thrives by perſecution. Yet his Majeſty is much addicted to uſeful reading; and, if I am not ill informed, has honoured the *Public Advertiſer* with particular attention. I have endeavoured therefore, and not without ſucceſs, (as perhaps you may remember), to furniſh it with ſuch intereſting and edifying intelligence, as probably would not reach him thro' any other channel. The ſervices you have done the nation,—your integrity in office, and ſignal fidelity to your approved good Maſter, have been

faith-

---

* By an intercepted letter from the Secretary of the Treaſury, it appeared, *that the friends of government were to be very active* in ſupporting the miniſterial nomination of ſheriffs.

faithfully recorded.    Nor have his own virtues
been entirely neglected.    These letters, my Lord,
are read in other countries and in other languages;
and I think I may affirm without vanity, that the
gracious character of the best of Princes, is by this
time not only perfectly known to his subjects, but
tolerably well understood by the rest of Europe.
In this respect alone I have the advantage of Mr
Whitehead.  His plan, I think, is too narrow.  He
seems to manufacture his verses for the sole use
of the hero who is supposed to be the subject of
them; and, that his meaning may not be export-
ed in foreign bottoms, sets all translation at defiance.

Your Grace's re-appointment to a seat in the
cabinet, was announced to the public by the ominous return of Lord Bute to this country.  When
that noxious planet approaches England, he never
fails to bring plague and pestilence along with
him.  The King already feels the malignant effect of your influence over his counsels.  Your
former administration made Mr Wilkes an alderman of London, and representative of Middlesex.
Your next appearance in office is marked with his
election to the shrievalty.  In whatever measure
you are concerned, you are not only disappointed
of success, but always contrive to make the government of the best of Princes contemptible in
his own eyes, and ridiculous to the whole world.
Making all due allowance for the effect of the minister's declared interposition, Mr Robinson's activity, and Mr Horne's new zeal in support of administration, we still want the genius of the Duke
of Grafton to account for committing the whole
interest of government in the city to the conduct
of Mr Harley.  I will not bear hard upon your
faithful friend and emissary Mr Touchit; for I
know the difficulties of his situation, and that a
few lottery-tickets are of use to his œconomy.
There

There is a proverb concerning perfons in the predicament of this gentleman, which, however, cannot be ftrictly applied to him : *They commence dupes,
and finifh knaves.* Now Mr Touchit's character is
uniform. I am convinced that his fentiments never
depended upon his circumftances, and that in the
moft profperous ftate of his fortune he was always
the very man he is at prefent.—But was there no
other perfon of rank and confequence in the city,
whom government could confide in, but a notorious Jacobite ? Did you imagine that the whole
body of the Diffenters, that the whole Whig intereft of London, would attend at the levee, and
fubmit to the directions, of a notorious Jacobite ?
Was there no Whig magiftrate in the city, to
whom the fervants of George the Third could intruft the management of a bufinefs fo very interefting to their mafter as the election of fheriffs ?
Is there no room at St James's but for Scotchmen
and Jacobites ? My Lord, I do not mean to queftion the fincerity of Mr Harley's attachment to
his Majefty's government. Since the commencement of the prefent reign, I have feen ftill greater
contradictions reconciled. The principles of thefe
worthy Jacobites are not fo abfurd as they have
been reprefented. Their ideas of divine right are
not fo much annexed to the perfon or family, as
to the political character of the Sovereign. Had
there ever been an honeft man among the *Stuarts*,
his Majefty's prefent friends would have been
Whigs upon principle. But the converfion of the
beft of Princes have removed their fcruples. They
have forgiven him the fins of his Hanoverian anceftors, and acknowledge the hand of Providence
in the defcent of the crown upon the head of a
true *Stuart*. In you, my Lord, they also behold,
with a kind of predilection which borders upon
loyalty, the natural reprefentative of that illuftrious family. The mode of your defcent from
Charles

Charles the Second, is only a bar to your pretenfions to the crown, and no way interrupts the re-
gularity of your fucceffion to all the virtues of the
*Stuarts.*

The unfortunate fuccefs of the Reverend Mr
Horne's endeavours, in fupport of the minifterial
nomination of fheriffs, will, I fear, obftruct his
preferment. Permit me to recommend him to your
Grace's protection. You will find him copioufly
gifted with thofe qualities of the heart, which u-
fually direct you in the choice of your friendfhips.
He too was Mr Wilkes's friend, and as incapable
as you are of the liberal refentment of a gentleman. No, my Lord—it was the folitary vindictive
malice of a monk, brooding over the infirmities of
his friend until he thought they quickened into
public life, and feafting with a rancorous rapture
upon the fordid catalogue of his diftreffes. Now
let him go back to his cloifter. The church is a
proper retreat for him. In his principles he is already a bifhop.

The mention of this man has moved me from
my natural moderation. Let me return to your
Grace. You are the pillow upon which I am determined to reft all my refentments. What idea
can the beft of Sovereigns form to himfelf of his
own government ?—In what repute can he conceive that he ftands with his people, when he fees,
beyond the poffibility of a doubt, that, whatever
be the office, the fufpicion of his favour is fatal to
the candidate ; and that when the party he wifhes
well to has the faireft profpect of fuccefs, if his
royal inclination fhould unfortunately be difcovered, it drops like an acid, and turns the election ?

This event, among others, may perhaps contribute to open his Majefty's eyes to his real honour and intereft. In fpite of all your Grace's ingenuity, he may at laft perceive the inconvenience
of felecting, with fuch a curious felicity, every
villain

villain in the nation to fill the various departments of his government. Yet I should be sorry to confine him in the choice either of his footmen or his friends.　　　　JUNIUS.

---

## LETTER LI.

FROM THE REVEREND MR HORNE TO JUNIUS.

SIR,　　　　　　　　　　　　· JULY 13. 1771·

*F*ARCE, *Comedy, and Tragedy—Wilkes, Foote,* and *Junius,* united at the same time against one poor Parson, are fearful odds. The two former are only labouring in their vocation; and may equally plead in excuse, that their aim is a livelihood. I admit the plea for the *second;* his is an honest calling, and my clothes were lawful game: but I cannot so readily approve Mr Wilkes, or commend him for making patriotism a trade, and a fraudulent trade. But what shall I say to *Junius?* the grave, the solemn, the didactic! Ridicule indeed has been ridiculously called the test of truth; but surely, to confess that you lose your *natural moderation* when mention is made of the man, does not promise much truth or justice when you speak of him yourself.

You charge me with " a new zeal in support " of administration," and with " endeavours in " support of the ministerial nomination of she- " riffs." The reputation which your talents have deservedly gained to the signature of *Junius,* draws from me a reply, which I disdained to give to the anonymous lies of Mr Wilkes. You make frequent use of the word *Gentleman;* I only call myself a *Man,* and desire no other distinction: If you are either, you are bound to make good your charges, or to confess that you have done me a hasty injustice upon no authority.

I put the matter fairly to issue.—I say, that so
far

far from any " new zeal in support of adminiſtration," I am poſſeſſed with the utmoſt abhorrence
of their meaſures; and that I have ever ſhown
myſelf, and am ſtill ready, in any national manner, to lay down all I have—my life, in oppoſition to thoſe meaſures. I ſay, that I have not,
and never have had, any communication or connection of any kind, directly or indirectly, with
any courtier or miniſterial man, or any of their
adherents: that I never have received, or ſolicited,
or expected, or deſired, or do now hope for, any
reward of any ſort, from any party or ſet of men
in adminiſtration or oppoſition. I ſay, that I never
uſed any " endeavours in ſupport of the miniſte-
" rial nomination of ſheriffs;" that I did not ſolicit any one liveryman for his vote for any one of
the candidates, nor employ any other perſon to ſolicit; and that I did not write one ſingle line or
word in favour of Meſſrs Plumbe and Kirkman,
whom I underſtand to have been ſupported by the
miniſtry.——

You are bound to refute what I here advance,
or to loſe your credit for veracity. You muſt produce facts: ſurmiſe and general abuſe, in however elegant language, ought not to paſs for proofs.
You have every advantage; and I have every diſ-
advantage: you are unknown; I give my name.
All parties, both in and out of adminiſtration, have
their reaſons (which I ſhall relate hereafter) for u-
niting in their wiſhes againſt me; and the popular prejudice is as ſtrongly in your favour, as it is
violent againſt the Parſon.

Singular as my preſent ſituation is, it is neither
painful, nor was it unforeſeen. He is not fit for
public buſineſs, who does not even at his entrance
prepare his mind for ſuch an event. Health, fortune, tranquillity, and private connections, I have
ſacrificed upon the altar of the Public; and the
only return I receive, becauſe I will not concur to

dupe

dupe and miſlead a ſenſeleſs multitude, is barely, that they have not yet torn me in pieces. That this has been the only return is my pride, and a ſource of more real ſatisfaction than honours or proſperity. I can practiſe, before I am old, the leſſons I learned in my youth; nor ſhall I ever forget the words of my ancient Monitor,

    " 'Tis the laſt key-ſtone
" That makes the arch: the reſt that there were put
" Are nothing, till that comes to bind and ſhut:
" Then ſtands it a triumphal mark! then men
" Obſerve the ſtrength, the height, the why and
  " when
" It was erected; and ſtill, walking under,
" Meet ſome new matter to look up and wonder!

  I am, Sir, your humble Servant,
     JOHN HORNE.

---

## LETTER LII.

### TO THE REVEREND MR HORNE.

SIR,       JULY 24. 1771.

I Cannot deſcend to an altercation with you in the newſpapers: but ſince I have attacked your character, and you complain of injuſtice, I think you have ſome right to an explanation. You defy me to prove that you ever ſolicited a vote, or wrote a word, in ſupport of the miniſterial aldermen. Sir, I did never ſuſpect you of ſuch groſs folly. It would have been impoſſible for Mr Horne to have ſolicited votes, and very difficult to have written in the newſpapers in defence of that cauſe, without being detected and brought to ſhame. Neither do I pretend to any intelligence concerning you, or to know more of your conduct than you yourſelf have thought proper to communicate to the public. It is from your own letters I con-

clude that you have sold yourself to the miniftry;
or if that charge be too fevere, and fuppofing it
poffible to be deceived by appearances fo very
ftrongly againft you, what are your friends to fay
in your defence? Muft they not confefs, that, to
gratify your perfonal hatred of Mr Wilkes, you
facrificed, as far as depended on *your* intereft and
abilities, the caufe of the country? I can make
allowance for the violence of the paffions; and if
ever I fhould be convinced that you had no motive
but to deftroy Wilkes, I fhall then be ready to do
juftice to your character, and to declare to the
world, that I defpife you fomewhat lefs than I do
at prefent. But as a public man, I muft for ever
condemn you. You cannot but know,—nay you
dare not pretend to be ignorant, that the higheft
gratification of which the moft deteftable  *  *
in this nation is capable, would have been the defeat of Wilkes. I know *that man* much better than
any of you. Nature intended him only for a good-
humoured fool. A fyftematical education, with
long practice, has made him a confummate hypocrite. Yet this man, to fay nothing of his worthy
minifters, you have moft affiduoufly laboured to
gratify. To exclude Wilkes, it was not neceffary
you fhould folicit votes for his opponents. We
incline the balance as effectually by leffening the
weight in one fcale, as by increafing it in the
other.

The mode of your attack upon Wilkes (though
I am far from thinking meanly of your abilities)
convinces me, that you either want judgment extremely, or that you are blinded by your refentment. You ought to have forefeen, that the charges you urged againft Wilkes could never do him
any mifchief. After all, when we expected dif-
coveries highly interefting to the community, what
a pitiful detail did it end in!—Some old cloaths—
a Welfh poney—a French footman, and a hamper



of

of claret. Indeed, Mr Horne, the public fhould, and *will* forgive him his claret and his footman, and even the ambition of making his brother chamberlain of London, as long as he ftands forth againft a miniftry and parliament who are doing every thing they can to enflave the country, and as long as he is a thorn in the King's fide. You will not fufpect me as fetting up Wilkes for a perfect character. The queftion to the public is, Where fhall we find a man, who, with purer principles, will go the lengths and run the hazards that he has done? The feafon calls for fuch a man, and he ought to be fupported. What would have been the triumph of that odious hypocrite and his minions, if *Wilkes* had been defeated! It was not *your* fault, reverend Sir, that he did not enjoy it completely.—But now, I promife you, you have fo little power to do mifchief, that I much queftion whether the miniftry will adhere to the promifes they have made you. It will be in vain to fay that I am a partizan of Mr Wilkes, or perfonally your enemy. You will convince no man, for you do not believe it yourfelf. Yet I confefs I am a little offended at the low rate at which you feem to value my underftanding. I beg, Mr Horne, you will hereafter believe, that I meafure the integrity of men by their conduct, not by their profeffions. Such tales may entertain Mr Oliver, or your grandmother; but, truft me, they are thrown away upon *Junius.*

You fay you are a *man.* Was it generous, was it manly, repeatedly to introduce into a newfpaper the name of a young lady, with whom you muft heretofore have lived on terms of politenefs and good-humour?—But I have done with you. In *my* opinion, your credit is irrecoverably ruined. Mr *Townfhend,* I think, is nearly in the fame predicament. Poor *Oliver* has been fhamefully duped by you. You have made him facrifice all the honour he got by his imprisonment. As for Mr *Sawbridge*, whose character I really respect, I am astonished he does not see through your duplicity. Never was so base a design so poorly conducted.—— This letter, you see, is not intended for the public; but if you think it will do you any service, you are at liberty to publish it.    JUNIUS.

*** This letter was transmitted privately by the Printer to Mr Horne, by Junius's request. Mr Horne returned it to the Printer, with directions to publish it.

---

## LETTER LIII.

### FROM THE REVEREND MR HORNE TO JUNIUS.

SIR,                 JULY 31. 1771.

YOU have disappointed me. When I told you, that surmise and general abuse, in however elegant language, ought not to pass for proofs, I evidently hinted at the reply which I expected: but you have dropped your usual elegance, and seem willing to try what will be the effect of surmise and general abuse in very coarse language. Your answer to my letter (which I hope was cool, and temperate, and modest) has convinced me, that my idea of a *man* is much superior to yours of a *gentleman*. Of your former letters I have always said, *Materiem superabat opus:* I do not think so of the present; the principles are more detestable than the expressions are mean and illiberal. I am contented, that all those who adopt the one should for ever load me with the other.

I appeal to the common sense of the public, to which I have ever directed myself: I believe they have it, though I am sometimes half-inclined to suspect that Mr Wilkes has formed a truer judgement of mankind than I have. However, of this I am sure, that there is nothing else upon which to place a steady reliance. Trick, and low cunning,

A a 2

'ning,

ning, and addreffing their prejudices and paffions, may be the fitteft means to carry a particular point; but if they have not common-fenfe, there is no profpect of gaining for them any real permanent good. The fame paffions which have been artful- ly ufed by an honeft man for their advantage, may be more artfully employed by a difhoneft man for their deftruction. I defire them to apply their common-fenfe to this letter of *Junius;* not for my fake, but their own : it concerns them moft near- ly ; for the principles it contains lead to difgrace and ruin, and are inconfiftent with every notion of civil fociety.

The charges which *Junius* has brought againft me, are made ridiculous by his own inconfiftency and felf-contradiction. He charges me pofitively with " a new zeal in fupport of adminiftration ;" and with " endeavours in fupport of the minifte- " rial nomination of fheriffs." And he affigns two inconfiftent motives for my conduct : either that I have "*fold* myfelf to the miniftry," or am inftigated " by the folitary vindictive *malice* of a " monk ;" either that I am influenced by a fordid defire of *gain,* or am hurried on by " perfonal *ha-* " *tred,* and blinded by *refentment.*" In his letter to the Duke of Grafton, he fuppofes me actuated by both : in his letter to me, he at firft doubts which of the two, whether intereft, or revenge, is my motive. However, at laft he determines for the former, and again pofitively afferts that " the miniftry have made me promifes :" yet he produces no inftance of corruption, nor pretends to have any intelligence of a minifterial connec- tion. He mentions no *caufe* of a perfonal hatred to Mr Wilkes, nor any *reafon* for my refentment or revenge; nor has Mr Wilkes himfelf ever hint- ed any, though repeatedly preffed. When *Junius* is called upon to juftify his accufation, he an- fwers, " He cannot defcend to an altercation with
" me

" me in the newſpapers." *Junius*, who *exiſts*
only in the newſpapers, who acknowledges " he
" has attacked my character" *there*, and thinks
" I have ſome right to an *explanation ;*" yet this
*Junius* " cannot deſcend to an altercation in the
" newſpapers !" And becauſe he cannot deſcend
to an altercation with me in the newſpapers, he
ſends a letter of abuſe by the printer, which he fi-
niſhes with telling me—" I am at liberty to *pub-*
" *liſh* it." This, to be ſure, is a moſt excellent
method to avoid an altercation in the newſpapers !

The *proofs* of his poſitive charges are as extraordinary : " He does not pretend to any intelli-
" gence concerning me, or to know more of my
" conduct than I myſelf have thought proper to
" communicate to the public." He does not ſuſpect me of ſuch groſs folly as to have ſolicited
votes, or to have written anonymouſly in the newſpapers ; becauſe it is impoſſible to do either of
theſe without being detected and brought to ſhame.
*Junius* ſays this !—who yet imagines that he has
himſelf written two years under that ſignature,
(and more under *others*), without being detected !
—his warmeſt admirers will not hereafter add,
without being brought to ſhame. But though he
did never ſuſpect me of ſuch groſs folly as to run
the *hazard* of being detected and brought to ſhame
by *anonymous* writing, he inſiſts, that I have been
guilty of a much groſſer folly, of incurring the
certainty of ſhame and detection, by writings *ſigned* with my name ! But this is a ſmall flight for
the towering *Junius :* " HE IS FAR from thinking
" meanly of my abilities," though he is " con-
" vinced that I want judgment extremely ;" and
can " really reſpect Mr Sawbridge's character,"
though he declares him * to be ſo poor a creature,

A a 3

as

---

* I beg leave to introduce Mr. Horne to the character of the
*Double*

as not to " see through the bafeft defign conduct-
" ed in the pooreft manner !" And this moft bafe
defign is conducted in the pooreft manner, by
a man whom he does not fufpect of grofs folly,
and of whofe abilities he is FAR from thinking
meanly !

Should we afk *Junius* to reconcile thefe contradictions, and explain this nonfenfe, the anfwer
is ready;—" He cannot defcend to an altercation
" in the newfpapers." He feels no reluctance to
attack the character of any man: the throne is not
too high, nor the cottage too low: his mighty
malice can grafp both extremes: he hints not his
accufations as *opinion, conjecture*, or *inference*, but
delivers them as *pofitive affertions*. Do the accufed complain of injuftice? He acknowledges they
have fome fort of right to an *explanation :* but if
they afk for *proofs* and *facts*, he begs to be excu-
fed ; and though he is no where elfe to be encountered—" he cannot defcend to an altercation in
" the newfpapers."

And this, perhaps, *Junius* may think " the *li-*
" *beral refentment of a gentleman :*" This fkulking
affaffination he may call courage. In all things, as
in this, I hope we differ.

" I thought that fortitude had been a mean
" 'Twixt fear and rafhnefs; not a luft obfcene
" Or

*Double Dealer.* I thought they had been better acquainted.—" A-
" nother very wrong objection has been made by fome, who have
" not taken leifure to diftinguifh the characters. The hero of the
" play (meaning *Mellefont*) is a gull, and made a fool, and cheat-
" ed.——Is every man a gull and a fool that is deceived ?——At
" that rate, I am afraid the two claffes of men will be reduced to
" one, and the knaves themfelves be at a lofs to juftify their title.
" But if an open honeft-hearted man, who has an entire confidence
" in one whom he takes to be his friend, and who (to confirm
" him in his opinion) in all appearance, and upon feveral trials,
" has been fo ; if this man be deceived by the treachery of the o-
" ther, muft he of neceffity commence fool immediately, only be-
" caufe the other has proved a villain ?"——Yes, fays parfon Horne:
No, fays Congreve; and he, I think, is allowed to have known
fome thing of human nature.

" Or appetite of offending ; but a fkill
" And nice difcernment between good and ill.
" Her ends are honefty and public good,
" And without thefe fhe is not underftood."

Of two things, however, he has condefcended
to give proof.  He very properly produces a *young
lady*, to prove that I am not a man ; and a good
*old woman*, my grandmother, to prove Mr Oliver
a fool.   Poor old foul !  fhe read her bible far
otherwife than *Junius !* She often found there,
that the fins of the fathers had been vifited on the
children; and therefore was cautious that herfelf,
and her immediate defcendents, fhould leave no
reproach on her pofterity :  and they left none.
How little could fhe forefee this reverfe of *Junius,*
who vifits my political fins upon my *grandmother !*
I do not charge this to the fcore of malice in him;
it procceded entirely from his propenfity to blun-
der;  that whilft he was reproaching me for introducing, in the moft harmlefs manner, the name
of *one* female, he might himfelf, at the fame inftant, introduce *two.*

I am reprefented alternately, as it fuits *Junius's*
purpofe, under the oppofite characters of a *gloomy
monk,* and a man of *politenefs and good-humour.*   I
am called " *a folitary monk,*" in order to confirm
the notion given of me in Mr Wilkes's anonymous
paragraphs, that I *never laugh.*   And the terms of
*politenefs* and *good-humour,* on which I am faid to
have lived heretofore with the *young lady,* are intended to confirm other paragraphs of Mr Wilkes,
in which he is fuppofed to have offended me by
*refufing his daughter.*   Ridiculous ! Yet I cannot
deny but that *Junius* has proved me *unmanly* and
*ungenerous,* as clearly as he has fhown me *corrupt*
and *vindictive :* and I will tell him more ; I have
paid the prefent miniftry as many *vifits* and *compliments* as ever I paid to the *young lady ;* and fhall
all

all my life treat them with the *same politeness and good-humour.*

But *Junius* " begs me to believe, that he mea-" sures the integrity of men by their *conduct*, not " by their *professions*." Sure this *Junius* must i-magine his readers as void of understanding as he is of modesty! Where shall we find the standard of HIS integrity? By what are we to measure the *conduct* of this lurking assassin?—And he says this to me, whose conduct, wherever I could per-sonally appear, has been as direct, and open, and public, as my words. I have not, like him, con-cealed myself in my chamber, to shoot my arrows out of the window; nor contented myself to view the battle from afar; but publicly mixed in the engagement, and shared the danger. To whom have I, like him, refused my name upon complaint of injury? What printer have I desired to conceal me? In the infinite variety of business in which I have been concerned, where it is not so easy to be faultless, which of my actions can he arraign? To what danger has any man been exposed, which I have not faced? *information, action, imprisonment,* or *death?* What labour have I refused? what ex-pence have I declined? what pleasure have I not renounced?—But *Junius, to whom no conduct be-longs,* " measures the integrity of men by their " *conduct,* not by their professions;" himself all the while being nothing but *professions,* and those too *anonymous!* The political ignorance or wilful falsehood of this *declaimer* is extreme. His own *former* letters justify both my conduct and those whom his *last* letter abuses: for the public mea-sures which *Junius* has been all along defending, were ours whom he attacks; and the uniform op-poser of those measures has been Mr Wilkes, whose bad actions and intentions he endeavours to screen.

Let *Junius* now, if he pleases, change his abuse;

and,

and, quitting his loose hold of *interest* and *revenge,*
accuse me of *vanity,* and call this defence *boasting.*
I own I have a pride to see statues decreed, and
the highest honours conferred, for measures and
actions which all men have approved; whilst those
who counselled and caused them are execrated and
insulted. The darkness in which *Junius* thinks
himself shrouded, has not concealed him; nor the
artifice of only *attacking under that signature those*
he would pull down, (whilst he *recommends by other
ways* those he would have promoted), disguised
from me whose partizan he is. When Lord Chatham can forgive the aukward situation in which,
for the sake of the public, he was designedly placed by the thanks to him from the city; and when
*Wilkes's name* ceases to be necessary to Lord Rockingham to keep up a clamour against the *persons* of
the ministry, without obliging the different factions now in opposition to bind themselves before-
hand to some certain points, and to stipulate some
precise advantages to the public; then, and not
till then, may those whom he now abuses expect
the approbation of *Junius.* The approbation of
the public for our faithful attention to their interest, by endeavours for those stipulations, which
have made us as obnoxious to the factions in opposition as to those in administration, is not perhaps to be expected till some years hence; when
the public will look back, and see how shamefully
they have been deluded, and by what arts they were
made to lose the golden opportunity of preventing
what they will surely experience,—a change of ministers, without a material change of measures, and
without any security for a tottering constitution.

But what cares *Junius* for the security of the
constitution? He has now unfolded to us his dia-
bolical principles. *As a public man, he must ever
condemn any measure which may tend accidentally
to gratify the Sovereign;* and Mr Wilkes is to be
supported

supported and aſſiſted in all his attempts (no matter how ridiculous and miſchievous his projects)
*as long as he continues to be a thorn in the King's
ſide !*—The *cauſe of the country*, it ſeems, in the o-
pinion of *Junius*, is merely to vex the King; and
any raſcal is to be ſupported in any roguery, provided he can only thereby plant *a thorn in the King's
ſide.*—This is the very extremity of faction, and
the laſt degree of political wickedneſs.  Becauſe
Lord Chatham has been ill treated by the King,
and treacherouſly betrayed by the Duke of Grafton, the latter is to be " the pillow on which *Ju-*
" *nius* will reſt his reſentment ;" and the public
are to oppoſe the meaſures of government from
mere motives of perſonal enmity to the Sovereign !
Theſe are the avowed principles of the man who,
in the ſame letter, ſays, " If ever he ſhould be
" convinced that I had no motive but to deſtroy
" Wilkes, he ſhall then be ready to do juſtice to
" my character, and to declare to the world, that
" he deſpiſes me ſomewhat leſs than he does at
" preſent !"   Had I ever acted from perſonal affection or enmity to Mr Wilkes, I ſhould juſtly
be deſpiſed :  but what does he deſerve, whoſe
avowed motive is perſonal enmity to the Sovereign ? The contempt which I ſhould otherwiſe feel
for the abſurdity and glaring inconſiſtency of *Junius*, is here ſwallowed up in my abhorrence of
his principles.  The *right divine* and *ſacredneſs* of
Kings is to me a ſenſeleſs jargon.  It was thought
a daring expreſſion of Oliver Cromwell in the time
of Charles the firſt, that if he found himſelf placed oppoſite to the King in battle, he would diſcharge his piece into his boſom as ſoon as into any
other man's.  I go farther : had I lived in thoſe
days, I would not have waited for chance to give
me an opportunity of doing my duty ; I would
have ſought him through the ranks, and, without
the leaſt perſonal enmity, have diſcharged my
piece

piece into his bosom *rather* than into any other man's. The King whose actions justify rebellion to his government, deserves death from the hand of every subject. And should such a time arrive, I shall be as free to act as to say : but till then, my attachment to the person and family of the Sovereign shall ever be found more zealous and sincere than that of his flatterers. I would offend the Sovereign with as much reluctance as the parent; but if the happiness and security of the whole family made it necessary, so far, and no farther, I would offend him without remorse.

But let us consider a little whither these principles of *Junius* would lead us. Should Mr Wilkes once more commission Mr Thomas Walpole to procure for him a pension of *one thousand pounds* upon the Irish establishment for thirty years, he must be supported in the demand by the public—because it would mortify the King !

Should he wish to see Lord Rockingham and his friends once more in administration, *unclogged by any stipulations for the people*, that he might again enjoy a *pension of one thousand and forty pounds* a-year, viz. from the *first Lord of the Treasury* 500 l. from the *Lords of the Treasury*, 60 l. each, from the *Lords of Trade* 40 l. each, &c. the public must give up their attention to points of national benefit, and assist Mr Wilkes in his attempt—because it would mortify the King !

Should he demand the government of *Canada*, or of *Jamaica*, or the embassy to *Constantinople*, and in case of refusal threaten to write them down, as he had before served another administration, in a year and a half, he must be supported in his pretensions, and upheld in his insolence—because it would mortify the King !

Junius may choose to suppose that these things cannot happen ! But that they have happened, notwithstanding Mr Wilkes's denial, I do aver.

I maintain that Mr Wilkes did commiffion Mr Thomas Walpole to folicit for him a penfion of *one thoufand pounds* on the *Irifh* eftablifhment for *thirty years;* with which, and a pardon, he declared he would be fatisfied: and that, notwithftanding his letter to Mr Onflow, he did accept a *clandeftine, precaricus,* and *eleemofinary* penfion from the Rockingham adminiftration; which they paid in proportion to, and out of their falaries: and fo entirely was it minifterial, that as any of them went out of the miniftry, there names were fcratched out of the lift, and they contributed no longer.   I fay, he did folicit the governments, and the embaffy, and threatened their refufal nearly in thefe words—" It coft me a year and a half to write " down the laft adminiftration; fhould I employ " as much time upon you, very few of you would " be in at the death." When thefe threats did not prevail, he came over to England to embarrafs them by his prefence: and when he found that Lord Rockingham was fomething firmer and more manly than he expected, and refufed to be -bullied—into what he could not perform, Mr Wilkes declared that he could not leave England without money; and the Duke of Portland and Lord Rockingham purchafed his abfence with *one hundred pounds a-piece,* with which he returned to Paris.   And for the truth of what I here advance, I appeal to the Duke of Portland, to Lord Rockingham, to Lord John Cavenifh, to Mr Walpole, &c.—I appeal to the hand-writing of Mr Wilkes, which is ftill extant.

Should Mr Wilkes afterwards (failing in this wholefale trade) choofe to dole out his popularity by the pound, and expofe the city offices to fale to his brother, his attorney, &c. *Junius* will tell us, it is only an *ambition* that he has to make them *chamberlain, town-clerk,* &c. and he muft not be oppofed in thus robbing the ancient citizens of

their

their birthright—becaufe any defeat of Mr Wilkes would gratify the King!

Should he, after confuming the whole of his own fortune, and that of his wife, and incurring a debt of *twenty thoufand pounds*, merely by his own private extravagance, without a fingle fervice or exertion all this time for the public, whilft his eftate remained ;  fhould he at length, being undone, commence patriot, have the good fortune to be illegally perfecuted, and in confideration of that illegality be efpoufed by a few gentlemen of the pureft public principles; fhould his debts (tho' none of them were contracted for the public) and all his other encumbrances be difcharged ; fhould he be offered 600 l. or 1000 l. a-year to make him independent for the future; and fhould he, after all, inftead of gratitude for thefe fervices, infolently forbid his benefactors to beftow their own money upon any other object but himfelf, and revile them for fetting any bounds to their fupplies ; *Junius* (who, any more than Lord Chatham, never contributed one farthing to thefe enormous expences) will tell them, that if they think of converting the fupplies of Mr Wilkes's private extravagance to the fupport of public meafures———they are as great fools as my *grandmother ;* and that Mr Wilkes ought to hold the ftrings of their purfes—*as long as he continues to be a thorn in the King's fide !*

Upon thefe principles I never have acted, and I never will act.  In my opinion, it is lefs difhonourable to be the creature of a court than the tool of a faction.  I will not be either.  I underftand the two great leaders of oppofition to be Lord Rockingham and Lord Chatham; under one of whofe banners, all the oppofing members of both houfes who defire to get places enlift.  I can place no confidence in either of them, or in any others, unlefs they will now engage, whilft they are OUT, to grant certain effential advantages for

the security of the public when they shall be in
administration. These points they refuse to stipulate, because they are fearful left they should
prevent any future overtures from the court. To
force them to these stipulations has been the uniform endeavour of Mr Sawbridge, Mr Townsend,
Mr Oliver, &c. and THEREFORE they are abused
by Junius. I know no reason but my zeal and industry in the same cause, that should intitle me to
the honour of being ranked by his abuse with persons of their fortune and station. It is a duty I
owe to the memory of the late Mr Beckford to
say, that he had no other aim than this, when he
provided that sumptuous entertainement at the
Mansion-house for the members of both houses in
opposition. At that time he drew up the heads of
an engagement, which he gave to me, with a request that I would couch it in terms so cautious
and precise, as to leave no room for future quibble
and evasion; but to oblige them either to fulfil the
intent of the obligation, or to sign their own infamy, and leave it on record: and this engagement he was determined to propose to them at the
Mansion-house, that either by their refusal they
might forfeit the confidence of the public, or by
the engagement lay a foundation for confidence.
When they were informed of the intention, Lord
Rockingham and his friends flatly refused any engagement; and Mr Beckford as flatly swore, they
should then—"eat none of his broth;" and he
was determined to put off the entertainment: But
Mr Beckford was prevailed upon by —— to indulge them in the ridiculous parade of a popular
procession through the city, and to give them the
foolish pleasure of an imaginary consequence, for
the real benefit only of the cooks and purveyors.

It was the same motive which dictated the
thanks of the city to Lord Chatham; which were

ex-

expreffed to be given for his declaration in favour of *fhort parliaments* ; in order thereby to fix Lord Chatham at leaft to that one conftitutional remedy, without which all others can afford no fecurity. The embarraffment, no doubt, was cruel. He had his choice either to offend the Rockingham party, who declared *formally* againft fhort parliaments, and with the affiftance of whofe numbers in both houfes he muft expect again to be minifter; or to give up the confidence of the public, from whom finally all real confequence muft proceed. Lord Chatham chofe the latter: and I will venture to fay, that, by his *anfwer* to thofe thanks, he has given up the people without gaining the friendfhip or cordial affiftance of the Rockingham faction ; whofe little politics are confined to the making of matches, and extending their family connections, and who think they gain more by procuring one additional vote to their party in the houfe of commons, than by adding their languid property and feeble character to the abilities of a *Chatham*, or the confidence of a public.

Whatever may be the event of the prefent wretched ftate of politics in this country, the principles of Junius will fuit no form of government. They are not to be tolerated under any conftitution. Perfonal enmity is a motive fit only for the devil. Whoever, or whatever, is Sovereign, demands the refpect and fupport of the people. The union is formed for their happinefs, which cannot be had without mutual refpect ; and he counfels malicioufly who would perfuade either to a wanton breach of it. When it is banifhed by either party, and when every method has been tried in vain to reftore it, there is no remedy but a divorce: But even then he muft have a hard and a wicked heart indeed who punifhes the greateft criminal merely for the fake of the punifhment; and

                                    who

who does not let fall a tear for every drop of blood
that is fhed in a public ftruggle, however juft the
quarrel.                              JOHN HORNE.

---

## LETTER LIV.

TO THE PRINTER OF THE PUBLIC ADVER-
TISER.

SIR,                              Aug. 15. 1771.

I OUGHT to make an apology to the Duke of
Grafton, for fuffering any part of my attention
to be diverted from his Grace to Mr Horne.  I
am not juftified by the fimilarity of their difpofitions.   Private vices, however deteftable, have not
dignity fufficient to attract the cenfure of the prefs,
unlefs they are united with the power of doing
fome fignal mifchief to the community.—Mr
Horne's fituation does not correfpond with his
intentions.—In my own opinion, (which, I know,
will be attributed to my ufual vanity and prefumption) his letter to me does not deferve an anfwer. But
I underftand that the public are not fatisfied with
my filence;—that an anfwer is expected from me;
and that if I perfift in refufing to plead, it will be
taken for conviction. I fhould be inconfiftent with
the principles I profefs, if I declined an appeal to
the good fenfe of the people, or did not willingly
fubmit myfelf to the judgment of my peers.

If any coarfe expreffions have efcaped me, I am
ready to agree that they are unfit for Junius to
make ufe of; but I fee no reafon to admit that they
have been improperly applied.

Mr Horne, it feems, is unable to comprehend
how an extreme want of conduct and difcretion
can confift with the abilities I have allowed him;
nor can he conceive that a very honeft man, with
a very good underftanding, may be deceived by a
knave.  His knowledge of human nature muft be
limited

limited indeed. Had he never mixed with the world, one would think that even his books might have taught him better. Did he hear Lord Mansfield, when he defended his doctrine concerning libels ?—or when he stated the law in prosecutions for criminal conversation ?—or when he delivered his reasons for calling the house of Lords together to receive a copy of his charge to the jury in Woodfall's trial ?—Had he been present upon any of these occasions, he would have seen how possible it is for a man of the first talents, to confound himself in absurdities, which would disgrace the lips of an idiot. Perhaps the example might have taught him not to value his own understanding so highly.—Lord Lyttleton's integrity and judgment are unquestionable;—yet he is known to admire that cunning Scotchman, and verily believes him an honest man.—I speak to facts, with which all of us are conversant—I speak to men, and to their experience; and will not descend to answer the little sneering sophistries of a collegian. —Distinguished talents are not necessarily connected with discretion. If there be any thing remarkable in the character of Mr Horne, it is that extreme want of judgment should be united with his very moderate capacity. Yet I have not forgotten the acknowledgment I made him. He owes it to my bounty; and, though his letter has lowered him in my opinion, I scorn to retract the charitable donation.

I said it would be *very difficult* for Mr Horne to write directly in defence of a ministerial measure, and not be detected; and even that difficulty I confined to *his* particular situation. He changes the terms of the proposition, and supposes me to assert, that it would be *impossible* for *any* man to write for the newspapers and not be discovered.

He repeatedly affirms, or intimates at least, that he knows the author of these letters.—With

B b 3                                  what

what colour of truth, then, can he pretend *that I
am nowhere to be encountered but in a newspaper?*
—I shall leave him to his suspicions.· It is not
necessary that I should confide in the honour or
discretion of a man who already seems to hate me
with as much rancour as if I had formerly been
his friend.—But he asserts that he has traced me
through a variety of signatures.  To make the dis-
covery of any importance to his purpose, he should
have proved, either that the fictitious character of
*Junius* has not been consistently supported, or that
the author has maintained different principles under different signatures.—I cannot recal to my memory the numberless trifles I have written;—but
I rely upon the consciousness of my own integrity,
and defy him to fix any colourable charge of inconsistency upon me.

I am not bound to assign the secret motives of
his apparent. hatred of Mr Wilkes : nor does it
follow that I may not judge fairly of *his* conduct,
though it were true *that I had no conduct of my
own.*—Mr Horne enlarges with rapture upon the
importance of his services ;—the dreadful battles
which he might have been engaged in, and the
dangers he has escaped.—In support of the formidable description, he quotes verses without mercy.
The gentleman deals in fiction, and naturally appeals to the evidence of the poets.—Taking him
at his word, he cannot but admit the superiority
of Mr Wilkes in this line of service.  On one side,
we see nothing but imaginary distresses.  On the
other, we see real prosecutions;—real penalties;
—real imprisonment;—life repeatedly hazarded ;
and, at one moment, almost the certainty of death.
Thanks are undoubtedly due to every man who
does his duty in the engagement ; but it is the
wounded soldier who deserves the reward.

I did not mean to deny that Mr Horne had been
an active partizan.  It would defeat my own purpose

pose not to allow him a degree of merit, which aggravates his guilt. The very charge *of contributing his utmost efforts to support a ministerial measure*, implies an acknowledgment of his former services. If he had not once been distinguished by his apparent zeal in defence of the common cause, he could not now be distinguished by deserting it.—As for myself, it is no longer a question, *whether I shall mix with the throng, and take a single share in the danger.* Whenever *Junius* appears, he must encounter a host of enemies. But is there no honourable way to serve the public, without engaging in personal quarrels with insignificant individuals, or submitting to the drudgery of canvassing votes for an election? Is there no merit in dedicating my life to the information of my fellow-subjects?—What public question have I declined? What villain have I spared?—Is there no labour in the composition of these letters? Mr Horne, I fear, is partial to me, and measures the facility of *my* writings by the fluency of his own.

He talks to us in high terms of the gallant feats he would have performed if he had lived in the last century. The unhappy Charles could hardly have escaped him. But living princes have a claim to his attachment and respect. Upon these terms, there is no danger in being a patriot. If he means any thing more than a pompous rhapsody, let us try how well his argument holds together.—I presume he is not yet so much a courtier as to affirm that the constitution has not been grossly and daringly violated under the present reign. He will not say, that the laws have not been shamefully broken or perverted;—that the rights of the subject have not been invaded, or that redress has not been repeatedly solicited and refused.—Grievances like these were the foundation of the rebellion in the last century; and, if I understand

Mr

Mr Horne, they would, at that period, have ju-ftified him to his own mind in deliberately attacking the life of his Sovereign. I fhall not afk him to what political conftitution this doctrine can be reconciled. But at leaft it is incumbent upon him to fhow, that the prefent King has better excufes than Charles the Firft for the errors of his government. He ought to demonftrate to us, that the conftitution was better underftood a hundred years ago than it is at prefent;—that the legal rights of the fubject, and the limits of the prerogative, were more accurately defined and more clearly comprehended. If propofitions like thefe cannot be fairly maintained, I do not fee how he can reconcile it to his confcience, not to act immediately with the fame freedom with which he fpeaks. I reverence the character of Charles the Firft as little as Mr Horne; but I will not infult his misfortunes by a comparifon that would degrade him.

It is worth obferving, by what gentle degrees the furious, perfecuting zeal of Mr Horne has foftened into moderation. Men and meafures were yefterday his objects. What pains did he once take to bring that great ftate-criminal *Macquirk* to execution!—To-day he confines himfelf to meafures only.—No penal example is to be left to the fucceffors of the Duke of Grafton.—To-morrow, I prefume, both men and meafures will be forgiven. The flaming patriot, who fo lately fcorched us in the meridian, finks temperately to the weft, and is hardly felt as he defcends.

I comprehend the policy of endeavouring to communicate to Mr Oliver and Mr Sawbridge a fhare in the reproaches with which he fuppofes me to have loaded him. My memory fails me, if I have mentioned their names with difrefpect;—unlefs it be reproachful to acknowledge a fincere refpect for the character of Mr Sawbridge, and

not

not to have queſtioned the innocence of Mr Oliver's intentions.

It ſeems I am a partiſan of the great leader of
the oppoſition. If the charge had been a reproach,
it ſhould have been better ſupported. I did not
intend to make a public declaration of the reſpect
I bear Lord Chatham.— I well knew what unworthy concluſions would be drawn from it. But I
am called upon to deliver my opinion; and ſurely
it is not in the little cenſure of Mr Horne to deter
me from doing ſignal juſtice to a man who, I confeſs, has grown upon my eſteem. As for the common, ſordid views of avarice, or any purpoſe of
vulgar ambition, I queſtion whether the applauſe
of *Junius* would be of ſervice to Lord Chatham.
*My* vote will hardly recommend him to an increaſe
of his penſion, or to a ſeat in the cabinet. But if
his ambition be upon a level with his underſtanding;—if he judges of what is truly honourable for
himſelf, with the ſame ſuperior genius which animates and directs him to eloquence in debate, to
wiſdom in deciſion, even the pen of Junius ſhall
contribute to reward him. Recorded honours ſhall
gather round his monument, and thicken over
him. It is a ſolid fabric, and will ſupport the lau-
rels that adorn it.—I am not converſant in the language of panegyric.—Theſe praiſes are extorted
from me; but they will wear well, for they have
been dearly earned.

My deteſtation of the Duke of Grafton is not
founded upon his treachery to any individual:
though I am willing enough to ſuppoſe, that, in
public affairs, it would be impoſſible to deſert or
betray Lord Chatham, without doing an eſſential
injury to this country. My abhorrence of the
Duke ariſes from an intimate knowledge of his
character; and from a thorough conviction that
his baſeneſs has been the cauſe of greater miſchief

to England, than even the unfortunate ambition of Lord Bute.

The ſhortening the duration of parliaments is a ſubject on which Mr Horne cannot enlarge too warmly; nor will I queſtion his ſincerity. If I did not profeſs the ſame ſentiments, I ſhould be ſhamefully inconſiſtent with myſelf. It is unneceſſary to bind Lord Chatham by the written formality of an engagement. He has publicly declared himſelf a convert to Triennial Parliaments; and though I have long been convinced, that this is the only poſſible reſource we have left to preſerve the ſubſtantial freedom of the conſtitution, I do not think we have a right to determine againſt the integrity of Lord Rockingham or his friends. Other meaſures may undoubtedly be ſupported in argument, as better adapted to the diſorder, or more likely to be obtained.

Mr Horne is well aſſured, that I never was the champion of Mr Wilkes. But though I am not obliged to anſwer for the firmneſs of his future adherence to the principles he profeſſes, I have no reaſon to preſume that he will hereafter diſgrace them. As for all thoſe imaginary caſes which Mr Horne ſo petulantly urges againſt me, I have one plain, honeſt anſwer to make to him.—Whenever Mr Wilkes ſhall be convicted of ſoliciting a penſion, an embaſſy, or a government, he muſt depart from that ſituation, and renounce that character, which he aſſumes at preſent, and which, in *my* opinion, intitle him to the ſupport of the public. By the ſame act, and at the ſame moment, he will forfeit his power of mortifying the King; and though he can never be a favourite at St James's, his baſeneſs may adminiſter a ſolid ſatiſfaction to the royal mind. The man I ſpeak of has not a heart to feel for the frailties of his fellow-creatures. It is their virtues that afflict, it is their vices that conſole, him.

I give every possible advantage to Mr Horne, when I take the facts he refers to for granted. That they are the produce of his invention, seems highly probable; that they are exaggerated, I have no doubt.  At the worst, what do they amount to, but that Mr Wilkes, who never was thought of as a perfect pattern of morality, has not been at all times proof against the extremity of distress. How shameful is it, in a man who has lived in friendship with him, to reproach him with failings too naturally connected with despair!  Is no allowance to be made for banishment and ruin? Does a two years imprisonment make no atonement for his crimes?—The resentment of a priest is implacable.  No sufferings can soften, no penitence can appease, him.—Yet he himself, I think, upon his own system, has a multitude of political offences to atone for.  I will not insist upon the nauseous detail, with which he so long disgusted the public.  He seems to be ashamed of it.  But what excuse will he make to the friends of the constitution for labouring to promote *this consummately bad man* to a station of the highest national trust and importance?  Upon what honourable motives did he recommend him to the livery of London for their representative;—to the ward of Faringdon for their alderman;—to the county of Middlesex for their knight? Will he affirm, that, at that time, he was ignorant of Mr Wilkes's solicitations to the ministry?—That he should say so, is indeed very necessary for his own justification; but where will he find credulity to believe him?

In what school this gentleman learned his ethics I know not.  His *logic* seems to have been studied under Mr Dyson. That miserable pamphleteer, by dividing the only precedent in point, and taking as much of it as suited his purpose, had reduced his argument upon the Middlesex election to something
thing

thing like the shape of a syllogism. Mr Horne has conducted himself with the same ingenuity and candour. I had affirmed, that Mr Wilkes would preserve the public favour, " as long as he " stood forth against a ministry and parliament " who were doing every thing they could to en- " slave the country, *and* as long as he was a thorn " in the King's side." Yet, from the exulting triumph of Mr Horne's reply, one would think that I had rested my expectation, that Mr Wilkes would be supported by the public upon the single condition of his mortifying the King. This may be logic at Cambridge or at the Treasury; but among men of sense and honour, it is folly or villainy in the extreme.

I see the pitiful advantage he has taken of a single unguarded expression, in a letter not intended for the public. Yet it is only the *expression* that is unguarded. I adhere to the true meaning of that member of the sentence, taken separately as *he* takes it; and now, upon the coolest deliberation, reassert, that, for the purposes I referred to, it may be highly meritorious to the public, to wound the personal feelings of the Sovereign. It is not a general proposition, nor is it generally applied to the chief magistrate of this or any other constitution. Mr Horne knows as well as I do, that the best of Princes is not displeased with the abuse which he sees thrown upon his ostensible ministers. It makes them, I presume, more properly the objects of his royal compassion; —neither does it escape his sagacity, that the lower they are degraded in the public esteem, the more submissively they must depend upon his favour for protection. This I affirm, upon the most solemn conviction, and the most certain knowledge, is a leading maxim in the policy of the closet. It is unnecessary to pursue the argument any farther.

Mr Horne is now a very loyal subject. He laments the wretched state of politics in this country; and sees, in a new light, the weakness and folly of the opposition. *Whoever, or whatever, is Sovereign, demands the respect and support of the people* *; it was not so *when Nero fiddled while Rome was burning.* Our gracious Sovereign has had wonderful success in creating new attachments *to his person and family.* He owes it, I presume, to the regular system he has pursued in the mystery of conversion. He began with an experiment upon the Scotch; and concludes with converting Mr Horne.—What a pity it is, that the *Jews* should be condemned by Providence to wait for a Messiah of their own!

The priesthood are accused of misinterpreting the scriptures. Mr Horne has improved upon his profession. He alters the text, and creates a refutable doctrine of his own. Such artifices cannot long delude the understanding of the people; and, without meaning an indecent comparison, I may venture to foretel, that the Bible and *Junius* will be read, when the commentaries of the Jesuits are forgotten.                    JUNIUS.

---

## LETTER LV.

TO THE PRINTER OF THE PUBLIC ADVERTISER.

SIR,                              AUG. 26. 1771.

THE enemies of the people, having now nothing better to object to my friend *Junius*, are at last obliged to quit his politics, and to rail at him for crimes he is not guilty of. His vanity and impiety are now the perpetual topics of their abuse. I do not mean to lessen the force of such charges, (supposing they were true); but to show

C c                                    that

* The very soliloquy of Lord Suffolk before he passed the Rubicon.

that they are not founded. If I admitted the pre-miffes, I fhould readily agree in all the confequen-ces drawn from them. Vanity indeed is a venial error; for it ufually carries its own punifhment with it:—but if I thought *Junius* capable of ut-tering a difrefpectful word of the religion of his country, I fhould be the firft to renounce and give him up to the public contempt and indignation. As a man, I am fatisfied that he is a Chriftian up-on the moft fincere conviction: as a writer, he would be grofsly inconfiftent with his political principles, if he dared to attack a religion efta-blifhed by thofe laws which it feems to be the purpofe of his life to defend.—Now for the proofs. —*Junius* is accufed of an impious allufion to the holy facrament, where he fays, that *if Lord Wey-mouth be denied the cup, there will be no keeping him within the pale of the miniftry.* Now, Sir, I affirm, that this paffage refers entirely to a ceremonial in the Roman-Catholic church, which denies the cup to the laity. It has no manner of relation to the Proteftant creed; and is in this country as fair an object of ridicule as *tranfubftantiation*, or any other part of Lord *Peter*'s hiftory in the Tale of the Tub.

But *Junius* is charged with equal vanity and im-piety, in comparing his writings to the holy fcrip-ture.—The formal proteft he makes againft any fuch comparifon avails him nothing. It becomes neceffary, then, to fhow that the charge deftroys itfelf.—If he be *vain*, he cannot be *impious*. A vain man does not ufually compare himfelf to an object which it is his defign to undervalue. On the other hand, if he be *impious*, he cannot be *vain*; for his impiety, if any, muft confift in his endeavouring to degrade the holy fcriptures by a comparifon with his own contemptible writings. This would be folly indeed of the groffeft nature; but where lies the vanity?—I fhall now be told,—

" Sir,

" Sir, what you fay is plaufible enough ; but ftill
" you muft allow that it is fhamefully impudent
" in *Junius* to tell us that his works will live as
" long as the Bible." My anfwer is, *Agreed; but
first prove that he has faid fo.* Look at his words,
and you will find, that the utmoft he expects is,
that the Bible and *Junius* will furvive the commentaries of the Jefuits ; which may prove true in a
fortnight. The moft malignant fagacity cannot
fhow that his works are, *in his opinion,* to live as
long as the Bible.—Suppofe I were to foretel, that
*Jack* and *Tom* would furvive *Harry*—does it follow that *Jack* muft live as long as *Tom ?* I would
only illuftrate my meaning, and proteft againft the
leaft idea of profanenefs.

Yet this is the way in which *Junius* is ufually
anfwered, arraigned, and convicted. Thefe candid critics never remember any thing he fays in
honour of our holy religion ; though it is true,
that one of his leading arguments is made to reft
*upon the internal evidence which the pureft of all re-
ligions carries with it.* I quote his words ; and
conclude from them, that he is a true and hearty
Chriftian, in fubftance, not in ceremony ; though
poffibly he may not agree with my Reverend Lords
the Bifhops, or with the head of the Church, *that
prayers are morality, or that kneeling is religion.*
                    PHILO JUNIUS.

---

## LETTER LVI.

FROM THE REVEREND MR HORNE TO JUNIUS.

                                    AUG. 17. 1771.

I Congratulate you, Sir, on the recovery of your
  wonted ftyle, though it has coft you a fortnight.
I compaffionate your labour in the compofition of
your letters, and will communicate to you the fecret of my fluency.——Truth needs no ornament ;

and, in my opinion, what she borrows of the pencil is deformity.

You brought a positive charge against me of corruption. I denied the charge, and called for your proofs. You replied with abuse, and reasserted your charge. I called again for proofs. You reply again with abuse only, and drop your accusation. In your fortnight's letter there is not one word upon the subject of my corruption.

I have no more to say, but to return thanks to you for your *condescension*, and to a *grateful* public and *honest* ministry for all the favours they have conferred upon me. The two latter, I am sure, will never refuse me any grace I shall solicit; and since you have pleased to acknowledge, that you told a deliberate lie in my favour out of bounty, and as a charitable donation, why may I not expect that you will hereafter (if you do not forget you ever mentioned my name with disrespect) make the same acknowledgment for what you have said to my prejudice?—This second recantation will perhaps be more abhorrent from your disposition; but should you decline it, you will only afford one more instance how much easier it is to be generous than just, and that men are sometimes bountiful who are not honest.

At all events, I am as well satisfied with your panegyric as Lord Chatham can be. Monument I shall have none; but over my grave it will be said, in your own words, " *Horne's situation did* " *not correspond with his intentions* *."

JOHN HORNE.

---

* The epitath would not be ill suited to the character;—at the best, it is but equivocal.

## LETTER LVII.

### TO HIS GRACE THE DUKE OF GRAFTON.

My Lord, Sept 28. 1771.

THE people of England are not apprifed of the full extent of their obligations to you. They have yet no adequate idea of the endlefs variety of your character. They have feen you diftinguifhed and fuccefsful in the continued violation of thofe moral and political duties, by which the little as well as the great focieties of life are collected and held together. Every colour, every character, became you. With a rate of abilities, which Lord Weymouth very juftly looks down upon with contempt, you have done as much mifchief to the community as *Cromwell* would have done, if *Cromwell* had been a coward; and as much as *Machiavel*, if *Machiavel* had not known that an appeaiance of morals and religion are ufeful in fociety.—To a thinking man, the influence of the Crown will, in no view, appear fo formidable, as when he obferves to what enormous fuccefſes it has fafely conducted your Grace, without a ray of real underftanding, without even the pretenfions to common decency or principle of any kind, or a fingle fpark of perfonal refolution. What muft be the operation of that pernicious influence, (for which our Kings have wifely exchanged the nugatory name of prerogative), that, in the higheft ftations, can fo abundantly fupply the abfence of virtue, courage, and abilities, and qualify a man to be the minifter of a great nation, whom a private gentleman would be afhamed and afraid to admit into his family! Like the univerfal pafsport of an ambaffador, it fuperfedes the prohibition of the laws, banifhes the ftaple virtues of the country, and introduces vice and folly triumphantly into all the departments of the ftate. O-

C c 3 ther

ther princes, befides his Majefty, have had the means of corruption within their reach ; but they have ufed it with moderation. In former times, corruption was confidered as a foreign auxiliary to government, and only called in upon extraordinary emergencies. The unfeigned piety, the fanctified religion, of *George the Third*, have taught him to new-model the civil forces of the ftate. The natural refources of the crown are no longer confided in. Corruption glitters in the van ;—collects and maintains a ftanding army of mercenaries, and at the fame moment impoverifhes and enflaves the country.—His Majefty's predeceffors (excepting that worthy family from which you, my Lord, are unqueftionably defcended) had fome generous qualities in their compofition, with vices, I confefs, or frailties, in abundance. They were kings or gentlemen, not hypocrites or priefts. They were at the head of the church, but did not know the value of their office. They faid their prayers without ceremony ; and had too little prieftcraft in their underftanding, to reconcile the fanctimonious forms of religion with the utter deftruction of the morality of their people.——My Lord, this is fact, not declamation.—With all your partiality to the houfe of *Stuart*, you muft confefs, that even *Charles the Second* would have blufhed at that open encouragement, at thofe eager, meretricious careffes, with which every fpecies of private vice and public proftitution is received at St James's.—The unfortunate houfe of *Stuart* has been treated with an afperity which, if comparifon be a defence, feems to border upon injuftice. Neither *Charles* nor his brother were qualified to fupport fuch a fyftem of meafures as would be neceffary to change the government and fubvert the conftitution of England. One of them was too much in earneft in his pleafures—the other in his religion. But the danger to this country

would

would ceafe to be problematical, if the crown fhould ever defcend to a Prince, whofe apparent fimplicity might throw his fubjects off their guard, —who might be no libertine in behaviour,—who fhould have no fenfe of honour to reftrain him,— and who, with juft religion enough to impofe upon the multitude, might have no fcruples of confcience to interfere with his morality. With thefe honourable qualifications, and the decifive advantage of fituation, low craft and falfehood are all the abilities that are wanting to deftroy the wifdom of ages, and to deface the nobleft monument that human policy has erected.—I know *fuch* a man :—My Lord, I know you both ; and with the bleffing of God (for I too am religious), the people of England fhall know you as well as I do. I am not very fure that greater abilities would not in effect be an impediment to a defign, which feems at firft fight to require a fuperior capacity. A better underftanding might make him fenfible of the wonderful beauty of that fyftem he was endeavouring to corrupt. The danger of the attempt might alarm him. The meannefs and intrinfic worthleffnefs of the object, (fuppofing he could attain it), would fill him with fhame, repentance, and difguft. But thefe are fenfations which find no entrance into a barbarous contracted heart. In fome men, there is a malignant paffion to deftroy the works of genius, literature, and freedom. The Vandal and the monk find equal gratification in it.

Reflections like thefe, my Lord, have a general relation to your Grace, and infeparably attend you in whatever company or fituation your character occurs to us. They have no immediate connection with the following recent fact, which I lay before the public, for the honour of the beft of Sovereigns, and for the edification of his people.

A

A prince, (whose piety and self-denial, one would think, might secure him from such a multitude of worldly necessities), with an annual revenue of near a million sterling, unfortunately *wants money.*——The navy of England, by an equally strange concurrence of unforeseen circumstances, (though not quite so unfortunately for his Majesty), is in equal want of timber. The world knows in what a hopeful condition you delivered the navy to your successor, and in what a condition we found it in the moment of distress. You were determined it should continue in the situation in which you left it. It happened, however, very luckily for the privy-purse, that one of the above wants promised fair to supply the other: Our religious, benevolent, generous Sovereign, has no objection to selling *his own* timber to *his own* admiralty to repair *his own* ships, nor to putting the money into *his own* pocket. People of a religious turn naturally adhere to the principles of the church. Whatever they acquire falls into *mortmain.*——Upon a representation from the admiralty of the extraordinary want of timber for the indispensable repairs of the navy, the surveyor-general was directed to make a survey of the timber in all the royal chaces and forests in England. Having obeyed his orders with accuracy and attention, he reported, that the finest timber he had anywhere met with, and the properest in every respect for the purposes of the navy, was in *Whittlebury Forest*, of which your Grace, I think, is hereditary ranger. In consequence of this report, the usual warrant was prepared at the treasury, and delivered to the surveyor, by which he or his deputy were authorised to cut down any trees in *Whittlebury Forest* which should appear to be proper for the purposes above-mentioned. The deputy, being informed that the warrant was signed and delivered to his principal in London, crosses the
country

country to Northamptonshire, and with an officious zeal for the public service begins to do his duty in the forest. Unfortunately for him, he had not the warrant in his pocket. The oversight was enormous; and you have punished him for it accordingly. You have insisted, that an active, useful officer should be dismissed from his place. You have ruined an innocent man and his family. —In what language shall I address so black, so cowardly, a tyrant;—thou worse than *one* of the *Brunswicks*, and all the *Stuarts!*—To them who know Lord North, it is unnecessary to say, that he was mean and base enough to submit to you.—This, however, is but a small part of the fact. After ruining the surveyor's deputy for acting without the warrant, you attacked the warrant itself. You declared that it was illegal; and swore, in a fit of foaming frantic passion, that it never should be executed. You asserted upon your honour, that in the grant of the rangership of *Whittlebury Forest*, made by *Charles the Second* (whom, with a modesty that would do honour to Mr Rigby, you are pleased to call your ancestor) to one of his bastards, (from whom I make no doubt of your descent), the property of the timber is vested in the ranger.—I have examined the original grant; and now, in the face of the public, contradict you directly upon the fact. The very reverse of what you have asserted upon your honour is the truth. The grant, *expressly, and by a particular clause*, reserves the property of the timber for the use of the crown.—In spite of this evidence,—in defiance of the representations of the admiralty,—in perfect mockery of the notorious distresses of the English navy, and those equally pressing and almost equally notorious necessities of your pious Sovereign,—here the matter rests.—The lords of the treasury recal their warrant; the deputy-surveyor is ruined for doing his

duty;

duty;—Mr John Pitt (whose name I suppose is offensive to you) submits to be brow-beaten and insulted;—the oaks keep their ground;—the King is defrauded, and the navy of England may perish for want of the best and finest timber in the island. And all this is submitted to—to appease the Duke of Grafton!—to gratify the man who has involved the King and his kingdom in confusion and distress, and who, like a treacherous coward, deserted his Sovereign in the midst of it!

There has been a strange alteration in your doctrines, since you thought it adviseable to rob the *Duke of Portland* of his property, in order to strengthen the interest of Lord *Bute*'s son-in-law before the last general election. *Nullum tempus occurrit regi,* was then your boasted motto, and the cry of all your hungry partisans. Now, it seems, a grant of *Charles the Second* to one of his bastards is to be held sacred and inviolable! It must not be questioned by the King's servants, nor submitted to any interpretation but your own.— My Lord, this was not the language you held, when it suited you to insult the memory of the glorious deliverer of England from that detested family, to which you are still more nearly allied in principle than in blood.—In the name of decency and common sense, what are your Grace's merits, either with King or ministry, that should intitle you to assume this domineering authority over both?—Is it the fortunate consanguinity you claim with the house of *Stuart?*—Is it the secret correspondence you have for so many years carried on with Lord Bute, by the assiduous assistance of your *cream-coloured parasite?*—Could not your gallantry find sufficient employment for him in those *gentle* offices by which he first acquired the tender friendship of *Lord Barrington?*—Or is it only that wonderful sympathy of manners which subsists between your Grace and one of your superiors,

periors, and does so much honour to you both?——
Is the union, of *Blifil* and *Black George* no longer a
*romance?*——From whatever origin your influence
in this country arises, it is a phenomenon in the
history of human virtue and understanding.——Good
men can hardly believe the fact. Wise men are
unable to account for it. Religious men find exercise for their faith; and make it the last effort of
their piety, not to repine against Providence.

JUNIUS.

----

## LETTER LVIII.

ADDRESSED TO THE LIVERY OF LONDON.

GENTLEMEN,       SEPT. 30. 1771.

IF *you* alone were concerned in the event of the
present election of a chief magistrate of the
metropolis, it would be the highest presumption
in a stranger to attempt to influence your choice,
or even to offer you his opinion. But the situation of public affairs has annexed an extraordinary importance to your resolutions. You cannot, in the choice of your magistrate, determine
for *yourselves only*. You are going to determine
upon a point in which every member of the community is interested. I will not scruple to say,
that the very being of that law, of that right, of
that constitution, for which we have been so long
contending, is now at stake. They who would
ensnare your judgment tell you, it is a *common,
ordinary* case, and to be decided by ordinary precedent and practice. They artfully conclude from
moderate peaceable times, to times which *are not*
moderate, and which *ought not* to be peaceable.——
While they solicit your favour, they insist upon
a rule of rotation which excludes all idea of election.

Let me be honoured with a few minutes of your
attention.

attention.—The queftion, to thofe who mean fairly to the liberty of the people, (which we all profefs to have in view), lies within a very narrow compafs.—Do you mean to defert that juft and honourable fyftem of meafures which you have hitherto purfued, in hopes of obtaining from parliament, or from the crown, a full redrefs of paft grievances, and a fecurity for the future?—Do you think the caufe defperate, and will you declare that you think fo to the whole people of England? If this be your meaning and opinion, you will act confiftently with it in choofing Mr *Nafh*.—I profefs to be unacquainted with his private character. But he has acted as a magiftrate,—as a public man.—As fuch I fpeak of him.—I fee his name in a proteft againft one of your remonftrances to the crown.—He has done every thing in his power to deftroy the freedom of popular elections in the city, by publifhing the poll upon a former occafion; and I know in general, that he has diftinguifhed himfelf, by flighting and thwarting all thofe public meafures which *you* have engaged in with the greateft warmth, and hitherto thought moft worthy of your approbation.—From his paft conduct, what conclufion will you draw, but that he will act the fame part as *Lord Mayor* which he has invariable acted as *Alderman* and *Sheriff?* He cannot alter his conduct without confeffing that he never acted upon principle of any kind.—I fhould be forry to injure the character of a man, who perhaps may be honeft in his intention, by fuppofing it *poffible* that he can ever concur with you in any political meafure or opinion.

If, on the other hand, you mean to perfevere in thofe refolutions for the public good, which, though not always fuccefsful, are always honourable, your choice will naturally incline to thofe men who (whatever they be in other refpects) are moft likely to co-operate with you in the great



purpofes

purpofes which you are determined not to relinquifh:—The queftion is not of what metal your
inftruments are made, but *whether they are adapted to the work you have in hand.*  The honours of
the city, *in thefe times*, are improperly, becaufe ex-
clufively, called a *reward.* You mean not merely to
*pay*, but to *employ.*—Are Mr *Crofby* and Mr *Sawbridge*
likely to execute the extraordinary as well as the ordinary duties of Lord Mayor?—Will they grant you
common-halls when it fhall be neceffary?—Will
they go up with remonftrances to the King?—
Have they firmnefs enough to meet the fury of a
venal houfe of commons?—Have they fortitude
enough not to fhrink at imprifonment?—Have
they fpirit enough to hazard their lives and fortunes in a conteft, if it fhould be neceffary, with
a proftituted legiflature?—If thefe queftions can
fairly be anfwered in the affirmative, your choice
is made.  Forgive this paffionate language.—I am
unable to correct it.—The fubject comes home to
us all.—It is the language of my heart.

J U N I U S.

---

L E T T E R  LIX.

TO THE PRINTER OF THE PUBLIC ADVERTISER.

S I R,                              Oct. 5. 1771.

NO man laments more fincerely than I do, the
unhappy differences which have arifen among
the friends of the people, and divided them from
each other.  The caufe undoubtedly fuffers as
well by the diminution of that ftrength which
union carries along with it, as by the feparate lofs
of perfonal reputation which every man fuftains
when his character and conduct are frequently
held forth in odious or contemptible colours.——
Thefe differences are only advantageous to the common enemy of the country.—The hearty friends

D d

of

of the cause are provoked and disgusted.——The lukewarm advocate avails himself of any pretence to relapse into that indolent indifference about every thing that ought to interest an Englishman, so unjustly dignified with the title of moderation. ————The false, insidious partisan, who creates or foments the disorder, sees the fruit of his dishonest industry ripen beyond his hopes, and rejoices in the promise of a banquet, only delicious to such an appetite as his own.——It is time for those who really mean the *Cause* and the *People*, who have no view to private advantage, and who have virtue enough to prefer the general good of the community to the gratification of personal animosities——it is time for such men to interpose. ——Let us try whether these fatal dissentions may not yet be reconciled; or, if that be impracticable, let us guard at least against the worst effects of division, and endeavour to persuade these furious partisans, if they will not consent to draw together, to be separately useful to that cause which they all pretend to be attached to.——Honour and honesty must not be renounced, although a thousand modes of right and wrong were to occupy the degrees of morality between Zeno and Epicurus. The fundamental principles of Christianity may still be preserved, though every zealous sectary adheres to his own exclusive doctrine, and pious ecclesiastics make it part of their religion to persecute one another.————The civil constitution too, that legal liberty, that general creed which every Englishman professes, may still be supported, tho' Wilkes, and Horne, and Townshend, and Sawbridge, should obstinately refuse to communicate; and even if the fathers of the church, if Savile, Richmond, Camden, Rockingham, and Chatham, should disagree in the ceremonies of their political worship, and even in the interpretation of twenty texts in Magna Charta.——I speak to the

people

people as one of the people.—Let us employ thefe men in whatever departments their various abilities are beft fuited to, and as much to the advantage of the common caufe as their different inclinations will permit. They cannot ferve *us*, without effentially ferving themfelves.

If Mr *Nafb* be elected, he will hardly venture, after fo recent a mark of the perfonal efteem of his fellow-citizens, to declare himfelf immediately a courtier. The fpirit and activity of the fheriffs, will, I hope, be fufficient to counteract any finifter intentions of the Lord Mayor. In collifion with *their* virtue, perhaps he may take fire.

It is not neceffary to exact from Mr Wilkes the virtues of a Stoic. They were inconfiftent with themfelves, who, almoft at the fame moment, reprefented him as the bafeft of mankind, yet feemed to expect from him fuch inftances of fortitude and felf-denial as would do honour to an apoftle. It is not however flattery to fay, that he is obftinate, intrepid, and fertile in expedients.— That he has no poffible refource, but in the public favour, is, in my judgment, a confiderable recommendation of him. I wifh that every man who pretended to popularity were in the fame predicament. I wifh that a retreat to St James's were not fo eafy and open as patriots have found it. To Mr Wilkes there is no accefs. However he may be mifled by paffion or imprudence, I think he cannot be guilty of a deliberate treachery to the public. The favour of his country conftitutes the fhield which defends him againft a thoufand daggers. Defertion would difarm him.

I can more readily admire the liberal fpirit and integrity, than the found judgment, of any man who prefers a republican form of government, in this or any other empire of equal extent, to a monarchy fo qualified and limited as ours. I am convinced, that neither is it in theory the wifeft syftem of government, nor practicable in this country. Yet, though I hope the Englifh conftitution will for ever preferve its original monarchical form, I would have the manners of the people purely and ftrictly republican.—I do not mean the licentious fpirit of anarchy and riot.—I mean a general attachment to the common-weal, diftinct from any partial attachment to perfons or families;—an implicit fubmiffion to the laws only, and an affection to the magiftrate, proportioned to the integrity and wifdom with which he diftributes juftice to his people, and adminifters their affairs. The prefent habit of our political body appears to me the very reverfe of what it ought to be. The form of the conftitution leans rather more than enough to the popular branch; while, in effect, the manners of the people (of thofe at leaft who are likely to take a lead in the country) incline too generally to a dependence upon the crown. The real friends of arbitrary power combine the facts, and are not inconfiftent with their principles when they ftrenuoufly fupport the unwarrantable privileges affumed by the Houfe of Commons.—In thefe circumftances, it were much to be defired, that we had many fuch men as Mr Sawbridge to reprefent us in parliament.—I fpeak from common report and opinion only, when I impute to him a fpeculative predilection in favour of a republic.—In the perfonal conduct and manners of the man, I cannot be miftaken. He has fhown himfelf poffeffed of that republican firmnefs which the times require; and by which an Englifh gentleman may be as ufefully and as honourably diftinguifhed, as any citizen of ancient Rome, of Athens, or Lacedemon.

Mr Townfhend complains, that the public gratitude has not been anfwerable to his deferts.—It is not difficult to trace the artifices which have fuggefted to him a language fo unworthy of his

under

understanding. A great man commands the affections of the people. A prudent man does not complain when he has loft them. Yet they are far from being loft to Mr Townshend. He has treated our opinion a little too cavalierly. A young man is apt to rely too confidently upon himself, to be as attentive to his miftrefs as a polite and paffionate lover ought to be. Perhaps he found her at firft too eafy a conqueft.—Yet, I fancy, fhe will be ready to receive him whenerer he thinks proper to renew his addreffes. With all his youth, his fpirit, and his appearance, it would be indecent in the lady to folicit his return.

I have too much refpeft for the abilities of Mr Horne, to flatter myfelf that thefe gentlemen will ever be cordially re-united. It is not, however, unreafonable to expeft, that each of them fhould aft his feparate part with honour and integrity to the public.—As for the differences of opinion upon fpeculative queftions, if we wait until *they* are reconciled, the aftion of human affairs muft be fufpended for ever. But neither are we to look for perfeftion in any one man, nor for agreement among many.—When *Lord Chatham* affirms, that the authority of the Britifh legiflature is not fupreme over the colonies in the fame fenfe in which it is fupreme over Great Britain ;——when *Lord Cambden* fuppofes a neceffity, (which the King is to judge of), and, founded upon that neceffity, attributes to the crown a legal power (not given by the aft itfelf) to fufpend the operation of an aft of the legiflature—I liften to them both with diffidence and refpeft, but without the fmalleft degree of conviftion or affent. Yet, I doubt not, they delivered their real fentiments; nor ought they to be haftily condemned.—*I too* have a claim to the candid interpretation of my country, when I acknowledge an involuntary, compulfive affent to one very unpopular opinion. I lament

the unhappy neceffity, whenever it arifes, of pro-
viding for the fafety of the.ftate, by a temporary
invafion of the perfonal liberty of the fubject.
Would to God it were practicable to reconcile
thefe important objects, in every poffible fituation
of public affairs!—I regard the legal liberty of the
meaneft man in Britain as much as my own, and
would defend it with the fame zeal. I know we
muft ftand or fall together. But I never can doubt,
that the community has a right to command, as
well as to purchafe, the fervice of its members.
I fee that right founded originally upon a neceffity,
which fuperfedes all argument. I fee it eftablifhed
by ufage immemorial, and admitted by more than
a tacit affent of the legiflature. I conclude there
is no remedy, in the nature of things, for the grie-
vance complained of; for, if there were, it muft
long fince have been redreffed. Though number-
lefs opportunities have prefented themfelves highly favourable to public liberty, no fuccefsful attempt has ever been made for the relief of the
fubject in this article. Yet it has been felt and
complained of ever fince England had a navy.—
The conditions which conftitute this right, muft
be taken together. Separately, they have little
weight. It is not fair to argue, from any abufe
in the execution, to the illegality of the power;
much lefs is a conclufion to be drawn from the
navy to the land fervice. A feaman can never be
employed but againft the enemies of his country.
The only cafe in which the King can have a right
to arm his fubjects in general, is that of a foreign
force being actually landed upon our coaft. Whenever that cafe happens, no true Englifhman will
inquire whether the King's right to compel him
to defend his country, be the cuftom of England,
or a grant of the legiflature. With regard to the
prefs for feamen, it does not follow that the fymp-
toms may not be foftened, although the diftem-

per

per cannot be cured.  Let bounties be increafed as far as the public purfe can fupport them.  Still they have a limit; and when every reafonable expence is incurred, it will be found, in fact, that the fpur of the prefs is wanted to give operation to the bounty.

Upon the whole, I never had a doubt about the ftrict right of preffing, until I heard that Lord Mansfield had applauded Lord Chatham for delivering fomething like this doctrine in the houfe of Lords.  That confideration ftaggered me not a little.  But, upon reflection, his conduct accounts naturally for itfelf.  He knew the doctrine was unpopular, and was eager to fix it upon the man who is the firft object of his fear and deteftation.  The cunning Scotchman never fpeaks truth without a fradulent defign.  In council, he generally affects to take a moderate part.  Befides his natural timidity, it makes part of his political plan, never to be known to recommend violent meafures.  When the guards are called forth to murder their fellow-fubjects, it is not by the oftenfible advice of Lord Mansfield.  That odious office, his prudence tells him, is better left to fuch men as Gower and Weymouth, as Barrington and Grafton.  Lord Hilfborough wifely confines *his* firmnefs to the diftant Americans.—The defigns of Mansfield are more fubtle, more effectual, and fecure.—Who attacks the liberty of the prefs?—Lord Mansfield.—Who invades the conftitutional power of juries?—Lord Mansfield.—What judge ever challenged a juryman, but Lord Mansfield?—Who was that judge, who, to fave the King's brother, affirmed that a man of the firft rank and quality, who obtains a verdict in a fuit for criminal converfation, is intitled to no greater damages than the meaneft mechanic?—Lord Mansfield:—Who is it makes commiffioners of the great feal?—Lord Mansfield.—Who is it forms a

decree

decree for thofe commiffioners, deciding againft Lord Chatham, and afterwards (finding himfelf oppofed by the judges) declares in parliament, that he never had a doubt that the law was in direct oppofition to that decree?—Lord Mansfield. —Who is he that has made it the ftudy and practice of his life, to undermine and alter the whole fyftem of jurifprudence in the court of King's-Bench?—Lord Mansfield.   There never exifted a man but himfelf, who anfwered exactly to fo complicated a defcription.   Compared to thefe enormities, his original attachment to the Pretender (to whom his deareft brother was confidential fecretary) is a virtue of the firft magnitude.   But the hour of impeachment *will* come, and neither he nor Grafton fhall efcape me.   Now let them make common caufe againft England and the houfe of Hanover.   A Stuart and a Murray fhould fympathife with each other.

When I refer to fignal inftances of unpopular opinions delivered and maintained by men who may well be fuppofed to have no view but the public good, I do not mean to renew the difcuffion of fuch opinions.   I fhould be forry to revive the dormant queftions of *Stamp-act*, *Corn-bill*, or *Prefs-warrant*.   I mean only to illuftrate one ufeful propofition, which it is the intention of this paper to inculcate;—*That we fhould not generally reject the friendfhip or fervices of any man becaufe he differs from us in a particular opinion*.   This will not appear a fuperfluous caution, if we obferve the ordinary conduct of mankind.   In public affairs there is the leaft chance of a perfect concurrence of fentiment or inclination.   Yet every man is able to contribute fomething to the common ftock; and no man's contribution fhould be rejected.   If individuals have no virtues, their vices may be of ufe to us.   I care not with what principle the new-born patriot is animated; if the

mea-

meafures he fupports are beneficial to the community.  The nation is interefted in his conduct. His motives are his own.  The properties of a patriot are perifhable in the individual; but there is a quick fucceffion of fubjects, and the breed is worth preferving.—The fpirit of the Americans may be an ufeful example to us.  Our dogs and horfes are only Englifh upon Englifh ground; but patriotifm, it feems, may be improved by tranfplanting.—I will not reject a bill which tends to confine parliamentary privilege within reafonable bounds, though it fhould be ftolen from the houfe of Cavendifh, and introduced by Mr Onflow.  The features of the infant are a proof of the defcent, and vindicate the noble birth from the bafenefs of the adoption.—I willingly accept of a farcafm from *Colonel Barre*, or a fimile from *Mr Burke*.  Even the filent vote of *Mr Calcraft* is worth reckoning in a divifion.—What though he riots in the plunder of the army, and has only determined to be a patriot when he could not be a peer?—Let us profit by the affiftance of fuch men while they are with us, and place them, if it be poffible, in the poft of danger, to prevent defertion.—The wary *Wedderburne*, the pompous *Suffolk*, never threw away the fcabbard, nor ever went upon a forlorn hope.  They always treated the King's fervants as men with whom, fome time or other, they might poffibly be in friendfhip.—When a man who ftands forth for the public has gone that length from which there is no practicable retreat,—when he has given that kind of perfonal offence which a pious monarch never pardons, I then begin to think him in earneft, and that he never will have occafion to folicit the forgivenefs of his country. —But inftances of a determination fo entire and unreferved are rarely met with.  Let us take mankind *as they are*.  Let us diftribute the virtues and abilities of individuals, according to the offices

they

they affect; and, when they quit the service, let us endeavour to supply their places with better men than we have lost. In this country, there are always candidates enough for popular favour. The temple of *fame* is the shortest passage to riches and preferment.

Above all things, let me guard my countrymen against the meanness and folly of accepting of a trifling or moderate compensation for extraordinary and essential injuries. Our enemies treat us as the cunning trader does the unskilful Indian. They magnify their generosity, when they give us baubles of little proportionate value, for ivory and gold. The same house of commons, who robbed the constituent body of their right of free election; who presumed to *make* a law, under pretence of *declaring* it; who paid our good King's debts, without once inquiring how they were incurred; who gave thanks for repeated murders committed at home, and for national infamy incurred abroad; who screened *Mansfield*; who imprisoned the magistrates of the metropolis for asserting the subject's right to the protection of the laws; who erased a judicial record, and ordered all proceedings in a criminal-suit to be suspended;—this very house of commons have graciously consented, that their own members may be compelled to pay their debts, and that contested elections shall for the future be determined with some decent regard to the merits of the case. The event of the suit is of no consequence to the crown. While parliaments are septennial, the purchase of the sitting member or of the petitioner makes but the difference of a day. —Concessions, such as these, are of little moment to the sum of things; unless it be to prove that the worst of men are sensible of the injuries they have done us, and perhaps to demonstrate to us the imminent danger of our situation. In the shipwreck of the state, trifles float and are preserved;

while

while every thing folid and valuable finks to the
bottom, and is loft for ever.

JUNIUS.

---

## LETTER LX.

### TO THE PRINTER OF THE PUBLIC ADVER-
### TISER.

SIR,                   Oct. 15. 1771.

I AM convinced that *Junius* is incapable of wilfully mifreprefenting any man's opinion, and
that his inclination leads him to treat *Lord Camden*
with particular candour and refpect. The doctrine
attributed to him by *Junius*, as far as it goes, cor-
refponds with that ftated by your correfpondent
*Scævola*, who feems to make a diftinction withcut
a difference. *Lord Camden*, it is agreed, did certainly maintain, that, in the recefs of parliament,
the King (by which we all mean the *King in council*, or the executive power) m'ght fufpend the o-
peration of an act of the legiflature; and he founded his doctrine upon a fuppofed neceffity, of which
the King, *in the firft inftance*, muft be judge. The
lords and commons cannot be judges of it in the
firft inftance, for they do not exift.—Thus far *Junius*.

But, fays *Scævola*, *Lord Camden* made *parliament*,
and not the *King*, judges of the neceffity.—That
parliament may review the acts of minifters, is unqueftionable; but there is a wide difference between faying that the crown has a *legal* power,
and that minifters may act *at their peril*. When
we fay that an act is *illegal*, we mean that it is
forbidden by a joint refolution of the three eftates.
How a fubfequent refolution of two of thofe
branches can make it *legal ab initio*, will require
explanation. If it could, the confequence would
be truly dreadful, efpecially in thefe times. There

is no act of arbitrary power which the King might not attribute to *necessity*, and for which he would not be secure of obtaining the approbation of his prostituted lords and commons. If *Lord Camden* admits that the subsequent sanction of parliament was necessary to make the proclamation *legal*, why did he so obstinately oppose the bill which was soon after brought in for indemnifying all those persons who had acted under it?—If that bill had not been passed, I am ready to maintain, in direct contradiction to Lord Camden's doctrine, (taken as *Scævola* states it), that a litigious exporter of corn, who had suffered in his property in consequence of the proclamation, might have laid his action against the custom-house officers, and would infallibly have recovered damages. No jury could refuse them; and if I, who am by no means litigious, had been so injured, I would assuredly have instituted a suit in Westminster-hall, on purpose to try the question of right. I would have done it upon a principle of defiance of the pretended power of either or both houses to make declarations inconsistent with law; and I have no doubt that, with an act of parliament on my side, I should have been too strong for them all. This is the way in which an Englishman should speak and act; and not suffer dangerous precedents to be established, because the circumstances are favourable or palliating.

With regard to *Lord Camden*, the truth is, that he inadvertently overshot himself, as appears plainly by that unguarded mention of *a tyranny of forty days*, which I myself heard. Instead of asserting that the proclamation was *legal*, he *should* have said, " My Lords, I know the proclamation was " *illegal;* but I advised it because it was indispen- " sably necessary to save the kingdom from fa- " mine; and I submit myself to the justice and " mercy of my country."



Such

Such language as this would have been manly, rational, and confiftent:—not unfit for a lawyer, and every way worthy of a great man.

PHILO JUNIUS.

P. S. If *Scævola* fhould think proper to write again upon this fubject, I beg of him to give me a *direct* anfwer, that is, a plain affirmative or negative, to the following queftions:—In the interval between the publifhing fuch a proclamation (or order of council) as that in queftion, and its receiving the fanction of the two houfes, of what nature is it?—is it *legal* or *illegal?* or is it neither one nor the other?—I mean to be candid, and will point out to him the confequence of his anfwer either way. If it be *legal*, it wants no farther fanction; if it be *illegal*, the fubject is not bound to obey it; confequently it is a ufelefs nugatory act, even as to its declared purpofe. Before the meeting of parliament, the whole mifchief, which it means to prevent, will have been completed.

---

## LETTER LXI.

### TO ZENO.

S I R,                              Oct. 17. 1771.

THE fophiftry of your letter in defence of Lord *Mansfield*, is adapted to the character you defend. But Lord *Mansfield* is a man of *form*, and feldom in his behaviour tranfgreffes the rules of decorum. I fhall imitate his Lordfhip's good manners, and leave you in full poffeffion of his principles. I will not call you *liar*, *jefuit*, or *villain:* but, with all the politenefs imaginable, perhaps I may prove you fo.

Like other fair pleaders in Lord *Mansfield's* fchool of juftice, you anfwer *Junius* by mifquo-

E e

ting

ting his words, and miſtating his propoſitions. If I am candid enough to admit that this is the very logic taught at *St Omer's*, you will readily allow that it is the conſtant practice in the court of *King's-Bench.*—JUNIUS *does not ſay*, that he never had a doubt about the ſtrict right of preſſing, *till he knew Lord Mansfield was of the ſame opinion.* His words are, *Until he heard that Lord Mansfield had applauded Lord Chatham for maintaining that doctrine in the houſe of Lords.* It was not the accidental concurrence of Lord Mansfield's opinion; but the ſuſpicious applauſe given by a cunning Scotchman to the man he deteſts, that raiſed and juſtified a doubt in the mind of *Junius.* The queſtion is not, Whether Lord Mansfield be a man of learning and abilities, (which *Junius* has never diſputed); but, Whether or no he abuſes and miſapplies his talents.

*Junius* did *not* ſay that Lord Mansfield had adviſed the calling out the Guards. On the contrary, his plain meaning is, that he left that odious office to men leſs cunning than himſelf.—Whether Lord Mansfield's doctrine concerning libels be or be not an attack upon the liberty of the preſs, is a queſtion which the public in general are very well able to determine. I ſhall not enter into it at preſent. Nor do I think it neceſſary to ſay much to a man, who had the daring confidence to ſay to a jury, " Gentlemen, you are to bring in a verdict " *guilty* or not *guilty;* but whether the defendant " be guilty or innocent, is not matter for *your* " conſideration." Clothe it in what language you will, this is the ſum total of Lord Mansfield's doctrine. If not, let *Zeno* ſhow us the difference.

But it ſeems, *the liberty of the preſs may be abuſed,* and *the abuſe of a valuable privilege is the certain means to loſe it.* The *firſt* I admit:—but let the *abuſe* be ſubmitted to a jury; a ſufficient, and indeed the only legal and conſtitutional check upon

on

on the licence of the preſs.  The *ſecond* I flatly
deny.  In direct contradiction to Lord *Mansfield*,
I affirm, " that the abuſe of a valuable privilege
" *is not* the *certain* means to loſe it."  If it were,
the Engliſh nation would have few privileges left;
for where is the privilege that has not, at one time
or other, been abuſed by individuals.  But it is
falſe in reaſon and equity, that particular abuſes
ſhould produce a general forfeiture.  Shall the
community be deprived of the protection of the
laws, becauſe there are robbers and murderers?
—Shall the community be puniſhed, becauſe individuals have offended?  Lord Mansfield ſays ſo,
conſiſtently enough with his principles; but I wonder to find him ſo explicit.  Yet, for one conceſſion, however extorted, I confeſs myſelf obliged
to him :—The liberty of the preſs is after all a *valuable privilege.*  I agree with him moſt heartily,
and will defend it againſt him.

You aſk me, What *juryman* was challenged by
Lord Mansfield ?—I tell you his name is *Benſon*.
When his name was called, Lord Mansfield ordered the clerk to paſs him by.  As for his reaſons, you may aſk himſelf, for he aſſigned none :
but I can tell you what all men thought of it.
This *Benſon* had been refractory upon a former
jury, and would not accept of the law as delivered
by Lord Mansfield;  but had the impudence to
pretend to think for himſelf.—But you, it ſeems,
honeſt *Zeno*, know nothing of the matter.  You
never read *Junius*'s letter to your patron: You
never heard of the intended inſtructions from the
city to impeach Lord Mansfield : You never heard
by what dexterity of Mr *Paterſon* that meaſure
was prevented.  How wonderfully ill ſome people
are informed !

*Junius* did *never* affirm, that the crime of ſedu-
cing the wife of a mechanic or a peer, is not the
ſame, taken in a moral or religious view.  What



he

he affirmed, in contradiction to the levelling principle so lately adopted by Lord Mansfield, was,
*that the damages should be proportioned to the rank
and fortune of the parties;* and for this plain reason, (admitted by every other judge that ever sat
in Westminster-hall), because, what is a compensation or penalty to one man, is none to another.
The sophistical distinction you attempt to draw
between the person *injured* and the person *injuring*, is *Mansfield* all over. If you can once establish the proposition, that the injured party is not
intitled to *receive* large damages, it follows pretty
plainly, that the party *injuring* should not be compelled to *pay* them; consequently the King's brother is effectually screened by Lord *Mansfield's*
doctrine. Your reference to *Nathan* and *David*
come naturally in aid of your patron's professed
system of jurisprudence. He is fond of introducing into the *court of King's-bench* any law that
contradicts or excludes the common law of England; whether it be *canon, civil, jus gentium,* or
*Levitical.* But, Sir, the Bible is the code of our
religious faith, not of our municipal jurisprudence;
and though it was the pleasure of God to inflict
a particular punishment upon David's crime (taken
as a breach of his divine commands), and to send
his prophet to denounce it, an English jury have
nothing to do either with David or the prophet.
They consider the crime only as it is a breach of
order, an injury to an individual, and an offence
to society; and they judge of it by certain positive rules of law, or by the practice of their ancestors. Upon the whole, the man *after God's
own heart* is much indebted to you for comparing
him to the Duke of Cumberland. That his Royal
Highness may be the man after Lord *Mansfield's*
own heart, seems much more probable; and you,
I think, Mr *Zeno,* might succeed tolerably well
in the character of *Nathan.* The evil deity, the

prophet,

prophet, and the royal sinner, would be very proper company for one another.

You say Lord Mansfield did not *make* the commissioners of the Great Seal, and that he only advised the King to appoint. I believe *Junius* meant no more; and the distinction is hardly worth disputing.

You say he *did not* deliver an opinion upon Lord Chatham's appeal.—I affirm that he *did*, directly in favour of the appeal.—This is a point of fact, to be determined by evidence only. But you assign no reason for his supposed silence, nor for his desiring a conference with the judges the day before. Was not all Westminster-hall convinced that he did it with a view to puzzle them with some perplexing question, and in hopes of bringing some of them over to him ?—You say the commissioners were *very capable of framing a decree for themselves*. By the fact, it only appears, that they were capable of framing an *illegal* one ; which, I apprehend, is not much to the credit either of their learning or integrity.

We are both agreed, that Lord *Mansfield* has incessantly laboured to introduce new modes of proceeding in the court where he presides ; but *you* attribute it to an honest zeal in behalf of innocence oppressed by quibble and chicane. I say, that he has introduced *new law* too, and removed the landmarks established by former decisions. I say, that his view is to change a court of common law into a court of equity, and to bring every thing within the *arbitrium* of a *prætorian* court. The public must determine between us. *But now for his merits. First*, then, the establishment of the judges in their places for life, (which you tell us was advised by Lord Mansfield), was a concession merely to catch the people. It bore the appearance of a royal bounty, but had nothing real in it. The judges were already for life, excepting in the



case

cafe of a *demife*.　Your boafted bill only provides, that it fhall not be in the power of the King's fucceffor to remove them.　At the beft, therefore, it is only a legacy, not a gift, on the part of his prefent Majefty, fince for himfelf he gives up nothing.—That he did oppofe Lord *Camden* and Lord *Northington* upon the proclamation againft the exportation of corn, is moft true, and with great ability. With his talents, and taking the right fide of fo clear a queftion, it was impoffible to fpeak ill.—His motives are not fo eafily penetrated.. They who are acquainted with the ftate of politics at that period, will judge of them fomewhat differently from *Zeno*. Of the popular bills, which you fay he fupported in the houfe of Lords, the moft material is unqueftionably that of Mr *Grenville*, for deciding contefted elections.　But I fhould be glad to know upon what poffible pretence any member of the Upper Houfe could oppofe fuch a bill after it had paffed the *houfe of commons ?*—I do not pretend to know what fhare he had in promoting the other two bills; but I am ready to give him all the credit you defire.　Still you will find, that a whole life of deliberate iniquity is ill atoned for, by doing now and then a laudable action upon a mixed or doubtful principle.—If it be unworthy of him, thus ungratefully treated, to labour any longer for the public, in God's name let him retire.　His brother's patron (whofe health he once was anxious for) is dead; but the fon of that unfortunate prince furvives, and, I dare fay, will be ready to receive him.　　　　PHILO JUNIUS.

## LETTER LXII.

### TO AN ADVOCATE IN THE CAUSE OF THE PEOPLE.

SIR,                                    Oct. 18. 1771.

YOU do not treat *Junius* fairly. You would not have condemned him so hastily, if you had ever read Judge *Foster*'s argument upon the legality of pressing seamen. A man who has not read that argument, is not qualified to speak accurately upon the subject. In answer to strong facts and fair reasoning, you produce nothing but a vague comparison between two things which have little or no resemblance to each other. *General warrants*, it is true, had been often issued; but they had never been regularly questioned or resisted until the case of Mr *Wilkes*. He brought them to trial; and the moment they were tried, they were declared *illegal*. This is not the case of *Press-warrants*. They have been complained of, questioned, and resisted in a thousand instances; but still the legislature have never interposed, nor has there ever been a formal decision against them in any of the superior courts. On the contrary, they have been frequently recognised and admitted by parliament; and there are judicial opinions given in their favour by judges of the first character. Under the various circumstances stated by *Junius*, he has a right to conclude *for himself*, that there is no remedy. If you have a good one to propose, you may depend upon the assistance and applause of *Junius*. The magistrate who guards the liberty of the individual, deserves to be commended. But let him remember, that it is also his duty to provide for, or at least not to hazard, the safety of the community. If in the case of a foreign war, and the expectation of an invasion, you would rather keep your fleet in harbour, than man it by

pressing

preſſing ſeamen who refuſe the bounty, I have done.

You talk of diſbanding the army with wonderful eaſe and indifference. If a wiſer man held ſuch language, I ſhould be apt to ſuſpect his ſincerity.

As for keeping up a *much greater* number of ſeamen in time of peace, it is not to be done. You will oppreſs the merchant, you will diſtreſs trade, and deſtroy the nurſery of your ſeamen. He muſt be a miſerable ſtateſman, who voluntarily by the ſame act increaſes the public expence, and leſſens the means of ſupporting it.

PHILO JUNIUS.

---

L E T T E R  LXIII.

Oct. 22. 1771.

A Friend of *Junius* deſires it may be obſerved, (in anſwer to *A Barriſter at Law*),

1*mo*, That the fact of Lord Mansfield's having ordered a juryman to be paſſed by (which poor *Zeno* never heard of) is now formally admitted.

When Mr *Benſon*'s name was called, Lord *Manſfield* was obſerved to fluſh in the face, (a ſignal of guilt not uncommon with him,) and cried out, *Paſs him by.* This I take to be ſomething more than a peremptory challenge. It is an *unlawful command*, without any reaſon aſſigned. That the counſel did not reſiſt, is true; but this might happen either from inadvertence, or a criminal complaiſance to Lord Mansfield.—You *Barriſters* are too apt to be civil to my Lord Chief Juſtice, at the expence of your clients.

2*do*, *Junius* did never ſay that Lord Mansfield had *deſtroyed* the liberty of the preſs. " That his " Lordſhip has *laboured to deſtroy*,—that his doc- " trine is an *attack* upon the liberty of the preſs,
—that

" —that it is an *invasion* of the right of juries,"
are the propositions maintained by *Junius*. His
opponents never answer him in point, for they never meet him fairly upon his own ground.

3*tio*, Lord *Mansfield's* policy, in endeavouring
to screen his unconstitutional doctrines behind an
act of the legislature, is easily understood.—Let
every Englishman stand upon his guard;—the right
of juries to return a general verdict, in all cases
whatsoever, is a part of our constitution. It stands
in no need of a bill, either *enacting* or *declaratory*,
to confirm it.

4*to*, With regard to the *Grosvenor cause*, it is
pleasant to observe, that the doctrine, attributed by
*Junius* to Lord Mansfield, is admitted by *Zeno* and
directly defended. The *Barrister* has not the as-
surance to deny it flatly; but he evades the charge,
and softens the doctrine by such poor contemptible
quibbles as cannot impose upon the meanest understanding.

5*to*, The quantity of business in the *court of
King's-Bench* proves nothing but the litigious spirit of the people, arising from the great increase
of wealth and commerce. These, however, are
now upon the decline, and will soon leave nothing
but *law-suits* behind them. When *Junius* affirms
that Lord Mansfield has laboured to alter the system of jurisprudence in the court where his Lordship presides, he speaks to those who are able to
look a little farther than the vulgar. Besides that
the multitude are easily deceived by the imposing
names of *equity* and *substantial justice*, it does not
follow, that a judge, who introduces into his court
new modes of proceeding and new principles of
law, intends, *in every instance*, to decide unjustly.
Why should he, where he has no interest?—We
say that Lord Mansfield is a bad *man*, and a worse
*judge*;—but we do not say that he is a *mere devil*.
Our adversaries would fain reduce us to the difficulty

culty of proving too much.—This artifice, however, shall not avail him. The truth of the matter is plainly this. When *Lord Mansfield* has fucceeded in his fcheme of changing a court of *common law* to a court of *equity*, he will have it in his
power to do injuftice *whenever he thinks proper.*
This, though a wicked purpofe, is neither abfurd
nor unattainable.

*6to,* The laft paragraph relative to *Lord Chatham's* caufe cannot be anfwered. It partly refers
to facts of too fecret a nature to be afcertained,
and partly is unintelligible. " Upon *one* point,
" the caufe is decided againft Lord Chatham.—
" Upon *another* point, it is decided for him."—
Both the *law* and the *language* are well fuited to a
*Barrifter!*—If I have any guefs at this honeft gentleman's meaning, it is, That " whereas the com-
" miffioners of the Great Seal faw the queftion
" in a point of view unfavourable to *Lord Chatham,*
" and decreed accordingly,—Lord Mansfield, out
" of fheer love and kindnefs to Lord Chatham,
" took the pains to place it in a point of view
" more favourable to the *appellant.*"—*Credat Ju-
dæus Appella.*—So curious an affertion would ftag-
ger the faith of *Mr Sylva.*

---

# L E T T E R  XLIV.

Nov. 2. 1771.

WE are defired to make the following declaration, in behalf of *Junius,* upon three material points, on which his opinion has been miftaken or mifreprefented.

*1mo, Junius* confiders the right of taxing the
colonies, by an act of the Britifh Legiflature, as
a *fpeculative* right merely, never to be *exerted,*
nor ever to be *renounced.* To *his* judgment it appears plain, " That the general reafonings which

" were

" were employed againſt that power went directly
" to our whole legiſlative right, and that one part
" of it could not be yielded to ſuch arguments
" without a virtual ſurrender of all the reſt."

2do, That, with regard to preſs-warrants, his
argument ſhould be taken in his own words, and
anſwered ſtrictly;—that compariſons may ſometimes illuſtrate, but prove nothing; and that, in
this caſe, an appeal to the paſſions is unfair and
unneceſſary. *Junius* feels and acknowledges the
evil in the moſt expreſs terms, and will ſhow himſelf ready to concur in any rational plan that may
provide for the liberty of the individual, without
hazarding the ſafety of the community. At the
ſame time, he expects that the evil, ſuch as it is,
be not exaggerated or miſrepreſented. In general, it is *not* unjuſt that, when the rich man contributes his wealth, the *poor* man ſhould ſerve the
ſtate in perſon;—otherwiſe the latter contributes
nothing to the defence of that law and conſtitution from which he demands ſafety and protection. But the queſtion does not lie between *rich*
and *poor*. The laws of England make no ſuch di-
ſtinctions. Neither is it true that the poor man
is torn from the care and ſupport of a wife and family, helpleſs without him. The ſingle queſtion
is, Whether the *ſeaman**, in times of public danger, ſhall ſerve the merchant, or the ſtate, in that
profeſſion to which he was bred, and by the exer-
ciſe of which alone he can honeſtly ſupport himſelf and his family.—General arguments againſt
the doctrine of *neceſſity*, and the dangerous uſe
that may be made of it, are of no weight in this
particular caſe. *Neceſſity* includes the idea of *inevitable*. Whenever it is ſo, it creates a law to
which all *poſitive* laws and all *poſitive* rights muſt
give

---

* I confine myſelf ſtrictly to *ſeamen*;—if any others are preſſed, it is a groſs abuſe, which the magiſtrate can and ſhould correct.

give way. In this sense the levy of *ship-money* by the King's warrant was not *necessary*, because the business might have been as well or better done by parliament. If the doctrine maintained by *Junius* be confined within this limitation, it will go but very little way in support of arbitrary power. That the King is to judge of the occasion, is no objection, unless we are told how it can possibly be otherwise. There are other instances, not less important in the exercise nor less dangerous in the abuse, in which the constitution relies entirely upon the King's judgment. The executive power proclaims war and peace, binds the nation by treaties, orders general embargoes, and imposes quarantines; not to mention a multitude of prerogative writs, which, though liable to the greatest abuses, were never disputed.

3*tio*, It has been urged as a reproach to *Junius*, that he has not delivered an opinion upon the Game Laws, and particularly the late *Dog Act*: But *Junius* thinks he has much greater reason to complain, that he is never assisted by those who are able to assist him; and that almost the whole labour of the press is thrown upon a single hand, from which a discussion of *every* public question whatsoever is unreasonably expected. He is not paid for his labour, and certainly has a right to choose his employment.—As to the *Game Laws*, he never scrupled to declare his opinion, that they are a species of the *Forest Laws ;* that they are oppressive to the subject; and that the spirit of them is incompatible with legal liberty:—That the penalties imposed by these laws bear no proportion to the nature of the offence; that the mode of trial, and the degree and kind of evidence necessary to convict, not only deprive the subject of all the benefits of a trial by jury, but are in themselves too summary, and to the last degree arbitrary and oppressive: That, in particular, the late acts to prevent dog-stealing, or killing game between sun and sun, are distinguished by their absurdity, extravagance, and pernicious tendency. If these terms are weak or ambiguous, in what language can *Junius* express himself?—It is no excuse for *Lord Mansfield* to say, that he *happened* to be absent when these bills passed the house of Lords. It was his duty to be present. Such bills could never have passed the house of commons without his knowledge. But we very well know by what rule he regulates his attendance. When that order was made in the house of Lords in the case of *Lord Pomfret*, at which every Englishman shudders, my honest *Lord Mansfield* found himself, *by mere accident*, in the court of King's Bench :— Otherwise he would have done wonders in defence of law and property! The pitiful evasion is adapted to the character. But *Junius* will never justify himself by the example of this bad man. The distinction between *doing wrong*, and *avoiding to do right*, belongs to Lord Mansfield. *Junius* disclaims it.

---

## L E T T E R   LXV.

TO LORD CHIEF JUSTICE MANSFIELD.

Nov. 2. 1771.

AT the intercession of three of your countrymen, you have bailed a man who, I presume, is also a *Scotchman*, and whom the Lord Mayor of London had refused to bail. I do not mean to enter into an examination of the partial, sinister motives of your conduct; but, confining myself strictly to the fact, I affirm, that you have done that which by law you were not warranted to do. The thief was taken in the theft ;—the stolen goods were found upon him, and he made no defence. In these circumstances, (the truth of which

you dare not deny, becaufe it is of public notriety),
it could not ftand indifferent whether he was guilty or not, much lefs could there be any prefumption of his innocence; and, in thefe circumftances, I affirm, in contradiction to YOU, Lord
Chief Justice Mansfield, that, by the laws
of England, he was *not bailable*. If ever *Mr Eyre*
fhould be brought to trial, we fhall hear what You
have to fay for yourfelf; and I pledge myfelf, before God and my country, in proper time and
place, to make good my charge againft you.

JUNIUS.

---

## LETTER LXVI.

### TO THE PRINTER OF THE PUBLIC ADVER-<br>TISER.

Nov. 9. 1771.

JUNIUS engages to make good his charge againft
*Lord Chief Juftice Mansfield* fome time before
the meeting of parliament, in order that the houfe
of commons may, if they think proper, make it
one article in the impeachment of the faid *Lord
Chief Juftice.*

---

## LETTER LXVII.

### TO HIS GRACE THE DUKE OF GRAFTON.

Nov. 27. 1771.

WHAT is the reafon, my Lord, that when almoft every man in the kingdom, without
diftinction of principles or party, exults in the ridiculous defeat of Sir James Lowther; when good
and bad men unite in one common opinion of that
baronet, and triumph in his diftrefs, as if the event
(without any reference to vice or virtue) were interefting to human nature; your Grace alone
fhould

should appear so miserably depressed and afflicted? In such universal joy, I know not where you will look for a compliment of condolence, unless you appeal to the tender, sympathetic sorrows of Mr Bradshaw. That cream-coloured gentleman's tears, affecting as they are, carry consolation with them. He never weeps but, like an April shower, with a lambent ray of sunshine upon his countenance. From the feelings of honest men upon this joyful occasion, I do not mean to draw any conclusion to your Grace. *They* naturally rejoice when they see a signal instance of tyranny resisted with success; —of treachery exposed to the derision of the world; —an infamous informer defeated, and an impudent robber dragged to the public gibbet—But, in the *other* class of mankind, I own I expected to meet the Duke of Grafton. Men who have no regard for justice, nor any sense of honour, seem as heartily pleased with Sir James Lowther's well-deserved punishment, as if it did not constitute an example against themselves. The unhappy Baronet has no friends, even among those who resemble him. You, my Lord, are not reduced to so deplorable a state of dereliction. Every villain in the kingdom is your friend; and, in compliment to such amity, I think you should suffer your dismal countenance to clear up. Besides, my Lord, I am a little anxious for the consistency of your character. You violate your own rules of decorum, when you do not insult the man whom you have betrayed.

The divine justice of retribution seems now to have begun its progress. Deliberate treachery entails punishment upon the traitor. There is no possibility of escaping it, even in the highest rank to which the consent of society can exalt the meanest and worst of men. The forced, unnatural union of Luttrell and Middlesex was an omen of another unnatural union, by which indefeasible



infamy

infamy is attached to the houfe of Brunfwick. If one of thefe acts was virtuous and honourable, the beft of Princes, I thank God, is happily rewarded for it by the other.—Your Grace, *it has been faid*, had fome fhare in recommending Colonel Luttrell to the King;—or was it only the gentle Bradfhaw who made himfelf anfwerable for the good behaviour of his friend? An intimate connection has long fubfifted between him and the worthy Lord Irnham. It arofe from a fortunate fimilarity of principles, cemented by the conftant mediation of their common friend Mifs Davis *.

Yet I confefs I fhould be forry that the opprobrious infamy of this match fhould reach beyond the family.—We have now a better reafon than ever

* There is a certain family in this country, on which nature feems to have entailed an hereditary bafenefs of difpofition. As far as their hiftory has been known, the fon has regularly improved upon the vices of his father, and has taken care to tranfmit them pure and undiminifhed into the bofom of his fucceffor. In the fenate, their abilities have confined them to thofe humble, fordid fervices in which the fcavengers of the miniftry are ufually employed. But, in the memoirs of private treachery, they ftand firft and unrivalled. The following ftory will ferve to illuftrate the character of this refpectable family, and to convince the world that the prefent poffeffor has as clear a title to the infamy of his anceftors as he has to their eftate. It deferves to be recorded for the curiofity of the fact, and fhould be given to the public as a warning to every honeft member of fociety.

The prefent Lord Irnham, who is now in the decline of life, lately cultivated the acquaintance of a younger brother of a family with which he had lived in fome degree of intimacy and friendfhip. The young man had long been the dupe of a moft unhappy attachment to a common proftitute. His friends and relations forefaw the confequences of this connection, and did every thing that depended upon them to fave him from ruin. But he had a friend in Lord Irnham, whofe advice rendered all their endeavours ineffectual. This hoary letcher, not contented with the enjoyment of his friend's miftrefs, was bafe enough to take advantage of the paffions and folly of a young man, and perfuaded him to marry her. He defcended even to perform the office of father to the proftitute. He gave her to his friend, who was on the point of leaving the kingdom, and the next night lay with her himfelf.

Whether the depravity of the human heart can produce any thing more bafe and deteftable than this fact, muft be left undetermined until the fon fhall arrive at the father's age and experience.

ever to pray for the long life of the beft of Princes, and the welfare of his royal *iffue.*—I will not mix any thing ominous with my prayers;—but let parliament look to it—A *Luttrell* fhall never fucceed to the crown of England.—If the hereditary virtues of the family deferve a kingdom, Scotland will be a proper retreat for them.

The next is a moft remarkable inftance of the goodnefs of Providence. The juft law of retaliation has at laft overtaken the little contemptible tyrant of the North. To the fon-in-law of your deareft friend the Earl of Bute you meant to tranffer the Duke of Portland's property; and you haftened the grant with an expedition unknown to the Treafury, that he might have it time enough to give a decifive turn to the election for the county. The immediate confequence of this flagitious robbery was, that he loft the election which you meant to infure to him, and with fuch fignal circumftances of fcorn, reproach, and infult, (to fay nothing of the general exultation of all parties), as (excepting the King's brother-in-law Col. Luttrell, and old *Simon* his father in-law) hardly ever fell upon a gentleman in this country.—In the event, he lofes the very property of which he thought he had gotten poffeffion, and after an expence which would have paid the value of the land in queftion twenty times over.—The forms of villainy, you fee, are neceffary to its fuccefs. Hereafter you will act with greater circumfpection, and not drive fo directly to your object. To *fnatch a grace* beyond the reach of common treachery, is an exception, not a rule.

And now, my good Lord, does not your confcious heart inform you, that the juftice of rettibution begins to operate, and that it may foon approach your perfon?—Do you think that *Junius* has renounced the Middlefex election?—or that the King's timber fhall be refufed to the Royal



Navy

Navy with impunity?—or that you fhall hear no more of the fale of that patent to *Mr Hine*, which you endeavoured to fkreen by fuddenly dropping your profecution of *Samuel Vaughan*, when the rule againft him was made abfolute? I believe indeed there never was fuch an inftance in all the hiftory of negative impudence.—But it fhall not fave you. The very funfhine you live in is a prelude to your diffolution. When you are ripe, you fhall be plucked.　　　　JUNIUS.

P. S. I beg you will convey to our gracious mafter my humble congratulations upon the glorious fuccefs of peerages and penfions, fo lavifhly diftributed as the rewards of Irifh virtue.

---

## L E T T E R LXVIII.

### TO LORD CHIEF JUSTICE MANSFIELD.

Jun. 21. 1772.

I HAVE undertaken to prove, that when, at the interceffion of three of your countrymen, you bailed *John Eyre*, you did that *which by law you were not warranted to do;* and that a felon, under the circumftances *of being taken in the fact, with the ftolen goods upon him, and making no defence, is not bailable* by the laws of England. Your learned advocates have interpreted this charge into a denial that the court of King's-bench, or the judges of that court during the vacation, have any greater authority to bail for criminal offences than a juftice of peace. With the inftance before me, I am fuppofed to queftion your power of doing wrong, and to deny the exiftence of a power at the fame moment that I arraign the illegal exercife of it. But the opinions of fuch men, whether wilful in their malignity, or fincere in their ignorance, are unworthy of my notice. You,

-Lord

Lord Mansfield, did not understand me so; and, I promise you, your cause requires an abler defence. —I am now to make good my charge against you. However dull my argument, the subject of it is interesting. I shall be honoured with the attention of the public, and have a right to demand the attention of the legislature. Supported as I am by the whole body of the criminal law of England, I have no doubt of establishing my charge. If, on your part, you should have no plain, substantial defence, but should endeavour to shelter yourself under the quirk and evasion of a practising lawyer, or under the mere insulting assertion of power without right, the reputation you pretend to is gone for ever;—you stand degraded from the respect and authority of your office, and are no longer, *de jure*, Lord Chief Justice of England. This letter, my Lord, is addressed, not so much to *you*, as to the public. Learned as you are, and quick in apprehension, few arguments are necessary to satisfy you, that you have done that which by law you were not warranted to do. Your conscience already tells you, that you have sinned against knowledge, and that whatever defence you make contradicts your own internal conviction. But other men are willing enough to take the law upon trust. They rely upon your authority, because they are too indolent to search for information; or, conceiving that there is some mystery in the laws of their country which lawyers only are qualified to explain, they distrust their judgment, and voluntarily renounce the right of thinking for themselves. With all the evidence of history before them, from *Tresillian* to *Jefferies*, from *Jefferies* to *Mansfield*, they will not believe it possible that a learned judge can act in direct contradiction to those laws which he is supposed to have made the study of his life, and which he has sworn to administer faithfully. Superstition is certainly not

the

the characteristic of this 'age. Yet some men are bigotted in politics who are infidels in religion.—I do not despair of making them ashamed of their credulity.

The charge I brought against you is expressed in terms guarded and well considered. They do not deny the strict power of the judges of the court of King's Bench to bail in cases not bailable by a justice of peace, nor replevisable by the common writ, or *ex officio* by the sheriff. I well know the practice of the court, and by what legal rules it ought to be directed. But, far from meaning to soften or diminish the force of those terms I have made use of, I now go beyond them, and affirm,

I. That the superior power of bailing for felony, claimed by the court of King's Bench, is founded upon the opinion of lawyers, and the practice of the court;—that the assent of the legislature to this power is merely negative,—and that it is not supported by any positive provision in any statute whatsoever—If it be, produce the statute.

II. Admitting that the judges of the court of King's Bench are vested with a discretionary power to examine and judge of circumstances and allegations which a justice of peace is not permitted to consider, I affirm that the judges, in the use and application of that discretionary power, are as strictly bound by the spirit, intent, and meaning, as the justice of peace is by the words, of the legislature. Favourable circumstances, alleged before the judge, may justify a doubt whether the prisoner be guilty or not; and, where the guilt is doubtful, a presumption of innocence should, in general, be admitted. But, when any such probable circumstances are alleged, they alter the state and condition of the prisoner. *He* is no longer that *all-but-convicted* felon whom the law intends, and who by law is *not bailable at all*. If

no

no circumſtances whatſoever are alleged in his favour;—if no allegation whatſoever be made to
leſſen the force of that evidence which the law
annexes to a poſitive charge of felony, and particularly to the fact of *being taken with the maner;*
I then ſay, that the Lord Chief Juſtice of England
has no more right to bail him than a juſtice of
peace. The diſcretion of an Engliſh judge is not
of mere will and pleaſure;—it is not arbitrary;—
it is not capricious; but, as that great lawyer,
(whoſe authority I wiſh you reſpected half as much
as I do) truly ſays*, " Diſcretion, taken as it
" ought to be, is, *diſcernere per legem quid ſit juſ-*
" *tum.* If it be not directed by the right line of
" the law, it is a crooked cord, and appeareth to
" be unlawful."—If diſcretion were arbitrary in
the judge, he might introduce whatever novelties
he thought proper. But, ſays Lord Coke, " No-
" velties, without warrant of precedents, are not
" to be allowed; ſome certain rules are to be fol-
" lowed;—*Quicquid judicis authoritati ſubjicitur,*
" *novitati non ſubjicitur:*" and this ſound doctrine
is applied to the Star chamber, a court confeſſedly
arbitrary. If you will abide by the authority of
this great man, you ſhall have all the advantage
of his opinion, wherever it appears to favour you.
Excepting the plain expreſs meaning of the legiſlature, to which all private opinions muſt give
way, I deſire no better judge between us than
Lord Coke.

III. I affirm, that, according to the obvious in-
diſputable meaning of the legiſlature, repeatedly
expreſſed, a perſon poſitively charged with *feloni-
ouſly ſtealing,* and taken *in flagrante delicto,* with
the ſtolen goods upon him, is *not bailable.* The
law conſiders him as differing in nothing from *a
convict,* but in the form of conviction; and (whatever a corrupt judge may do) will accept of no ſecurity

* 4 *Inſt.* 41. 66.

curity but the confinement of his body within four walls. I know it has been alleged in your favour, that you have often bailed for murders, rapes, and other manifeſt crimes. Without queſtioning the fact, I ſhall not admit that you are to be juſtified by your own example. If that were a protection to you, where is the crime, that, as a judge, you might not now ſecurely commit? But neither ſhall I ſuffer myſelf to be drawn aſide from my preſent argument, nor *you* to profit by your own wrong.—To prove the meaning and intent of the legiſlature, will require a minute and tedious deduction. To inveſtigate a queſtion of law, demands ſome labour and attention; though very little genius or ſagacity. As a practical profeſſion, the ſtudy of the law requires but a moderate portion of abilities. The learning of a pleader is uſually upon a level with his integrity. The indiſcriminate defence of right and wrong contracts the underſtanding, while it corrupts the heart. Subtlety is ſoon miſtaken for wiſdom, and impunity for virtue. If there be any inſtances upon record, as ſome there are undoubtedly, of genius and morality united in a lawyer, they are diſtinguiſhed by their ſingularity, and operate as exceptions.

I muſt ſolicit the patience of my readers. This is no light matter; nor is it any more ſuſceptible of ornament, than the conduct of Lord Mansfield is capable of aggravation.

As the law of bail, in charges of felony, has been exactly aſcertained by acts of the legiſlature, it is at preſent of little conſequence to inquire how it ſtood at common law before the ſtatute of Weſtminſter. And yet it is worth the reader's attention to obſerve, how nearly, in the ideas of our anceſtors, the circumſtance of being taken *with the maner* approached to the conviction of the
felon.

felon*. "It fixed the authoritative stamp of ve-
"risimilitude upon the accusation; and, by the
"common law, when a thief was taken *with the*
"*maner* (that is, with the thing stolen upon him,
"*in manu*) he might, so detected *flagrante delicto*,
"be brought into court, arraigned and tried, *with-*
"*out indictment*; as, by the Danish law, he might
"be taken and hanged upon the spot, without ac-
"cusation or trial." It will soon appear that our
statute-law, in this behalf, though less summary
in point of proceeding, is directed by the same
spirit. In one instance, the very form is adhered
to. In offences relating to the forest, if a man
was taken with vert, or venison†, it was declared
to be equivalent to indictment. To enable the
reader to judge for himself, I shall state, in due
order, the several statutes relative to bail in criminal cases, or as much of them as may be material to the point in question, omitting superfluous
words. If I misrepresent, or do not quote with fidelity, it will not be difficult to detect me.

The statute of Westminster the first‡, in 1275,
sets forth, that "Forasmuch as sheriffs and others,
"who have taken and kept in prison persons de-
"tected of felony, and incontinent have let out
"by replevin such as were *not replevisable*, because
"they would gain of the one party and grieve the
"other; and forasmuch as, before this time, it
"was not determined which persons were reple-
"visable, and which not, it is provided, and by
"the King commanded, that such prisoners, &c.
"as be *taken with the maner*, &c. or for *manifest*
"offences, shall be *in no wise* replevisable by the
"common writ, nor without writ." §—Lord
Coke,

---

* *Blackstone*, 4. 303.
† 1 *Ed.* III. *cap.* 8.—— and 7 *Rich.* II. *cap.* 4.
‡ "*Videtur que le statute de mainprise ne'st que reberful del comen*
"*ley.*" Bro. Mainp 61.
§ "There are three points to be considered in the construction
"of all remedial statutes;——the old law, the mischief, and the
remedy:

Coke in his expofition of the laft part of this quotation, accurately diftinguifhes between *replevy* by the common writ, or *ex officio*, and *bail* by the King's Bench. The words of the ftatute certainly do not extend to the judges of that court. But, befides that the reader will foon find reafon to think that the legiflature, in their intention, made no difference between *bailable* and *replevifable*, Lord Coke himfelf (if he be underftood to mean nothing but an expofition of the ftatute of Weftminfter, and not to ftate the law generally) does not adhere to his own diftinction. In expounding the other offences which, by this ftatute, are declared *not replevifable*, he conftantly ufes the words *not bailable*.—" That outlaws, for inftance, are " *not bailable at all;*—that perfons who have ab-" jured the realm, are attainted upon their own " confeflion, and therefore *not bailable at all by* " *law;*—that provers are *not bailable;*—that no-" torious felons are *not bailable.*" The reafon why the fuperior courts were not named in the ftatute of Weftminfter, was plainly this, " becaufe an-" ciently moft of the bufinefs touching bailment " of prifoners for felony or mifdemeanours, was " performed by the fheriffs, or fpecial bailiffs of " liberties, either by writ, or *virtute officii*;*" confequently the fuperior courts had little or no opportunity to commit thofe abufes which the ftatute imputes to the fheriffs.—With fubmiffion to Dr Blackftone, I think he has fallen into a contradiction; which, in terms at leaft, appears irreconcileable. After enumerating feveral offences not bailable, he afferts, without any condition or limitation whatfoever †, " All thefe are clearly not

ad-

" remedy:———that is, how the common law ftood at the making " of the act, what the mifchief was for which the common law " did not provide, and what remedy the parliament hath provided " to cure this mifchief. It is the bufinefs of the judges fo to conftrue " the act, as to fupprefs the mifchief and advance the remedy."

*Blackftone,* 1. 87.

* 2 *Hale,* P. C. 128. 136.          † *Blackftone,* 4. 296.

"admiffible to bail." Yet, in a few lines after, he says, "*it is agreed* that the court of King's Bench "may bail for any crime whatfoever, *according* "*to circumftances of* the cafe." To his firft pro-pofition he fhould have added, *by Sheriffs or Ju-ftices:* otherwife the two propofitions contradict each other; with this difference, however, that the firft is abfolute, the fecond limited by *a confi-deration of circumftances.* I fay this without the leaft intended difrefpect to the learned author. His work is of public utility, and fhould not hafti-ly be condemned.

The ftatute of 17 *Richard* II. *cap.* 10. 1393, fets forth, that "Forafmuch as thieves notoriouffy "defamed, *and others taken with the maner,* by "their long abiding in prifon, were delivered by "charters, and favourable inquefts procured, to "the great hindrance of the people, two men of "law fhall be affigned, in every commiffion of "the peace, to proceed to the deliverance of fuch "felons, &c." It feems by this act, that there was a conftant ftruggle between the legiflature and the officers of juftice. Not daring to admit felons *taken with the maner* to bail or mainprize, they evaded the law by keeping the party in prifon a long time, and then delivering him without due trial.

The ftatute of 1 *Richard* III. in 1483, fets forth, that "Forafmuch as divers perfons have been "daily arrefted and imprifoned for *fufpicion* of fe-"lony, fometime of malice, and fometime of a "*light fufpicion,* and fo kept in prifon without "bail or mainprize, be it ordained, that every "juftice of peace fhall have authority, by his dif-"cretion, to let fuch prifoners and perfons fo ar-"refted to bail or mainprize."—By this act it ap-pears, that there had been abufes in matter of im-prifonment, and that the legiflature meant to pro-
<br>G g                    vide

vide for the immediate enlargement of perſons arreſted on *light ſuſpicion* of felony.

The ſtatute of 3d Henry VII. in 1486, declares,
that, " under colour of the preceding act of Ri-
" chard the Third, perſons, *ſuch as were not main-*
" *pernable*, were oftentimes let to bail or main-
" prize by juſtices of the peace, whereby many
" murderers and felons eſcaped, the King, &c.
" hath ordained, that the juſtices of the peace,
" or two of them at leaſt, (whereof one to be of
" the *quorum*), have authority to let any ſuch
" priſoners or perſons, mainpernable by the law,
" to bail or mainprize."

The ſtatute of 1ſt and 2d of Philip and Mary,
in 1554, ſets forth, that, " notwithſtanding the
" preceding ſtatute of Henry the Seventh, *one*
" juſtice of peace hath oftentimes, by ſiniſter la-
" bour and means, ſet at large the greateſt and
" notableſt offenders, *ſuch as be not repleviſable*
" *by the laws of this realm;* and yet, the rather to
" hide their affections in that behalf, have ſigned
" the cauſe of their apprehenſion to be but only
" for *ſuſpicion* of felony, whereby the ſaid offen-
" ders have eſcaped unpuniſhed, and do daily, to
" the high diſpleaſure of Almighty God, the great
" peril of the King and Queen's true ſubjects,
" and encouragement of all thieves and evil-
" doers ;—for reformation whereof be it enacted,
" that no juſtices of peace ſhall let to bail or main-
" prize any ſuch perſons, which, for any offence
" by them committed, be declared *not* to be *re-*
" *pleviſed*, or *bailed*, or be forbidden to be *reple-*
" *viſed* or *bailed* by the ſtatute of Weſtminſter the
" firſt ; and furthermore, that any perſons, ar-
" reſted for manſlaughter, felony, *being bailable*
" *by the law*, ſhall not be let to bail or mainprize
" by any juſtices of peace, but in the form there-
" in after preſcribed."—In the two preceding ſtatutes, the words *bailable*, *repleviſable*, and *main-*

*pernable*, are ufed fynonimoufly *, or promifcu-
oufly, to exprefs the fame fingle intention of the
legiflature, viz. *not to accept of any fecurity but
the body of the offender;* and when the latter ftatute prefcribes the form in which perfons arrefted on *fufpicion* of felony (*being bailable by the law*)
may be let to bail, it evidently fuppofes, that
there are fome cafes *not* bailable by the law.—It
may be thought, perhaps, that I attribute to the
legiflature an appearance of inaccuracy in the ufe
of terms, merely to ferve my prefent purpofe.
But in truth it would make more forcibly for my
argument, to prefume, that the legiflature were
conftantly aware of the ftrict legal diftinction between *bail* and *replevy*, and that they always meant
to adhere to it †. For if it be true that *replevy* is
by the fheriffs, and *bail* by the higher courts at
Weftminfter, (which I think no lawyer will deny),
it follows, that when the legiflature exprefsly fays,
that any particular offence is by law *not bailable*,
the fuperior courts are comprehended in the prohibition, and bound by it. Otherwife, unlefs
there was a pofitive exception of the fuperior
courts (which I affirm there never was in any ftatute relative to bail), the legiflature would grofsly
contradict themfelves, and the manifeft intention
of the law be evaded. It is an eftablifhed rule,
that when the law is *fpecial*, and reafon of it general, it is to be *generally* underftood; and though
by cuftom a latitude be allowed to the court of
King's Bench, (to confider circumftances induc-
tive of a doubt, whether the prifoner be guilty or
innocent), if this latitude be taken as an arbitrary
power to bail, when no circumftances whatfoever
are alleged in favour of the prifoner, it is a power

G g 2

without

* 2 *Hale*, P. C. ii. 124.

† *Vide* 2d Inft. 150. 186.———" The word *replevifable* never fig-
" nifies *bailable*. *Bailable* is in a court of record by the King's
" juftices; but *replevifable* is by the Sheriff.

*Selden*, State Tr. vii. 149.

without right, and a daring violation of the whole Englifh law of bail.

The act of the 31ft of Charles the Second (commonly called the *Habeas Corpus act*) particularly declares, that it is not meant to extend to treafon or felony plainly and fpecially exprefled in the warrant of commitment. The prifoner is therefore left to feek his *habeas corpus* at common law; and fo far was the legiflature from fuppofing that perfons (committed for treafon or felony plainly and fpecially exprefled in the warrant of commitment) could be let to bail by a fingle judge, or by the whole court, that this very act provides a remedy for fuch perfons, in cafe they are not indicted in the courfe of the term or feffions fubfequent to their commitment. The law neither fuffers them to be enlarged before trial, nor to be imprifoned after the time in which they ought regularly to be tried. In this cafe the law fays, " It fhall and may be lawful to and for the judges " of the court of King's Bench, and juftices of " oyer and terminer, or general gaol delivery, and " they are hereby required, upon motion to them " made in open court, the laft day of the term, " feffion, or gaol-delivery, either by the prifoner " or any one in his behalf, to fer at liberty the " prifoner upon bail; unlefs it appear to the jud- " ges and juftices, upon oath made, that the wit- " neffes for the king could not be produced the " fame term, feffions, or gaol-delivery."—Upon the whole of this article, I obferve, 1. That the provifion made in the firft part of it, would be, in a great meafure, ufelefs and nugatory, if any fingle judge might have bailed the prifoner *ex arbitrio* during the vacation; or if the court might have bailed him immediately after the commencement of the term or feffions.—2. When the law fays, *It fhall and may be lawful* to bail for felony under particular circumftances, we muft prefume,

that

.that before the paffing of that act, it was *not* lawful to bail under thofe circumftances.   The terms ufed by the legiflature are *enacting*, not *declaratory.*—3. Notwithftanding the party may have been imprifoned during the greateft part of the vacation, and during the whole feffion, the court are exprefsly forbidden to bail him from that feffion to the next, if oath be made that the witneffos for the King could not be produced that fame term or feffions.

Having faithfully ftated the feveral acts of parliament relative to bail in criminal cafes, it may be ufeful to the reader to take a fhort hiftorical review of the law of bail, through its various gradations and improvements.

By the ancient common law, before and fince the Conqueft, all felonies were bailable, till murder was excepted by ftatute; fo that perfons might be admitted to bail, before conviction, almoft in every cafe.   The ftatute of Weftminfter fays, that before that time, it had not been determined which offences were replevifable, and which were not, whether by the common writ *de homine replegiando*, or *ex officio* by the fheriff.  It is very remarkable, that the abufes arifing from this unlimited power of replevy, dreadful as they were, and deftructive to the peace of fociety, were not corrected or taken notice of by the legiflature, until the commons of the kingdom had obtained a fhare in it by their reprefentatives; but the houfe of commons had fcarce begun to exift, when thefe formidable abufes were corrected by the ftatute of Weftminfter.  It is highly probable, that the mifchief had been feverely felt by the people, although no remedy had been provided for it by the Norman Kings or Barons.  "The iniquity of the " times was fo great *, as it even forced the " fubjects to forego that, which was in account

G g 3

<hr>

* *Selden,* by *N. Bacon,* 182.

" a great liberty, to ſtop the courſe of a growing
" miſchief." The preamble to the ſtatutes, made
by the firſt parliament of Edward the Firſt, aſſigns
the reaſon of calling it†, " becauſe the people
" had been otherwiſe entreated than they ought
" to be, the peace leſs kept, the laws leſs uſed,
" and *offenders leſs puniſhed*, than they ought to be,
" by reaſon whereof the people feared leſs to of-
" fend :" and the firſt attempt to reform theſe
various abuſes, was by contracting the power of
replevying felons.

For above two centuries following, it does not
appear that any alteration was made in the law
of bail, except that *being taken with vert or veni-
ſon* was declared to be equivalent to indictment.
The legiſlature adhered firmly to the ſpirit of the
ſtatute of Weſtminſter. The ſtatute of 27th of
Edward the Firſt, directs the juſtices of aſſize to
inquire and puniſh officers bailing ſuch as were
*not bailable*. As for the judges of the ſuperior
courts, it is probable, that in thoſe days they
thought themſelves bound by the obvious intent
and meaning of the legiſlature. They conſidered
not ſo much to what particular perſons the prohibition was addreſſed, as what the *thing* was which
the legiſlature meant to prohibit; well knowing,
that in law, *quando aliquid prohibetur, prohibetur
et omne, per quod devenitur ad illud.* " When any
" thing is forbidden, all the means by which the
" ſame thing may be compaſſed or done, are e-
" qually forbidden."

By the ſtatute of Richard the Third, the power
of bailing was a little enlarged. Every juſtice of
peace was authoriſed to bail for felony; but they
were expreſsly confined to perſons arreſted *on light
ſuſpicion*; and even this power, ſo limited, was
found to produce ſuch inconveniences, that, in
three years after, the legiſlature found it neceſſary

to

<hr>

† Parliamentary Hiſtory, i. 82.

to repeal it. Inftead of trufting any longer to a single juftice of peace, the act of 3d Henry VII. repeals the preceding act, and directs, " that no " prifoner (*of thofe who are mainpernable by the* " *law*) fhall be let to bail or mainprife by lefs " than *two* juftices, whereof one to be of the " quorum." And fo indifpenfably neceffary was this provifion thought for the adminiftration of juftice, and for the fecurity and peace of fociety, that at this time an oath was propofed by the King, to be taken by the knights and efquires of his houfehold, by the members of the houfe of commons, and by the peers fpiritual and temporal, and accepted and fworn to *quafi una voce* by them all; which, among other engagements, binds them " not to let any man to bail or mainprife, " knowing and deeming him to be a felon, upon " your honour and worfhip. So help you God " and all faints*."

In about half a century, however, even thefe provifions were found infufficient. The act of Henry the Seventh was evaded, and the legiflature once more obliged to interpofe. The act of 1ft and 2d of Philip and Mary, takes away entirely from the juftices all power of bailing for offences declared *not bailable* by the ftatute of Weftminfter.

The illegal imprifonment of feveral perfons who had refufed to contribute to a loan exacted by Charles the Firft, and the delay of the *habeas corpus*, and fubfequent refufal to bail them, conftituted one of the firft and moft important grievances of that reign. Yet when the houfe of commons, which met in the year 1628, refolved upon meafures of the moft firm and ftrenuous refiftance to the power of imprifonment affumed by the King or privy-council, and to the refufal to bail the party on the return of the *habeas corpus*, they

did

* Parliamentary Hiftory, ii. 419.

did exprefsly, in all their refolutions, make an exception of commitments, where the caufe of the
reftraint was expreffed, and did by law juftify the
commitment. The reafon of the diftinction is,
that whereas, when the caufe of commitment is
expreffed, the crime is then known, and the offender muft be brought to the ordinary trial; if,
on the contrary, no caufe of commitment be expreffed, and the prifoner be thereupon remanded,
it may operate to perpetual imprifonment.  This
conteft with Charles the Firft produced the act of
the 16th of that king; by which the court of
King's Bench are directed, within three days after
the return to the *habeas corpus*, to examine and
determine the legality of any commitment by the
King or privy-council, and to do *what to juftice
fhall appertain*, in delivering, bailing, or *remanding* the prifoner.—*Now*, it feems, it is unneceffa-
ry for the judge to do what appertains to juftice.
The fame fcandalous traffic, in which we have
feen the privilege of parliament exerted or relaxed,
to gratify the prefent humour, or to ferve the immediate purpofe, of the crown, is introduced into
the adminiftration of juftice.  The magiftrate, it
feems, has now no rule to follow, but the dictates
of perfonal enmity, national partiality, or perhaps
the moft proftituted corruption.

To complete this hiftorical inquiry, it only remains to be obferved, that the *habeas corpus* act
of 31ft of Charles the Second, fo juftly confidered
as another Magna Charta of the kingdom *, " ex-
" tends only to the cafe of commitments for fuch
" criminal charge, as can produce no inconve-
" nience to public juftice by a temporary enlarge-
" ment of the prifoner."—So careful were the legiflature, at the very moment when they were pro-
viding for the liberty of the fubject, not to furnifh any colour or pretence for violating or eva-
ding

* Blackftone, iv. 137.

ding the eftablifhed law of bail in the higher criminal offences.   But the exception, ftated in the
body of the act, puts the matter out of all doubt.
After directing the judges how they are to proceed to the difcharge of the prifoner upon recognizance and furety, having regard to the quality
of the prifoner and nature of the offence, it is exprefsly added, " unlefs it fhall appear to the faid
" Lord Chancellor, &c. that the party fo commit-
" ted is detained for fuch matters or offences, for
" the which, BY THE LAW, THE PRISONER IS
" NOT BAILABLE."

When the laws, plain of themfelves, are thus
illuftrated by facts, and their uniform -meaning
eftablifhed by hiftory, we do not want the authority of opinions, however refpectable, to inform
our judgment, or to confirm our belief.   But I
am determined that you fhall have no efcape.   Authority of every fort fhall be produced againft you,
from *Jacob* to Lord *Coke*, from the dictionary to
the claffic.—In vain fhall you appeal from thofe
upright judges whom you difdain to imitate, to
thofe whom you have made your example.   With
one voice they all condemn you.

" To be taken with the *maner*, is where a thief,
" having ftolen any thing, is taken with the fame
" about him, as it were in his hands, which is
" called *flagrante delicto*.   Such a criminal is *not*
" *bailable by law*."—*Jacob, under the word* Maner.

" Thofe who are taken with the *maner* are ex-
" cluded, by the ftatute of Weftminfter, from
" the benefit of a replevin."—*Hawkins, P. C.* ii.
98.

" Of fuch heinous offences, no one, who is no-
" torioufly guilty, feems to be *bailable* by the in-
" tent of this ftatute."—*Ditto,* ii. 99.

" The common practice and allowed general
" rule is, that bail is only then proper where it
                                          " ftands

" ftands *indifferent*, whether the party were guil-
" ty or innocent."—*Ditto, ditto*.

" There is no doubt, but that the bailing of a
" perfon, *who is not bailable by law*, is punifhable,
" either at common law as a negligent efcape, or
" as an offence againft the feveral ftatutes relative
" to bail."—*Ditto*, 89.

" It cannot be doubted, but that neither the
" judges of this, nor of any other fuperior court
" of juftice, are ftrictly within the purview of
" that ftatute; yet they will always, in their dif-
" cretion, pay a due regard to it, and not admit
" a perfon to bail, who is exprefsly declared by
" it irreplevifable, *without fome particular circum-*
" *ftance in his favour;* and therefore it feems dif-
" ficult to find an inftance, where perfons, at-
" tainted of felony, or notorioufly guilty of trea-
" fon or manflaughter, &c. by their own confef-
" fion, or *otherwife*, have been admitted to the
" benefit of bail, without fome fpecial motive to
" the court to grant it."—*Ditto*, 114.

" If it appears that any man hath injury or
" wrong by his imprifonment, we have power to
" deliver and difcharge him;—if otherwife, *he is*
" *to be remanded* by us to prifon again."—*Lord Ch.*
" *J. Hyde, State Trials*, vii. 1115.

" The ftatute of Weftminfter was efpecially for
" direction to the Sheriffs and others; but to fay
" courts of juftice are excluded from this ftatute,
" I conceive it cannot be."—*Attorney General.*
*Heath, Ditto*, 132.

" The court, upon view of the return, judgeth
" of the fufficiency or infufficiency of it. If they
" think the prifoner *in law* to be *bailable*, he is
" committed to the Marfhal and bailed; if not,
" he is remanded."—Through the whole debate,
the objection on the part of the prifoner was,
that no caufe of commitment was exprefled in the
warrant; but it was uniformly admitted by their
" counfel,

counfel, that if the caufe of commitment had been expreffed for treafon or felony, the court would then have done right in remanding them.

The Attorney-General having urged, before a committee of both houfes, that, in Beckwith's cafe and others, the lords of the council fent a letter to the court of King's Bench to bail, it was replied by the managers of the houfe of commons, that this was of no moment; "for that either "the prifoner was *bailable by the law*, or *not bail-* "*able*.—If bailable by the law, then he was to "be bailed without any fuch letter;—if not bail- "able by the law, then plainly the judges could "not have bailed him upon the letter, without "breach of their oath, which is, *that they are to* "*do juftice according to the law, &c.—State Trials*, vii. 175.

"So that in bailing upon fuch offences of the "higheft nature, a kind of difcretion, rather than "a conftant law, hath been exercifed, when it "ftands *wholly indifferent* in the eye of the court, "whether the prifoner be guilty or not." *Selden*, *St. Tr.* vii. 230. 1.

"I deny that a man is always bailable when "imprifonment is impofed upon him for cufto- "dy." *Attorney-General Heath, ditto*, 238.—By thefe quotations from the State Trials, though otherwife not of authority, it appears plainly, that in regard to *bailable* or not *bailable*, all parties agreed in admitting one propofition as incontrovertible.

"In relation to capital offences, there are efpe- "cially thefe acts of parliament that are the com- "mon *landmarks**  touching offences bailable or "not bailable." *Hale*, ii. *P. C.* 127. The enumeration includes the feveral acts cited in this paper.

"Perfons

* It has been the ftudy of Lord Mansfield to remove land-marks.

" Perſons taken with the *manoeuvre* are not
" bailable, becauſe it is *furtum manifeſtum*." *Hale*,
ii. *P. C.* 133.

" The writ of *habeas corpus* is of a high nature:
" for if perſons be wrongfully committed, they
" are to be diſcharged upon this writ returned ;
" or, if bailable, they are to be bailed ;—*if not*
" *bailable, they are to be committed.*" *Hale*, ii. *P.C.*
143. This doctrine of Lord Chief-Juſtice Hale
refers immediately to the ſuperior courts from
whence the writ iſſues.—" After the return is filed,
" the court is either to diſcharge, or bail, or *com-*
" *mit* him, as the nature of the cauſe requires."
*Hale*, ii. *P. C.* 146.

" If bail be granted *otherwiſe than the law al-*
" *loweth*, the party that alloweth the ſame ſhall
" be fined, impriſoned, render damages, or forfeit
" his place, as the caſe ſhall require." *Selden by*
*N. Bacon*, 182.

" This induces an abſolute neceſſity of expreſ-
" ſing, upon every commitment, the reaſon for
" which it is made ; that the court, upon a *ha-*
" *beas corpus*, may examine into its validity, and,
" *according to the circumſtances of the caſe*, may
" diſcharge, admit to bail, or *remand* the priſo-
" ner." *Blackſtone*, iii. 133.

" Marriot was committed for forging indorſe-
" ments upon bank-bills, and upon a *habeas cor-*
" *pus* was bailed, becauſe the crime was only a
" great miſdemeanor ;—for though the forging
" the bills be felony, yet forging the indorſement
" is not." *Salkeld*, i. 104.

" Appell de Mahem, &c. ideo ne fuit leſſe a
" baille, nient plus que in appell de robbery ou
" murder ; quod nota, et que in robry et murder
" le partie n'eſt baillable." *Bro Mainpriſe*, 67.

" The intendment of the law in bails is, *Quod*
" *ſtat indifferenter*, whether he be guilty or no ;
" but when he is convict by verdict or confeſſion,

2

" then

" then he muſt be deemed in law to be guilty of
" the felony, and therefore *not bailable at all.*"
*Coke*, ii. *Inſt.* 188.—iv. 178.

" Bail is *quando ſtat indifferenter*, and *not* when
" the offence is open and manifeſt." ii. *Inſt.* 189.

" In this caſe, *non ſtat indifferenter* whether he
" be guilty or no; being taken with the *Maner,*
" that is, with the thing ſtolen, as it were in his
" hand." *D°. D°.*

" If it appeareth that this impriſonment be juſt
" and lawful, he *ſhall* be *remanded* to the former
" gaoler; but if it ſhall appear to the court that
" he was impriſoned againſt the law of the land,.
" they ought, by force of this ſtatute, to deliver
" him; if it be *doubtful* and under conſideration,
" he may be bailed." ii. *Inſt.* 55.

It is unneceſſary to load the reader with any
farther quotations. If theſe authorities are not
deemed ſufficient to eſtabliſh the doctrine maintained in this paper, it will be in vain to appeal
to the evidence of law-books, or to the opinions
of judges. They are not the authorities by which
Lord Mansfield will abide. He aſſumes an arbitrary power of doing right; and if he does wrong,
it lies only between God and his conſcience.

Now, my Lord, although I have great faith in
the preceding argument, I will not ſay that every
minute part of it is abſolutely invulnerable. I am
too well acquainted with the practice of a certain
court, directed by your example, as it is governed
by your authority, to think there ever yet was an
argument, however conformable to law and reaſon,
in which a cunning quibbling attorney might not
diſcover a flaw. But, taking the whole of it together, I affirm, that it conſtitutes a maſs of de-
monſtration, than which nothing more complete
or ſatisfactory can be offered to the human mind.
How an evaſive, indirect reply will ſtand with
your reputation, or how far it will anſwer, in

H h

point

point of defence, at the bar of the houfe of Lords, is worth your confideration. If, after all that has been faid, it fhould ftill be maintained, that the court of King's Bench, in bailing felons, are exempted from all legal rules whatfoever; and that the judge has no direction to purfue but his private affections, or mere unqueftionable will and pleafure; it will follow plainly, that the diftinction between *bailable* and *not bailable*, uniformly expreffed by the legiflature, current through all our law-books, and admitted by all our great lawyers without exception, is in one fenfe a nugatory, in another a pernicious diftinction. It is nugatory, as it fuppofes a difference in the bailable quality of offences, when, in effect, the diftinction refers only to the rank of the magiftrate. It is pernicious, as it implies a rule of law, which yet the judge is not bound to pay the leaft regard to; and impreffes an idea upon the minds of the people, that the judge is wifer and greater than the law.

It remains only to apply the law, thus ftated, to the fact in queftion. By an authentic copy of the *Mittimus* it appears, that John Eyre was committed for felony, plainly and fpecially expreffed in the warrant of commitment. He was charged before Alderman Halifax, by the oath of Thomas Fielding, William Holder, William Payne, and William Nafh, for *felonicufly ftealing* eleven quires of writing-paper, value fix fhillings, the property of Thomas Beach, &c.—By the examinations upon oath of the four perfons mentioned in the *mittimus*, it was proved, that large quantities of paper had been miffed, and that eleven quires (previoufly marked from a fufpicion that Eyre was the thief) were found upon him. Many other quires of paper, marked in the fame manner, were found at his lodgings; and after he had been fome time in Wood-ftreet Compter, a key was found in his
room

room there, which appeared to be a key to the closet at Guildhall, from whence the paper was stolen. When asked what he had to say in his defence, his only answer was, *I hope you will bail me.* Mr Holder, the clerk, replied, *That is impossible. There never was an instance of it, when the stolen goods were found upon the thief.* The Lord Mayor was then applied to, and refused to bail him.—Of all these circumstances it was your duty to have informed yourself minutely. The fact was remarkable; and the chief magistrate of the city of London was known to have refused to bail the offender. To justify your compliance with the solicitations of your three countrymen, it should be proved that such allegations were offered to you, in behalf of their associate, as honestly and *bona fide* reduced it to a matter of doubt and indifference whether the prisoner was innocent or guilty. Was any thing offered by the Scotch triumvirate that tended to invalidate the positive charge made against him by four credible witnesses upon oath?—Was it even insinuated to you, either by himself or his bail, that no felony was committed;—or that *he* was not the felon;—that the stolen goods were *not* found upon him;—or that he was only the-receiver, not knowing them to be stolen?—Or, in short, did they attempt to produce any evidence of his insanity?—To all these questions I answer for you, without the least fear of contradiction, positively NO. From the moment he was arrested, he never entertained any hope of acquittal; therefore thought of nothing but obtaining bail, that he might have time to settle his affairs, convey his fortune into another country, and spend the remainder of his life in comfort and affluence abroad. In this prudential scheme of future happiness, the Lord Chief Justice of England most readily and heartily concurred. At sight of so much virtue in distress, your

H h 2

natural

natural benevolence took the alarm. Such a man as Mr Eyre, struggling with adversity, must always be an interesting scene to Lord Mansfield.—Or was it that liberal anxiety, by which your whole life has been distinguished, to enlarge the liberty of the subject?—My Lord, we did not want this new instance of the liberality of your principles. We already knew what kind of subjects they were for whose liberty you were anxious. At all events, the public are much indebted to you for fixing a price at which felony may be committed with impunity. You bound a felon, notoriously worth 30,000l. in the sum of 300l. With your natural turn to equity, and knowing as you are in the doctrine of precedents, you undoubtedly meant to settle the proportion between the fortune of the felon and the fine, by which he may compound for his felony. The ratio now upon record, and transmitted to posterity under the auspices of Lord Mansfield, is exactly one to a hundred.—My Lord, without intending it, you have laid a cruel restraint upon the genius of your countrymen. In the warmest indulgence of their passions, they have an eye to the expence; and if their other virtues fail us, we have a resource in their œconomy.

By taking so trifling a security from John Eyre, you invited and manifestly exhorted him to escape. Although, in bailable cases, it be usual to take four securities, you left him in the custody of three Scotchmen, whom he might have easily satisfied for conniving at his retreat. That he did not make use of the opportunity you industriously gave him, neither justifies your conduct, nor can it be any way accounted for but by his excessive and monstrous avarice. Any other man but this bosom-friend of three Scotchmen, would gladly have sacrificed a few hundred pounds, rather than to submit to the infamy of pleading guilty in open court. It is possible indeed that he might have

flattered

flattered himself, and not unreasonably, with the hopes of a pardon. That he would have been pardoned, seems more than probable, if I had not directed the public attention to the leading step you took in favour of him. In the present gentle reign, we well know what use has been made of the lenity of the court and of the mercy of the crown. The Lord Chief Justice of England accepts of the hundredth part of the property of a felon taken in the fact, as a recognizance for his appearance. Your brother *Smythe* browbeats a jury, and forces them to alter their verdict, by which they had found a Scotch sergeant guilty of murder; and, though the Kennedies were convicted of a most deliberate and atrocious murder, they still had a claim to the royal mercy.—They were saved by the chastity of their connections.—They had a sister;—yet it was not her beauty, but the pliancy of her virtue, that recommended her to the King. —The holy Author of our religion was seen in the company of sinners; but it was his gracious purpose to convert them from their sins. Another man, who in the ceremonies of our faith might give lessons to the great enemy of it, upon different principles keeps much the same company. He advertises for patients, collects all the diseases of the heart, and turns a royal palace into an hospital for incurables.—A man of honour has no ticket of admission at St James's. They receive him like a virgin at the Magdalene's;—*Go thou and do likewise.*

My charge against you is now made good. I shall however be ready to answer or to submit to fair objections. If, whenever this matter shall be agitated, you suffer the doors of the house of Lords to be shut, I now protest, that I shall consider you as having made no reply. From that moment, in the opinion of the world, you will stand self-convicted. Whether your reply be quibbling



and

and evasive, or liberal and in point, will be matter for the judgment of your peers ;—but if, when every possible idea of disrespect to that noble house (in whose honour and justice the nation implicitly confides) is here most solemnly disclaimed, you should endeavour to represent this charge as a contempt of their authority, and move their Lordships to censure the publisher of this paper, I then affirm that you support injustice by violence, that you are guilty of a heinous aggravation of your offence, and that you contribute your utmost influence to promote on the part of the highest court of judicature a positive denial of justice to the nation.

---

## LETTER LXIX.

### TO THE RIGHT HON. LORD CAMDEN.

My Lord,

I TURN with pleasure from that barren waste, in which no salutary plant takes root, no verdure quickens, to a character fertile, as I willingly believe, in every great and good qualification. I call upon you, in the name of the English nation, to stand forth in defence of the laws of your country, and to exert, in the cause of truth and justice, those great abilities with which you were intrusted for the benefit of mankind. To ascertain the facts set forth in the preceding paper, it may be necessary to call the persons mentioned in the *mittimus* to the bar of the house of Lords. If a motion for that purpose should be rejected, we shall know what to think of Lord Mansfield's innocence. The legal argument is submitted to your Lordship's judgment. After the noble stand you made against Lord Mansfield upon the question of libel, we did expect that you would not have suffered that matter to have remained undetermined. But it was said that Lord Chief Justice Wilmot had been *prevailed*

*vailed upon* to vouch for an opinion of the late Judge Yates, which was suppofed to make againft you; and we admit of the excufe. When fuch deteftable arts are employed to prejudge a queftion of right, it might have been imprudent, at that time, to have brought it to a decifion. In the prefent inftance, you will have no fuch oppofition to contend with. If there be a judge, or a lawyer of any note in Weftminfter-hall, who fhall be daring enough to affirm, that, according to the true intendment of the laws of England, a felon, taken with the *maner, in flagrante delicto,* is bailable; or that the difcretion of an Englifh judge is merely arbitrary, and not governed by rules of law;—I fhould be glad to be acquainted with him. Whoever he be, I will take care that he fhall not give you much trouble. Your Lordfhip's character affures me that you will affume that principal part, which belongs to you, in fupporting the laws of England againft a wicked judge, who makes it the occupation of his life to mifinterpret and pervert them. If you decline this honourable office, I fear it will be faid, that, for fome months paft, you have kept too much company with the Duke of Grafton. When the conteft turns upon the interpretation of the laws, you cannot, without a formal furrender of all your reputation, yield the poft of honour even to Lord Chatham. Confidering the fituation and abilities of Lord Mansfield, I do not fcruple to affirm, with the moft folemn appeal to God for my fincerity, that, in my judgment, he is the very worft and moft dangerous man in the kingdom. Thus far I have done my duty in endeavouring to bring him to punifhment. But mine is an inferior, minifterial office in the temple of juftice:—I have bound the victim, and dragged him to the altar.

JUNIUS.

THE

THE Reverend Mr John Horne having, with his ufual veracity and honeft induftry, circulated a report that Junius, in a letter to the Supporters of the Bill of Rights, had warmly declared himfelf in favour of long parliaments and rotten boroughs, it is thought neceffary to fubmit to the public the following extract from his letter to John Wilkes, Efq; dated the 7th of September 1771, and laid before the Society on the 24th of the fame month.

" WITH regard to the feveral articles, taken
" feparately, I own I am concerned to fee, that
" the great condition which ought to be the *fine*
" *quâ non* of parliamentary qualification,—which
" ought to be the bafis (as it affuredly will be the
" only fupport) of every barrier raifed in defence
" of the conftitution, I mean *a declaration upon*
" *oath to fhorten the duration of parliaments*, is re-
" duced to the fourth rank in the efteem of the
" fociety; and, even in that place, far from be-
" ing infifted on with firmnefs and vehemence,
" feems to have been particularly flighted in the
" expreffion, *You fhall endeavour to reftore annual*
" *parliaments !*—Are thefe the terms which men,
" who are in earneft, make ufe of, when the *fa-*
" *lus reipublicæ* is at ftake?—I expected other lan-
" guage from Mr Wilkes.—Befides my objection
" in point of form, I difapprove highly of the
" meaning of the fourth article as it ftands. When-
" ever the queftion fhall be ferioufly agitated, I
" will endeavour (and if I live will affuredly at-
" tempt it) to convince the Englifh nation, by ar-
" guments to *my* underftanding unanfwerable,
" that they ought to infift upon a triennial, and
" banifh the idea of an annual parliament. . . . .
" . . . . I am convinced, that, if fhortening the
" duration of parliaments (which in effect is keep-
" ing the reprefentative under the rod of the con-
" ftituent)

" ftituent) be not made the bafis of our new par-
" liamentary jurifprudence, other checks or im-
" provements fignify nothing.  On the contrary,
" if this be made the foundation, other meafures
" may come in aid, and, as auxiliaries, be of con-
" fiderable advantage.  Lord Chatham's projeĉt,
" for inftance, of increafing the number of knights
" of fhires, appears to me admirable. . . . . . .
" As to cutting away the rotten boroughs, I am
" as much offended as any man at feeing fo many
" of them under the direĉt influence of the crown,
" or at the difpofal of private perfons.  Yet, I
" own, I have both doubts and apprehenfions in
" regard to the remedy you propofe.  I fhall be
" charged, perhaps, with an unufual want of po-
" litical intrepidity, when I honeftly confefs to
" you, that I am ftartled at the idea of fo exten-
" five an amputation.—In the firft place, I quef-
" tion the power, *de jure*, of the legiflature to
" disfranchife a number of boroughs, upon the
" general ground of improving the conftitution.
" There cannot be a doĉtrine more fatal to the li-
" berty and property we are contending for, than
" that which confounds the idea of a *fupreme* and
" an *arbitrary* legiflature.  I need not point out
" to you the fatal purpofes to which it has been,
" and may be, applied.  If we are fincere in the
" political creed we profefs, there are many things
" which we ought to affirm cannot be done by
" King, Lords and Commons.  Among thefe I
" reckon the disfranchifing of boroughs with a
" general view of improvement.  I confider it as
" equivalent to robbing the parties concerned, of
" their freehold, of their birth-right.  I fay, that
" although this birth-right may be forfeited, or
" the exercife of it fufpended in particular cafes,
" it cannot be taken away by a general law, for
" any real or pretended purpofe of improving the
" conftitution.  Suppofing the attempt made, I
" am

" am perfuaded you cannot mean that either
" King, or Lords, fhould take an active part in
" it.   A bill, which only touches the reprefenta-
" tion of the people, muft originate in the houfe
" of commons.   In the formation and mode of
" paffing it, the exclufive right of the commons
" muft be afferted as fcrupuloufly as in the cafe
" of a money-bill.   Now, Sir, I fhould be glad to
" know by what kind of reafoning it can be pro-
" ved, that there is a power vefted in the repre-
" fentative to deftroy his immediate conftituent.
" From whence could he poffibly derive it ? A
" courtier, I know, will be ready to maintain the
" affirmative.   The doctrine fuits him exactly,
" becaufe it gives an unlimited operation to the
" influence of the crown.   But we, Mr Wilkes,
" ought to hold a different language.   It is no an-
" fwer to me to fay, that the bill, when it paffes
" the houfe of commons, is the act of the majori-
" ty, and not the reprefentatives of the particular
" boroughs concerned.   If the majority can dis-
" franchife ten boroughs, why not twenty, why
" not the whole kingdom ? Why fhould not they
" make their own feats in parliament for life ?—
" When the feptennial act paffed, the legiflature
" did what, apparently and palpably, they had no
" power to do : but they did more than what
" people in general were aware of ; they, in ef-
" fect, disfranchifed the whole kingdom for four
" years.

" For argument's fake, I will now fuppofe that
" the expediency of the meafure and the power
" of parliament are unqueftionable.   Still you
" will find an infurmountable difficulty in the ex-
" ecution.   When all your inftruments of am-
" putation are prepared, when the unhappy pa-
" tient lies bound at your feet without the poffi-
" bility of refiftance, by what infallible rule will
" you direct the operation ? When you propofe to
" cut

" cut away the *rotten* parts, can you tell us what
" parts are perfectly *found ?*—Are there any cer-
" tain limits in fact or theory, to inform you at
" what point you muft ftop, at what point the
" mortification ends? To a man fo capable of ob-
" fervation and reflection as you are, it is unne-
" ceffary to fay all that might be faid upon the
" fubject.   Befides that I approve highly of Lord
" Chatham's idea *of infufing a portion of new health*
" *into the conftitution to enable it to bear its infirmi-*
" *ties,* (a brilliant expreffion, 'and full of intrinfic
" wifdom), other reafons concur in perfuading me
" to adopt it.   I have no objection, &c."
The man who fairly and completely anfwers
this argument fhall have my thanks and my ap-
plaufe.   My heart is already with him.—I am
ready to be converted.—I admire his morality,
and would gladly fubfcribe to the articles of his
faith.—Grateful as I am, to the GOOD BEING,
whofe bounty has imparted to me this reafoning
intellect, whatever it is, I hold myfelf proportion-
ably indebted to him, from whofe enlightened
underftanding another ray of knowledge commu-
nicates to mine.   But neither fhould I think the
moft exalted faculties of the human mind a gift
worthy of the Divinity, nor any affiftance in the
improvement of them a fubject of gratitude to
my fellow-creature, if I were not fatisfied, that
really to inform the underftanding corrects and
enlarges the heart.

J U N I U S.

I N-

# INDEX.

## A.





*Bing-*

### C.





*Carle-*

*Carleton-house*, the tutelage and dominion of the heir-apparent laid there many years ago, 173.

*Charles* I. lived and died a hypocrite, 76.

*Charles* II. a hypocrite, though of another sort, ib.

*Chatham*, Lord, introduces the Duke of Grafton on the political stage, 77—obliged to withdraw his name from an administration formed on the credit of it, 78.—the motive of giving the thanks of the city to him, 290—an encomium on him by Junius, 297.

*Clergy*, their incapacity to sit in the house of commons, 120.

*Coke*, Sir Edward, his opinion with regard to the power of the house of commons committing for contempt, 261.

*Colonies*, those of America alienated from their natural affection to the mother-country, 33—receive spirit and argument from the declaration of Mr Pitt and Lord Camden, 34—the stamp-act repealed, and a new mode of taxing the Colonies invented, ib.—the Colonists equally detest the pageantry of a king and the hypocrify of a bishop, 181.

*Commons*, house of, the situation they are reduced to by their vote on the Middlesex election, 119—said to have transferred their gratitude from their parents to their benefactors, 179—have assumed an authority equal to an act of the legislature, 185—have transferred the right of election from the collective to the representative body, 186—they are only interpreters to convey the sense of the people to the crown, 209—did not dare to assert their own dignity when grossly attacked, 215—would best consult their dignity by appealing to the laws when they are offended, 255.

*Corsica* would never have been invaded if the British court had interposed with dignity and firmness, 80.

*Cromwell*, Oliver, with all his crimes, had the spirit of an Englishman, 244—an expression of his in the time of Charles I. 286.

*Cumberland*, the late Duke of, in his time parliamentary influence prevailed least in the army, 50.

### D.

*Dingley* Mr. becomes a candidate for the county of Middlesex, 65.

*Dodd*

*Dodd*, Captain, applied to Captain Garth for the affiftance of his guard to refcue General Ganfel, 162.
*Draper*, Sir William, his defence of the Marquis of
Granby againft the charges of Junius, 39—his letter
to Junius, 49—refers him to the united voice of the
army, and all Germany, for inftances of the military
fkill and capacity of the Marquis of Granby, 50—
his anfwer on his own account, 52—accufed of making a traffic of the royal favour, 54—Another letter
to Junius, 57—his anfwer to a queftion of Junius, ib.
To Junius, 136—complains of the affertion of Junius, that he had fold the companions of his fuccefs,
ib.—that it is a malicious falfehood, and bids the
writer ftand forth and avow the charge, ib.—appeals
to the gentlemen to whom he had made application
in this affair, 137—To Junius, 141—that he has
read his letter to the Duke of Bedford with horror
and aftonifhment, wherein an affectionate father is
upbraided with the lofs of an only and moft amiable
fon, 142—that Junius goes wantonly out of his way
to torment declining age, ib.—he is called upon to
prove the Duke's avarice before he makes his hafty
and wicked conclufions, 143—but if an ambaffador
loves money too much, is this a proof that he has taken any to betray his country ? 145—Sir William's
account of the minifterial quarrels, 144—that the
Duke however, potent as he is, is amenable to juftice, and the parliament is the high and folemn tribunal, 144.

### E.

*Ellis*, Mr Welbore, whether he makes or fuppreffes a
motion, is fure of his difgrace, 206.
*Expulfion* from the houfe of commons, whether it creates
incapacity of being re-elected, 109 & feq.—Mr Walpole's cafe confidered as a precedent, 112.
*Eyre*, John, bailed by Lord Mansfield, 337—this affair
ftated and examined according to the ftatutes in fuch
cafes, 362.

### F.

*Felony*, whether or not bailable, 344—the ftatutes rela-

tive

tive to bail in criminal matters ſtated in due order, 347.

*Foote*, Mr. Surgeon, his evidence on the trial of M'Quirk, 62.

### G.

*Game-laws* oppreſſive to the ſubject, 336.

*Ganſel*, General, his reſcue from the bailiffs near the Tilt-yard in St James's Park, 157—he ſolicited a corporal and other ſoldiers to aſſiſt him in making his eſcape, 162.

*Garth*, Captain, declined appearing himſelf, but ſtood aloof while Captain Dodd took upon him to order out the King's guard to reſcue General Ganſel, 162.

*Giſborne*, Colonel, a regiment ſaid to be ſold to him, 48 —Colonel Draper reſigned it to him for his half-pay, 54—accepts of a penſion for the government of Kinſale, 222.

*Grafton*, Duke of, upon what footing he firſt took, and ſoon after reſigned, the office of ſecretary of ſtate, 31 —the only act of mercy to which he adviſed his Sovereign, received with diſapprobation, 61—his eſtabliſhment of a new tribunal, 64—one fatal mark fixed on every meaſure wherein he is concerned, 65—a ſingular inſtance of youth without ſpirit, 66—obliged either to abandon a uſeful partiſan, or to protect a felon from public juſtice, 67—accuſed of balancing his non-execution of the laws with a breach of the conſtitution, 71—the ſeating Mr Luttrell in the houſe of commons entails on poſterity the immediate effects of his adminiſtration, ib.—in his ſyſtem of government he addreſſes himſelf ſimply to the touch, 75— his character, conſidered as a ſubject, of curious ſpeculation, ib.—reſemblance thereof to that of his royal progenitors, 76—at his ſetting out, a patriot of no unpromiſing expectations, 77—has many compenſations to make in the cloſet for his former friendſhip with Mr Wilkes, ib.—his union by marriage not imprudent in a political view, 78—his Grace's public conduct as a miniſter the counterpart of his private hiſtory, 79—in the whole courſe of his life a ſtrange endeavour to unite contradictions, 84—his inſult on
public

public decorum at the Opera-house, 86—his reasons
for deserting his friends, ib.—his political infant-state,
childhood, puberty, and manhood, 87—if his Grace's
abilities had been able to keep pace with the principles of his heart, he would have been a formidable
minister, 88—the people find a resource in the weakness of his understanding, ib.—charged with being the
leader of a servile administration, collected from the
deserters of all parties, 90—his coyness in rejecting
Mr Vaughan's proposals is said to resemble the termagant chastity of a prude, 166—is called upon to
tell the price of the patent purchased by Mr Hine,
167—will he dare (says Junius) to prosecute Vaughan
whilst he is setting up the royal patronage to auc-
tion? 187—in his public character has injured every
subject in the empire, 189—the event of all the sa-
crifices he made to Lord Bute's patronage, ib.—at
the most active period of life obliged to quit the
busy scene, and conceal himself from the world, 190
—the neglect of the petitions and remonstrances a
part of his original plan of government, 191—was
contented with pronouncing Colonel Luttrell's panegyric, 229—is restored to his rank under the royal
standard, 265—is acknowledged by Junius to have
great intrinsic merit, but is cautioned not to value it
too highly, 266—in vain would his Majesty have
looked round for a more consummate character, ib.
—he remembers with gratitude how the Duke accommodated his morals to the necessity of his service, 267
—the abundance of merit in the Duke to secure the
favour of his sovereign, 268—a striking peculiarity
in his character, 270—his Grace's re-appointment in
the cabinet announced to the public by the ominous
return of Lord Bute, 271—in whatever measure concerned, he makes the government of the best of princes
contemptible and ridiculous, ib.—his baseness affirmed
to be the cause of greater mischief to England than
even the unfortunate ambition of Lord Bute, 297—
to what enormous excesses the influence of the crown
has conducted his Grace without a spark of personal
resolution, 305—in what a hopeful condition he delivered the navy to his successor, 308—the navy be-

### H.

nomination of sheriffs, 273—in his principles already
a bishop, ib.—His letter to Junius, 274—it is the reputation gained under this signature which draws from
him a reply, ib.—that he is ready to lay down his
life in opposition to the ministerial measures, 275—
that he did not solicit one vote in favour of Messrs
Plumbe and Kirkman, ib.—A letter to him from Junius, 276—accused of having sold himself to the ministry, from his own letters, 277—his mode of attack
on Mr Wilkes censured, ib.—is blamed for introducing the name of a young lady into the newspapers, 278
—is charged with having duped Mr Oliver, ib.—Another letter to Junius, 279—charges him with inconsistency and self-contradiction, 280—that he feels no
reluctance to attack the character of any man, 282—
that the darkness in which he thinks himself shrouded
has not concealed him, 285—reflections on the tendency of Junius's principles, 287—that Mr Wilkes
did commission Mr Thomas Walpole to solicit a pension for him, 288—that, according to Junius, Mr
Wilkes ought to hold the strings of his benefactors
purses *so long as he continues to be a thorn in the King's
side*, 289—that the leaders of the opposition refused
to stipulate certain points for the public in case they
should get into administration, ib.—A letter in reply
to Mr Horne, 292—is charged with changing the
terms of Junius's proposition when he supposes him
to assert it would be impossible for any man to write
in the newspaper and not to be discovered, 293—
that he deals in fiction, and therefore naturally appeals to the evidence of the poets, 294—is allowed a
degree of merit which aggravates his guilt, 295—
his furious persecuting zeal has by gentle degrees soft-
ened into moderation, 296—shameful for him who
has lived in friendship with Mr Wilkes to reproach
him for failings naturally connected with despair, 299.
*Humphrey*, Mr. his treatment of the Duke of Bedford on
the course at Litchfield, 131.

## I.

*Ireland*, the people of, have been uniformly plundered
and oppressed, 180.

*Irnham*, Lord, father of Colonel Luttrel, 340.

*Judge*, one may be honeſt enough in the deciſion of private cauſes, yet a traitor to the public, 37.

*Junius*, letter from, to the printer of the Public Adver- tiſer, on the ſtate of the nation, and the different departments of the ſtate, 29—To Sir William Dra- per, 44—approves of Sir William's ſpirit in giving his name to the public, but that it was a proof of nothing but ſpirit, ib.—requires ſome inſtances of the military ſkill and capacity of Lord Granby, 45—puts ſome queries to Sir William as to his own conduct, 48 —called upon by Sir William to give his real name, 49 —Another letter to Sir William Draper, 55—ex- plains Sir William's bargain with Colonel Giſborne, 56—Letter to Sir William Draper, 58—declares himſelf to be a plain unlettered man, ib.—calls upon Sir William to juſtify his declaration of the Sove- reign's having done an act in his favour contrary to law, 59—takes his leave of Sir William, ib.—Let- ter to the Duke of Grafton, 60—that the only act of mercy to which the Duke adviſed his Majeſty meets with diſapprobation, 61—that it was hazard- ing too much to interpoſe the ſtrength of prerogative between ſuch a felon as M'Quirk and the juſtice of his country, 62—the pardoning of this man, and the rea- ſons alleged for ſo doing, conſidered, 64—To the Duke of Grafton, 65—that one fatal mark ſeems to be fix- ed on every meaſure of his Grace, whether in a per- ſonal or political character, ib.—that a certain mini- ſterial writer does not defend the miniſter as to the pardoning M'Quirk upon his own principles, 66— that his Grace can beſt tell for which of Mr Wilkes's good qualities he firſt honoured him with his friend- ſhip, 67—To Mr Edward Weſton, 68—a citation from his pamphlet in defence of the pardoning of M'Quirk, with remarks, 69—To the Duke of Graf- ton, 70—that his Grace was at firſt ſcrupulous of even exerciſing thoſe powers with which the executive power of the legiſlature is inveſted, ib.—that he re- ſerved the proofs of his intrepid ſpirit for trials of greater hazard, 71—that he balanced the non-execu- tion of the laws with a breach of the conſtitution, ib.

—To

him, 147—admitting the single instance of hi Grace's generosity, the public may perhaps demand some other proofs of his munificence, 148—though there was no document left of any treasonable negotiation, yet the conduct and known temper of the minister carried an internal evidence, ib.—To the printer of the Public Advertiser, 150—Junius applauds the spirit with which a lady has paid the debt of gratitude to her benefactor, ib.—this single benevolent action is perhaps the more conspicuous from standing alone, ib.—To the Printer of the Public Advertiser, 155—the present ministry singularly marked by their fortune as their crimes, ib.—they seem determined to perplex us with the multitude of their offences, 156—a Major-General of the army arrested for a considerable debt, and rescued by a serjeant and some private soldiers, ib.—that this is a wound given to the law, and no remedy applied, 157—the main question is, how the ministry have acted on this occasion, 158—the aggravating circumstances of this affair, ib.—that the regiments of guards as a corps are neither good subjects nor good soldiers, 159—the marching regiments the bravest troops in the world, ib.—To the Printer of the Public Advertiser, 165—that he admits the claim of Modestus in the Gazetteer, ib.—that Modestus having insinuated that the offenders in the rescue may still be brought to a trial, any attempt to prejudge the cause would be highly improper, 166—if the gentlemen whose conduct is in question are not brought to a trial, the Duke of Grafton shall hear from him again, ib.—leaves it to his countrymen to determine whether he is moved by malevolence, or animated by a just purpose of obtaining a satisfaction to the laws of the country, ib.—To his Grace the Duke of Grafton, ib.—Junius gives his Grace credit for his discretion in refusing Mr Vaughan's proposals, ib.—asks what was the price of Mr Hine's patent, 167—and whether the Duke dares to complain of an attack upon his own honour while he is selling the favours of the crown, ib.—To his Grace the Duke of Grafton, 168—Junius is surprised at the silence of his Grace's friends to the charge of having sold a patent-place

advifed

John-

John Eyre, who was committed for felony, 362—
To the Right Hon. Lord Camden, 365—Junius calls
upon his Lordship to stand forth in defence of the
laws of his country, 366—extract of a letter from
Junius to Mr Wilkes, 367.

## L.

*Ligonier*, Lord, the army taken from him much against
his inclination, 47.

*London*, city of, has given an example in what manner
a king of this country should be addressed.

*Lottery*, the worst way of raising money upon the people, 33.

*Loyalty*, what it is, 29.

*Luttrell* Mr. patronized by the Duke of Grafton with
success, 71—the assertion, that two-thirds of the nation approve of his admission into parliament, cannot
be maintained nor confuted by argument, 85—the
appointment of, invades the foundations of the laws
themselves, 91—a strain of prostitution in his character admired for its singularity, 221.

*Lynn*, burgesses of, re-elect Mr Walpole after being expelled, 97.

## M.

*M'Quirk*, the King's warrant for his pardon, 62—the
pardoning of him much blamed, and the reasons alleged for so doing refuted, 64.

*Manilla* ransom dishonourably given up, 45—the ministers said to be desirous to do justice in this affair, but
their efforts in vain, 53.

*Mansfield*, Lord, extracts from his speech in the court
of King's-Bench, in regard to the offer of money made
by Vaughan to the Duke of Grafton for the reversion
of a place, 171—a tribute paid by Junius to his Scotch
sincerity, 224—that his Lordship had some original
attachments which he took every opportunity to acknowledge, ib.—is charged with reviving the maxims
of government of his favourite family, 225—that he
follows an uniform plan to enlarge the power of the
crown, ib.—that he labours to contract the power of
the jury, 226, 228—that instead of positive rules by
which

## N.



## O.



## P.

de-camp to the King, and had the rank of colonel before he had the regiment, 55.

*Philo-Junius* to the printer of the Public Advertiser, 82 —that the Duke of Grafton's friends, in the conteſt with Junius, are reduced to the general charge of ſcurrility and falſehood, ib.—the truth of Junius's facts of importance to the public, ib.—a reviſal and conſideration of them as they appeared in letter xii. ib. —Another letter of his to the printer of the Public Advertiſer, 84—that in the whole courſe of the Duke of Grafton's life there is a ſtrange endeavour to unite contradictions, ib.—a violation of public decorum ſhould never be forgiven, 86—the Duke of Grafton's conduct in this reſpect, ib.—his Grace has always ſome reaſon for deſerting his friends, ib.—To the printer of the Public Advertiſer, 99—the objections of G. A. to Junius's ſtate of the queſtion as to the Middleſex election conſidered, ib.—To the printer of the Public Advertiſer, 107—that a correſpondent of the St James's Evening Poſt miſunderſtood Junius, ib. —that it appears evident that Dr Blackſtone never once thought of his Commentaries when ſpeaking in the houſe of commons, until the contradiction was urged, 108—Philo-Junius defends Junius's conſtruction of the vote againſt Mr Walpole, 117—charges the miniſtry with introducing a new ſyſtem of logic, which he calls argument againſt fact, 123—To the printer of the Public Advertiſer, 151—that he is aſſured Junius will never deſcend to a diſpute with ſuch a writer as Modeſtus, ib.—an examination of the inſtances brought to ſupport the charge of Junius being an Iriſhman, ib. &c.—that Modeſtus miſquotes what Junius ſays of conſcience, and makes the ſentence ridiculous by making it his own, 153—To the printer of the Public Advertiſer, 243—that Anti-Junius triumphs in having, as he ſuppoſes, cut off an outpoſt of Junius, ib.—that Junius does not ſpeak of the Spaniſh nation, but the Spaniſh court, as the natural enemies of England, ib.—if it were not the reſpect he bears the miniſter, he could name a man who, without one grain of underſtanding, can do half as much as Oliver Cromwell, 245—as to a ſecret ſyſtem in the

cloſet,

ference

F I N I S.